T0012800

That Jewish Thing

About the Author

Amber Crewe is the alter-ego of Nicole Burstein, who lives in North London with her family and multiple bichon frises. In the past, Nicole has worked as a gallery attendant at the Natural History Museum, a bookseller for Waterstones, and used to present the traffic and travel news on various radio stations including LBC and local BBC Radio. Her current day job is in Customer Support for a financial technology company. She completed her Creative Writing Masters with Birkbeck College in 2011 and has been trying to make the writing career happen ever since. In her spare time, Nicole is a keen embroiderer and consumer of pop culture (in other words, she does cross-stitch whilst binge watching series on Netflix). She has a total of three Blue Peter badges, has an unending appetite for sourdough bread, and has never seen any *Die Hard* films. When the world gets too much, she watches YouTube videos of rollercoasters to relax.

Also by Amber Crewe:

Adult Virgins Anonymous

AMBER CREWE

That Jewish Thing

CORONET

First published in Great Britain in 2021 by Coronet
An Imprint of Hodder & Stoughton
An Hachette UK company

This paperback edition published in 2022

1

Copyright © Nicole Burstein 2021

The right of Nicole Burstein to be identified as the Author of the Work has been asserted by her in accordance with the Copyright, Designs and Patents Act 1988.

All rights reserved. No part of this publication may be reproduced, stored in a retrieval system, or transmitted, in any form or by any means without the prior written permission of the publisher, nor be otherwise circulated in any form of binding or cover other than that in which it is published and without a similar condition being imposed on the subsequent purchaser.

All characters in this publication are fictitious and any resemblance to real persons, living or dead, is purely coincidental.

A CIP catalogue record for this title is available from the British Library

Paperback ISBN 978 1 529 36692 1
eBook ISBN 978 1 529 36691 4

Typeset in Plantin Light by Hewer Text UK Ltd, Edinburgh
Printed and bound in Great Britain by Clays Ltd, Elcograf S.p.A.

Hodder & Stoughton policy is to use papers that are natural, renewable and recyclable products and made from wood grown in sustainable forests. The logging and manufacturing processes are expected to conform to the environmental regulations of the country of origin.

Hodder & Stoughton Ltd
Carmelite House
50 Victoria Embankment
London EC4Y 0DZ

www.hodder.co.uk

For my grandmothers, Jackie and Iris,
For their mothers, and all the mothers before them.

I

Heavesdon Manor in Hertfordshire is one of those grey-stone country houses that wouldn't look out of place in an expensive Jane Austen adaptation. From looking at Google Maps, it's about equidistant between North West London and Essex, and therefore optimally inconvenient for both sides of the family.

I was almost disappointed when Mum and Dad said I could stay at theirs afterwards. Living in grimy East London has its perks, one of the best ones being a perfect 'get out of family events scot-free' card. But I knew I couldn't miss this. Not the longed-for fairy-tale wedding of my first cousin Abigail Galinski. She's been talking about this wedding ever since she knew what a wedding was. We played 'weddings' with our Barbies, and she always got annoyed when I inevitably decided it would be far more fun for my doll to pretend to rock-climb her chest of drawers rather than aim for the happily ever after. I guess it never really seemed that important for me. But for Abigail Galinski, I know this day means absolutely everything.

Feeling like a teenager all over again stuffed in the cramped backseat of my dad's car (a sporty one picked not for practicality, but for the enjoyment of a comfortable retirement), we drive through tall gates and generous parkland as Heavesdon appears in the distance. I haven't reread the classics since my degree, but even so, I feel the stirrings of romanticism somewhere inside of me. Long lost, but maybe not quite forgotten.

Is this what Lizzie felt like when she first saw Pemberley? Hadn't *Emma* been set in Hertfordshire? I can imagine someone like Emma living here. An idle, frivolous life filled with luxury. Dreamlike rolling lawns punctuated with ancient trees and crumbling follies to explore and stroll through under bonnets and lacy white parasols.

But whatever costume drama I'm managing to conjure internally is quickly ruined by Mum stating loudly and without provocation: 'It wouldn't suit me living somewhere like this. What if you had to pop to the shops?'

There are young men wearing visibility jackets directing cars to parking spaces, which instantly manages to annoy Dad as he wanted to park closer to the entrance of the house.

'I'm sure they're saving those spaces for the less abled,' I say, already feeling like my patience is wearing thin, and the event hasn't even begun.

'And what am I? An acrobat? It's my sister's daughter getting married, for goodness sake.' His grumbling fades into mostly indiscernible nonsense as Mum and I share a look.

I do manage to convince my parents to crowd together with me for a selfie in the bright May sunshine before we head inside. I like the way my skin is glowing in the light, and my parents look pretty cute too. Dad in his sharpest dark navy suit (he was very annoyed that it wasn't a black-tie affair so he could parade around in his tux) and Mum in a pink two-piece and flowery print blouse I picked out for her, one she still isn't quite sure of no matter how many times I tell her she looks fabulous.

'It's a bit bright and modern though, isn't it?' she wondered aloud when she tried it on, before I pointed out that yes, that was the idea.

She's always said that she likes to trust my fashion opinions, but when I give them, it's as if I've forced an outfit on her at gunpoint. Even now, I know she's waiting for someone to make a comment, a backhanded compliment or give her a look she can interpret as odd, so that she can turn to me with an 'I told you so'.

I miss Ross as we walk up the steps and into the manor's grand entrance. Stupid brother. He hates these big, lavish family events as much as I do, but at least he has a sense of humour about it. He should be here next to me making quiet, snide comments about my cousins or sending me stupid texts to diffuse my irritability instead of remaining up in Edinburgh. The rest of the family are so annoyed about it I can't even bring it up.

'What's so important that he can't come down for one weekend to celebrate his cousin's special day?' my auntie Davina, the bride's mother, had lamented.

'His PhD,' is what I wanted to say. But instead, Mum managed something far more diplomatic.

Mum is annoyed too, of course. But I imagine she's also a little relieved she doesn't have to parade two unmarried grown-up children in front of everyone. One is already too much to handle. Then I wonder if perhaps she'd prefer if Ross were the one here. He may be unmarried, but at least he's trying to cure cancer. What am I doing? I'm just working at a magazine. Not even a glamorous one people actually read, but a *trade* magazine.

I'm under strict instructions not to mention Ross at all, for fear of reminding everyone that he isn't here. We're to pretend he doesn't exist and to deflect conversations quickly in case anyone asks about him. It's not often that I get to be the 'good child' and he ends up being the 'bad one', but here we are.

I miss him so much though. I messaged him while I was curling my hair earlier on. One word: *loser*.

Dillweed he replied, which made me laugh.

We've arrived early because Dad wants to take part in the Tisch, which is happening in a room upstairs. I've never gone to the trouble of finding out what happens at a Tisch, but as far as I can tell it involves booze, some loud singing, and a lot of thumping on tables. Girls aren't allowed, of course, which means that in my head it's the Las Vegas weekender of Jewish traditions. They could have a stripper up there, for all I know. But probably not. I'm not sure that rabbis appreciate strippers.

Mum and I treat ourselves to a glass of pink champagne served by waiters in waistcoats before we move into the room that's being used for the ceremony.

It might have been a library before it was swathed in acres of white draping. I wonder how much Mum will scold me if I peek behind to have a look.

'Now is not the time to be delinquent,' I can hear her saying. That's how well trained I am now after thirty-odd years. I can hear my mother's voice in my head before I've even done anything. 'Now is the time to prove to everyone that I did my job properly when I raised you.'

And because this is first cousin Abigail Galinski's wedding (and also because I haven't got my baby brother to pin any blame on), I behave.

The room is beautiful. Like a Renaissance vision of heaven. At the end of the room, placed beneath a golden cupola surrounded by high windows letting in bright sunbeams, is the chupah. Tall and graceful and surrounded by white flowers, some of the leaves of which seem to have been spray-painted gold.

'Oh! Isn't it lovely,' Mum sighs as we take our seats on the women's side of the aisle.

'It's really pretty,' I agree.

'Don't you want this?' she turns to me then. My mother, her eyes already glittering with emotion, already playing through possibilities in her head, wondering why I'm not as perfect as my cousin. Abigail, who went on Tour to Israel at sixteen and loved it so much she decided to spend part of her gap year on a kibbutz. Abigail, who attended every event at Hillel House throughout university and kept kosher the entire time. Abigail, who found her husband on Jdate and now teaches at a Jewish nursery.

'Of course, she won't be there long,' I remember Auntie Davina telling Mum when I last saw her. 'Once she has kids she won't want to work.'

I wanted to ask what the point of working so hard on her degree had been then, but of course, I knew the answer. To be in the right place with the right people, and to find herself a husband. Nobody literally said it in those words of course, but we all knew that's what it was for.

At least Mum could say I had been to university. Unfortunately, she could never say that I'd attended even one Jewish Society social or been to Israel other than for a family holiday when I was nine, or even downloaded Jdate. I've been eating bacon since I was fourteen (my parents do not know this part).

This is why Ross is a bit of a problem child, too. Sure, he's going to be a doctor soon enough, but not the right kind of doctor. He went to university and liked it so much he decided to stay there forever. I'm pretty sure that Mum would agree that introverted academics don't make the best Jewish husbands. Especially ones stuck in Edinburgh.

I'm looking at Mum now. Already tearful, asking me why I don't want a heavenly chupah and a nice Jewish boy to stand under it with me, and I wish I could lie to her. I really wish I could, but I also don't want to set her up for disappointment later on. She shouldn't get her hopes up. Not when it comes to this kind of thing.

'It's not for me Mum,' I tell her. 'You know that.'

Mum blinks away the forming tears (there'll be more later, I'm sure) and grabs my hand, giving it a loving squeeze.

'I love that you've never been scared to do your own thing,' she tells me, but I hear the sadness behind the smile. 'You and your brother, both on your own paths.'

I imagine the next words she would say though, unspoken but clear as anything in my head: 'but don't you think you're going to regret it someday, and want all of this once it's too late?'

The room is filling up. Men on the right, and women on the left. In the third row on the other side of the aisle, sitting all alone, I see a familiar face.

'Is Uncle Doodle okay?' I ask Mum. She turns to follow my gaze.

Uncle Doodle is really David Rutman, and he's Dad's uncle, the brother of my Grandpa Irving. But Ross and I have called him Uncle Doodle ever since he happened to reveal to us his Hebrew name: Dudel Aharon. I can't remember how it came up, but when I was eleven and Ross was six, this was the funniest thing we had ever heard, and we have called him Uncle Doodle ever since.

'He had a fall a couple of weeks ago, I don't think he's been the same since,' Mum reveals.

'Why didn't you tell me?' I ask her.

'Why am I telling you every time your great-uncle has a fall? People that age have falls all the time.'

But he doesn't look well. In his late eighties, Uncle Doodle looks grey and withdrawn. Both palms are fixed over his walking stick, holding himself steady, as if he's not sure of himself even sitting down.

'Where's Paul and Terry?' I ask, referring to his son and daughter, my cousins.

'How am I meant to know? We just got here.'

I get up and squeeze past Mum to go over to him.

'Tamsyn, shayna meydeleh,' he says, his expression instantly warming as I come to sit by his side.

'You're all on your own Uncle Doodle?' I ask, as I lean over to centre his kippah, which is at risk of sliding right off his head..

'I was keeping an eye,' says a man sitting behind. I don't know him, but he seems familiar. 'Your cousin just had to pop out for a bit.'

'Thank you,' I say, still trying to place the guy. He must be my age, sweet-looking, one of those bright, happy-face kinds of people. But I don't dwell on him too much. He seems to know Uncle Doodle, or at least one of my cousins (he could be referring to any of Paul or Terry's children, Paul or Terry themselves, or relatives of their spouses, for all I know), so the chances of us being distantly related are horribly high.

'You look very dapper Uncle Doodle,' I say, turning back to my uncle.

'And you are beautiful, as always,' he responds.

'I have a bone to pick with you though.'

'You do?' One corner of his mouth quirks up; he knows I'm about to tease him.

'Mum tells me you had a trip recently. And you didn't even think to send me a postcard?'

There it is, the full gleaming Uncle Doodle smile. I like imagining what he must have been like before he got old and frail, before his wife, my Great Aunt Gloria, passed away. It was such a long time ago I can barely remember her, but it's family lore that losing her changed Uncle Doodle forever. He's always said that I remind him of her, but he can't mean in the physical sense as I'm not even genetically related to her. From what I gather from stories, Great Aunt Gloria was quite the raging anarchic feminist in her day. But she ended up marrying the Jewish guy down the road, so I guess she wasn't that anarchic. Going by my family's standards, it could just mean that she wore trousers to synagogue once.

'Oh, you should have seen it!' Uncle Doodle continues, playing into my line. 'Rode past the pyramids on a camel!'

'Did you swim in the Nile?'

'Swim in the Nile? We skinny dipped!'

'Uncle Doodle!' I exclaim.

'But we got out quick before the crocodiles came snapping.'

'I'm pleased to hear it,' I wait a moment, watching how his eyes glitter when he's having fun. 'But you're okay now?' I add warmly, so that he knows what I'm referring to.

'You mustn't worry, meydeleh,' he sighs. 'You're young. You should be enjoying yourself, not worrying about alte kackers like me.'

'Of course, I worry about you Uncle Doodle,' I say. 'And I'm pleased that you got back from your trip in time to be here. I know Abigail will be pleased you're here too.'

I make eye contact with the guy behind, who turns away suddenly as though he'd been caught staring. 'You okay to keep on watching him?' I ask.

'Sure,' he replies.

'Uncle Doodle, I'm going to go back and sit with the women again, okay?'

'You think I can't sit here on my own without a babysitter?' he counters, gesturing towards the friendly stranger.

'Course not, but it gives him something to do,' I shrug. 'You'll save a dance for me later, right?'

'I won't get a look in. You'll have all the boys wanting to dance with you!'

'Now on that front, you couldn't be more wrong,' I assure.

I lean into him so that our shoulders meet and press. The closest we're going to get to a hug when we're sitting in folding chairs packed in tight. Then I offer a grateful nod to the stranger behind and go back to my place next to my mother.

'He's not well,' I tell her.

'I know. But he's got that whole side of the family to look after him.'

'Do they look after him though? Paul and Terry aren't even there. They've got some Joe Schmo sitting behind him keeping watch.'

'I only hope you care about me so much when I get old and frail.'

'Ross and I already have the care home picked out,' I tease.

'Scoundrels, both of you,' Mum huffs.

The wedding is beautiful. Abigail looks soft and ethereal in a flowing silk gown, her parents proud as they accompany her down the aisle. A string quartet is positioned behind the chupah so that it seems to emanate sweet sounds, and standing just before the platform, his tallis neat and his kippah straight, is Dominic Cohn, the handsome groom. He stares at Abigail as she walks towards him in a way that almost makes me want to sigh. Almost, because I don't want Mum to think I'm finding this romantic. She'll start wedding planning for me the moment she thinks I'm in any way amenable to all this romance and spectacle.

Even so, I look behind me and across the aisle to see where my dad is, and if he's enjoying the moment too. He's sitting a couple of seats away from Uncle Doodle, and as I'm looking, my eye falls again on the kind stranger who is sitting behind him, and I'm overcome once more with a feeling of familiarity.

I scan back over any event where I might have seen him before. Previous weddings, bar mitzvahs, that one summer I was sent to Jewish camp in an attempt to force me to make more Jewish friends. But nothing. When he catches my gaze and gives me a soft, friendly smile back, I look away, embarrassed.

The bride circles around her husband seven times. It's a tradition I'm not fond of; it feels strangely awkward for those of us who have to sit and watch. Maybe I'd like it more if the bride and groom circle each other together. The bride doing all the work, revolving herself around the groom, has never felt particularly feminist to me, but it's not a tradition you see at every wedding. The party under the chupah (bride and groom, rabbi, both sets of parents, Abigail's sister Sarah and one of Dominic's grandparents, who is an Auschwitz survivor) have all clearly rehearsed the proceedings, but it appears none of them gave much thought to the size of Abigail's skirts. They start winding up and Dominic has to help her along, swooshing the skirts around his own legs so that they don't get caught up.

Finally, after the service has concluded and the rabbi has said his lovely words about the happy couple, Dominic stamps his foot upon the wine glass, and the room erupts in applause and song. During the happy uproar I grab the chance to pull out my phone and text Ross to tell him that Mum is crying already.

You know what she's like, he replies almost instantly. *She loves it.*

We've grown apart since he went away, but at times like this, when surrounded by the lunacy of our family and all this intensity, we've always stuck together, watching from the sidelines and making our own quiet fun.

There's a lengthy reception whilst the bride and groom, plus their close family, are whisked away for photographs. The weather is nice, so we've all been shifted out into the formal gardens behind the manor house. Those perfectly waistcoated waiters are back, not only serving pink champagne but now platters of tiny food too. The string quartet are also back playing their charming melodies, and I make my own private entertainment by watching as the women wearing high-heeled shoes grapple with their tendency to sink into the soft lawn (the trick is to walk on your toes).

I stay close to Mum and Dad. I know most of the people here, but it's not really the kind of environment where I feel like I can comfortably mingle and enjoy myself. If not Ross, then Abigail and Sarah might have been some of the people I could feasibly hang out with, but they're not here either of course. I recognise plenty of family members and family friends, but they'd only ask about my job, or my love life, and if I dared to ask them back, I'd be considered rude and churlish. It's weird – I may be thirty-one years old but as long as I'm attending these events with my parents (and no significant other) I guess I'll always be the child.

'And look at Tamsyn!' Mum is chatting with Deborah Dreyer, someone whose connection to the family I've never been able to place. It's possible we're related (she's been around at family functions for as long as I can remember) but nobody has ever told me how exactly. 'How are you?'

'I'm doing well,' I tell Deborah. Her face is flushed with suntan and too-pink lipstick.

'Still at that magazine?' she asks me.

'Yep,' I smile as warmly as I can muster, even though I want nothing more than to run away and hunt down the miniature salmon bagel bites I've seen floating around on one of those waiter's trays.

'When are you going to write that novel then?' I try to recall if I ever mentioned I planned on writing a novel, even in jest, before Deborah continues: 'I remember when you were small and all you ever wanted to do was read out your poetry and talk about being a writer.'

'Well, that must have been twenty years ago,' I say.

'A magazine is good though. Do you still get to do lots of writing there?'

'Tamsyn is a managing editor,' Dad offers proudly. I'm not sure he's helping.

'Do managing editors do much writing?' Deborah asks.

'No,' I say. 'My role is more about making sure the magazine runs smoothly and organising the rest of the staff, editing their work rather than writing my own.'

'Ah, that's a shame.'

Except I don't think it's a shame, not really. I'm good at what I do, and people seem to like me. Okay, it's not the most glamorous magazine in the universe, and it's not publicly available. Our budget has dropped significantly with the advertising downturn, along with the many perks we used to get back in the day, and a lot of the tasks I do are repetitive, but it's going to pay off one day. It can't be long before my boss Gareth decides to retire, and then I'm in a prime position to take over. Besides, as much as I liked making up stupid rhymes when I was younger, I've never considered myself a writer.

But I don't tell Deborah any of this.

'And how are your children doing?' Mum asks, noticing my irritation, and making me really want to hug her.

'Oh, you know. I hardly ever see them nowadays of course, which breaks my heart! But Jasper is off being this big-shot lawyer gallivanting all over the place, and Nina is into photography now. She's flying to Milan next week for a shoot – can you believe it?'

I wish I could disbelieve it, but alas, Nina's Instagram is a catalogue of glamorous locations and gorgeous models.

'You should get my Nina to do photos for your magazine!' Deborah exclaims.

'We only really have photos of hotel rooms,' I say.

'But what about models actually being in those hotel rooms? Make it sexy! You'll sell more copies!'

'We're not really that kind of magazine.' We're a trade magazine, the only people who read us are hoteliers and people who want to be hoteliers.

'Anyway, I must go and speak with Rita over there. I haven't seen her in yonks! It was lovely seeing you all,'

Deborah beams to my parents before turning directly to me again and adding: 'and Please God by you, Tamsyn!'

I must have the same conversation three or four times over the next hour, each one a brief chat about my career before a comment regarding my love life, always punctuated by a hopeful 'please god by you', as if being unmarried at my age were some sort of curse. And I never manage to find the waiter with the tiny salmon bagel bites. Mum and Dad are great and watching them deflect any questions about Ross (despite Mum clearly being desperate to talk about how her son is going to cure cancer one day) is admirable.

'You'd think they'd provide more seating,' Dad moans to me during a break between schmoozing.

'I think there are seats inside,' I say. I imagine that's where Uncle Doodle is, as he could never cope standing this long in the sunshine.

'But if you're inside then how are you meant to talk with everybody?'

'We'll be going in for dinner soon,' I soothe. Dad gets irritable when he's hungry, and I know he had a light lunch in anticipation of the meal tonight.

Sure enough, I notice that the string quartet have stopped playing, and a bell is rung calling us all inside to enter the ballroom.

On a table outside the grand ballroom doors, I find my seating card, and immediately go to compare it with my parents.

'We're table four,' Mum says proudly. The higher the number, the more important you are. Which makes my table number all the more disappointing.

'Table twenty-two,' I grumble.

'I'm sure they've put you at the interesting one!' Mum says.

If by interesting she means the awkward single people and distant friends and relatives they couldn't fit anywhere else, she might be right. I'm a little annoyed that Abigail did me badly there, to be honest. We're not the closest, and I'm not a part of the bridal party, but I am still a first cousin.

I'm pretty much resigned to this wedding dinner being an absolute nightmare and am seriously considering feigning a headache and seeing if Uber will come out this far, but then the doors to the ballroom open and I'm too flabbergasted by the spectacle to think of anything else.

2

There are trees. In the ballroom. It's like walking into a magical spring-time woodland, except we're in a Georgian country house.

I honestly can't believe it. The whole library thing was a lot, but at least it was elegant. Now I'm wondering why they picked this venue in the first place if they were only going to transform it into some kind of decadent arboreal wonderland.

Every table is built around a whole tree so big that even though the tables are spaced comfortably apart, the branches and leaves reach out to each other creating a canopy so lush you can barely see the ceiling. The trees are then decked with fairy lights, which, along with the spotlights that stream through the canopy, create a soft, dappling effect across the tablecloths. I think some of the foliage is fake, but it effectively heightens the drama and instantly makes you feel like you've stepped from the formal English garden into something obscenely dreamlike.

'What is this, a sukkah?' I hear someone mutter beside me in disbelief as I take out my phone to snap pictures. They're not wrong. It's not a stretch to imagine that Abigail and Dominic might have been inspired by the traditional huts built for the festival of Sukkot, with their leafy roofs left open just enough to see the stars.

The tables are arranged around a dance floor, at the head of which is the stage where a band is playing a funky jazz version of 'I Gotta Feeling' by the Black Eyed Peas.

'Isn't that . . .?' I turn to Mum, nodding towards the lead singer and too dumbfounded to finish the sentence.

'He was in the finals of *Britain's Got Talent* a couple of years ago,' Mum confirms. 'It's nice to know he's working! Do you think he earns a lot from things like this?'

Opposite the band on the other side of the dance floor is the head table. It's long instead of circular, so doesn't have a tree at the centre, however there is the most incredible flower wall behind it, probably about eight feet high. The wall is made up entirely of roses, mostly white but some painted gold.

White and gold is clearly the theme, but under the constellation of lighting everything is at once shiny and multicoloured.

'How are you meant to see anything?' Dad is complaining already. 'Everywhere you look, you have a tree to get your head around!'

'I'm sure it's fine when you're sitting down,' I say.

'But what if you're not sitting down? What if you want to see what's happening?'

I leave my parents to find the dreaded table twenty-two. As I'm the first to get there, I have a chance to walk around and check out the name plates. Like I feared, I don't know anyone. Fun. We're about as far away as you can get from the action too. It really feels like Abigail has decided that she doesn't know what to do with me and has plonked me in the sticks. The moment I find my place setting, I grab the nearest bottle of red wine and pour some into one of the three glasses (one for red, one for white, one for water) in front of me.

On my left will be sitting someone called Paige, and on my right, someone called Ari. Seeing as I've never knowingly encountered anyone by those names before, I presume they're from the groom's side of the guest list.

The band has moved on and are now performing a smooth jazz rendition of Amy Winehouse's version of 'Valerie'.

My tablemates slowly start to arrive. Some much older friends of Dominic's parents who have flown over from America (they came all this way and they're stuck on table twenty-two? Something tells me that nobody expected that invite to be accepted); Dominic's old maths teacher (which really is sweet but I also feel sorry for him as he came alone and looks entirely out of his depth); Abigail's father's accountant and his wife (again, I'm guessing the invite was a gesture never meant to be followed up on); another couple whose connection to the wedding party I'm not able to ascertain; and then Paige, who is a white woman wearing a bindi jewel between her eyebrows. No sign of Ari.

'Ladies and gentlemen,' the *Britain's Got Talent* finalist hushes the music and calls for our attention. 'I'm pleased to welcome, for the first time as a married couple, Mr and Mrs Cohn!'

They appear from behind the flower wall, one from each side, Dominic now without his tallis and jacket, and Abigail in an entirely new dress, this one all frothy tulle exploding from a tight corset. They meet in the centre of the dance floor, gazing intently at each other with happy grins, and then proceed to do the dance from *Pulp Fiction*. You can't really see what Abigail's legs are doing under all that skirt, but it seems Dominic has some impressively flexible hips. I'm not sure that the Uma Thurman/John Travolta dance sequence is the most romantic thing they could have rehearsed, but it's entertaining for the rest of us at least.

Then the band switches the music, and we get the rhythms of '(I've Had) the Time of My Life'.

'No,' I'm muttering under my breath. 'They're not going to do it.'

'This is amazing!' Paige is squealing next to me, tears in her eyes.

They do it. The full lift. Dominic looks like he's being smothered by Abigail's skirts, but her arms are extended and her face is the happiest I have ever seen it.

They did the Dirty Dancing *dance*, I text Ross hurriedly.

This is a joke, right? he replies almost instantly.

We're eating dinner in a forest, I quickly send back, along with a photo to prove it.

Once the applause for the spectacle has died down, the *Britain's Got Talent* finalist announces: 'The bride and groom would like to welcome everyone to the dance floor!'

Everyone rushes forward as the band starts firing up the klezmer music, 'Hevenu Shalom Aleichem' and 'Hava Nagila' among others, the latter of which is perhaps the only Jewish song I know all the words to. And when I say I know all the words, I mean I know all the words to the chorus.

The fact that Jews can assemble themselves into perfect concentric circles so quickly is honestly a miracle in itself. The women surround the bride, and the men the groom, and as I'm a first cousin, I'm pulled to the front to be a part of the closest circle.

We dance the horah, spinning around the bride as she twirls within us, beaming with satisfaction. And I have to say, Abigail does look spectacular. This is the closest I've been to her today, and her hair and make-up are impeccable. The corset she's wearing fits so well that it manages to be sexy without ever being inappropriately revealing, despite all the dancing she's doing. I don't know how she's managing to move so much and yet not even have the barest hint of perspiration.

We stop moving so that we can lift Abigail's skirts as she continues to twirl in the centre of the circle, whilst in the men's circle Dominic is committing to some impressive Russian-like low leg kicks.

Then the moment we've all been waiting for. Someone brings the chairs, and four men invade the women's circle so that they can heave Abigail up on one of them. She squeals in genuine terror as there's nothing to hold on to other than the seat, and the men are bouncing her rather vigorously. I've never seen a bride dropped before, but it's not hard to imagine it happening.

'Oy gevult,' Auntie Davina, who is standing close to me, says, terrified.

Then the chair stops being bounced up and down and is brought closer to the groom's chair. His shirt has become untucked, his kippah askew, as he tries to maintain composure throughout the bedlam. Dominic is holding a white silk handkerchief, and Abigail grabs the other end of it, both of them clutching on as they are bounced around each other, the chairs looking almost like they're flying.

All the while, the band is egging on the hurly-burly with the klezmer music, until it finally starts to die down and the crowd dissipates back to their tables to grab a drink and get ready for their meals.

There's a man sitting in the place next to mine at table twenty-two. It's the guy from before, the one who was keeping an eye on Uncle Doodle.

'Hi,' he says chirpily as I sit down next to him.

'Hello,' I say back.

'Nice to see you again. You're Tamsyn, right?'

I am immediately suspicious of this situation, because it's evident from the table arrangement that we're two single people of a similar age, and he's been placed right next to me. I'm also suspicious because Ari is really quite good-looking. He's tall, with thick black hair grown out on top that looks like it needs a lot of effort to keep tame, and that open-faced, jolly quality that instantly screams 'I'M A NICE PERSON'. Problem is, there's too much of a familiarity and similarity there too, along with a very irritating 'I'd make a perfect son-in-law' demeanour. I smell a set-up and I'm determined not to fall for it.

'I am. And you are?'

'Ari. Ari Marshall.'

'Nice to meet you Ari Marshall. How do you know the happy couple?'

'I'm a cousin of Dominic's. My brother was one of the groomsmen. The rest of my family are sitting somewhere on the other side of the room.' He looks sheepish as he says this, so I can't help but try and make him feel at ease.

'I'm Abigail's cousin and my parents are at table four.' I laugh. 'So, what did you do to end up here in the Siberian wilderness?'

'Siberian wilderness?' he looks at me, quirking an eyebrow in mock surprise before leaning in more closely. 'You mean that this isn't the cool table? The table so powerful it had to be placed out of the way for fear of overwhelming the rest of the party?'

'So powerful we're closer to the fire exit than the table next to us?'

'Hey, one rogue candle and these trees will go up faster than the burning bush. I'm telling you, this close to the fire exit? We're the lucky ones here. I wouldn't want to be anywhere else.'

Okay, he's got charm, I'll give him that. But I'm not falling for it. I'm not going to let myself get set up at a family wedding like this is some shidduch.

The food is good. Gourmet chicken soup and kneidlach (it may be fancy but it's nowhere near as tasty as the kind my grandma used to make), followed by a dish that is essentially breaded chicken but served so ornately on a tower of finely sliced potatoes that it seems cruel to destroy the presentation. Even the vegetables have been arranged to look like roses. It's impressive. Throughout all this, I'm treating myself to more red wine. At least one large glass with each course, and then another to finish it all off. When a bottle runs out, a waiter is quick to bring another, and I figure that if it's here and already open, it would be a shame to leave any to waste.

The best man delivers not so much a speech as a PowerPoint presentation, complete with home-movie clips and a professionally edited video of the groomsmen performing a version of a One Direction song as if they were an early '00s boy band, complete with choreography.

'That's my brother!' Ari points out proudly when a guy appears on the large projector screen grinding obscenely (yet comically) during one of the verses.

Then a toast from the father of the bride, my Uncle Mark, who starts crying in front of everyone. I've never seen him cry before (except maybe once when Tottenham Hotspur made it to the Champions League final) and I peer through the woodland to try and see how my parents are reacting. Dad was right, it is hard to see around all the tree branches and fairy lights, but if I lean in a certain way (into Ari, as it happens) then I can see my dad's face flushed with emotion, and my mum fanning her eyes with her hands to stop her eye make-up from running.

I wonder if they knew about where I was going to be sitting, if they had a part in encouraging what I really think might be an attempt at a set-up. I love them for caring, I really do, but no matter how many times I express my determination to go my own way, I always feel like they're trying to force me down this one path. The path that my mother and all the mothers before her took. The path that Abigail has just taken now.

'That was really nice,' Ari says with a soft sigh. Are his eyes sparkling with tears too? For goodness sake.

I nod in agreement, but when a toast is raised to the bride and groom, I down the whole glass instead of just taking a polite sip.

'Do you want to dance?' he asks me when the band start a bold fanfare that leads into a very jubilant version of Pink's 'Get the Party Started'. Ari doesn't look serious. He's slouched in his chair and phrased it like he had just arrived at the bus stop and was asking if I had been waiting long.

'Maybe later,' I say, knowing that if he gets around to asking again, I'll have to let him down a little more firmly. 'I'm just going to see how my parents are doing.'

I head over to my parents' table, surprised at how unsteady I am on my feet when I first stand up, and sit in a currently vacated chair next to Mum.

'Your father thinks the music is too loud,' she tells me.

'What?' I feign not being able to hear her.

'I said, YOUR FATHER THINKS . . .' then she realises what I'm doing and gives me a playful punch on the side of my arm.

'It's a nice wedding,' I offer, looking at all the people who are enjoying themselves on the dance floor.

'Very nice,' Mum says, in a way that makes me think that she's going to want to dissect and criticise every tiny moment in the car on the way back home.

'The chicken was dry!' Dad says, a touch too loudly.

'You didn't have enough of the sauce. You should have asked for more sauce!' says cousin Paul, also at the table. 'Of course it was dry if you didn't have the sauce!'

'The sauce was too sticky,' Dad grumbles.

'So, tell me about your table,' Mum asks me. 'Any interesting people?'

'Not really.'

'No one at all?' And the way she says this, with so much sly intention, I know that she's been in on this stupid set-up from the outset.

'The guy I'm sitting next to is *urgh*,' I say, making sure that nobody else can hear us.

'Oh, really?'

'Nice guy. Just, a bit weirdly cheerful, you know?'

Mum leaves it at that, but I can see that she's trying to hide her disappointment.

I'm still sitting with my parents when Abigail and Dominic make their rounds to greet the guests.

'You look beautiful,' I tell her as she leans in for a kiss on the cheek. 'That dress is miraculous!'

'Thank you,' Abigail says. 'We took your suggestion on the honeymoon hotel by the way. Thank you for the tip!'

'A lot of people think eco-hotels are low star and rustic, but there are some incredible luxury ones out there if you know where to look,' I say. 'I think you're going to have a great time out there.'

'We fly out in two days. But we must have you round for dinner after we get back. We've barely seen anything of each other lately, have we?'

'We've both been busy,' I reply, thinking that we've never really spent time together other than for family events.

'Well, now the wedding stress is over, I insist that we arrange something. I'll invite Dominic's cousin Ari over too. You're sitting next to him, right? How's that going?'

I steady myself from a light-headed moment and feel the heat of the wine in the tips of my ears.

'Oh, Ari's a great guy. A real mensch, one of the good ones!' Dominic chimes in.

'Tamsyn thought he was *too* nice,' Mum says. I'm pretty sure I would have responded with a little more tact, if given the opportunity.

'Nice is great Tamsyn! Nice guys are the ones you want to stick with!' Abigail says, squeezing my shoulder and looking behind her at Dominic.

'He's fine,' I say, hearing the words come out forced as I say them, but eager not to let this conversation go on much longer.

'We'll have a proper catch up once we're back from honeymoon. But I'm so pleased to hear that you and Ari are getting on. I thought you'd make a great couple, didn't I Dominic? And who knows, maybe it'll be your turn for all this next?'

'Ha ha!' I accidentally slam my hand down on the table as I laugh, leaving Abigail and Dominic a little stunned.

'Well then, we'd best say hello to the others. It was so nice to see you! I'm so glad you're here to enjoy our special day with us!'

Abigail leans in to hug me again, and then goes to hug my mum and dad.

'That was a dig against Ross,' Mum says as the couple walk over to the next table.

'What was? And anyway, no it wasn't,' I say. 'They forgot Ross even exists.'

'They pointedly said that they were glad we're *all* here to enjoy the special day. And what, Abigail Cohn nee Galinski suddenly forgets her genius cousin in Scotland?'

'You're reading too much into it. Have more wine,' I encourage.

'I dare say you've had enough! Look at you. You're shickered! You think that Ari person is going to like you when you're like this?'

'I don't want that Ari person to like me.'

'Well, you should. I have no idea why you're so against people trying to help you.'

'Come on Mum. This isn't the shtetl and I don't need anyone to help me.'

'All I'm asking is that you're open to the idea. That you give it a chance. Because you just don't know.'

'Give it a rest, Lydia,' Dad warns Mum. 'You think you're helping?'

'I think some things need to be said,' Mum replies to him. 'Punkt.'

'You can say them, but I don't need to hear them,' I say. Getting up with a wobble, I make my way across the room to where I can see Uncle Doodle at a table with nobody sitting either side of him.

'Always by yourself Uncle Doodle,' I say once I reach him.

'My darling,' he says to me, a little sadness in his voice.

'You promised me a dance?'

'I'm too old even for a little tentsl.'

'We'll stay close to your table. Besides, I'm sure you can show me a thing or two on the dance floor.'

'Oh, you should have seen me. Your Auntie Gloria and I used to go wild. She'd keep me up dancing until two in the morning!'

I help Uncle Doodle to his feet and support him as he finds his balance. After a gentle shift from side to side for a moment, he puts one hand on my waist, and then holds my other one with his own.

'None of this modern dancing nonsense,' he tells me. 'When I dance, I really dance!'

'Backstreet's Back' by the Backstreet Boys is playing behind us, the *Britain's Got Talent* finalist crooning as if it's a Sinatra ballad, but it doesn't matter. We find a rhythm, and I let Uncle Doodle do his thing. He's clearly in his element.

'Did you and Auntie Gloria use to dance a lot?' I ask.

'Every week. We'd go swing dancing. I had all these lessons; that was the thing back then. Tea dances they used to call them, after the war. You know that's where I met her? She had skirts that would fly up all over the place! All the boys liked her.'

'I love hearing about Auntie Gloria,' I say, enjoying the moment.

'Always put everyone in their place. Made a lot of people angry with her opinions, but that's why I loved her. She never let anyone tell her no.'

'Whenever I try and stand up for myself, people get annoyed with me.'

'Annoyed with you? Never!' he gives me one of those glittery-eyed grins.

'Mum just wants me to meet a guy and get married. You know they tried to set me up tonight? And I'm sure the guy is perfectly nice, it's just that whenever someone forces me to do something, it just makes me want to do the opposite.'

'Parents are always the same. My parents were the same, and I was the same with my kids,' Uncle Doodle says. 'Although mine needed it, the meshuggenehs.'

'But it's so old-fashioned. My priorities are completely different.'

'Be patient with them.'

'It's just that I feel like it's not mine, whatever it is they cling on to.'

'What's not yours?' Uncle Doodle asks.

'All this,' I gesture as best I can whilst still being held. 'You know, the Jewish stuff.'

'Eh, you'll find it at some point. It's there with you, even when you don't feel it. I promise. And until then, we dance!' He moves to dip me, and although he can't manage much, I exaggerate my response to make it look more impressive. He laughs at the effort, which makes me smile.

'I'm sorry. I know I should be grateful,' I say once we're swaying together again. 'I feel guilty about it, I promise I do, but I'm tired of it too. You know?'

'*A yid hot akht un tsvantsik protsent pakhed, tsvey protsent tsuker, un zibetsik protsent khutspe*,' Uncle Doodle says sagely. 'A Jew is twenty-eight percent fear, two percent sugar, and seventy percent chutzpah. And maybe you have a little more chutzpah, I don't know. You certainly don't have as much fear! But perhaps that's how things are nowadays. Maybe it's a bad thing, but hopefully a good thing. All anyone wants is for you to be happy, kinderlech.'

'I want that too. I just want to find it on my own.' He misses a step and I reach out to grab hold of him. 'Let's sit you back down and get you a drink of water.'

Uncle Doodle thanks me, holding on tight to my arm as I guide him back to his chair, before Terry comes to make sure that he's okay. She gives me a quick look as if to say that I've put him through too much, but I know that Uncle Doodle loved to dance, and still does. I go to kiss him on the cheek before returning to my table for the dessert course.

'How's it going?' Ari asks me as I come to sit down.

'Swell!' I say, pouring myself another glass of red.

'Listen, I was thinking, and I can't help but feel that we know each other from somewhere,' Ari says.

'I'm not sure that we do.'

'Really? Because either we've met before, or my brain is going funny.'

'Definitely the funny brain.'

We're served a ruby chocolate mousse, shaped exquisitely into the most perfect velveteen rose.

'Did you go to JFS? FZY or Maccabi? Do Israel tour in 2006?'

'Nope, nope, nope and nope.'

'Weird. I could swear I know you from somewhere. It's been bugging me ever since I saw you at the ceremony.'

I don't admit that I recognise him too. I don't want the feeling that I'm giving my family satisfaction by getting on with him.

'Never seen you before in my life.'

'Huh.'

The mousse is like something from another planet. It's so good. But Ari hasn't touched his.

'You going to eat that?' I ask him.

'Lactose intolerant,' he says by way of explanation. Because of course he is.

'Can I have it?'

'Sure.'

'You're missing out.'

'No really, I'm fine.' Although he sounds a little pissed off as he says it. I like him better when he's a little pissed off. I tend to like most people when they're a little pissed off. It seems more honest somehow. No more nicey-nice pretences to hide behind.

There's more dancing, and cake cutting, and yet more dancing after that. I spend most of the rest of the evening at my parents' table, until we reach the perfect point where my father's despair over the volume of the music matches the point where my mother believes we can leave without seeming rude. I don't look for Ari as we make our rounds saying goodbye to the relatives and to the bride and groom. I pretend I haven't noticed when my mother gestures towards him, suggesting I go and give him my number, and I blank him entirely when he happens to walk past us as we head to the grand foyer of Heavesdon Manor and on to the car park. I don't care if I'm being rude. It's not as if I'm ever going to see him again.

3

I hate Monday mornings at the best of times. But waking up on a Monday morning in my old bedroom doesn't make it any better. At least I don't have to go to work, I suppose. With Jewish weddings usually being on Sundays, I'm pretty good at making sure I book the following Monday off as holiday as soon as I get the invitation.

Correction – I actually didn't get the invitation. My parents did. Mine and Ross' names were squeezed on the line in tiny writing, like the afterthought we apparently are.

It's 10am. I can hear my parents downstairs. Mum pottering in the kitchen and clanging dishes around as passive aggressively as she can, and my Dad getting vocal about something he must be listening to on the radio. At least I've woken up too late to hear him raging at whatever politician they've got on *Good Morning Britain*. I don't know why he bothers exposing himself to these things if he knows he's just going to get riled up.

My sheets are still the same ones I had when I was a teenager. Perfectly clean of course, just faded and dated. There's one of those grey fuzzy teddy bears printed on the pillowcase, the kind you used to be able to get on the counter at Clinton Cards and hoped a best friend might buy you on your birthday to symbolise your eternal friendship.

On the floor is my overnight case, a trusty little pull-along open like a spatchcocked chicken, with an explosion of belongings scattered across my carpet (beige but speckled with the remnants of my teenage years: nail varnish spillages and drips from various colours of hair dye, now all the same shade of grey-brown, and a particularly atrocious splodge of navy paint from a school project gone wrong). The dress I was wearing last night is discarded upon my dressing table chair. My bra trailing after it. Make-up palettes are left open on the dressing table itself, brushes unwashed.

I lament the fact that not only do I have to actually get up, but somehow I have to clean up and get myself back to Hoxton at some point today too. All I want is to wrap myself in my duvet and listen to podcasts about murders and conspiracy theories until my blood alcohol level has gone back to normal and I'm miraculously rehydrated.

My phone buzzes. It's Mum: *Are you up yet?*

How does she know? I swear she's psychic, but only in ways that can annoy me. I groan and decide to answer her by letting her hear me get in the shower (the pipes creak around the whole house when the hot water starts up).

Everything hurts. My feet hurt from where my heels were pinching. My throat hurts from how loud I had to speak to be heard above the music. My head hurts from . . . everything else.

Drinking used to be so much fun. I don't think I ever had a proper hangover until I was in my late twenties. All through uni and then through the party years, I was up for anything. Nothing seemed to hurt me. It's like you pass the thirty mark and suddenly your body starts to give up on you. Everything in the gym becomes harder. Belly paunches refuse to flatten. You need just that little bit more concealer to hide the purple sins under your eyes.

Sometimes I don't know what's happening. I definitely don't feel like a child anymore, that's for certain, but it's like I don't feel like a proper grown-up yet either. The feeling is especially heightened when I'm with my family. It's oppressive right now, back in my family home. All I want when I'm here is to be free. To do what I want in my own time, and to have nobody tell me no. And yet when I'm out there, completely untethered – I don't know. That doesn't always feel right either.

Mum is having a cup of tea and playing sudoku when I head downstairs. She's using the little book of extra-hard puzzles I got her for her last birthday.

'There you are!' she exclaims.

'Here I am,' I say.

'How are you feeling?'

'Fine.'

'Do you want something to eat now or do you want to wait for lunch? Seeing as you're here, I thought I'd make something. Deborah Dreyer said she might be popping over at some point too.'

Oy vey. Deborah Dreyer and a hangover are not what I need.

'What were you planning for lunch?'

'Nothing fancy. Bagels and egg salad. I've got some smoked salmon in the fridge too. Need to pop out to Grodzinski's to get the bagels though.'

'I prefer the ones from Sharon's!' Dad yells through from the living room.

'We do challah from Sharons's and bagels from Grod's!' Mum calls back.

'I thought it was the other way around,' Dad shouts. 'What did we have last time?'

'Those were Grodz!'

'Why don't I go out to get them?' I offer. I need the walk and the fresh air, and my parents' voices are going right through me.

'Are you sure, lovely?'

'It's fine. Just need to dry my hair and I'll head out.'

I brought 'off duty' clothes with me. My comfy leggings, and a giant sweater that's basically a dress. I blow-dry my hair with the diffuser on to help with volume (my dark brown hair falls just below the shoulders and has a distinct wave, but there's not much of it) and then pull it back into a loose bun. I don't bother with make-up, just some tinted moisturiser. I make a mental note to treat myself to an eye mask and a hair treatment later when I get back to my flat.

'Oh Tamsyn, put something nice on,' Mum says to me as I open the door to leave.

'I'm just heading down the road,' I reply. 'It doesn't matter.' But I know she disapproves. For her, popping to the shops is an event, just because of the likelihood of bumping into someone she knows. If she has to go to Brent Cross, she plans her ensemble the night before.

It's a twenty-minute walk down Edgwarebury Lane to the shops. Ross and I used to joke and call this part of Edgware the shtetl, and honestly, I don't think it's far off. If a shop or restaurant isn't outright kosher, then it's still Jewish owned, and even though the rest of the parade up to the small shopping centre next to Edgware station feels like every other grey, decaying high street around the country, this tiny patch is thriving. There's an old man in full black robes, stockings, peyot and wide-brimmed Russian hat, sitting outside a cafe sipping on a tiny cup of espresso. He looks like he's leaped straight out of Barbra Streisand's *Yentl.* A stressed mother is heaving a chain of small children, all with tiny peyot swaying by their ears and the trails of their tzitzit dangling around their trousers, out from one shop and into the next. Two teenage girls, both wearing skirts that reach down to their shins and long-sleeve-tops that stretch to their wrists under their more fashion-forward shirts, are chatting excitedly outside the fishmongers.

Is it strange to know you belong to a world, and feel next to no attachment to it? I sometimes wonder what the strictly Orthodox types think of Jews like me and my family, the ones that do all the high holy ceremonial stuff, without all the religious observant stuff that goes along with it. We eat the food and bounce around atop the chairs at parties, but it's just another weird tradition passed through the ages. I've never really felt like it meant anything. Or that I'm really a part of it. Can you appropriate your own culture? Sometimes I wonder if just dancing the horah like I did last night is disrespectful to the people who really believe and follow all the rules.

I've had one Jewish boyfriend. My *only* Jewish boyfriend.

His name was Simon Schaffler. He came from a haimishe family, as Mum liked to say. Our dads knew each other from some social club they used to go to when they were teenagers. Needless to say, every adult involved wildly approved.

Simon and I met when we were both seventeen, at a party held by one of the girls from my school. We both joked about the fact that neither of us were really party types. I was there purely because I had this cool new dress and wanted to be seen, and he had been dragged there by a friend who was a cousin of the girl throwing the party. He found me perched on the arm of the living room sofa, trying to look like I didn't give a damn, when the truth was, I gave a damn and a lot more the moment I saw him.

He had a mop of shaggy dark blonde hair that framed a round, nervous face. The face of a kid who shied away from the ball when it was thrown at him instead of reaching out to catch it. My hair was poker straight back then, ironed to oblivion and parted right down the centre. I liked to outline my whole eye with the darkest black eyeliner I could find, which resulted in having to nip off to the loo every fifteen minutes to top it up and check that I hadn't turned into a smudgasaurus. I thought I was so cool and imagined myself being with a guy who was equally so. But when I saw Simon, something about his goofiness just appealed. When I was around him, I relaxed. He never made me feel like I had to pretend. And when I did try to impress him by making a cutting remark I thought was terribly witty, but was probably just silly and mean, he'd just call me weird.

Simon Schaffler was the perfect first boyfriend. He had a car but we had nowhere to go. So, we'd just head off on these random drives and listen to CDs on his car stereo. We kissed. A lot. And eventually did a lot more in that car than just kiss.

My parents were desperate to have him round for dinner, and my mum would chat with his mum often. I don't even want to know what they talked about.

It always grated on me just how happy the whole situation made my parents. I'd get back from our dates and Mum would quiz me on how everything went. I could tell that she was trying to live vicariously through me, and then one evening it suddenly occurred to me that Simon wouldn't look unlike Dad when he grew to that age. It freaked me out, but I didn't stop seeing him. The kissing (and everything else) was too good for that, plus I had great cred in sixth form for having a boyfriend who could drive already and went to another school. It seemed better to have a boyfriend than to not have one back then, despite knowing that it was likely going to be ending soon enough anyway.

We always knew that we weren't going to go to the same university, that the relationship would have to end at some point, but we never discussed it. We never discussed any important stuff. We just kissed and listened to music and then kissed some more.

But then it was Deborah's daughter Nina Dreyer (of all people) who came to tell me that she was going on the same Israel trip as Simon.

'Haven't you already done Tour?' I asked him that night, referring to the trip to Israel that most sixteen-year-old Jewish kids take after GCSEs. One that I resolutely refused to go on because I'd grown up hearing stories from my parents of grimy hostels and remote kibbutzes with no running water. They had both done their Tours in the late seventies and early eighties, and told me these tales as if they might inspire me with a sense of adventure, but they did nothing but put me off, no matter how many times I heard afterwards about how modern the facilities had become.

'But now I'm going to be a guide,' Simon told me. 'I get to do Tour again, and this time be a leader!'

'I thought we'd have the whole summer,' I said.

'It's only one month.'

'A whole month?'

'Well, I have to do the training first, and I might stay on a little bit after. We'll still have some of the summer together. But this is really important to me.'

I was young and stupid and didn't understand why it was important. I'd been to Israel on a family holiday when I was younger and found it too hot. I just wanted to nap under an umbrella by the pool all afternoon whilst my parents took us around Yad Vashem, demanding that we feel something. But the Holocaust was far too big and difficult for me to comprehend at that age, and it was touching 40 degrees Celsius most days, so I was miserable most of the time. I had no idea why Simon would want to go back there. Why he would want to spend a month away from me, especially when it was a month with no school to keep us apart.

I was miserable for a bit, until I wasn't. When he did return, I had to force myself back into the girlfriend groove, because we hadn't officially broken up, and it was weird.

He came back looking so good. Leaner and browner and his curls grown out just a bit too much, in a way I thought looked kind of rugged and unpredictable. But he also came back not able to talk about anything but Israel.

'It's just a place we belong,' he told me.

'I'm British, I belong here,' I remember telling him, so confused.

'You do, but Israel's like a homeland. A spiritual homeland.'

'My ancestors came from Prague and Poland. Maybe you need to go there to get it. It's about your roots. It's about something that's meaningfully ours. I'm going to live out there one day. I'm going to make aliyah.'

'I want to live in a loft conversion in New York City,' I retorted, very much still in my *Friends* and *Sex and the City* phase.

'I think it's important that I'm with someone who feels the same way I do.'

Simon Schaffler hurt me that day. It took me far too long to realise that he was breaking up with me. After all the waiting I did, he was going to be the one to dump me? I was furious. But he said other things too. Painful and confusing things that made me angry and are tough to really think about, even now.

Simon Schaffler met his beshert at university and they made aliyah two years after graduating. I might have looked him up on Facebook a few times. But even if I hadn't, Nina Dreyer was always quick to give me updates whenever I saw her for years after. I hear they're still living in Israel and have four children now. Good for them.

I buy the bagels from Grodzinski's, and then start the walk back up Edgwarebury Lane to home.

Deborah Dreyer, Nina's mother, is already sitting on the couch with Mum when I get in. I didn't think she'd be round until later.

'I wish I'd have known you were in Edgware! I could have given you a lift!' she says.

'It's all right, I needed the walk,' I reply, taking the bagels through to the kitchen.

'Was it busy out?' Mum calls after me.

'Seemed pretty normal for midday on a Monday.'

'Did you see anyone?' I know what she really means is 'Did anyone I know catch you looking like a schloch?'

'No one I knew. Want me to slice the bagels ready?'

'If you wouldn't mind?'

I hear Mum and Deborah Dreyer's conversation as I dig through the cupboard to find the bagel slicer. They think they're being subtle.

'She'll come around. You just have to give her a chance,' says Deborah.

'I just worry about her,' Mum replies.

I don't know if the discomfort I'm feeling inside is just Monday tiredness or something else. Perhaps they're not talking about me. Perhaps they're gossiping about a mutual friend.

'But did she have to dismiss him so quickly? His family are so nice as well.'

The discomfort spikes to anger. Of course, they're talking about me. Simon Schaffler had a 'nice' family too and look how that ended up.

'Anyone want coffee?' I stroll into the living room and pretend that I haven't heard anything. Even though I'm annoyed and hurting.

'We're good, thank you,' Mum informs before she and Deborah hold up their coffee cups to indicate that they're looked after. 'But why don't you come and chat with us for a bit. Did you see what Rivka Martin was wearing? That dress?'

'With the sequins and the cleavage?' Deborah leans forward, riveted.

'She looked like she was ready to go on stage in Las Vegas!'

'Las broyges, more like.'

'Who wears something like that at her age?'

'I thought the dress was nice,' I chime in. It was over the top and revealing, yes, but it certainly wasn't the disaster Mum and Deborah seem to think it was.

'Oh Tamsyn, you don't wear dresses like that once you're past a certain age,' Mum chides. 'And you're meant to know about fashion things.'

What I know is that what you choose to wear doesn't really matter all that much as long as you feel good, and that being too prescriptive over clothing isn't in the least bit fun. But I also know Mum is a traditionalist who believes otherwise.

'You looked lovely by the way,' Deborah tells Mum. 'Was it new?'

'Yes, Tamsyn picked it out for me.'

'Well then, Tamsyn certainly knows something about fashion.' I'm somewhat surprised with Deborah for sticking up for me and smile at her in thanks. 'You can style me for the next simcha,' she continues. 'I haven't decided what I'm wearing for Jacob's bar mitzvah yet. Any suggestions, throw them my way!'

'That's not until August. You've got months,' Mum scoffs.

'But I like to plan these things. You know what I'm like.' Then, turning to me again: 'If you spot something Tamsyn, don't tell your mother, you tell me. Got it?'

'Got it,' I say.

I'm just about ready to think that Deborah Dreyer isn't really that bad after all, and that I was wrong to let myself get wound up by the part of the conversation I overheard, when the subject gets changed.

'I heard you met Ari Marshall last night,' she says. 'He's such a lovely boy. You know he worked with my Jasper for a bit?'

'Oh, is he a lawyer?' Mum asks.

'Not the same kind as Jasper. He does more small-scale stuff.'

'Did you know that Tamsyn? That Ari Marshall is a lawyer?'

'Mum.'

'What? I'm just saying.'

'I'm not interested in Ari Marshall.'

'She thought he was a drip,' Mum tells Deborah.

'I never said that.'

'The Marshall family are lovely,' Deborah intervenes.

'Haimish?' Mum asks.

'Oh, definitely. And they're all lawyers or doctors. Very hard working.'

'But Tamsyn thinks she knows better, of course,' Mum tuts between sips of her coffee.

'And you know how much I hate being set up,' I say.

'I just want you to be happy, darling.'

'And you think that meddling will make me happy?'

'It's not meddling. You can't meddle if you're not even with someone. Find yourself a nice Jewish boy and then you can call me a meddler!'

'That reminds me,' Deborah interjects. 'That Bette Midler film is on BBC2 next week.'

'The crying one? With the song?'

'Wind Beneath My Wings.'

'Is that the name of the film or the song?'

'The film is called *Beaches*,' I say.

'Oh Tamsyn, you're so clever to just be able to think about things quickly like that!'

'Tamsyn could have been a lawyer if she wanted to. Or a doctor,' Mum says sagely. 'She's got one of those brains.'

'There's still time Tamsyn!' Deborah exclaims.

'I'm very happy being an editor,' I inform with a sigh, before adding: 'I'm going to grab a bagel, and then I'm going to get going.'

'I thought you were going to stay for dinner and go home after?' Mum asks.

'I'm really tired,' I reply. Mentally I add, 'and if I stay one more hour, I'm going to explode with resentment and frustration.'

As I walk into the kitchen, I hear Mum say to Deborah: 'I just don't understand her at all,' and it makes me so annoyed because I feel like all my life I've told her what I want and need. She just refuses to listen.

4

My job isn't all that hard, but it is more stressful than I'd like it to be. Nine years ago, there were two senior staffers plus an assistant doing the job I currently do alone. I do technically still have an assistant, but rather than just work for me, I have to share her with the rest of the editorial department too.

Hotelier Monthly isn't a magazine at the cutting edge of journalism. We don't deal in scoops or scandals. What we do deal with is the travel industry and providing news to the travel industry. We review hotels and interview financiers, interior designers and concierges. We report on the world economy and how it might be impacting the travel industry, on the share prices of airlines and the latest tech billionaires to invest in luxury island resorts. We do features on how to woo influencers, the latest hot tourism trends, and sometimes do paid-for puff pieces for whoever wants a little bit more positive exposure. We've been doing more and more of those lately, especially since our advertising revenue started diminishing. It's been slowly pouring down the drain for years, despite the fact that more people are travelling around the world now than ever.

When I started as a fresh-faced intern, only a year out of university, I saw all the senior staffers going on their fancy trips to conduct their reviews, and all the meals at top hotel restaurants and thought, 'This is where I want to be.' There was a time where I thought I might be writing shocking exposés as an investigative reporter at some broadsheet, but I was quickly wooed by the prospect of tiny food on large plates and high-thread-count Egyptian cotton sheets.

And now I'm here. Nine years later, pulling my hair out wrangling freelancers and fighting to meet deadlines. Once in a blue moon, I'll get to go to a party at a new opening, maybe to a restaurant as a guest of someone else I know, but I haven't seen a genuine freebie in years. Nowadays, instead of flying to exotic locations to review new hotels, we have to make do with scouring Trip Advisor and Google Streetview. There's just no budget for anything grander, and nobody out there in the big wide world seems to care what *Hotelier Monthly* has to say about anything. I wish that wasn't the case. I know there's so much more we could do, especially online. Hotel managers don't want to impress other hotel managers in print anymore, they just want someone from Instagram to come and show off how pretty their lobbies and throw pillows are on the internet. I've been pushing with the execs upstairs to start thinking about widening our remit, so that we don't just publish for the trade but to the wider world too, pushing and pushing for more online and social content, but to call them traditionalists would be putting it mildly. As far as the men in suits are concerned (and they are all men), publishing hasn't evolved in decades. We're in a smart but crumbling Bloomsbury building with a bunch of other trade publications and journals owned by the same parent company. The lift rocks from side to side as it climbs the floors. We still have a fax machine in the corner of the office, and every few months I have to teach another intern how to use it because Gareth still has contacts who don't know how to scan a document and attach it to an email. They stare at me wide-eyed, like they've somehow stepped out of the lift and into the early nineties. But this place could be so much more.

'Meeting in five!' Kerry-Ann pops her head around my office door to warn me and I give her a nod in acknowledgment.

I remember being Kerry-Ann. Bright-eyed and bouncy and ready to help with anything. Not yet beaten down by years of pushback. I bet she'll be out within a year and working as a junior reporter for one of those funky upstart celeb news websites, or maybe as an assistant editor at a boutique publishing house. She'll flit from job to job, never establishing real roots, never seeing a big project through from the start to the very end. I could have done that too, and maybe I would have been high flying and famous and far wealthier than I am now, but I can see that happening if I stay at *Hotelier Monthly* too, if only I were actually in charge of the direction. If only they listened to me. Nine years has to mean something. I can't have spent the last nine years diligently hanging around for nothing.

I take my seat in the conference room at the right hand of the editor-in-chief, Gareth Parkinson. He's a ruddy-cheeked man who's been working here for nearly thirty years and is considered a true authority on the hotel industry. Once in a while he makes appearances on *BBC Breakfast* to give his take on the latest industry downturn or big takeover bid, his father ran the Commodore in London before it got taken over by one of the big chains, and his knowledge of fine wines is comparable to any of London's finest sommeliers. Trouble is, even after all this time, he knows practically nothing about running a magazine. Gareth could go away for a month on a Nile cruise and nobody would notice. It's not him who's panicking about deadlines, approving typefaces and layouts, liaising with the printers or sorting through invoices. And yet he has one hundred percent of the creative control.

'So, whip me through the agenda!' he asks the team gathered around the table.

'I'm just finishing the final draft of my piece on the history of the Savoy cocktail bar,' Mark, one of our writers says, a twenty-four-year-old Oxford graduate who also happens to be Gareth's nephew.

'Sounds good! Remind me to take you there one evening soon so that we can really get the atmosphere for it,' Gareth comments. He's never offered to take me to the Savoy for cocktails.

'I'm working on that piece about Airbnb and how it's pushing up local rental prices,' Nadine Kaur, another of my writers says. She's probably my best; full of great ideas and a passion for stories. But she's also wretched when it comes to hitting the deadlines I need. Plus, Gareth never takes her seriously enough.

'Intriguing,' Gareth says. We all know this is what he says when he isn't interested.

'We've also got a few freelance pieces in the works,' I add. 'The copy on "sleepover experiences" at country houses is nearly finished, and I've also commissioned a piece on airline compensation.'

'Airline compensation?' Gareth looks at me sceptically.

'It's a bit dry, I know, but there was some data recently that was published on the amount big airlines pay out annually, and we thought it was worth highlighting.'

He's still looking at me. I try again, not because I think this story is particularly great, but because I'm not about to let down a freelancer and because, let's face it, if we don't run the story it means I have a gap in the next issue that I don't want to have to fill with more puff pieces on old rich chums of Gareth's, who happen to also belong to his private members' club.

'The story actually has some mainstream news potential,' I say. 'The amounts have been going up. Is it because customers are getting more savvy and know how to ask for compensation, or is it because airline standards are slipping? Could be something worth looking into in case you're asked to give a talking point on the TV or radio?'

Gareth's already ruddy cheeks get ruddier, and he smiles, pleased with himself. I make a mental note to prepare some easy-to-digest bullet points once the freelancer has delivered.

'I have some issues with the planned piece on Euan Hegarty,' another of my writers, Carmella Quincey-Wright, says whilst chewing on her pen. She looks nervous.

'Who's Euan Hegarty?' Gareth asks.

'He's the new chef they've installed at the Clarence. He was on that professional chef battle show on Channel 4. They think he's going to be the next Gordon Ramsay, but hopefully without the swearing,' I inform the boss. 'What's the issue Carmella?'

'The Clarence can only give us two hours on the 3rd of June. And . . . I can't make it.'

'Why can't you make it?' Gareth asks.

'Hospital appointment,' Carmella replies.

I wince because I know what's coming next.

'What kind of appointment?'

There it is. Damn it. I'm annoyed because I know Gareth went through a whole course of sensitivity training last year and is well aware that he shouldn't be asking personal questions like that. Looks like he didn't learn a thing.

'I'll do the interview,' I say before Carmella has a chance to reply.

'Don't be silly Tamsyn,' Gareth says to me. 'You have far too much work already. Plus, do we really have to be flittering about over celebrity chefs? You know how I hate all this reality TV nonsense.'

'It's less about the reality TV angle,' I say carefully, knowing how popular the chef is and how we could do with a celebrity feature to liven up the next issue. 'More about the reinvention of the Clarence.'

'Dreary place,' Gareth scoffs.

'But it's on the up. It's an interesting story. Will a young chef reinvigorate a tired hotel? That's the hook. Not the TV appearances.'

'I suppose it could work. Why don't you give the interview to Mark?'

The last thing I want to do is allow Mark to sweep in and bask in more glory with his uncle. I would give the piece to Nadine, but I know that the Clarence won't want to wait another two or three issues before they see the story in print. She's far better at investigative stories where she can take her time, rather than interviews.

'No really, it's fine,' I insist. 'It's been a while since I've stretched my legs writing a piece. Also, it means I can get it written up and copyedited myself, in time to go to print the following week.'

'They've sent over press shots, so we don't even need to do photos,' Carmella adds. I'm thankful for this, but I really wish she'd given me some forewarning, and at the very least not brought this issue up in front of Gareth.

'Great! We save money on hiring a photographer too! I'll be in and out of there in a jiffy and give the Clarence all the publicity they want.'

'Well, suit yourself,' Gareth concedes. 'I'd rather you not spend your afternoon fawning over a reality TV star. I guess it's up to the Clarence what they do with themselves, but I'd rather not see them fawning over TV stars either, especially if it means they have to end up in my magazine, but hey-ho!'

I wish Gareth would understand that whilst subscription rates and advertising are dropping, splashy profile interviews with rising stars in the business is one of the few areas that keep people coming back to the magazine. Besides which, Euan Hegarty is hardly a celebrity. He was on one TV show barely anyone watched, was already a professional and likely only went on the show to raise his profile enough to land him a better long-term gig. All we should be caring about is how well he cooks and what that means for the fortunes of the Clarence, not his celebrity status.

'Carmella, can I have a word?' I ask once the meeting is adjourned and everyone is leaving the conference room.

'Did I mess up?' she asks. She's chewing on that biro again.

'I just could have done with a heads-up, that's all.'

'We're still a week away from the interview. I figured we'd be able to find someone else to do it anyway,' she says.

'But how long have you known about the hospital appointment?'

'Oh, only since last week.'

'And when did the Clarence get back to you confirming the interview?'

'Last Friday.'

'So that means you've known you can't do the interview for five days, and you didn't come to let me know? Didn't even drop me an email?'

'I didn't think it would be a big deal,' Carmella says. I don't know what kind of game she's playing, but she genuinely looks perplexed. She's twenty-five years old. Surely, she knows that this is something she should have come to me about straight away?

'I'd just really appreciate not hearing something like that in front of Gareth. He doesn't need to hear it, you know what he's like.'

'Right, I get it. I'm sorry.' She doesn't sound sorry.

'Seriously Carmella, do you know how much rearranging I have to do to get this sorted? I thought I could trust you with this interview.'

'Okay, I said I'm sorry.'

'I don't appreciate that attitude either.'

She sighs. A big, can't-be-bothered sigh that takes me by surprise.

'Okay then. Fine. I wasn't going to do this now, but it seems as good a time as any. Thing is, I got another job.'

'You did?'

'And it's not a hospital appointment. It's a meet-the-team lunch.'

'A meet-the-team lunch? Before you've handed in your notice here?'

'Well, the timing was weird. But they were having this lunch anyway, and they thought it would be nice if I joined, even though my official start date isn't for another few weeks. Because of working off my notice period here.'

'Carmella!' I really can't believe her. 'You haven't handed in your notice yet! This is the first I'm hearing about it!'

'I know, sorry, but I've been so busy with everything. And you know how I hate confrontation and awkwardness.'

'You don't think this is awkward?'

'Well, it obviously is. But this is precisely what I was hoping to avoid.'

I bring a palm to my forehead, pressing to ease the tension. Carmella is as perplexing as she is annoying, but I know that there's not going to be much point getting angry with her now. It's not as if I can fire her.

'So, where are you going then?' I ask with a sigh.

'Condé Nast,' she reveals.

'Condé Nast?' My throat goes dry with envy.

'*Tatler*, to be more specific.'

'You got a job at *Tatler*?'

'Junior staff writer. Lots of social media-type stuff. You know that Mummy once modelled for them when she was my age? Amazing right?'

'Amazing.'

'So, yeah, sorry about the interview thing. Landing you in it like that. But I think you're really going to enjoy interviewing Euan. He's so dishy. Have you seen him?'

I have in fact seen him and am fully aware of his dishiness. This definitely did not factor into my decision to step in and interview him. Not one bit.

'Carmella, when am I actually going to be getting your resignation?'

'This is it.'

'It's verbal, yes, but I also need it in writing.'

'Like a letter?'

'Or an email. I just need something written down.'

'Really?'

I stare at her.

'What do I write?'

'You write that you're leaving. You say why. With regret . . . yadda yadda yadda.'

'I really can't just tell you in person? I have to do a whole thing?'

I stare at her even harder. It's just an email for goodness sake. I can't remember what it said on Carmella's CV when I hired her, but I'm starting to suspect that this is the first job she's ever had to leave.

Then I realise that I've never written a resignation letter either.

'Leave it with me,' I tell Carmella.

'You sure?'

I tell her I am and then immediately regret it as soon as she leaves the room.

Back in my office I start to dawdle over my keyboard, imagining all the things I'd say if I had the courage to leave this job. But what exactly would I even be able to do? Become another managing editor at another trade magazine? I'm pretty sure I'm too old to go for the jobs my underlings are gunning for, and even in the nine years I've been here, the industry has changed so much. I want to move this magazine forward, without any doubt, but I have no actual experience in the online sector, apart from my own social media profiles, and I don't think they count because everybody has those. Besides which, I love the hotel and travel industry. I've spent nearly a decade learning everything about it, and it would be a shame to let all that go to waste. It can't be too long before Gareth decides to retire to his country house in Chipping Norton and I'll get to step up. I just need to hold out a little longer.

'Dear Gareth,' I start writing, my heart feeling a little hollow. 'My time at *Hotelier Monthly* has been an exciting and invaluable learning curve, but I'm afraid that I must leave to pursue a new opportunity. I'm incredibly grateful for all you've done for me, and hope that you'll wish me well going forward.'

I polish the letter a little and then print it off. I'll get Carmella to sign it before she finishes today and then make sure that Gareth has it on his desk in the morning.

I'm lucky here, I really am. I have everything I need, and who knows, maybe we'll be in a position one day where the perks will come back? Maybe I'll be able to go to exotic beach resorts every other month or try out the tasting menus at fancy Michelin-starred restaurants. It's not out of the question.

But as things stand right now, it is unlikely.

I look down at the letter on my desk and imagine myself in another nine years. In another couple of decades. Once I make my mind up on something, I very rarely change it and when I started here, I made my mind up that this was where I needed to be. I know my family think I should leave and find something else. But what would that say about me?

When I was ten, I insisted to my mum that I wanted to go to a two-week roller-skating camp after seeing some cool girls on skates in the park. It wasn't a real camp as such, just a daily summer school that was being run at the local leisure centre, but I was insistent that it was absolutely what I wanted and where I needed to be. Mum signed me up and got me the skates but warned me that it would be hard. Having never expressed any interest in physical activity before, I'm sure she was a little stunned that this was now my dearest wish and goaded me frequently in the run up to camp starting.

'You're not going to like it, I promise you. You'll come home after day one hating it,' she told me.

Sure enough, my mother was right. I fell over within the first half an hour of the first day and bruised my knees pretty badly, and then discovered that I had a terrible sense of balance and coordination. Other kids were flying past me whilst I was battling to get any sort of momentum going. I felt like a fool.

'Told you,' Mum said when I got home miserable. 'I told you and you didn't listen to me.'

That was all it took to make me want to push further, and to try harder. It didn't matter that I wasn't very good, and that I'd never shown any aptitude for sporting endeavours before or since. I had an image of myself flying around on roller-skates alongside those cool girls, and even though I was rubbish at it and knew that my parents thought I was a crazy kid, I also knew that the most important thing I could do was to see the week through and do all I could to realise my dream.

Just the thought of my mum ever saying that she was right and I was wrong was enough to motivate me into surviving all two weeks of that camp, and by the end I was speed skating around the rink playing capture the flag with the rest of them. I can't say that I enjoyed every single minute, but I felt proud of myself regardless. I learnt that I could endure. And that it was worth enduring for the sake of being right and feeling justified.

I've been pretty stubborn ever since. Tell me I can't do something, and I'll try and do it. When I make a resolution, I keep it. Every time it's suggested I should I think about giving up, I just imagine the glee I'll feel proving myself right.

This is how I know that I won't be writing my own resignation letter any time soon. As much as I'd like to, I know that it shows more character to stick it out. Momentary blips of unhappiness are just the adult version of falling down and scraping my knees. Give me another few years and I will have made it to the finish line, Gareth gone and me in charge, proving to everybody that I can do it once again.

Apart from all that, I also feel like I've sunk far too much of myself into this place to be able to just leave now. It has to be worth it in the end.

'I'm going on a coffee run, want anything?' Kerry-Ann offers.

'I'm good thanks,' I reply, but before she goes, I add, 'When you get back are you able to gather everything Carmella collected on Euan Hegarty? For the interview?'

'It's probably not organised,' Kerry-Ann suggests, in a way that makes me sense that she's trying to drop Carmella in it without seeming like she's doing so. Not that it matters anymore. She can drop Carmella in it as much as she likes now.

'If she's got notes and papers you can bring them to me. Ask her to email you anything she has stored on her computer. If you could compile it into one folder and send it over by the end of the day?'

'I heard you're doing the interview now, is that right?'

'Apparently so. And I need to read up.'

'I'm honestly so jealous,' Kerry-Ann says, lingering in my doorway.

I very, very nearly offer Kerry-Ann a chance to do the interview instead. It would be the right thing to do, as a boss.

I'm already losing one writer, so it makes sense to prepare the next one down the ladder to step up. And Kerry-Ann is definitely hungry for it. I can see it now in her eyes. She's eager to please and desperate for a chance.

But I'm also currently looking at Euan Hegarty on Google Images and scrolling through photo after photo of him in various forms of compelling attractiveness. Here in a suit and tie, expertly tailored with his beard groomed to perfection; many photos of him in chef whites with sleeves rolled up, revealing a catalogue of intriguing tattoos; and even more from his time on that TV show, all hot determination and raw, monstrous energy.

I try to think of the last time I got any perks from this job. Sure, I'm a little rusty on my interview skills, but I can't imagine two hours with this guy in a swanky London hotel will be all that much of a challenge. Quite the opposite in fact.

'I'll tell you all about it when I get back,' I say to Kerry-Ann, who smiles sweetly at me before she goes to finish gathering coffee orders.

5

'What are you going to wear?' Helene asks me.

Helene is my flatmate. We live three storeys up in a building that was once offices adjoining an old stone-brick warehouse not far from Shoreditch High Street. The warehouse part was turned into trendy, expensive loft space, whereas this side building is small and pokey, with thin walls and a cramped central staircase that won't allow more than one person walking on it at once, so it was considered 'affordable housing'. Honestly, I think it's the best find in all of London. We get light streaming in throughout the afternoon, and then at sunset the living room-come-dining room-come-kitchen is flooded with the most gorgeous molten glow. I love it here. I did one of those part-buy-part-rent things, so it's officially part-mine. Except that I still can't really afford it solo, and that's where Helene comes in.

Helene has been living with me for a couple of years now, and she's great. We found each other on Twitter after I was lamenting the need to fill my spare room, and a mutual from the publishing world put us in touch. They knew Helene was looking for a place to live as she'd just secured her first job in London after a few years of post-grad freelancing, and thought we'd be a good fit. She's from a rural village in Devon, so introducing her to the multicultural hubbub of London was good fun and we quickly became friends. We'd go to the touristy exhibitions and art events on the weekends, and then in the evenings I'd take her to the bars, clubs and restaurants only people who have lived in London all their lives know about.

I found out early on that she really doesn't like it when you accidentally call her Helen. The longer you draw out the last syllable of her name, the more impressed she seems to be. She's an illustrative designer and has approximately seven pairs of dungarees (that I know of) and made an organiser to hold all her various types of pens and markers out of loo rolls, which she has propped up against the wall on the desk in her room and looks remarkably professional. She's crafty and funny and doesn't seem to take anything too seriously, which I appreciate, considering how grouchy I can be at times.

'Maybe that dress with the little dots? Or my dark jeans with the bomber jacket?' I say. I hadn't really given it much thought.

'Don't you have anything more colourful?' Helene checks. She has one personal fashion rule and that is: if a toddler would wear it, then so would she. She's currently adorned by some bright, dangly earrings in pink and red that she made herself from polymer clay, and a necklace featuring a lobster. I think she looks amazing, but it's not really my style. 'Or if not colourful, then at least something slinkier, or more dangerous. What about those leather trousers you have?' She's weirdly excited about all this, and I also had no idea that she was so aware of what I had in my wardrobe.

'They're not real leather, they're from ASOS,' I reply, digging through the back of my cupboard to find them. 'And they're a bit much for a work thing, aren't they?'

'This isn't just a work thing,' she says, her voice low and serious. 'This is Euan Hegarty. He's like a Hemsworth. And he can cook!'

'This isn't a date Helene.'

'Doesn't mean you can't dress like it is?'

Helene politely averts her eyes as I change into the leather-look trousers. They're not the awkwardly tight and shiny kind, but a more relaxed fit with a cinched waist and tailored towards the ankles. I bought them at 3am whilst scrolling Instagram when I saw an influencer with the same kind of hair as mine wearing a similar pair.

'No, not that one,' Helene says when I pull out a T-shirt to go with it. 'Try this!' She hands me a much tighter top, one that would require me to wear a much less comfortable bra.

'Now this is getting scandalous,' I laugh.

'Can you imagine if you started dating him?'

'My mum would have a fit.'

'Why?'

'A big, blonde, bearded man with tattoos? Do me a favour. It's bad enough I'm not being a good Jewish daughter and providing her with grandchildren as it is. If I ever came home with him, she'd have a heart attack on the spot.'

'Is your family really that religious?' Helene asks. 'They don't seem it.'

Helene is of course referring to the times my mum has brought round food, or whenever my dad has schlepped over to fix something.

'Oh no, my family isn't religious at all. I don't even think my parents believe in God. Although, to be honest, we've never actually talked about it.'

'Then why is it such a big deal?'

There's a reason I don't talk to Helene about in-depth family stuff, I remember. Whenever she asks me questions about my family or Judaism, I always end up feeling like this exotic creature she's never come across before. A month or so after she moved in she caught me frying bacon, and after a confused moment, started asking all these questions about kosher food laws.

'But why can't you mix milk and meat?' she said.

'Because it says so, I think? I'm not sure on the specifics. And my family have never stuck to that rule anyway.'

She pressed on: 'But there must be a reason? Don't you think it's strange? That the rule is in there?'

'There are lots of rules in there,' I told her. 'Most of them are strange. But they're in there, and so they get followed.'

'But you don't follow them?'

'I don't. Mum goes through a big kosher phase once in a while, only buying chicken from kosher butchers, but she always goes back to the supermarkets eventually. My parents have never eaten pig or shellfish as far as I know, but beyond that, it's not really a big deal in my family.'

I remembered one of my Mum's cousins who had two whole different kitchen set-ups, one for milky meals, and one for meaty, and then another whole set of crockery and utensils to be used only at Pesach. But I didn't tell Helene about all that. I didn't want to confuse her or lead her into asking me more questions about it.

'But you're still Jewish? Even when you don't follow the rules?'

'Yes.'

But she needed yet more clarification: 'Have I got this right? Even if you do nothing, don't follow any of the rules, and don't believe in God, you're still Jewish?'

'Sounds about right!'

'But I'm Christian, and if I stopped believing in Jesus, then I'd be an atheist.'

'You can be Jewish and atheist. It's sort of a cultural thing as much as it is a religious thing.'

'That's just insane.'

I remember feeling rattled by her sense of wonder. The way she looked at me like I was something brand new to be figured out. Yes, she's from a small village and maybe she hadn't had the chance to come across many Jewish people before, plus I know her interest is always well meaning, but it never sat right that what was perfectly normal to me was 'insane' to her, so I ignored it and decided to just be careful about bringing up Jewishy things around her again.

'I know right? It's totally weird,' I said at the time, just to try and bring the conversation to an end.

'It's just tradition,' I tell her now, berating myself for being the one to bring up my mother and her desire to have me dating Jewish boys who look like accountants. 'Tradition, tradition!' I sing for good measure, trying to signal that I'm done. Helene's face is blank. I don't think she's aware of *Fiddler on the Roof*.

'If he asked you out, would you date him?' Helene asks, going back to Euan Hegarty. 'He is single right now. I looked it up.'

'I'm not sure it's wholly ethical for me to date the person I'm interviewing.'

'What, like you suddenly work for *The Times*? Who's going to care if you break journalistic ethics? Does *Hotelier Monthly* even count as journalism?'

I know it's a silly joke, but I look in the mirror and catch the hurt on my own face. I didn't think that Helene thought that way about my job.

She helps with my make-up. Something about her skill in graphic design and illustration means she's a dab hand at these kinds of things. She picks out a blush-red lipstick from her collection that complements my dark hair and eyes, and then guides me through a half-up, half-down style that somehow manages to make my often wild waves seem under control and even rather pretty.

'He's going to fancy you rotten,' Helene says proudly.

'It's not a date. Plus, I have to get through the morning at work first. I'm not even seeing him until after lunch.'

'Even so,' Helene sighs, before I put on my shoes, grab my bag, and head out.

'You never dress up like that for me,' Gareth comments when I see him in the kitchenette in the office.

'You're not a celebrity chef,' I say carefully.

'Maybe it would be a good thing,' he ponders, his face red and his silly cheeks even redder, 'if we got the women to dress up again. Men too of course, suits and ties and whatnot, but wouldn't it be nice to see all the women in skirts and heels for a change? I miss those times.'

I'm sure he does.

'I'm wearing trousers,' I say, eager to get out of the conversation.

'Yes,' Gareth responds with a half-smile, looking me up and down. 'I can see that.'

I give him a friendly broad grin in return and get back to my office as quickly as possible. It's been a long while since Gareth spoke to me like that. Usually, he tries it on with the more junior members of the team, not with me.

There are a few raised eyebrows and pointed looks when people see my outfit, but I'm not self-conscious. I bought these trousers for me and I love how they look. I'm pleased that I finally have a good excuse to wear them, and just wish that I felt comfortable enough to dress in a way that made me feel this good every day. Once again, I find myself daydreaming of Gareth retiring, of finally getting the chance to take this magazine where I want it to be, both inside and out.

After lunch, I head out to the Clarence. It's a relatively small hotel, tucked away just around the corner from Bond Street; quiet but chic. The kind of celebrities who stay here are the ones you don't really know about, the ones who crave privacy. If you want to be splashy and show off, you go to

Park Lane or one of the hip new stylish hotels littered around the West End. If you want to be discreet, you come here.

There's a doorman out front in a smart navy top hat who opens the door for me, and inside, the lobby is luxuriously quiet, the soft furnishing and fittings buffering sounds and providing an atmosphere of soothing calm. Even the entrance chandelier, large and imposing, manages to be refined and elegant at the same time. I'm instructed to take a seat on the couches, upholstered in the most delicate peach silk, and I marvel that I don't even feel like I'm in London anymore, but perhaps in a remote summer palace belonging to a minor European royal.

'Tamsyn Rutman? From *Hotelier Monthly*?' It's a lady who has come to meet me, Florence Biddulphe, from the Clarence's PR team. 'Mr Hegarty is running a little late, but come with me, I'll take you into the parlour where you'll be having your interview.'

The parlour is the name they give to their tea rooms. As I'm led through, I marvel again at the understated opulence. The dark mahogany finishes, the barest flicker of gold gilding hiding within all the rich creams and peaches. I can imagine what this hotel might have been like in its heyday, when society's elite would gather here to tittle-tattle whilst swirling silver spoons in tiny china cups. The kind of place my Uncle Doodle might have taken my great-aunt Gloria on a date when they were courting.

'Would you like anything to drink?' Florence asks me. I ask for a glass of water, and she goes to instruct one of the staff to wait on me.

I arrange my phone on the table in front of me and get the voice memo app ready to record. My leather trousers lightly squeak on the chair I'm sitting on and I try not to move again after that.

I'm nervously tapping my fingers on the chair's armrest when I see a figure standing in the entryway. The light is behind him, so I can only see his silhouette, but he's tall and broad, almost hulking, and moves like a boxer or a fighter, heavy but self-aware.

Euan Hegarty stalks towards me, and my breath catches. I've seen him on television, been re-watching clips on YouTube, and have hunted through his photos dozens of times now over the past week or so, but nothing prepares me for the piercing blue of his eyes, or his presence. He's like a real star with real gravity, with everything in the room captured and falling in towards him.

'Tamsyn? Right?' A Northeast accent. My heart flutters when he says my name.

'Hi, Mr Hegarty!' I say too quickly.

'It's okay, call me Euan.'

His tone and his smile are so gentle, and so friendly, and I'm amazed by it. Amazed that someone who looks like they might have been easily cast as an extra in *Game of Thrones* can have that kind of cheeky twinkle in his eye, and that warmth in his voice.

I'm obsessed and the interview hasn't even actually started yet. To be honest, I'm not even sure I should be conducting an interview when I'm feeling this way. Every part of me is fluttering.

'Did you have to travel far?' he asks me.

'No, our offices are in Bloomsbury.'

'That's good.'

His eyes. Oh my god, his eyes. When he looks at you it's like there's nothing else in the room. And his arms – did I mention his arms? Bulging and barely an inch that isn't covered by tattoos.

'What about you? Are you local? Do you have to travel far for work?'

That was not the first question I was meant to be asking. It's an atrociously awful first question.

'I live South West, Barnes in fact. Just moved in. But I have a room here too, for when I finish really late.'

'Fancy.'

'It's more of a cupboard really. I think it's where the servants used to sleep. Which, I suppose, is what I am.'

'You're not a servant, you're the executive chef,' I blush, and I see him smile when he notices.

'So, what kind of questions have you got for me then? What do you want to know?' he asks, the smile not leaving his face.

'I'd say *Hotelier Monthly* readers mainly come to our magazine for the business side of things, but that's not to say they aren't partial to gossip too. Obviously, they'd be curious about how Euan Hegarty fits with the Clarence's image, and what it means for the hotel's future. And then, how that reflects on the hotel industry as a whole right now, and some predictions going forward.'

'Sounds pretty heavy.'

'They'll be interested in you as a person as well of course.'

'Would they now?'

I smile and look down at my notes.

'I suspect our readers would have lots of questions for you.'

'And what kinds of questions do *you* have?'

His big arms are now folded across his chest, but I don't get the sense he's being defensive. I feel like he's challenging me. I feel like he's having fun.

A million things flash through my mind, all the things I'd really like to ask him, all entirely inappropriate.

I look down at my notepad again, self-conscious, and he chuckles to himself.

'Tell me about what drew you to the Clarence?' I ask after I've regained my composure.

'Well, they offered a lot of money,' he says. I can't tell if he's joking with me or not, but he continues before I can question him: 'and I was looking for a new challenge. I've worked at some incredible places, but all a lot smaller and more rural. The Clarence has the prestige and history, and that's certainly an impressive draw, but what's really important to me is capturing the soul of the city. What I want to do with this restaurant is explore a diverse range of food styles. Create a literal melting pot that's representative of the culture here in London.'

'You don't think that's going to clash with the Clarence's more traditional values?'

'The top brass here are as passionate as I am about the vision I see. They want to attract new visitors, new customers, and I really feel like this could be a great way to do it. The world is opening up, and I want to embrace it.'

He seems so noble. Nice, but not in the way that annoys me. Nice, but with passion and fire. There's softness there, but it's hidden beneath this bravado and intention that draws me in and makes me hungry for more. I honestly really didn't expect this, but I don't want to be a fool. He challenged me earlier, and now it's time for me to challenge him. I can't wait to see how he reacts.

'Some would say that the restaurant industry has a problem when it comes to the types of people who get the top jobs, that opportunities might be harder to come by for people from different backgrounds. Do you think there's a diversity issue in your field?'

There's a flicker of something, not quite annoyance, in his face as he takes in the question. Then he focuses his laser beam-blue eyes back on me. Challenge accepted.

'Do I wish there were more women in these jobs? Absolutely. More people of colour? Yes. I want to help make that happen. And so part of what I'll be doing here at the Clarence is making sure that I'm working with people who know these recipes, and then training those people to a standard where they can hopefully get the next top spot that opens. I don't want to replicate or reinterpret dishes, I want to get to the heart of them. Employing and working with the right people is a part of that.'

Colour me impressed. I take some notes, check again that my phone is still recording, and move on with more of my questions.

'Big time chefs have a bit of a reputation nowadays. Do you feel like you have to be hyper-masculine and aggressive to get what you want?' I ask.

'I'm someone who tends to get what they want,' Euan is looking right at me again, that challenge in his eyes, that hint of a gentle smirk at the corners of his mouth. 'But do I roam around my kitchen swearing and barking like a military commander? No, that's not my style. The kitchen is a tough place, it gets hot in there and emotions tend to always be high, but I've found you get more out of people with encouragement, constructive feedback, and a hefty amount of praise when it's deserved.'

'Don't take this the wrong way, but you seem like the kind of person that people might mistake for aggressive and confrontational. Has that happened, in your experience?'

'Do I come across as aggressive and confrontational to you?'

'No,' I say, staring back at him, feeling emboldened. 'You come across as intriguing.'

I feel like I want to turn the recorder on my phone off. I'm worried in case anyone back at the office happens to hear it. Who knows what they'd think? But then again, what am I thinking?

'Intriguing?'

I know I'm blushing again, but I pretend that I'm not.

'Well, I am interviewing you. Shouldn't I be intrigued? It'll be rather boring to our readers if I'm not.'

He chuckles, and rubs at his beard, considering me.

'If you wanted people to know one thing about you, one true thing, what would it be?' It's an off-the-cuff question, after another run of basic ones, but it feels like a good one.

'*Hotelier Monthly* is interested in knowing my deepest, darkest secrets, are they?'

'They are,' I reply, letting myself smile.

'Well, I'm not too sure about this kind of thing being on the record,' he glances down at my phone on the table. 'But I'm happy to discuss this further, perhaps over dinner some time?'

Holy cow – I feel hot and bothered in the most tremendous way. Sitting still in this posh chair in these synthetic leather trousers is making me itchy and jumpy and if we weren't in public, and I wasn't here in a professional capacity, I'm pretty sure I would lunge right into him, so it takes all of my strength to just sit still.

'You seem . . .' he's looking at me, questioning me with those intense eyes. God, even his eyebrows are sexy. This is ridiculous. 'You seem like someone I would like to get to know.'

'I'm that good at interviewing, am I?' I joke.

'You've made me smile today. How's that?'

'A pretty good reason to ask someone out, I guess.'

'Well, I usually hate being interviewed, so you've definitely done something right.'

'I'm not sure how much usable material I have.'

'You haven't answered my question yet, either.'

I know I haven't. Mainly because I have no idea how to. I can't remember the last time I agreed to go on a date with someone that didn't involve a few half-hearted text messages after swiping right. I didn't think that actually asking someone out in the real-life sense was something that really happened anymore.

'Dinner would be nice,' I say gently, not wanting to appear too eager.

'Well, I'll be honest with you. I'm pretty busy and chefs work most evenings. But I'm free next Friday night if you're up for it? We can go somewhere else, not here. That would be a bit too weird.'

'You're not going to cook for me?' I flirt.

'Well, we'll have to see about that. I don't just cook for anyone.'

'Not unless you're being paid thousands of pounds, I guess.'

He laughs, the first proper laugh I've heard from him. It's guttural and jolly. He seems like the kind of person for whom every emotion is laid bare, and I like it.

'But next Friday should be good,' I confirm before reaching for my phone.

I'm slightly embarrassed that the last part has been caught on microphone, but I can always go and scrub that later. Or maybe I'll keep it. Maybe I'll want to remember this first encounter at some point in the future.

'So that's the 11th June?' I say, confirming the date. Euan is checking his phone too.

'It's the only night off I have in a while,' he says apologetically. 'At least until we settle into a routine here and I can hand off to others.'

'That should be fine—' I stop myself, looking at my calendar. It's not fine.

'What is it?' Euan asks.

'I actually have plans.'

'You could have just said no if you don't want to,' he teases. God, he's even sexy when he teases.

'I have dinner with my cousins that night. But don't worry, it's not important.'

Already I'm thinking about this in my head. If I tell Abigail that I have a date with Euan Hegarty, then surely she'd let me off? I know that preparing her first Friday night dinner as a wife is a bit of a big deal for her, but this is Euan Hegarty. Sexiest-man-alive Euan Hegarty. She'd be mad not to understand, surely?

'You shouldn't cancel dinner with your family,' Euan says, but he sounds disappointed. I wonder if he's going to back out, if he's lost interest already.

'I really can, I'm sure it would be fine!'

'So, the 11th June then?'

'It's a date.'

We swap numbers. And then we shake hands. It's a strange gesture, especially when coupled with those hungry Viking eyes of his, but it feels loaded with the promise of exciting things, and somewhat electric too.

'It was nice meeting you,' I say, feeling overwhelmed and embarrassed, and also very conscious of Florence Biddulphe and a couple of waiting staff lingering on the other side of the room. She starts coming closer when she realises that I'm getting ready to leave.

'Very nice meeting you too,' Euan says. The handshake lasts just a little longer than it should. I will it to last forever.

'How long until the piece comes out?' Florence asks me. Her question shocks me back into professional mode.

'We have a deadline in a couple of weeks, and then we go to print for July shortly after that,' I reply.

'You'll keep me up to date?' she asks.

'Of course,' I reply. Then I turn to Euan again and, without thinking, reach out for another handshake. 'Very nice meeting you.'

I'm squirming with embarrassment until he clasps my hand again, smiles that devilishly quirky smile, and repeats the gesture, clearly amused with my awkwardness.

'Very nice indeed,' he chuckles.

'Right, I'd better be going,' I say. He still hasn't broken the handshake, and I swear my insides are melting.

'I'll speak to you soon,' he promises.

'Definitely,' I assure.

I turn to head back to the lobby of the Clarence, scrunching my face with embarrassment as I strut away, praying that my bum looks as good as I imagine it does in these trousers, and that Euan is liking what he sees.

6

Peanut butter. Smooth or crunchy? Euan texts me.

It's been like this for days. There'll be silence for a while, and then suddenly a barrage of silly questions that make me smile. Lots are food related. Every time I feel that sense of intention, an eagerness that oozes through my phone screen and makes my heart beat faster. I've never found texting so exhilarating.

Smooth, I reply, grinning.

I'm afraid that's the wrong answer. Damn, and I had such high hopes for us too.

How does this man manage to be so sexy even when he's being ridiculous?

'You're blushing again,' Helene comments from behind her Nintendo Switch. She's splayed out on the sofa, avoiding the desk in her room. I think one of the reasons we get on so well is that we both understand the stress of deadlines.

'I'm not.'

'I can tell whenever he messages you. You transform into a horny tomato.'

'I'm being pathetic,' I say to her, wincing. 'I'm sorry.'

'You're not pathetic. I just keep telling myself it's the horniness and you'll get over it the moment you sleep together. It's like the pressure and humidity building up before a storm. Once the lightning hits and breaks it, everything will be calm again.'

'You think this is just about sex?'

'I don't think it's *just* about sex. I think it's *a lot* about sex, but not *just* about it. Come on, how long has it been?'

'Since I was last with a guy?'

'Yeah.'

'Nine months? Nearly ten?'

'So that guy from Tinder then? The one with the name?'

'His name wasn't that bad.'

'What was it again? Randy? Rufus?'

'Ryder.'

'Ryder! That was it. Wow. The last guy you slept with was called Ryder.'

'It's not that bad a name.'

Helene gives me a look that reminds me far too much of the 'Sure Jan' meme.

'Anyway, I don't think it's just about the sex,' I tell her. 'Euan seems really cool too. One of those gentle giant types. All grizzly bear on the outside but teddy bear on the inside. He's got values, and he's passionate about them. Do you know how rare it is to meet a guy like that?'

'Look, if it turns out that you spend some proper time together and you end up falling deeply, madly in love, then great. All I'm saying is that you don't really know him yet, that's all.'

'You don't believe in love at first sight?'

'I believe in lust at first sight, that's for certain.'

I know she's only teasing me. During the moments where I'm not being much of a blatant 'horny tomato', she's been searching the *Daily Mail* sidebar of shame for mentions of him. She forwards me the links with flourishes of excited emojis.

I guess I'm in even more of a mood because I could be seeing him instead of being with my family. I really didn't think the Friday night dinner with Abigail and Dominic would be a big deal, but the earful I got when I told Mum I was planning to postpone was uncomfortable to say the least.

'What do you mean postpone?' Mum asked.

'I mean, something has come up and I have other plans.'

'This is the first time Abigail's making Friday night. And she wanted you to be there. You have no idea how she's going to feel if you cancel.'

'It's not cancelling, it's postponing. Come on, there's going to be plenty of other opportunities. It's not as if Friday nights don't come up every week. This is Abigail, I'm sure she'll be fine.'

'It's not just Abigail though. What am I meant to say when Auntie Davina calls me asking where you were? What am I meant to say if the machatunim ever ask?'

'Why would Dominic's parents ask why I can't make Friday night? I'll just say I'm busy. That something came up, a work thing.'

'Is it a work thing?'

'In a way.'

'Tamsyn, darling. I know you don't understand these things. But this is Abigail's first Friday night. She wants you there with her. Maybe one day when you're married and making dinner you'll understand.'

'Mum.'

'God forbid, you'll be postponing on Seder night next.'

'Well, if I could bow out of Seder night then I would.'

'Tamsyn!'

'Oh, come on, remember that one Mandy Galinski made a few years ago? We didn't eat until 11pm!'

'I know you don't want to hurt me.'

'Mum.'

'I'm just saying that I can't imagine anything you've got going on that would be more important than supporting your cousin, than being there for your family.'

I knew she was never going to let it go. And this is why I'm heading to Finchley tonight rather than out to see Euan. He didn't mind, in fact he seemed to like the idea of me having a large family that I was sociable with. Even so, I'd much rather be sharing longing looks over glasses of red wine, instead of listening to honeymoon stories and pretending to gush over wedding photos.

'I shouldn't be back too late,' I tell Helene.

'If the food is good bring me leftovers?' she calls after me as I leave.

The Cohns are living in a fancy new-build gated apartment block, a few roads away from Tally-Ho Corner. It's all sleek glass, uniform pale bricks and minimal steel finishes. I've brought a bottle of wine with me, and I'm under strict instructions from Mum to see if Abigail drinks any. I doubt she'd be pregnant yet, but Mum is desperate to be first in the know just in case.

Dominic greets me at the door and gives me a warm hug.

'Tamsyn! Cousin-in-law!' he says. 'And you brought wine! Amazing, amazing. Come in!'

Abigail emerges from the kitchen wearing a modest skirt that comes past her knees and a long-sleeved blouse. Considering how much skin was on display at the wedding, I'm a little surprised to see her so covered up.

'Shabbat shalom!' she embraces me too. She smells of roast chicken.

'Good Shabbos,' I return.

'You're the first one here but come in. I'll open the wine and we'll get the photo album out. Have you got the photo album ready Dom?'

'I'm right on it, sweetheart!'

Dom takes me into the lounge and presents to me the photo album, already laid out on the coffee table.

'So, who's coming tonight?' I ask, whilst flicking through

the pages. I know that this evening is strictly 'our generation only', so no parents, which made me think that things should be a lot more relaxed. I'm wearing my jeans with rips at the knees along with Doc Martens, something I'm starting to regret considering that Dominic is wearing a suit. There's no tie and the top button is undone, but even so, it's still smarter than what most of my colleagues at the office wear.

'Some married couple friends of Abigail's, Yael and Ed, plus my brother Michael and his wife Becca,' Dominic responds.

'Ahh, lots of couples then.'

'Oh well, my cousin Ari might be coming too, but he's been snowed under at work so we're not quite sure how that's turning out yet.'

'The guy I was sitting next to at your wedding?'

'Yes! You remember him! Such a great guy.'

'A great guy. Really great,' I say, through a tense smile.

'Definitely. One of the best! I'm pleased you remember him so well. But he hasn't even confirmed yet.'

'Flaky, is he?'

'Oh no! He's not flaky!' Abigail comes into the lounge with a large glass of wine for me. 'He's just so busy. But I wouldn't call him flaky. He's going to try and make it if he can.'

We light the candles once the other guests arrive, which coincides with sunset, Abigail's head covered with a scarf, her gestures over the new flames dramatic until she covers her eyes and seems like she's about to cry.

'That's my first time bringing in Shabbos as a married woman in my own home, with my husband, and I'm so happy that you could be here with me,' she says through soft tears.

I look around at the other guests, Yael and Ed, and at Michael and Becca. They've dressed up too, the men in suits and the women in dresses.

'It's such a wonderful thing to welcome in the Shabbos bride as a new bride yourself,' Yael says.

I look closely at Yael's hairline. I think she's wearing a sheitl, but I can't be certain. If it is one, then it's really good. If it's not a sheitl, then I need to know what products she uses to relax her hair. A Jewish woman with thick, dark hair that sits so perfectly straight in a humid flat in June? I'm immediately suspicious.

The kiddush cup looks like it's been lifted from the set of *Star Trek*. As Dominic pours the wine, it filters down through tiny tubes into smaller cups that surround it.

'You're going to have to tell me where you got that!' Michael declares as Dominic hands the tiny kiddush cups to each of us.

Abigail gazes adoringly at her husband as he says the bracha for wine. Except he doesn't just say it like we would do at home, he sings it with acrobatic flourish. I don't recognise the words when they're all drawn out like that but I do say amen when the others do, chugging the wine back in one.

'Now, go easy on me, I made the challah myself and I haven't made my own in years,' Abigail says.

'I'm sure it's going to be lovely,' Becca says warmly.

Dominic says Harmotzi, drawing out the vowels and performing acrobatic runs with the melody that would make Beyoncé proud, before the challah cover is removed to reveal a flat lump of bread, the braids barely distinguishable.

'Stunning, really great work!' Yael says in a voice that reminds me of a primary school teacher.

I remember again that I could be with Euan right now. I could be gazing into his blue eyes and he could be telling me about his glorious tattoos. We could be going back to his place (there's no way I'd be bringing him back to mine to be scrutinised by Helene) and I could be seeing how far the tattoos spread. I imagine his chest, his abs, and lower. I imagine his fierceness, and what that must be like in the bedroom.

'You okay Tamsyn?' Abigail asks me as she passes around the basket of sliced challah. 'You've gone all red!'

'Just a bit hot,' I say, bringing up a hand to fan myself and bring my body temperature down.

'Could be the perimenopause,' Becca says to me. 'It's starting younger and younger these days. You should get that checked out.'

'I don't think it's the perimenopause,' I say back to her, aware that all the attention on me is just making me blush more.

'Seriously. Women don't talk about it enough,' she goes on. 'Hormones can be your best friend, or your worst enemy. Best to get them on side as early in the battle as you can.'

'It's not hormones,' I say. Although, I guess it is. Just maybe not the hormones she's thinking about.

It feels a little weird that everyone else at the table is a couple. Abigail has optimistically left the place setting laid out next to me in case Ari happens to turn up, but I'm hoping he doesn't arrive. I'd rather the weirdness of being the only single among couples than the weirdness of having to potentially deal with another matchmaking attempt.

'Have you heard from Ari?' I ask my cousin.

'Looking forward to seeing him, are you?' She looks so pleased with herself.

'Just think it's a little rude that he hasn't let you know,' I reply.

'I tried to call before we lit the candles, but the line went straight to voicemail. I guess he's underground. Must be on his way!'

Something twigs in me when Abigail mentions calling before lighting the candles. I think she's keeping Shabbos. Not just making a nice Friday night meal, but actually keeping Shabbos. I glance around the room. All the lights are on dimmer switches. I know right then that they're not going to be fully switched off before sunset tomorrow night. I peer back into the kitchen and see a huge pot on the hob, no doubt full of cholent she spent the entire day making. This isn't some weird little marriage performance; I really didn't realise how frum Abigail Cohn had become lately. She was always super involved in Jewish things, but I thought it was more of a social or cultural thing. I didn't realise how keen she was to actually be a perfect Jewish housewife. As appalled as I am, I start to feel even worse for turning up tonight in ripped jeans.

'So, Tamsyn,' Yael turns to me. I'm studying her hairline again, watching for the tell-tale signs of a wig. 'Your cousin tells me you're a bit of a modern bachelorette?'

'I wouldn't say that,' I reply, wondering what exactly Abigail has been telling her.

'What do you do?' her husband Ed asks me.

'I work for a magazine. Not one you've heard of,' I add this quickly. I've suffered through enough of these conversations to know exactly how they tend to go down. Everyone is fascinated about the magazine business until they find out it's something they can't find on the shelves. 'An industry magazine. For people in the hotel business.'

'Doesn't Ari work in magazines too?' Becca chips in.

'No, Ari works in law,' Michael says. 'I think he litigates against newspapers and magazines. He doesn't work for them.'

'It's nice that you're so career focused,' Yael continues to me. 'I would have liked to work, I think, but I find raising kids so much more fulfilling.'

'Oh, I need to work,' Becca interrupts. 'If I didn't leave the house every day, I think I'd go mad. Which reminds me Yael,' she turns to her friend. 'You must give me the number of that nursery you were telling me about. Eliana just isn't settling where she is now.' Then turning back to me: 'Sorry Tamsyn, what must you think? I swear, I've forgotten how to have conversations that aren't about children. It's infuriating, I know!'

'How old are yours?' I ask Becca.

'We have a five-year-old and Eliana is two,' Michael says proudly.

'And ours has just turned one,' Yael adds. She squeezes Ed's hand whilst she says it.

'Your turn next pal!' Michael nudges Dominic in the side and everyone laughs. I drink more wine.

'But seriously,' Yael continues to me. 'I know that you must love your lifestyle. I loved my lifestyle back then too. I really didn't think I needed anything to be happy. But then I met Ed, and everything suddenly made sense. Baruch Hashem I found him so quickly! It's like I was just half a person before, but now I'm whole.'

'Do you want kids?' Becca asks me next.

'Maybe, I don't know. I haven't really given it that much thought.'

'You're in your thirties though, right?'

'Thirty-one,' I clarify.

'Your mother must want grandchildren?'

'I'm sure she does.'

'You don't want to wait too late.'

'Nope. I sure don't.'

There's something about Becca's glare, as if she's genuinely concerned for me and my lack of wanting children, that makes me uneasy.

'Especially if it's perimenopause,' Yael adds with a knowing nod.

The doorbell rings and it takes all my willpower not to make a cheesy 'saved by the bell' joke.

But when Abigail goes to answer it and announces a cheery 'Ari!' my heart sinks. I look to the empty place setting beside me and realise that he's going to be sitting there. And that we're going to be the only single people here at this dinner. The one spot of brightness? As Ari comes into the dining room, I notice that he's in dressed-down work wear too. Jeans and sneakers and a hoodie.

'Sorry I'm so late. These are for you,' he presents Abigail with a box of chocolates. 'I only realised when I was already heading over here that they're milky.'

'You've only missed making kiddush, and you're just in time for soup! Don't worry about the chocolates,' Abigail reassures. 'We'll just have them another night.'

'Hi everyone,' he comes all the way into the dining room and waves at the table.

I catch his face when he notices me. He's shocked maybe, or repulsed, I'm not sure. Either way, he looks at me for just a moment too long, and then he goes back to greeting the other guests. I'm the only person he doesn't reach towards for a hug or a kiss on the cheek. Finally, he comes and sits down next to me.

'Hi,' he says.

'Hi,' I say back.

'How have you been?'

'I've been fine. You?'

'Fine.'

Abigail starts serving the chicken soup almost as soon as Ari's sat down.

'Tamsyn was just telling us about her job,' Yael prompts.

'Really?' Ari does a good job of pretending he's interested; I'll give him that.

'And Michael was trying to explain what you do. Something in law?'

'Oh, we don't want to talk about that. I've come here to be free of all that nonsense.'

'Michael said something about litigating newspapers?' Becca carries on regardless.

'Don't bother the man,' Michael scolds, 'he only just got in!'

'Ari's case was in the news!' Abigail says brightly, as she serves more people at the table, presenting bowls of steaming, honey-coloured soup with neat, golf ball-sized kneidlach bobbing within.

'Really?' Yael asks, leaning forward.

'It's just a libel thing,' Ari says. 'It's very dull really. I don't want to bore you all with it.'

He's being more polite than he needs to be, classic humble 'nice guy' move. I think of Euan, how if he were here, I'm sure he'd be happy to provide confident explanations of what his job entails, his body language oozing masculine dominance.

Even so, my interest is piqued, but only slightly. If there's a libel case against a newspaper that's making the news, then I've probably heard about it. But I don't want to show Ari that I'm interested in him or his life. I just file away the knowledge and promise myself that I'll ask Abigail about it another time.

As the other couples start talking about family life and how blessed they all are to have their children (and how Abigail and Dominic have so much to look forward to) I begin to feel like Ari and I are the naughty kids at the table. The conversation so rarely comes our way, and I don't feel particularly inclined to join in lest I start getting questioned about my life choices again.

'How long have you been single for, Ari?' Michael asks, at which point I decide to stare fiercely at the pattern on the bottom of the now empty china bowl in front of me.

'A while.'

'That's insane!' Yael says. 'A nice guy like you? Who wouldn't want you?'

Ari smiles meekly into the soggy remnants of his kneidlach.

'Why don't you ask Tamsyn out?' Becca asks.

'Becca!' Abigail fumes. I look at her making faces at Becca, silently asking her to keep schtum.

'I'm not really looking,' I interrupt suddenly, hoping to save both mine and Ari's dignity.

'Everybody says they're not looking. But that's only true if you have someone,' Yael comments.

'No, really. I'm not looking,' I say it more firmly this time. Maybe a little too firmly.

It's funny, the things you hear during an awkward silence. The scraping of spoons against china. The swallow of someone on the other side of the table when they take a drink. The tentative shuffle of the person sitting right next to you, suddenly far too close, his leg just inches from yours, almost touching your bare arm as he reaches forward for his glass of water.

I know it's not fair, because I can't imagine that he's to blame for any of this, or even a part of it. I bet he didn't even know I was going to be here tonight, just like I didn't know about him. But even so, I resent him immensely. Just for existing. For making me feel uptight, and for making me so angry at everyone else at the table.

'This looks amazing,' I tell Abigail once she sits down after serving the main course, eager to diffuse the tension. We have roast chicken with farfel on the side, along with a range of salads, one made with chickpeas and edamame beans, another featuring beetroot and avocado, plus a lush green tabbouleh. I'm reminded so much of the feasts my grandmother, Mum's mother, used to make before she became too frail to cook, although she would never venture far away from serving roast potatoes and boiled veg with her chicken. Mum cooks like this once in a while, but I can't remember the last time I saw food like this under the light of Shabbos candles. I can't remember when I was last home for a Shabbos meal.

'Oh, it's really nothing,' Abigail brushes off the compliment.

The others get deep into a heated conversation about whether they think citrus fruits belong in a salad, when Ari nudges me and says softly: 'Would you pass me the pickles?'

I pass them and offer him a polite smile as I do.

'Thank you,' he says, his words oddly purposeful and too polite.

'You're welcome,' I return, just as polite.

Then, after a moment of silence between us (the others are now talking about nurseries again. I'm beginning to wonder if there's anything else they have in common other than domestic labour), he says: 'Did you have a good week?'

I don't know what makes me fume so much at his question. I want him to be as angry and uncomfortable as I am by this whole mishigas. Maybe if we spent the meal in cold silence like a couple of surly teenagers, I'd feel vindicated somehow, but instead he has to go and be *nice*?

'It was okay,' I say.

In actual fact, it was not okay. Carmella finally officially left for Condé Nast, and it turns out she left a trail of messy, half-finished projects behind her, as well as a catalogue of claimed expenses for items that were almost certainly personal and not work related. Kerry-Ann has been taking up a lot of the slack, but we're now down a staff writer and Gareth has been hinting that we're unlikely to get the budget for another one. Which means everyone's going to have to work harder to fill the same number of pages.

The only bright spot has been the messages with Euan, but I can hardly tell anyone sitting here all about that.

'That's nice,' Ari says.

I hate that he's trying. I hate that I'm feeling sorry for his trying.

'How was your week?' I ask him out of politeness. Not because I'm interested.

His face falls for a moment, small lines of stress crossing his brow in a way that almost – almost – has me genuinely intrigued, but then he fixes his polite, easy-going smile back in place and shrugs.

I remember him being more upbeat and funny at the wedding, but then again that was a wedding. I was probably more upbeat and funny too. I start to wonder if something is wrong.

When I hear Becca and Yael start to talk about what Jewish schools they're thinking of going on the waiting lists for, and notice Abigail alone in the kitchen, I excuse myself from the table and follow her in there.

7

'So, what do you think about Ari? Must be nice to spend some proper time with him. You couldn't have had the chance to talk much at the wedding?'

'Abigail, I don't want to seem ungrateful,' I know I have to word this carefully so that I don't cause any offence, 'but I'm not interested in being set up.'

'Everyone says that. But it's just about meeting the right person at the right time. What if it's here and now?'

Her kitchen is cramped, the small flat not designed for large-scale entertaining. Even with just the two of us in here, I'm feeling crowded. I keep my voice low so there's no risk of being heard at the dining table just outside.

'I promise you, it's not,' I tell her, in as firm a voice as I can manage at this volume.

'That's a shame. I got the impression that Ari was quite smitten with you at the wedding.'

'Really?'

'I know, beats me too. With that scowl?'

I wind the scowl down, but still feel irritated.

'He was chatting with Dominic, was asking about you, what you're like and everything.'

'What did Dominic say?'

'That you were the independent type.'

'Well, thanks.'

'What? I thought you weren't interested?'

'I'm not. But calling me an independent type makes me sound like some kind of loner.'

'He didn't mean it like that. He meant free-spirited, not traditional. But really, it doesn't matter what Dominic said. I'm telling you . . .' she comes close and lowers her voice to a whisper, 'he got the distinct impression that Ari liked you.'

'Well, I'm not getting that kind of impression this evening.'

'I'm surprised you're not more relieved.'

Abigail fills up the sink with hot water and suds, and I hand her plates and cutlery to be lightly rinsed.

'Not using the dishwasher?' I ask her, a little confused.

'Shabbos,' she replies. 'I'll soak everything now so things don't get too grimy, then load it into the dishwasher to put on for a proper clean tomorrow night.'

'Seems like extra work,' I say.

I think I see a flash of something as Abigail rearranges the hairband she's wearing. I'd love it to be regret. I'd love her to suddenly break down with me and admit that being a good Jewish wife is far too much hard work, and she wants to be normal, but it's not that. She's not regretful, if anything she seems annoyed with me. But in a moment, the flash of anger has gone and the happy serenity has returned.

'I know you don't understand,' she says. 'I know you're *independent*. But just like how you are makes you happy, please understand that how I am makes me happy too. That Dominic and I chose this, and we're happy together.'

'Abigail, I'm sorry if I—'

'It's okay,' she looks at me, as if suddenly aware that she might have risked ruining her otherwise perfect first Friday night, and reaches towards me for a hug, her hands still damp and sudsy.

'I just need everyone to stop trying to marry me off, okay?' I mumble into the back of her head.

'Is Ari really that terrible?' she checks, pulling away from me but still holding me by the shoulders. 'He's a lawyer!'

'He's really not my type,' I say, hoping not to get drawn on what my type is.

'A decent, attractive guy isn't your type? I know you're straight Tamsyn, so don't try and play that one here.'

'It's not that he's not attractive . . .' I glance behind me into the dining room, making sure again that there's no chance of anybody listening in. I can hear Michael talking quite animatedly with Ed about the football, and the faint chatter of Becca and Yael, no doubt still talking about their babies, and schools, and any and every other thing associated with babies and schools.

'What then?'

I glance down at my watch and notice the time.

'I really should get going. It's getting late.'

'Tamsyn, stay a little longer? Have another glass of wine?'

'I really shouldn't.'

Abigail looks a little distressed, the bridge of her nose is wrinkled with concern. 'It was lovely to have you share this night with us,' she says. 'Sorry if I made you feel uncomfortable at any point.'

'Don't worry about it. And your cooking is impeccable. You're going to make a fine bubbe one day, I'm sure.'

'The challah will be better next time, I promise!'

Heading back out into the living room where everybody else is chatting, I announce my intention to leave and start hunting around the sofa for where I left my bag.

'Didn't you just say you had to make a move?' Yael nudges Ari.

'If we're both heading to the tube station, I can walk you there?' he suggests with a small, hopeful smile.

'Oh, I'm fine really.'

'Nonsense!' Becca intervenes. 'It's dark and nowhere is safe anymore. You must let Ari walk you.'

I glance towards the kitchen where Abigail is wincing apologetically. 'It would be a good idea,' she says. 'I know it's Finchley, but even I wouldn't walk about on my own this late at night.'

I only concede because I don't want to make a scene and because Ari doesn't look like the type to try anything with me.

As we say goodbye to everyone, I'm hyper-conscious that leaving together makes us look like a couple, and then suddenly we're walking down a suburban street together, heading in the direction of West Finchley tube station. The June night is balmy, almost tropical, the sky heavy with clouds that reflect the sodium yellow of the streetlights and mask everything in amber-purple. If I wasn't so vehemently against the idea, this would seem almost romantic.

'So, that was fun,' he says. We have at least another ten minutes walking together until we reach the tube station, and I suppose it would be weird if we didn't talk at all.

'Rock and roll,' I offer back with a sigh.

'You and your cousin seem pretty different.'

'In what way?' I challenge, side-eyeing him carefully.

'Oh, just, you know. Different.'

There go all my hopes for any sort of witty repartee. I find myself wondering if he still likes me, or if Abigail was just trying to wind me up. Ari looks off into the road, avoiding taking the conversation any further, which just makes me want to shake him. What kind of person starts a conversation, only to abandon it moments later? I thought he was meant to be a lawyer. I suddenly worry for his firm.

Conversation seemingly over, I take out my phone and find just one message from Euan, which to be honest is a little disappointing.

Hope the food is good, he says, followed by a cheeky wink.

I look at Ari again, who is looking down towards the pavement. Abigail isn't wrong, he is an attractive guy, but he's not exciting, not like Euan is. He's taller than most Jewish guys I tend to meet, and his hair is pretty outstanding, the type of texture I'm pretty sure would get awfully fluffy if it wasn't tamed regularly with a comb and various products, and I'm sure would be hilarious first thing in the morning. He looks kind when he smiles, and kind when he's not smiling too. But that doesn't mean he's my type. The fact that my family are all so keen for me to get on with him is precisely what rules him out as my type.

Euan comes into my head again, with all that vigour and fire in his eyes. The way he threw back to me every time I challenged him, the way he manages to excite me with almost every message he sends.

And then, out of nowhere, Ari says to himself with a sigh: 'Why is this night different from every other night?'

'Excuse me? Are you about to recite the "Ma Nishtana" or something?'

'Sorry, I was just thinking out loud.'

'About Pesach?'

'No, I just thought that tonight was an interesting night, that's all.'

'So, it wasn't a pick-up line?'

'A pick-up line? Do me a favour. If I was going to try a pick-up line, I'd say something like: I don't care what the Torah says, I'm not leaving any of your four corners unploughed.'

Despite myself, I'm laughing. 'Please don't tell me that line has ever worked?'

'Surprisingly, absolutely not. Never. One hundred percent failure record.'

'And that record continues undefeated.' I push the hair out of my eyes, realising that this is the first time I've genuinely smiled all evening.

'Damn, that's a shame. And I was so certain you were into me.'

'Oh really? What gave you that impression?'

'It wasn't you who set up the Jewish matchmaking brigade back there?'

'Are you serious? Abigail was in the kitchen after dinner begging me to give you a chance.'

'Wow. There I was thinking I would have to do this whole it's not you, it's me speech. Guess you are actually doing me a favour. Thanks!'

He's being funny, and I like that the ice is broken now. His posture is relaxed, and he seems more like himself. Not that I know what his real self is, but at least this version is easier to be around. I find myself relaxing too. It's like the pressure is off. Being able to talk so openly about how awkward that whole stupid dinner was, how obvious and annoying everyone else was being, is a huge relief.

'I'm sorry that you had to get roped into my family's determination to marry me off,' I tell Ari, trying to sound him out further.

'Well, you're one of the nicer ones they've tried for me, that's for sure.'

'You get it too?'

'Not so often since I decided to be busy with work all the time, but there's always someone I'm told I'm bound to hit it off with.'

'Is that what they did with me? They thought we'd hit it off?'

'Well, if we're being frank about things, there was a good chunk of time where I thought we actually might.'

So, he did like me at the wedding. Does he still fancy me now?

'Really?'

'Well,' he pauses, looking like he's thinking about how to phrase things. 'I don't think it would be a terrible idea if we took time to get to know each other better?'

I search for the words to help me with a careful let-down.

'I'm not sure,' I manage to say, before Ari quickly jumps back in.

'I said I didn't think it would be a terrible idea. However, I'm also not entirely convinced it would be a good idea either.'

Momentarily thrown, I ask: 'Why not?'

'Because you're a little . . .' he pauses again, scratching his head.

'What?'

'You're a little . . . cruel.'

I stop walking, stunned. That's not what I expected to hear. Ari stops a few steps ahead, and turns to face me, rolling his eyes with a shrug to indicate that he's really just teasing.

'Not all of the time, obviously,' he says. 'Not cruel like you're a nasty person, I don't think that at all. But you know, a little cold. Stubborn. Haughty maybe. And harsh with it.'

'I see,' I pout, because I really want to be able to argue with it, but I'm not sure how I can. I've been called stubborn my entire life. Kerry-Ann in the office once even called me an ice queen. Even so, I'm still floored that he actually said it. Ari Marshall, supposedly the nicest guy in the universe, meant to be smitten with me, called me out like that?

'I guess you could say I prefer a little more warmth?'

'Well, if we're being honest, I should let you know that you're really not my type either,' I tell him, fully intending to retaliate with all of my power.

'Let me guess, it's the nose.'

'What?' I'm startled, caught off-guard, again. I'm starting to hate when he does that.

'Not literally the nose, obviously. But you know what I mean.'

'I'm not sure that I do?' I'm finding this less and less funny by the moment.

'Okay, it was just a joke, but I can see it's touched a nerve.'

'Well, it wasn't funny. You're implying that I'm not into you because you look too Jewish? You don't even know me.'

'So, there's another reason?'

'Right now, I don't like you because you won't stop talking.'

We start walking again, my boots heavy on the pavement.

'Have you ever noticed,' Ari says, filling the silence, 'how on TV and in Hollywood there are all these Jewish leading men, but they never end up with Jewish girls? Woody Allen would be the archetype but let's not go there. But you know what I mean, right? The obviously Jewish guy, Adam Sandler, Andy Samberg or Seth Rogen, always going for the obviously non-Jewish girl. Not always blonde, but almost always WASPY and definitely Not Jewish.'

'Can't say I've ever really thought about it.'

'I have.'

'It's make-believe. It's not the real world. People end up with who they end up with.'

'You don't think it's strange though? That we don't see it all that often?'

'I don't think that Jewish people have to end up with Jewish people. It's really old fashioned to think like that. I don't want to be limited when it comes to falling in love.'

'As long as you're not limiting it the other way and ruling Jewish people out, I suppose.'

'Seriously? Is that what you think is happening here?'

'I just get a vibe from you about all this, that's all.'

'I promise you, I'm not sending out any vibes, positive or negative. I just want to get home, okay?'

I fold my arms across my chest and start walking faster.

'Do you even have any Jewish friends?' he asks.

'Why does it matter if I have Jewish friends or not?'

I've never had many Jewish friends, but he doesn't need to know that, and it's not as if it really means anything. I just didn't want to stay in the North West London bubble, and once you're out of it, there aren't an awful lot of Jewish people to befriend. When it came to deciding where to go for university, I knew I wanted to get as far away from what I knew as possible, which meant travelling across the country to Exeter. I'm not even sure they had a Jewish Society when I studied there.

'Come on, we were having fun,' Ari says.

'I'm not having fun,' I reply.

'Did it suddenly get really, really cold?' he teases, rubbing his hands on his arms as if he's freezing.

'Did you ever think that maybe I'm coming across as cold and cruel, or however you put it, because I'm just not interested? That it's a *you* problem rather than a *me* problem?'

'Eh, maybe. But I also think you didn't give me much of a chance either, and that's what makes me wonder.'

'You really think you're all that?'

'I think *you* think you're all that.'

'Whatever. This schtick is really boring me now.'

'Or it's just making you uncomfortable because it's true.'

'I'll tell you something true. You think you're one of these know-it-all people who has life sussed. You make everyone think you're the nice guy, playing the mild-mannered mensch who people fall over themselves to impress. You just can't stand being rejected, and you're desperate to find a reason that has nothing to do with you. How am I meant to like someone who's just spent a whole walk basically insulting me? You're the one with the problem Ari, not me.'

'Oof,' he puts a hand on a pretend bullet wound over his heart but continues smiling. He seems to be liking my ranting, is taking it too lightly, which only serves to infuriate me further.

'And why does everything have to be about being Jewish anyway?' I say. 'Why this push to marry Jewish people together? As if we have no other options in the world? Nature likes diversity. I like diversity. I want to meet other people, experience life in different backgrounds, get some perspective on life that isn't uniquely centred on one tiny minority community. The world is bigger than Jewishness, and it's not even something I particularly like about myself.'

I see the bright blue glow of the West Finchley underground sign ahead.

'Hmm,' Ari says, still smiling curiously to himself.

'What?'

'Nothing. Just thinking that what you said there was pretty telling.'

'Come off it. You're not about to psychoanalyse me too? What is this, a competition to see just how intensely Jewish you can actually be? It's not winning me over buddy.'

'I'm not going to psychoanalyse you Tamsyn, I'm just getting to know you.'

'Seems to me you're just being a dick.'

'Ouch, there's another hit.'

'It's not like you didn't hit me first.'

We scan our Oyster cards and go through the gates, crossing the bridge to the southbound platform where we wait in silence.

'Listen,' I say to him. 'I just want to make sure that we're on the same page here. I didn't know you before, and that's fine. But I know you now, and I think you're pretty insufferable. I'm sorry that our families set us up. I hope they both leave us alone from now on. And you know what? You're right. I don't date Jewish guys. But it's not for the reasons you think. It's a preference, that's all. And it's mainly come about because I've met so many Jewish men just like you. Happy now?'

He's smiling at me amiably, a sly half-quirk of the mouth.

'You think I'm funny?' I ask him.

'I think you're interesting,' he says. I catch a look in his eye, a sparkle of genuine curiosity. It's a look that might make me blush, if the circumstances were different. If this guy wasn't absolutely one hundred percent the worst.

The tracks below start their electrical splutter as the tube train approaches.

'Are you going via Bank?' I ask him, indicating the approaching train.

'I'm Charing Cross,' he says, and I look up to the sky in relief.

'In which case, goodbye then,' I say as I board the train. 'And I mean this in the most genuine and straightforward way possible, but I sincerely hope we're never forced together like this again.'

'I'll see you around Tamsyn Rutman,' Ari laughs after me as the tube door closes.

I'm boiling the whole way home.

'You okay?' Helene asks me when I get in.

'You know what, no. No, I am not,' I tell her.

'Do I need to get the gin?'

'Is there anything stronger in the flat?'

'Stronger than gin?'

'I just want to scream!'

'What on earth happened?'

I take a few breaths when I notice how concerned Helene looks. She's seen my temper in flashes, like when I spill a drink or get the answer in a quiz show wrong, but I don't think I've ever been this angry in front of her.

'You want to know something?' I ask her. She makes herself comfy on our sofa and nods. 'My whole life I was never allowed out on a Friday night. All through my teens, when other people were hanging out and going to parties, I wasn't allowed. Why? Because I was Jewish. Because Friday night was family time. And almost every week we didn't even do anything! We'd have a brisk Friday night dinner, light the candles and have some challah, and then after dinner we'd sit in front of the TV like every other night. It made no sense to me. Meanwhile, my friends were all out having fun, and I missed out every single time. So tonight, I tell the most incredible, amazingly attractive man in the universe, who barely gets any evenings off, that I can't go on our first ever date because I have a family obligation. Once again, I am a good girl. A good Jewish girl. And look where that gets me?'

'Tamsyn, what happened?' Helene still has this look of abject shock on her face, like I'm going to tell her the most awful thing in the world.

'I had a bad night, that's what happened!' I say.

'Yes, but what happened that got you so worked up like this? What *actually* happened?'

'This stupid guy,' I say.

'A guy?' Helene's mouth does the same little upward quirk thing that Ari's did.

'No Helene. Don't even start. This man, he is the worst. Someone I wish I'd never met. And I was stuck with him walking back to the tube station, where he spent the entire time insulting me for no reason! Just taking apart my character and being, well, just wretched!'

'Did he hurt you?' Helene asks, the concern back in her voice.

'Oh god no, he wasn't like that. He didn't hurt me at all. He was just talking.'

'Why would someone just insult you like that? I don't get it. What were you talking about?'

'It's so complicated, honestly. But we were fixed up. Actually, it was the second time we were fixed up. I wasn't firm enough the first time. But we were chatting on the way back and everything just descended. He called me cruel!'

'He called you cruel?'

'And cold, and stubborn! Outrageous, right?'

Except Helene is laughing. Or at least, she's trying not to laugh.

'What?' I yell at her.

'Sounds like this guy really pushed your buttons.'

'This guy makes me want to scream and punch things!'

'More so than Euan?'

'Don't you dare bring that amazing angel of a man's name into this. That situation is totally different. When Euan winds me up, it makes me want to rip his clothes off. With Ari? It makes me want to kill him!'

'Noted.'

Helene looks smug. Too smug. I sigh all the air out of myself and then collapse down on the sofa next to her.

'You're making the same face he did,' I say.

'Who, Ari?'

'It's that same "I've got your number" kind of face. Like either of you know what's actually going on in my head. You're both completely wrong.'

'I think I like this Ari guy,' Helene laughs before I reach over and smack her with a cushion.

8

He chose the restaurant, and I can honestly say this is the first time I've ever felt like a place is sexy. Or maybe it's just being with him, I don't know.

Euan is waiting at the bar when I turn up and looks so good, I feel like I've slipped outside of myself and into a place where I'm watching my life as a movie. His blonde hair is swooped back, his beard clearly freshly groomed and oiled, and he's wearing a swish dark-velvet blazer that I swear on anyone else would be far too much, but on him is impressively cool. I'm wearing a sleek, black, halterneck jumpsuit, the fit wide around the legs so that the fabric swishes like a gown, and with a slit down the front so potentially revealing that I considered using double-sided tape to make sure everything stayed where it was meant to. When we hug, he wraps both arms around me, and he smells faintly of syrup and burning pinecones. My body is humming just from the contact.

The lights in the restaurant are turned down low, the blacks and forest greens of the walls and panelling offset by understated copper fixtures and fittings. The layout – plush booths separated by dark wooden screens – dampens all sound, so that when we're facing each other, looking into each other's eyes, it's as if there's nobody else here but us.

I realise suddenly that this meal is foreplay, and my body starts humming once again.

'Tell Davide that I'm here,' Euan tells the waiter, whose cheeks go pink when she realises who she's talking to. Even the curl of his Geordie inflection is doing something to me.

'Davide?' I ask, suspicious.

'He's the chef here. We go way back. I let him know that we were coming, and he's got something special prepared. I hope that's okay?'

'My, it sounds like you're trying to impress me Mr Hegarty,' I tease.

'And what if I am?' he teases back with a grin.

I've gone from humming to melting. I didn't know it was possible to go weak at the knees when you're sitting down.

Despite the intensity I'm already feeling, I'm determined to stick to the plan for tonight. And that plan mostly involves being cool. It's like we're playing a game with each other, a game we both know is going to end up in bed, but all of this (the texts, the restaurant) is just a grand, meticulous plan to prolong the pleasure. I know it from the way he doesn't take his eyes off me; the way he smiles when I match the eye contact; the way I'm aware of every inch of his body, from the shape of his lips to the lean of his shoulders, and right down to where he's currently placed his feet. They're next to mine under the table, not touching but still so close I feel like if I just shuffled slightly, they'd be knocking into his. Not letting our feet touch is just a part of this game. The same way he takes a drink whenever I do, the same way he raises an annoyed eyebrow whenever the waiter comes back to check how we're doing.

So, I must keep cool. Despite wanting to explode, I'm determined to not be the one who breaks. I will be the cool girl he wants me to be right now, someone who has played this kind of game before, maybe even several times.

'I'm so pleased we've been able to do this,' he says, his voice almost a growl.

'I was scared you were never going to get another evening off,' I admit.

'They can get by without me for one night,' he takes a drink. 'So, how's the article going?'

'Oh, you know, just making sure everyone knows how boring and mean you are,' I smile wickedly.

'Hey, as long as you don't say anything about my kitchen, then I'll be happy.'

'You know I've been checking up on things, and technically this whole situation we have might be a breach of journalistic ethics?'

'Oh really?'

'They could say you're just trying to buy a good story,' this time I take a drink, watching him over the rim of my glass.

'You've already written it, right?' Euan checks.

'It's been filed. Goes to print next week.'

'In which case, my job is done and I'll be off. Waiter!'

He gets up and starts to signal for the staff, but I pull him down back into his seat by his incredibly lush velvet jacket and laugh.

'Now, now, you're not getting away that easily,' I say.

He gives me another of those devilishly hungry smiles and I wonder if it's enough to make the cool girl facade break. Nearly, very nearly, but I hold on.

'So, tell me more about yourself Ms Rutman,' he says.

'What would you like to know?'

'Where did you grow up? What's your family like? Did you always want to work for *Hotelier Monthly*?'

'I grew up in North West London. My family are very normal. And yes, it was my lifelong dream to work for a magazine like this.'

Truth, lie and lie. But he doesn't have to know.

'Did you always want to be a chef?' I ask him.

'Always. I remember once being really young, maybe only five or six, and I raided all the kitchen cupboards for ingredients to experiment with. I had no idea what I was doing, but it felt like exploring.'

'You didn't eat any of the experiments, did you?'

'You bet! Never anything that would have made me seriously ill, mind, but I can't say I wasn't a bit sick a few times. Speaking of being sick, it's Davide!'

A man dressed in a black chef's outfit has approached the table along with a team of wait staff. He greets Euan comfortably, like the old friends they are. They clasp hands and reach into one of those terribly manly hugs where no one actually ends up hugging anyone.

'Euan Hegarty, as I live and breathe!' Davide announces, his voice a little too loud for the ambience.

'What you got for us pal?' Euan asks once he's sat back down.

'A tasting menu. Nothing but the best for Mr Hegarty of the Clarence and his guest.' Davide turns to me, eyes shining. 'Anyway, I don't want to interrupt, just wanted to say hello. Please enjoy! I must get back in the kitchen. Some of us have work to do.'

'Easy pal, you don't know how hard it was to get this night off!' Euan laughs. I blush slightly, thinking about the effort he might have gone through to be with me.

There's one more handshake between the friends, and then Davide heads back into the kitchen. Almost at once a waiter presents the first dish in front of me.

'Grilled octopus with black bean and pear sauce,' she says before leaving us.

'Wow, I've never had octopus before,' I admit, relinquishing a tiny bit of my cool girl energy in order to let Euan help me.

'Oh, you'll love it. It's a bit like lobster?'

'Don't really have much experience with lobster either.'

At least I've tried lobster. Just once though. But I've never pulled one apart like I've seen people do on TV. When I was younger, pig and shellfish were completely off the menu. My parents wouldn't let them in the house, and if we were eating out, I could never order them. I understood why, but at the same time I didn't, and put it down to just being another quaint, old-fashioned tradition that never made much sense to me.

'Well then, someone is going to just have to teach you.'

There it is again, the hungry flirt loaded with so much intention I nearly miss my mouth when I go to eat the first bite. I'm surprised by the crispiness, followed by the tender inside, but it tastes good. I wish I could tell my parents what they're missing out on.

I get him to talk about his family and growing up just outside Newcastle throughout the meal. After we're done with every course, someone attentively whisks the plates away and provides the next serving, each one more lavish and bizarre than the last.

Whenever Euan asks about me, I answer as simply as I can before I deflect back to him. He's an easy talker, so he doesn't seem to mind. Plus, I end up learning lots about the kind of kid he was in school, why he decided not to go to university and nearly ended up joining the navy instead, and how seeing his brother deal with depression and anxiety led him to lead a more compassionate lifestyle and take notice of the world. Everything he tells me just sounds so perfect. If I could write a list of all the qualities that would make up my ideal man, it would add up to Euan Hegarty.

'You're a great listener, but you've not said much,' he says softly during a break between courses.

'That's because I'm interested in you,' I tell him in my best cool girl voice.

'But I'm interested in you too,' he says back, just as coolly.

'I don't think I have much to say.' Or at least, not much that I want to tell.

'Tell me about the first boy you kissed,' he asks cheekily.

I'm not going to let Simon Schaffler, and how much he hurt me, ruin the mood.

'You don't want to hear about that,' I smile, hoping that I come across as seductively coy, rather than uncomfortable.

'I do. I want to hear about every man you've been with. I want to know what you did and how badly you broke their hearts.'

I don't think any sentence has made my heart stop quite as urgently as that one. I'm thrumming again.

'Scared I'm going to break yours?'

'If I need to arm myself, I need to know what I'm up against.'

We look at each other. A long, daring stare. If the dessert course hadn't arrived at precisely that moment, I would have suggested we leave right away and get a cab back to his place. The urgency feels like it's boiling my blood.

I destroy the dark chocolate orb in front of me by pouring violet-scented cream over it. There's a small brownie-like cake inside that tastes of vanilla and caramel.

'This is divine,' I admit between mouthfuls. 'Seriously, the best thing I've ever tasted.'

'You dare say that in front of another chef?'

'Well, I might change my mind when you cook for me. But right now, nothing is beating this.'

He laughs while I make faces, devouring the dessert. Finally, when I put my fork down, he says: 'Want to get out of here?'

I nod, without saying anything, never losing his gaze.

Euan tells me to wait outside for him whilst he stays back to say goodbye to Davide, but I'm only alone on the pavement for a brief moment before he's back with me, one large arm around me as we head down the street looking for a taxi. The closeness is exhilarating, we fit together so perfectly. That slight pinecone scent again, warm in a way that makes me want to snuggle in as close as I can and let myself be completely absorbed.

Then I start to wonder when he's going to kiss me, if our mouths will still taste of violets and vanilla, and whether his arms will be strong enough to hold me when I'm inevitably overwhelmed and my legs start to buckle.

I think he can tell that I'm nervous because he suddenly stops and, in the glare of a streetlight, he swivels me around so that I'm facing him, and then he's leaning down and we're kissing. The richness and softness of him, it's like watching that chocolate orb melt under the hot cream all over again.

'Wow,' I say when he pulls away.

'I just had to,' he replies. I see now that he's blushing and realise that he must have been nervous too.

'I'm pleased that you did.'

There are glimmers, underneath all that vigorously sexy bravado, of something more like a wholesome boyishness. Of someone who wants comfort and security, a romantic who yearns for something more fulfilling. But I don't think Euan wants me to see this, at least not yet. He takes a deep breath, steeling himself and fixing the mask of confidence back in place.

He holds my hand in his as he hails a black cab, and then suddenly we're heading West.

To say that Euan's flat is sparse is an understatement. There's nothing in here. Everything is bare minimum. The last rays of a midsummer twilight fall lilac through the French windows, revealing a plain, generic sofa placed over one of those cheap beige rugs you can get from Ikea. The kitchen slash living area is open plan, making the relatively small space feel doubly wide but also doubly empty. The only piece of art is an unframed poster for *Eternal Sunshine of the Spotless Mind* tacked to the wall.

'The hotel arranged this place for me,' Euan says by way of explanation. 'I only moved in about three months ago, but I've been so busy I haven't had a chance to do anything with it.'

'It's a great blank canvas,' I say. It really is. Spending so much time going through reviews for hotels and stalking holiday destinations has given me a keen eye for the potential of a space. For Euan, I'm imagining rich upholstery, leathers and woods, and a feature wall of dark teal. 'Have you brought many girls back here yet?'

'No,' he admits, which surprises me. 'Back to the hotel on occasion? Can't confirm or deny. But you're the first to see where I actually live.'

Despite everything that's happened so far, this is the first hint I've had that something serious is happening, beyond just being a fun, sexual gallivant. I now look at the way he's groomed, the expert tailoring of his velvet jacket, and the suddenly shy look across his face and I realise *he likes me*. I knew he liked me, in as much as I'm absolutely certain that we're going to sleep together. But I never thought for a moment that I was anything other than another conquest. I never thought that he *liked me*, liked me.

'Shall I open a bottle of wine?' he asks, and I wonder if he's noticed the trepidation on my face.

'Go for it,' I say.

We clink glasses and, after a long drink, I feel the rhythm is back. It's darker now, the only light coming from the soft strips hidden under the kitchen cabinets, and he's standing close to me, nearly over me, the broadness of his chest right there, asking for me to touch it.

'I'm not usually a first date kind of girl,' I lie, my voice low and breathy.

'It's the second date if you count the interview,' he replies.

'That was work. It doesn't count.'

'It wasn't work for me,' he says, except the final word doesn't quite make it, because he's kissing me, and I'm letting him push me back towards the sofa.

I knew this was going to feel good, I was anticipating it from the moment I locked eyes with him in the Clarence, but I really had no idea. There's no denying that he's well practised, but then I'm not exactly a novice either. I let him move however he wants, because for me the pleasure is just being in his presence. The heat and the energy and the dark urgency of his kissing, as if he's scared I might escape and disappear in the blink of an eye. I love that he wants me this much. His wanting me is what makes me want him.

'I still feel like I hardly know you,' he says between kisses. But I don't want to stop to talk, I just want him to keep going. 'Tell me a secret. What's the baddest thing you've ever done?'

'Sleeping with an interviewee comes pretty close to the top,' I admit with a knowing smirk.

'Is that so?' he asks, pulling back from me.

'I shouldn't really have even been the one to do the interview. My boss tried to stop me. I was really very naughty.'

'Well, I'm pleased you did.'

'So am I.'

'Fated,' Euan murmurs before going back to kissing. Something squirms in me at the word 'fated', but I push past it, too hungry for him to think. The Hebrew word is beshert, and I know this isn't that.

We pull apart to move to the bedroom, another stark affair, the sheets dark grey.

I realise as he's undressing me that this is going to be the best sex I've ever had, despite the fact we haven't got to the good part yet. My body is on fire with urgency, and every tiny, slow movement of his is making me absolutely furious. I hate that he seems to know this too. When I clamour for more, he just pulls back. Every sign of my yearning just seems to amuse him. Euan's mouth crooks into a one-sided smile as he realises that any teasing he does makes me want to scream. And I do scream.

Lying beside him afterwards, I'm scared that it's never going to be that good again. That it will be impossible to ever fancy a man that much again. That my body will never feel as good as it does now.

'Amazing,' he pants, staring at the ceiling. He's still holding my sweaty hand.

'Wow,' I agree.

'Thank you for coming into my life.'

'Thank you for getting such a great job and letting me come into your life.'

'You keep bringing everything back to work.' He's not saying it in an accusatory way, but I know he's accusing me, and I also know that cool girls probably don't talk about work all the time either. Cool girls talk about drinking and hanging out with friends, the cool Instagrammable events they go to and how rebellious they were as children.

'It takes up a big chunk of my day,' I laugh.

'But what about you? Who you are and what you like? Tell me something I don't already know.'

'Okay, here's something,' I pause, hoping the extra time will help me come up with something that will impress him and not make me sound too lame. 'I once nearly got chucked out of Chessington World of Adventures for harassing one of those costumed mascots.'

'You what?'

I worry suddenly that I've got it wrong, that I should have told him something that was sexier, but then he's laughing, and peering at me with such admiration and humour that I can't help but laugh back.

'I was eighteen, it was the summer before we started university, and a group of us went on a trip to Chessington. A couple of us snuck a load of these tiny alcohol miniatures in so that we could get drunk. It wasn't even that much, but I was eighteen and I don't think it took much back then. Anyway. Next thing you know, I think it's hilarious to start trying to take the head off one of the costume characters. A big, furry, red monkey thing. They gave me a warning the first time, but then when I saw the same character towards the end of the day, I just went for it. I don't even know if it was the same person in the costume – they must switch out during the day, right? I guess I was drunk and desperate to impress my friends, which is completely stupid I know, but I ended up in this kind of holding room to sober up. I had to wait there until the end of the day and my friends collected me on the way home. You asked me earlier about the baddest thing I have ever done, and I think that's probably it.'

I don't tell him that this was the summer I was trying to forget that Simon Schaffler was having the time of his life in Israel, that I was drinking and trying to impress my friends because I felt lonely and angry.

He squeezes my hand. I look down at his arm, covered in all these intricate tattoos, Celtic knots and geometric patterns, and somewhere in there, a lion roaring, and I start to feel daunted by how much he seems to like me.

'Here's something about me,' he says. 'Something that I trust you to keep firmly off the record.'

I mimic zipping my mouth shut with my free hand.

'I've always wanted to be a chef, but I never thought I actually would be. At least, nothing at this level. This is a dream come true. But I had a backup plan, and it's something only my mother knows about me.'

'Go on.'

'I wanted to be a veterinary nurse.'

'You mean a vet?'

'Nope. A veterinary nurse. I knew I didn't have the grades in school to go to university and study to be a vet. I wasn't interested in all that. All I wanted was to look after puppies and kittens and help them get well.'

'Oh my god, you are so soft!'

'Completely and totally soft.'

'How did you end up a living, breathing *Game of Thrones* character then?'

'This is just a beard. I eat so much in my job I need to work out to keep it all under control. I got a lot of tattoos. But it's not who I am. Just like I know you're not the suave, frosty femme fatale woman you pretend to be.'

'If I'm not really who I pretend I am, then why do you like me?'

'Because I know there's something else. And getting to know that something else is exciting to me. Isn't it exciting to you too?'

I mumble in the affirmative, without agreeing out loud. Because what if he sees what's underneath and doesn't like it? Seeing underneath would mean seeing something he may not be ready for. And what's so wrong with pretending anyway? I want to be the person I am when I'm around him. I don't want to be someone who has a family to answer to, who has to hold off a pervy boss and spends most Saturday nights watching reality shows with their flatmate. I want to be cool, exciting and mysterious. I want to be with someone who is cool, exciting and mysterious too.

'I've enjoyed this evening,' I say.

'I have as well. You don't have to go so soon?'

'I do. I live on the other side of London. And I have work tomorrow.'

'Then at least let me get you a cab?'

'All the way to Hoxton?'

'One of the perks of dating the hottest new chef at the Clarence. I have no time to spend all the money they pay me. Let me spend it on you.'

I feel uncomfortable with this. The lavish meal was enough, and I don't want anyone to think I'm only dating someone like Euan because they have money. I've always been as forthright as I can about paying my own way, however I also don't want to ruin the magic by explaining why this is to him.

'Oh, we're dating are we?' I tease instead. Euan doesn't answer me, he only smirks.

He watches me as I get dressed and it doesn't feel creepy. The opposite in fact. I know he's taking me in, studying me, working out what he wants to do to me next time he has me naked. It's so hot it makes me want to take my clothes off all over again. By the time I'm ready, there's an Uber close by.

Euan gets out of bed, naked and glorious, and holds my face in his hands, his forehead close to mine.

'You're someone I could learn to adore,' he says, and I'm melting all over again, wondering how bad it would be if I turned up to work the following morning wearing these clothes, my hair flat and greasy.

'I should go,' I breathe, and he kisses me one more time, hard and intense.

I feel drunk as I walk down the steps to the road where the cab is waiting, despite knowing the wine must have worn off ages ago. Drunk and thrilled and excited about whatever is going to come next. But once I'm in the cab, the space next to me feeling pointedly empty, I realise too how exhausted I feel, and how much hard work it was to be the girl I imagined he wanted for the whole evening. He's already texted me to check that I got into the cab safely and that the driver isn't a creep, and instead of replying straight away, maintaining the connection, I decide to put my phone on silent and wait to reply until I get home.

9

It's a double page spread, barely more than two thousand words and loaded with flattering pictures, not just of Euan Hegarty, but of the Clarence Grill as well, but even so, I'm really proud of how it turned out. Nobody I care about will read it, but it doesn't matter. Euan looks hot in the photos and I gave him a gleaming write-up, being sure to focus on his values in the kitchen and why he'll make the restaurant a big success.

'I heard a rumour,' Kerry-Ann says, coming into my office. 'Is Euan Hegarty your boyfriend?'

'What? No! Don't be ridiculous,' I reply, trying not to look flustered. I know they're all going to know eventually, but I'd rather the gossip not reach Gareth or the rest of the senior team quite so soon. Plus, 'boyfriend' is a little extreme a term for what we're doing, which is essentially just eating in fancy restaurants and having a lot of sex.

'You know we have a shared calendar,' Kerry-Ann points out.

'Those were follow-up interviews. Fact checking.'

'Right. Fact checking. Over dinner?'

'He's a chef.'

Kerry gives me a sly smile but doesn't push any further. I allow myself the rare privilege of daydreaming in my office. Of running away with Euan to travel the world, maybe on a motorbike or a moped, zipping through old European cities and along mountain trails. I don't even know if he rides a motorbike, but that's what I want for him. Sunglasses and a leather jacket, looking mean and me being swept off my feet every single day.

Later in the afternoon I have a meeting with Gareth, which makes me a little nervous. We have regular catch-ups and of course there are the weekly team pitch meetings, but this one is unscheduled.

Gareth Parkinson's office hasn't changed since the nineties. Dented grey filing cabinets, a weird textured surface on the walls, those white square polystyrene tiles on the ceiling for some reason even more noticeable than they are elsewhere. He's had the same spider-plant on the windowsill for years, so it's now a veritable bush with offshoot tendrils reaching out left and right. Behind his desk he's hung up his diplomas and his degree from Cambridge, and on the desk is one of those executive toys with silver balls that move constantly once pushed. Everything is a little bit dusty in here, and a little bit murky. It's not been legal to smoke inside for years, and yet I swear everything is just a little bit yellower than it should be. Everything that is, apart from Gareth's cheeks, which are solidly pink.

'Everything okay?' I ask Gareth, taking a seat in front of his desk.

'Some lovely news actually,' my heart rate instantly goes down, relieved that he's not about to tell me about some impending doom or plans for downsizing. 'I wanted to make sure that you were in the loop prior to a proper announcement.'

I know I'm frowning. I also know that my heart rate has leapt back up again. Immediately, I wonder if Gareth is announcing his retirement, if it's finally time for me to step up to be editor-in-chief. It would make sense. He's in his early sixties, it's only a matter of time before someone files historic sexual harassment claims against him, and it's clear that he doesn't have the same interest in the business as he used to. I just wasn't expecting this to happen today, right now.

'Have you come across a young chap called Cooper Radcliffe?'

'I don't think I've heard that name.' It's the kind of name you'd remember if you heard it once.

'Lovely lad. Attended my alma mater, son of a good friend. Has been doing some good work over at the *Spectator* too, but he's after a new challenge, and I thought that it might be time to start thinking about my own next steps. Timing's perfect, don't you think?'

My internal frown intensifies, but I keep my face as placid as I can for the sake of this meeting.

'So, here's the plan. Bring him in as a deputy editor-in-chief, get him trained up and ready, and then, in due course, we'll have a solid line of succession. What say you?'

I think it's nepotism. I think it makes a mockery of everything I've done for most of the last decade. I think he has blinders on to seeing a woman, especially a non-Oxbridge educated one like me, possibly succeed him. I think he's living in the 1950s.

'I think it sounds interesting,' I say.

He wets his lips. 'So, if I arrange to bring Cooper in, you'll show him the ropes?'

'Of course. I'd be happy to help.'

'Well, that's swell then, isn't it? I'm really excited about this. It's a great move forward. Cooper will do wonderful things, I'm sure.'

I leave Gareth's office fuming, and when I get back to mine, I immediately make sure that my LinkedIn profile is on private mode before I start looking him up. Cooper Radcliffe is two years younger than me and has only been editing for a year. He's vastly under-qualified, but as soon as I notice his profile picture, I understand exactly what's happening. Floppy brown hair, the blue eyes, and the salmon pink shirt. The man looks like a dictionary definition of 'young Tory'. He even has the kind of complexion that makes me think he's going to be as ruddy faced as his predecessor as he gets older.

I think about texting Euan about my fury, but I don't want to bring my real-life problems into whatever it is that we have. Euan is who I can turn to when I need to escape all of this. I send a link to the profile to my brother Ross instead.

Who is this schmendrick? Ross texts back almost immediately. *Please don't tell me you're dating him?*

I'll be training him up to be my boss, apparently, I reply.

I don't know whether I'm relieved or more worried. Remind me why you haven't quit that place yet?

I'm not a quitter. Especially not after all the hard work I've put in.

Ross doesn't respond after that. But I know him well enough to know what he's thinking. My brother has always mocked my choices, but then I'm not the one who decided to pursue an academic career as far away from North West London as I could manage. I'm the one with the resilience, and the determination. I won't let Gareth or Cooper get the satisfaction of watching me leave. When everything goes wrong, I'll be there, the one who will fix everything and then can grab the glory.

I think about telling Ross about Euan, but I don't want to make a big thing of it. We're dating. We're having sex. But he's not my boyfriend and it's not serious. At least it's not yet. I haven't told Ross about a guy I'm seeing in ages, and he hasn't spoken to me about a girl in years. At all, come to think about it. But it's understandable. We both grew up in the same household. I have my issues, and I'm sure he has his.

My fury regarding Gareth's plan sits with me throughout the afternoon and onwards into my dinner with Euan. Tonight he's cooking for me.

In the couple of weeks since I was last here, he's been busy making his flat feel more like a home. I like how the simple fact of my presence has driven him to feel more settled, as if he can impress me with soft furnishings. Which, to be honest, he can. There are a few plants now (still in their freshly bought brown plastic pots), an array of fresh herbs to help him in the kitchen, and the film poster has come down, to be replaced with pictures of his family in thick black frames. There are cushions on the sofa, bright orange and earthy brown, and in the bedroom, some new expensive sheets. I very much like how they feel under me.

It's cute that he's nervous about cooking for me. When I arrive, he's got a proper chef's apron on, blue-and-white stripes, and his face is red from the heat. I know that he's frustrated by his home kitchen, that he doesn't have enough space nor the quality of appliances, but he's determined, and he wants me to be happy.

'I'm hungry,' I say in a cute voice, coming behind him whilst he's working at the stove. I have no idea what he's cooking, but it smells divine.

'Not much longer to wait,' he says.

'I'm not talking about the food.'

I've never considered myself a particularly sexually adventurous person, but there's something about him. Something that makes me want to test his boundaries, and my own. I reach down the front of his jeans as he cooks. They're tightly fitted, but he doesn't stop me as I press.

'What are you doing?' he asks, and I know he's smiling even though I can't see his face.

'Nothing,' I say, all innocence.

'I'm trying to cook here,' he says, the sentence fading as I find what I'm looking for. 'It's going to get burnt.'

'You want me to stop?' I ask, pressing myself into his back, one arm wrapped around him, the other still busy.

He can't say anything and knowing that I have this power over him is all I want right now.

'We can do this later,' he says between heavy breaths.

'Or we do it now? Skip to dessert?'

'I've been preparing for this all day. Please, stop. Just for now.'

I pull my hand back and step away from him. The rejection feels brutal. He turns around and catches my pout with a deep kiss, leaning me back into the fridge.

'I've been working hard on this dinner,' he says when he pulls away. 'Cooking means a lot to me. Cooking for you means even more.'

I nod, a naughty child scolded, and go to sit on the sofa as he finishes preparing. Doesn't he realise that I'm not overly interested in the food? That the food is not what I'm here for? Except he does look even more attractive when he's frowning over the stove, the muscles in his arms beautifully tense as he chops vegetables.

'What did you do with your day off?' I ask him.

'Not an awful lot. Slept in late, then went to the shops to get ingredients. Had a long chat with my parents, then the gym.'

'Are your parents well?' I ask, less from interest, more from wanting to make sure he knows I'm not at all bothered by his rejection just now. Plus, I think he likes talking about his family. He always smiles when I ask after them.

'They're good. Really well. I told them all about you actually.'

'You did? What did you say?'

'Just that I met someone really special. That we should all get together next time they come down to London. Or maybe, if I get some time off in the near future, we could head up there and say hello? I think you'd like Newcastle.'

'Oh, that would be nice.'

'You'd get on with my mum. She's a bit of a battle-axe, doesn't take any shit from anyone, but in a quiet, clever kind of way. Cool, calm and collected. Reminds me of you a bit.'

'Careful, there are implications in comparing me to your mother. And to a battle-axe, for that matter.'

'I'm well aware. You're very different people, trust me. And she looks nothing like you. But there's an energy. Maybe that's what I'm attracted to? Take that however you like. A hard shell on the outside, with all this soft gooeyness inside.' He sounds more Geordie when he talks about home.

'Well, now I sound like a chocolate bar.'

'You're my chocolate bar.'

'Nope. Too much corniness. Take that back!'

'A little corniness doesn't hurt once in a while.'

Euan serves me the most perfect seared salmon with a sauce I don't have the words to describe. There's also asparagus and gratin potatoes cooked so perfectly that they melt in my mouth before I've even had the chance to chew.

'Oh my god,' I moan as I take mouthful after mouthful.

'See what you nearly ruined?' he goads playfully.

'How do you do this? I can't imagine doing anything without having the recipe right in front of me.'

'Years and years of training and practise. In the early years, it's like being drilled in the military. You're shouted at until everything is perfect.'

'That doesn't sound like fun,' I point out.

'But it's worth it when I get to see your face after taking a bite.'

There's that corniness again.

'Tell me about your parents,' Euan asks as we're finishing up.

'Not sure there's much to say. They're just normal parents. Mum and Dad.'

'What are their names?'

'Lydia and Joseph.'

'And what do they do?'

'Mum is a retired medical secretary. My dad is a forensic accountant. But it's more like part-time consultant work these days.'

'And?'

'And what?'

'Wow, it's like drawing blood from a stone with you. Don't you get on with your parents?'

'We get on fine.'

'So?'

'So what?'

'So why don't you like to talk about them?'

'Because it's boring. I'm here with you. Why would I want to talk about my parents?'

I'm scared that this is going to turn into an argument. Not a serious one, but Euan really does look frustrated. I reach over the table to put my hand on his face, stroking away any creases I see there. 'This is time for me and you,' I tell him. 'Talking about our parents just seems . . . well, to put it frankly, it's not really very romantic.'

'I'm just trying to get to know you,' he says softly, turning his head slightly so that he can kiss my palm.

'You don't need to know about my parents to know about me,' I laugh.

'Just one more question then,' he starts. I decide to let him have it. It's not worth getting into an argument about. 'Do they know about me?'

'In what sense?'

'As in, have you talked to them about me.'

'We don't chat about stuff like that.'

'It just seems strange that if you get on with your parents, that you haven't let them know that you're seeing me.'

'I don't tell them about every guy I date.'

'I understand that. It's just,' he pauses, looks to the ceiling for inspiration.

'What?' I ask.

'Nothing.' Except that I know it's not nothing.

'Euan, I don't tell my parents everything that happens in my life. They're the kind to worry, or else they'd just irritate me by getting overly involved. We get on, but only because I keep them a certain distance away from me. When the time is right, I'm going to tell them all about you.'

'And what will you say?'

There's the cheeky challenge I've been yearning for all evening. The twinkle in the eye, coupled with the tiny half-smirk.

'I'll say I've met the last good man on earth. He touches me in places I didn't even know were capable of sensation.' I'm on my feet now, moving to sit on his lap, and taking him in for an intense kiss. I'm almost scared that he won't kiss me back, but there's the fire, alive and hot. 'He also cooks the best salmon I've ever had in my life.'

Without warning, and with my lips still attached to his, Euan picks me up and carries me to the bedroom.

'What do you want me to do?' he asks in a low voice once I'm naked and underneath him.

'Whatever you want,' I say.

'If you tell me what you like, then that's what I want to do.'

I'd rather not have to think and just let him have his way with me however he pleases. There's not a single thing this man could do to me that wouldn't turn me on, that wouldn't feel electric, but I give him instructions anyway, because I can feel the tension in his question and I don't want more arguments. When I'm with him, it's like there's a feedback loop of pleasure. The more he can see I'm enjoying myself, the more he enjoys himself. And when he intensifies with enthusiasm, I find myself sinking into a million tiny bubbles of electric feeling. Being with him is the most exhilarating experience of my life. I don't want to have to give him instructions, I just want him to know, and for me to be able to relax into it.

In the quiet aftermath, I turn to look at him and marvel at what a perfect specimen he is. Every inch of him a warrior. Why he wants to ruin what we have right now with lovey-dovey talk of parents and corny sentimentality, I have no idea.

'What's that noise?' he asks suddenly. 'Is that your phone?'

I focus over the sound of my own recovering breathing to try and pick up what he's hearing. Maybe it's a phone vibrating, but I can't be sure.

'I left it on the kitchen table,' I say.

'I'll go and get it.'

I hate the emptiness of the bed without him in it and run my hand over the sheets just to feel the leftover warmth.

'Who's Ross?' Euan asks, his voice sharp and concerned. Again, another jolt of brand-new pleasure at realising that he's jealous. I try to remember the last time I had a man feel so possessive over me.

'Ross is my brother,' I explain.

'You have a brother?' he asks, collapsing back into the bed and tossing me the handset.

I ignore his question, more concerned about the fact that there are three missed calls on the screen.

'I hope everything is okay?'

I don't reply and don't bother listening to the voicemail Ross has left either. I call him back straight away.

'Where were you?' Ross asks. 'I've been calling.'

'I was busy. What's happened? Are you okay?'

'I'm fine. But I'm just arranging a flight back to London first thing in the morning.'

'A flight?' This just makes me more concerned, as usually Ross would take the train.

'You need to call Mum for all the details, but I thought it would be best coming from me.'

'Ross, just tell me what's happened. Tell me now!'

'Tamsyn, it's Uncle Doodle. He's collapsed and he's in the hospital. It's his heart. It's too soon to know exactly how bad everything is, but I'm coming home straight away.'

'Right. I understand.'

If Uncle Doodle were to die, the funeral would be within twenty-four hours. Ross is getting home as quick as he can because he fears the worst.

'What's happened?' Euan asks me once I end the call. But I don't want to tell him. I don't want to ruin things, especially not here, in his bed where we've just had another round of earth-shattering sex. I don't want to bring reality into this space.

'Tamsyn,' Euan says again, taking my hand and impatient with my pause. 'You need to tell me what's happening. You need to let me in.'

'It's my great-uncle,' I say. 'I don't know all the details but it's bad enough that my brother is flying home from Edinburgh. I'm sorry, I need to go.'

If the worst happens, I want to be with my family, and not find out via a telephone call.

'I'll come with you.'

'No, no, I'll be fine. I need to get home – my parents' home I mean – and understand what's going on.'

'Let me pay for a cab?'

'I think the tube is quicker, with the traffic and everything.'

The tube is not quicker, but I'm counting on him not living in London long enough to know about the journey times. He's paid for the cab fare home twice already, and I don't want him to do it again. Also, the thought of being cooped up in a car for the next hour as it winds its way around the North Circular is not something that's particularly appealing. At least on the tube nobody will try and talk to me, and I can stick my headphones in and try and drown out the world. But Euan's face falls when I turn his offer down, and I realise that he feels helpless. That he's only trying to help.

'I promise I'll call you when I know something.'

'Even if it's late, I don't care. You know I'll be there for you, right?'

'I know. Thank you.'

He draws me in for a gentle kiss, one that I don't want to leave behind. I love how warm he is, how his large hand cradles the back of my head. I want to cry because of how scared I am, and of how quickly I'm being ripped away from his world.

Back to reality, I tell myself as I rush to the tube, praying that Uncle Doodle is going to be okay.

10

I sleep restlessly at my parents' place, and when I wake up in the morning the fuzzy teddy bear sheets are tossed across my bedroom floor. The house is already too hot, and I head downstairs in the oversized T-shirt I've borrowed from Dad to wear as a night dress.

It's hard to remember how sweaty and rotten I feel though when I see Ross sitting at the kitchen table eating breakfast. It's been months since I've seen him in the flesh and I cling to him like a limpet when he stands to hug me. We're about the same height, Ross maybe half an inch taller, and look as similar as siblings can be considering our genders. We have the same dark, wavy hair, but whilst mine is tousled about my shoulders (well, right now it's a frizzy cloud about my shoulders), his is cut conservatively trim. The same dark hazel eyes, the same infuriatingly pale skin tone that goes red in the sun rather than brown. He's filled out whilst he's been away, but he looks comfortable, happy.

'Urgh, put some trousers on,' he moans whilst still hugging me. 'You're disgusting.'

'You're disgusting too, bum-head.'

Mum comes over to us with a mug of instant coffee for me (I only ever drink instant here, and it's the only place I don't mind it) and gives me an affectionate pat on the shoulder.

'What's the latest?' I ask her.

'They're probably going to let him out of the hospital,' she replies.

'That's good, right?'

'It's positive. His vitals were good overnight. As long as he has the support at home, they're happy to let him go.' She purses her lips and shrugs as if maybe she thinks they've all made the wrong decision. Her years spent as a medical secretary sometimes make her think she knows more than she really does. 'Your father has gone to the hospital to help Paul and Terry with everything.'

'He's coming home though. That's good? That's definitely good?' I look at Ross, who looks tired.

'They don't want him to be in the hospital unnecessarily,' Mum confirms.

I should probably text Euan to let him know. Once I got to my parents last night and we realised that the worst wasn't going to happen, I sent him a quick message: *Everything is going to be fine, sorry for worrying you.*

It's ok. More than ok. Let me know if there's anything you need, he replied.

Of course, by that point Ross had already booked his flight, and with the dozens of days of unspent holiday at my disposal, I decided it would be worth claiming a day so that I could be with my family in case anything changed.

'Do they know what happened to him?' I ask Mum, taking a sip of my Gold Blend.

'It's hard to say at his age. Possibly a mini-stroke, possibly his heart.'

'How can they not know?'

'He's in his late eighties,' Ross explained, microbiologist doctoral hat firmly on. 'I'm sure there are dozens of tests they could put him through to find out exactly what happened, but they may end up being more traumatic and invasive than the original issue. At Uncle Doodle's age, the best thing they can do is make sure he's safe, stable, and that there's family at home to help him.'

'When can we go and visit?'

'If he's home this afternoon, you can go and visit later. But not for long. He'll be tired,' Mum informs me, and I agree.

'We'll go together,' Ross offers.

'That'll be nice,' I say.

Ross and I take our usual positions on the sofa in the living room after I've called work to explain what's happening, the same spots we'd sit in when we were kids. He picks up the satellite remote and starts flicking through the sports channels, looking for something interesting.

'Turn the telly off, let's chat,' I say, but he looks back at me sideways, as if to say 'Really?'

'Come on,' I try again, poking him with my foot.

'I was on the first flight this morning at 6am. I am not in the mood for a cosy chit-chat.'

'O. M. G.' I say, noticing something.

'What?'

'Your voice. Was that a Scottish lilt?'

'I don't think Scots "lilt".'

'I swear, you've been living up there so long you're starting to sound Scottish. Have Mum and Dad noticed? They'll be livid.'

'They will not be livid,' he pauses. 'Besides, we've barely spoken. I've been far too tired.'

'Guess I'll have to wait until later to tell you about the guy I'm seeing then.'

He sighs, reluctantly interested, and then puts the telly on mute before turning to me.

'Spill.'

I bring up a picture of Euan on my phone, one of his publicity photos, not one I've taken of him.

'This guy?' Ross asks me, almost sounding impressed. 'Why do I recognise him?'

'He's a minor celebrity,' I gloat. 'And actually, a much bigger celebrity in the chef world.'

'A chef? Wait, didn't I see him last year on that cooking show?'

'On Channel Four? That's the one. He cooked a sirloin blindfolded. He's the head chef at this fancy boutique hotel in Mayfair. Euan Hegarty.'

'How long has this been going on?'

'Just a couple of weeks. It's really new,' I say proudly.

'Do Mum and Dad know?'

'Absolutely not. And you're not going to tell them.'

'Why, worried they're going to frown on you for dating a member of the master-race?'

'Ross! Will you stop it. It's really upsetting to hear you say things like that.' I know he's teasing, but even so. 'So, who are you dating then? Would Mum and Dad approve of the kind of girls you see?'

Ross reddens and changes the subject. 'Don't worry, I won't tell them,' he says. 'But only because I'm terrified they'll end up shooting the messenger.'

'It's not like you're doing great work being the model Jewish son. You haven't been to a function in years.'

'Well, this Euan fella is certainly bringing out the best in you Sis.'

'Nice to know I have your unconditional support as always, Little Bro,' I reply.

He takes the television off mute and starts flicking through the sports channels again, which gets seriously annoying after a couple of rotations.

I hate how everyone always tries to make a fool of me, waiting to see when they're suspicions will be proved correct. I hate how my life is just one giant tenterhook, with everyone around me waiting with bated breath for their 'I told you so' moment. At least, that's how it feels. I know that Ross doesn't take my love life seriously, he never has done, but it would be nice if he was enthusiastic just this once, instead of making out like I've made yet another foolish decision that's only going to backfire on me someday. I'd do anything for him, and I know he'd do anything for me too, if push came to shove, but he'll also find any possible excuse he can to mercilessly tease.

Why do we always revert to being such absolute children when we're around each other? Especially in this house?

We borrow Mum's car to go to Uncle Doodle's flat later in the afternoon, Ross driving. Uncle Doodle lives in a smart apartment building in Hendon with gates out front that you have to be buzzed through. We're greeted at the door by our cousin Terry, his daughter, who embraces us warmly.

'How is he?' I ask in a hushed voice.

'Tired,' she replies. 'A little tsedrayte, but that's only to be expected.'

She places her fingers to the mezuzah on the frame of the living door and then kisses her fingers as we walk through.

'Have you slept since yesterday?' Ross asks, concerned.

'Oh, you don't want my tsuris. I'm fine. I'm staying here until we get a new nurse and they're settled in with the whole routine. Paul wants my dad to live with him, but you know my brother has no patience, and I really haven't got the space at mine.'

'Can we see him?' I ask. 'Is now a good time?'

'He's awake,' Terry tells us. 'Just be easy with him.'

The living room is a museum of tchotchkes. Uncle Doodle's wife Gloria used to collect tiny bells, and even though she's been gone a long time, they're still all on display in a glass fronted cabinet, along with an array of loving cups and toby jugs collected over the years. Then, on the other open surfaces, collections of books with browned, sun-stained pages, arrangements of glass paperweights placed carefully on doilies, as well as lots of other random ceramic ornaments and glass animals: tiny caricature-like heads, plants with crystal flowers, and a bejewelled egg I've been told is absolutely, definitely not a Fabergé.

Uncle Doodle himself is sitting in his recliner, propped up by pillows and covered in a thick blanket. His pallor is startling, the skin underneath his eyes almost translucent and vaguely bruised. He's awake, but barely. Even so, as Ross and I approach, his eyes light up with a dark sparkle.

'Meyne kinder,' he says, his voice raspy.

'How are you feeling Uncle Doodle?' I ask, taking a seat beside him, Ross standing up behind me, his hands on my shoulders.

'Eh,' Uncle Doodle replies with a slight shrug. 'Could be better.'

'You had us scared. Ross came down from Edinburgh!'

'All that fuss? You really thought I was done for I guess.'

'We care about you Uncle Doodle,' Ross reassures.

'I'll be dancing a samba tomorrow, you watch me,' the old man replies.

Ross squeezes one shoulder and leans down: 'I'll be in the kitchen with Terry. Shout if you need us, okay?'

Ross has always found it difficult talking to people. He thought he would overcome it by the time he actually became a doctor, but nobody was surprised when he went into research after completing his undergrad degree at medical school.

'Your brother looks healthy,' Uncle Doodle says to me after he's gone. 'Meat on his bones.'

'I think he enjoys life up in Scotland,' I reply.

'All that haggis, I bet.'

'Are you insinuating that my dear brother doesn't keep kosher?' I pretend to be shocked, but to be honest Uncle

Doodle is one of the few people in my extended family who doesn't seem to care about what anyone eats.

'You'd think if I was this close to dying my daughter would let me have a ham sandwich,' he mumbles. Then he takes one of my hands in his. I'm shocked by how cold it is, along with the damp waxiness, only feeling the warmth in there when I press. 'Tell me something happy, bubbeleh,' he asks sincerely.

'Well,' I start. 'I just got back from hiking the Alps. You should have seen the goats on the trail, all wearing tiny bells.'

He smiles sadly at me and says, 'Something real darling. Tell me something real.'

So, I do.

'I've met a man. A very nice man who seems to like me a lot.'

'But?'

'I didn't say but,' I point out.

'It was there anyway,' Uncle Doodle explains with a gentle sigh.

'He's not Jewish,' I say it quickly, unexpectedly nervous. 'He's a chef, and he's doing well. Earns a good living. Have you ever been to the Clarence? That's where he works.'

'The Clarence? Mayfair?'

'That's the one.'

'I know the place. Do they still have a band play in the Great Room on Tuesday nights?'

'I think they turned the Great Room into the Grill back in the nineties. That's the restaurant now.'

'Eh,' Uncle Doodle mutters. I wonder if I should have elaborated with the usual fictional flourish that accompanies our conversations, before he continues: 'Does he make you happy, bubbeleh?'

I pause before I reply, not wanting to lie, but not sure I want to be honest either.

'I don't know yet. It's not been long enough to tell. But when I'm with him, then I'm very happy. Does it matter that he's not Jewish? I mean, it doesn't matter to me. But does it *matter*?'

'You're asking me what I think about him, so this must be important.'

'It's still very new. Really early days, but signs are good. I just want to get this right.'

'Let me tell you something. When I met your Great-Aunt Gloria, when I saw her dancing – oy, you should have seen her dancing! When I saw her dancing, and then I danced with her, I knew there and then that there was nobody else in the world for me. Beshert. All I want is for the children in this family to find such happiness. You find that, and do you think I or anyone else should care whether they are Jewish or not?'

'It's always seemed important to my parents,' I point out.

'Parents can have hopes and wishes for their children but hopes and wishes aren't the same as reality. I'm sorry if they're being fools about this.'

'Well, I haven't told them about him yet. Apart from Ross, you're the first to know.'

'Tamsyn,' he doesn't often use my name, so I know he's being serious. 'If you can honestly and truthfully tell me that this is the right man, that he understands you, and loves you anyway, that you understand him and love him anyway, then that's all I need to know. That's all anyone needs to know.'

'It means a lot to hear you say that Uncle Doodle.'

'Here's the thing you need to remember about who we are,' he continues to explain. 'Not just our family, but about the Jewish people. We came very close to not being here at all. And before the Shoah, there are centuries worth of people who don't want us to be here. After the Shoah? Much the same. So, what happens after centuries of persecution? You become defensive and protective. It's a natural instinct.'

'Inherited trauma,' I say.

'That's a fancy way to say it. People, not just Jewish people, but all people, have a survival instinct. Now there are some people who fear we could lose the Jewish ways anyway. You hear about it all the time, young people marrying out and Jewish numbers going down. But here's what I say to that: it's the goyim who made us this way. The goyim forced us into ghettos, out of countries or into camps. You know what would really stick it to the goyim?'

'What Uncle Doodle?'

'That we expand through love. That we bring other people in, through love. That we finally allow ourselves to be free from what their hate has forced us to become.'

'What's he wittering on about now?' Terry comes in with a cup of tea for me.

'Just a very progressive treatise on the history of antisemitism,' I reply.

'Oh, don't let him talk to you about all that! He's just going to get worked up!'

'Worked up?' Uncle Doodle says. 'Who's going to pass on my knowledge when I'm gone, eh?'

'Well, you'll be gone a lot sooner if you get yourself all emotional like that.'

'The only one working me up is you.' Uncle Doodle dismisses his daughter with a hand gesture. 'You want me gone I bet. Make life easier for you I'm sure.'

'Oh Dad,' Terry sighs, but Uncle Doodle gives me a sly, mischievous wink.

'I'll give you a moment to rest,' I tell him, getting up to follow Terry back into the kitchen. 'I'll be back in a bit.'

The three of us cluster in Uncle Doodle's tiny galley kitchen, me clutching my mug of tea, still too hot to drink. The microwave in here looks like an original from the seventies and the plastic fixtures around the oven and stove have yellowed with age.

'He's talkative?' I say hopefully, my voice hushed.

'He's always talkative. That's not really saying much,' Terry says.

'What did the doctors say?' Ross asks.

'That there may be more false alarms like this. Hearts are like that. There's not much we can do except make sure he's comfortable and well cared for.'

'But he seems fine?' I know how naively hopeful I sound when I say this and realise afterwards that it's not quite what I mean. Because he doesn't seem fine. His skin is clammy yet cold at the same time, his face pale and his voice raspy. Maybe what I'm recognising is the aliveness in his eyes, and in what he's telling me. Sometimes I think I can imagine Uncle Doodle as a young man, maybe even see exactly what he was like, how he held himself and how he must have looked to others around him. Confident and mischievous and compassionate. I wish I could have known him then.

'There must be some medicine they can give him? What would they give to anyone else with his condition? Just because he's old doesn't mean he shouldn't be treated,' I keep my voice as hushed as possible, making sure that there's no way Uncle Doodle can hear me.

'They're treating him in the best way,' Ross says, not meeting my eyes.

'You'd never know he just had a small heart attack just from speaking with him,' Terry adds. 'We must remember this blessing.'

Ross goes into the living room and starts telling Uncle Doodle all about his life in Edinburgh, leaving me alone with Terry in the kitchen.

'It's so lovely how close you two are with him,' she says.

'Well, I never got to meet one of my grandfathers, and the other wasn't around too much either before he died. Being with Uncle Doodle always felt special, at least to me.'

'I love how you both still call him that. I don't even remember when it started. You know you're the only ones?'

'It's always made him smile, so we never stopped.'

'He likes it. And he likes you in particular. Sometimes I think better than he likes me.'

'Stop, you're his daughter. It's a different thing.'

'I know you aren't related, but you remind him of Mum. It's a lovely thing, for sure. But Mum wasn't perfect.' I sip on my tea and give Terry space to continue. 'She could never admit she was wrong, for starters. Couldn't be taught, everything had to be done her way. Can you believe, she thought she could do better than Evelyn Rose? Would always start on one of her recipes, but then switch everything up halfway through. Added some ingredients, left others out, played fast and loose with oven times. One year she threw a dinner party, and every single guest came down with food poisoning. I was too young to attend, would watch the parties through the bannisters at the top of the stairs. But up until the moment she passed, she swore blind that it was impossible that her cooking could have been the issue. That they all must have caught food poisoning from something else.'

'But she knew though, right? She must have known, deep down inside, that it was her fault?'

'Who knows.' She shrugs. 'But God, I loved her. And it would have saved a lot of arguments between her and my dad if she took the opportunity, sometimes, to admit when she had messed up.'

'They fought?' I ask. I'd always imagined that they had the most perfect relationship.

'Every week a new drama,' Terry reveals. 'They were mad about each other, but that doesn't mean they weren't sometimes just plain mad.'

'I'm surprised.'

'I hated it growing up, but looking back now, I think that's just how they communicated. All passion and loud voices. I miss it. The world is too quiet without them both together.'

'I'm sorry Terry.'

'I miss my mum,' she says to me, tears in her eyes. 'And as much as that old fart annoys me, I'm not ready to miss him too.'

'We should be heading off,' Ross says, coming back into the kitchen. 'I think Uncle Doodle is getting tired now.'

I go back to him to say goodbye.

'Will you tell them all to stop making a fuss?' he asks me. 'They act like this is my deathbed.'

'The doctor's given their orders and everyone just wants to look after you.'

'I'm fine. The only one the doctor is looking after is himself. Have you seen the number of pills I have to take? The man is on a commission, I swear.' I smile knowingly and his mock-fury breaks for a moment. 'You'll come and visit me?' he asks.

'I'll come soon,' I reply.

Ross and I are quiet on the way back to our parents' house. I don't know if he just needs to focus on the road, or if he's thinking about something else.

'What did you talk about with him?' I ask.

'Not much,' Ross replies. He's never been the most forthcoming of people.

'I told him about Euan,' I say.

'Who?'

'The guy I'm seeing.'

'Oh, him,' and then, as if suddenly realising that he should be more inquisitive: 'what did he say?'

'That I should be happy. That he didn't care if Euan wasn't Jewish, as long as I was happy.'

'It's nice to have his blessing. If the worst happens.'

'Hmmm,' I reply, watching the streets of Hendon merge into Mill Hill. I feel sad suddenly, along with that sense you get when you've inadvertently forgotten something. I pat at my pockets, feeling for anything out of place, and then dive into my handbag to check for my keys, wallet and phone.

'Everything okay?' Ross asks, the barest hint of that Scottish lilt creeping through again.

'Everything's fine,' I reply, still feeling tense but settling back into my seat.

11

Cooper Radcliffe is having takeout lunch with Gareth Parkinson in Gareth's office.

Nobody has been introduced to him yet, but I swear Cooper's laugh will haunt us all in our dreams for the next few nights. It's one of those unnecessarily uproarious laughs, an old-fashioned guffaw. We can hear it even though Gareth's door is closed. I've been working with Gareth for years and the man isn't all that funny. Which means the intention of the laugh is to announce his presence. He wants us all to know that he's here, and that he's having a great time with the boss.

'He's not that bad looking,' Kerry-Ann says. I'm hovering by her desk out in the bullpen, waiting for the lunch to finish so that I'm in the best spot when Gareth brings Cooper out on a tour to meet the team. 'He looks like Hugh Grant did in those old films.'

'Old films?' I clarify.

'The ones with the weddings and the funerals. He seems awfully posh, doesn't he? Dreamy, but very posh.'

Kerry-Ann had the good fortune to greet Cooper when he emerged from the lift and was the one who directed him to Gareth's office. As such, she's our current leading source on any potential scoop.

'I heard that his Uncle is an aristocrat. And that he once went skiing with Prince William,' Nadine chimes in.

'Where did you hear that?' I ask.

'I reached out to a pal of mine at the *Spectator*.'

I hate that I work with people who have pals at the *Spectator*. I also hate that I'm soon going to be working with someone who might have skied with royals and who does, irritatingly, look remarkably similar to a young Hugh Grant. My insides seethe with fury that another posh white dude is going to be taking over the magazine I've poured my last decade into. That despite everything I've done and am still trying to do to save it, I'm not being recognised. That Gareth feels like he has to go and get someone in to do a job I've been doing for the last few years anyway.

Then, the editor-in-chief's door opens.

Cooper guffaws again as Gareth leads him out into the bullpen. I stand a little straighter and put on my best cool-girl smile. I'm wearing my cream silk blouse with a pussy bow, but I've paired it with tight black trousers and biker-style ankle boots. I want to seem girly, but still indicate that he won't be able to walk all over me. I can be pretty, and chic, but still mean business. I want Cooper to see me and instinctively feel like he should want to be on my good side.

But Gareth doesn't give him a tour, nor introduce him to anyone on the team. Instead, they head directly over to the lifts, then Cooper says something I don't catch, and Gareth roars with laughter, his cheeks flaming red. The lift pings when it arrives, and then suddenly Cooper is gone.

Those of us who have gathered for any potential introductions let out a collective sigh of disappointment.

'Back to work everyone,' I announce, trying my best to seem like I didn't care in the first place.

'Do you think he'd take me skiing?' Kerry-Ann asks, I'm sure only half-jokingly.

'Depends on the proximity of your flat to the Kings Road,' I say.

'I live in New Cross.'

'Then that will be a no.'

Back in my office, I wait for Gareth to call me in for a catch-up. He's never been the kind of boss I have ever been able to drop in on without an invitation or for anything other than serious official business, but I'm desperate to find out how the meeting went. The afternoon passes, and nothing. It's infuriating.

I tell Euan as much over dinner. It's rare that he has a night off during the week, and the ones he does have, we try and spend together.

'I don't know why you didn't put yourself forward and go and talk to him?' he says. We're eating at a trendy ramen place in Soho, waiting for our food to arrive.

'Because that's not how it works. I can't just go and speak to Gareth. He's not that kind of boss. Either you're summoned, or it's not important enough to bother him with.'

'And knowing more about this Cooper guy wasn't important enough?'

'No. He'd say I was being petty. Or a gossip. Which, technically, I was.'

'I don't think it's petty or gossipy to know more about what's happening in your own workplace. You're not an underling, you're the managing editor. How does he expect you to stop gossip and do your job effectively when you're left in the dark. I think you should have been more assertive on this one.'

'This is why I don't tell you about work stuff. It's not like a kitchen. There are subtle dynamics and politics to play.'

'I'm going to call you out on two fronts there. One, if you don't think there are subtle dynamics and politics in a kitchen, then you really need to spend some time in a kitchen. And two, why would you not tell me about work stuff? I want to know these things, if I can help. And especially if it's causing you stress.'

The server brings our ramen, which is a dish that to me has always seemed like a big bowl of chicken soup with tons of extra good stuff. I'm hoping that the interruption and the arrival of good, hot food will put a swift halt to the conversation, but it quickly becomes apparent that Euan is waiting for me to continue.

'I don't want to bother you with my silly work stuff,' I try.

'So, it's gone from subtle dynamics and politics to silly?'

'It's just not worth talking about when we're meant to be spending time together.'

The first time we went out, it was all hungry eyes and dangerous flirting. That's what I want. I miss the sexiness. Even the way I'm eating this ramen, clumsily with the big wooden spoon they provide along with the chopsticks, feels cack-handed. I want to know if he fancies me. I want to find a way to let him know that I still fancy him. But instead, he just wants to talk about my day and how he can help.

'You remember the person who does PR at the Clarence? Florence Biddulphe? She doesn't actually work at the hotel, but for a PR agency. You could do that you know, work in hotel PR. I know she was really impressed with your piece on me. I could give her a call if you like? See if there's a vacancy there?'

'Euan,' I start, feeling tired suddenly. I don't like it when he's like this. He thinks he can be all Superman, swooping in to save me. It's precisely this reason that I don't tell him about what's bothering me. I don't want saving, nor his advice. But if I tell him this, he'll think I'm being defensive and foolish.

'Tammy,' he says softly. That's another thing. He's started calling me Tammy, something I've always faintly hated but never actually had to deal with on a recurring basis, and I have no idea how to let him know that I don't like it without making it awkward. It feels like he's said it too many times now for me to suddenly bring it up. 'I want to be here for you. It's okay to talk about this kind of thing.'

'I appreciate you trying to help,' I say diplomatically, and when I look up at him and see his head tilt with a frustrated sigh, I know he's realised I want to put a full stop on that conversation. 'But how about you just tell me about your day instead?'

'It was okay,' he says. 'The usual stuff. Training the new guys. Clearing out the fridge. A few admin things with the hotel. Worked the lunch service. I've been looking forward to seeing you all day.'

'I've been looking forward to seeing you, too.'

'You have?' he checks.

'Of course,' I reassure.

A bit later, after we've finished, we're wandering around Soho when Euan suggests we go back to my flat instead of his. My mind races, thinking about the state of my room and how messy I left it, and then I remember that Helene is out at a concert, so I can't even use her as an excuse to say no.

'I want to see where you live,' he says softly, taking my hand in his and bringing it to his mouth for a courtly kiss. 'I just want to get to know you better.'

I can't say no to that. Not without him thinking something's off.

Euan Hegarty in my flat feels incongruous. I associate him with sleek, expensive and minimal surroundings. My place is none of that. The wall behind the sofa (scattered with five bright fluffy cushions) is painted a gleaming yellow to reflect the light that comes in through the window during the day, with an up-cycled stepladder in the corner serving as makeshift shelving for an array of houseplants in multicoloured pots. I may not have the same dress sense as Helene, but letting her have some say with regards to decoration has definitely helped encourage a happy atmosphere. There are magazines scattered and piled high on the coffee table, some going back months, and one shameful mug with a dried-out herbal tea bag that I think has been sitting there for three days now (this I can't attribute to Helene. The mess is always mine). Half of the kitchen is taken up by the airer, moved temporarily from the bathroom where it usually lives, which is displaying quite the collection of bras and knickers, and then, most shamefully considering that I'm dating a chef, is the bowl of gone off fruit on the dining table. The fruit isn't rotten exactly, but the bananas have gone dark brown and the oranges are a little sunken.

'I wish I'd had some warning,' I say apologetically as Euan looks around curiously.

'This is nice. I like seeing where you live.'

'A lot of this stuff is Helene's. She's a graphic artist. Does lots of illustration. And I promise it's usually less of a tip.'

'Relax, Tammy.' Euan looks back at me, smiling playfully. 'This is what I wanted to see.'

'You wanted to see this?' I lift up the fluffiest of the cushions, which looks like a pink muppet was murdered to make it.

'I wanted to see you.'

Euan steps back towards me, takes the cushion from my hand, and lets it fall back to the sofa. He then wraps his big, impressive arms around me and pulls me into him for the kind of kiss I've been looking forward to all day.

'I want to see everything that you are,' Euan continues to say between kisses. 'I want to know every part of you.'

'You already know every part of me,' I say with a sly smile.

'I want to know about what's in here, too,' and with that he breaks away from my mouth to kiss me gently on my forehead.

I lead him into my bedroom, but Euan doesn't start to get undressed. Instead, he sits on the end of my bed, looking around my room with a serene kind of smile.

'What?' I ask him, feeling nervous.

'I mean it,' he says.

'Mean what?'

'Let's not have sex tonight. Let's get to know each other better. Let's stay up all night talking. I haven't done that in years.'

'I don't think you can ask or plan for something like that.' I take a seat next to him on my bed. 'I think it just happens.'

'But we haven't done that yet. Every single time we see each other, it's just sex. Don't you want something more?'

No, is my instinctual gut reaction, but I don't tell him this. I look down at the floor instead.

'Tamsyn,' he's using my full name again, his voice low and serious. 'I really, really like you.'

'I really, really like you too.'

'Then what's the problem? Please, be honest with me.'

So, I decide to be honest. I think about Uncle Doodle wanting me to be happy, of the chance of showing him how happy I can be before he leaves us. I did tell him about Euan after all, and he didn't react badly, the opposite in fact. I know I've been working really hard to keep Euan at arm's length, but I'm not sure that I can articulate why. I'm not sure what's stopping me from bringing him all the way in, from letting him see who I really am.

'I'm scared that my family might ruin things,' I say, a slight stutter in my voice.

Pleased with the fact that he's broken through whatever barrier he was aiming for, Euan shuffles himself back so that he's fully reclining on my bed. He holds one of my throw cushions in front of him for comfort, and then pats the side of the bed next to him, forcing me to recline with him.

'Is your family really that bad?' he asks sensitively.

'No, not really. But they can be a little intense. And I guess they're different.'

'Different?'

'Culturally I mean. I don't think they'd be altogether happy with me dating you, for example.'

'Oh, now I'm curious,' he teases.

'Euan, I'm Jewish,' I say finally. I don't know why it's such a big deal. I've told countless other people in many different situations. Some have guessed from my name combined with the way I look, and in the diverse melting pot that is London, it's never been particularly significant. But there's something about this, with Euan, that feels like a big deal. Somehow, I feel like I might be ruining everything.

'And you were scared to tell me that?' he asks.

'Kinda.'

'Can you say why?'

'Not really.' He laughs at my response.

'Did you think that I wouldn't like the fact that you're Jewish?'

'Not exactly. Although I can't say that I haven't had some weird experiences when I've told men in the past.'

'What do you mean, weird?'

'Well, there was one guy who found out I was Jewish on the second date and proceeded to tell me Hitler jokes for most of the evening. I think he thought I would find them funny? But one joke involved him doing a 'heil Hitler' right there in the middle of the bar. Then there was another guy who thought I must be rich because I was Jewish. It was before I had this flat. I was living in a really crummy house share in Cricklewood at the time, and he was utterly convinced that I was a millionaire who was slumming it. Started to refuse to pay for me when we went out for meals. He said it was all a joke, but it wasn't.'

'I had no idea you'd gone through things like that. But you know I'm not like that, right? That your background doesn't matter to me?'

'Those guys, they were just stupid. Never went past a few dates with either of them. And those kinds of things happen to everyone, right? I bet you get all sorts of stick for being a Geordie, don't you?'

'Yes, but those kinds of jokes aren't based on years of hatred?'

I shuffle in closer to Euan, finding a comfortable place in the crook of his arm. He's so warm, and so strong. Of course, I knew that he'd never have a problem with who I was and where I'd come from. That doesn't mean my family wouldn't have a problem with him though.

'The other night, when I had to leave to see my great-uncle? When I saw him the next day, we had a great little talk. I told him about you, asked if he would mind that you weren't Jewish.'

'And what did he say?'

'He said that he wanted me to be happy.'

'Well, that's that then. Nothing to worry about!'

'My great-uncle is far more progressive than my parents. I'm sorry I haven't told them about you. There are a couple of reasons for that.'

'Go on.'

'Well firstly, I didn't know how serious you were. I didn't know how serious I felt either.'

He takes one of my hands in his and holds it tightly.

'And secondly, once they know, they're going to be all over you. All over both of us. They're going to want to impress you, and find out everything about you, and it's kind of game over for what we have right now.'

'Sounds intense, but it's nothing I can't cope with.'

'It's not about what you can cope with. It's me who might not be able to cope with it.' I pause for a moment, thinking, trying to make sure I'm saying things right. 'The thing is, ultimately, I'm scared they're going to make it very clear – not to you, but definitely to me – that whilst they'll be happy to play along and make a happy fuss over you, that they'll never take you – us – seriously. They'll think you're a shiny distraction, but they won't ever really believe that we'll work out.'

'Because I'm not Jewish?'

'I don't mind. I don't think anyone should mind. But I wonder if they will.'

'I see.'

'And you can't charm offensive them either. Their minds will be made up the moment I tell them who you are.'

'Well, that sounds like quite the challenge.'

'I'm not kidding, Euan.'

'I know.' He brings the hand he's holding up to his mouth so that he can kiss it.

'I've never brought someone home to my parents. Not since I was a teenager. They know I've been dating, and they've tried to set me up with eligible men countless times. But I've never told them about anyone. I've never wanted to bring all that on anyone I'm seeing.'

I feel like adding that I'd rather not bring it on him too, that we're nowhere near ready for all that, that he's the one who has pushed me into this situation. I've been cornered into telling him the truth.

'You don't have to introduce me yet,' he says with a sigh.

'I just want to enjoy what we have right now,' I tell him. 'What we're doing is fun, isn't it?'

'It really is.'

'I don't think I'm ready for all the serious stuff yet. We can go slow, can't we?'

Euan chuckles. 'Normally when people ask to go slow, they're talking about the physical stuff. I guess we're doing things the opposite way around.'

He shifts and leans down so that he can kiss me properly. We're wrapped up in each other for several minutes before we break away. 'Did you really think I'd care if you were Jewish?' he checks.

'I thought the best of you, but it's not an unreasonable thing to worry about these days,' I reply carefully.

'I'm sad that it's not unreasonable.'

I give my best impression of an old Jewish guy giving a careless shrug. Then we go back to some more kissing. I'm really hoping that the making out will lead to us taking our clothes off and getting to what we're good at, but once again Euan pauses to have another chat.

'I'm happy to go slow, on one condition.'

'Go on,' I say cautiously.

'I want to learn more about your culture.'

'Okay, like what?'

'Well, most importantly food. I must have made nearly every one of Ottolenghi's dishes at some point. There's got to be some incredible original recipes in your family. Israeli salads, shakshuka, falafel?'

'That's not really the kind of food I grew up with. My ancestors lived in Eastern Europe and Russia, so it's more stews and chicken soup.'

'Do you eat holler?'

'Challah?'

'That's what I said. Holler.'

'No, you really have to get the 'h' sound raspy, right at the back of your throat. Challah.'

'Holla.'

I wince, and he laughs.

'See,' he says. 'If I'm going to be a good boyfriend, then I want to learn all about this stuff. When your family meet me, they're not going to be able to say anything about my background.'

I meet his face with another kiss so that he can't see my wince continue. I know he said the word 'boyfriend' on purpose. I know that's what he wants. I wouldn't be surprised if he's already imagining marriage proposals and the kind of house we'll live in when we're old and grey. And maybe I'll want those things too, in time. But until that time comes, I guess I'll just have to live with the uncomfortable curdle in my belly whenever he starts bringing up the future. He wants me so badly, and I want him, but we're just in different places, and going at a different pace. I'll get there with him. As long as I'm patient with myself, and make sure that he's still interested in me, I'm sure I'll catch up soon enough.

'Why don't you cook for me?' he asks between kisses.

'Excuse me?' I check.

'Cook for me. An old family recipe. Something Jewish.'

'I don't cook,' I inform him.

'I'm not expecting chef-level stuff. But I'd like to try your traditional food. Something that reminds you of home or your childhood. I want to try it.'

'I really, really don't cook.'

'I'll go slow for you, if you cook something for me?'

'That's not fair,' I warn with a light laugh. But no, it's really not fair. Added to this, he now has his hand under my shirt, reaching around to unclasp my bra. Damn him and his incredible hands.

'Come on, cook for me,' he's whispering into my neck, planting light kisses there as his hand that unclasped my bra reaches lower.

'I don't know what,' I'm gasping.

'Surprise me.'

And then my thoughts become incoherent as he gives me the release I've been craving all evening. In that moment, I swear to give him whatever he wants, and if that means cooking a five-course dinner, I'll do it. All I know is that I won't dare risk the chance of losing this.

12

Euan is being the sweetest he has ever been. I guess he really feels like we had a breakthrough with our relationship, whereas I feel like I worked my utmost to keep a tiger at bay. I just don't understand how I can want a person so badly, only for that person to want something else. Or at least, want something that I don't know how to envision.

'You? You're actually going to cook for him?' Helene asks me as I'm getting ready to go out the following Sunday morning. The year is about to turn from June to July and the sky outside is a gleaming bright blue. Ordinarily, I'd be finding my floatiest, most ethereal summer dress and looking for excuses to meet pals for brunch and drink gin-in-a-tin in Victoria Park, but instead I'm going 'off duty' in yoga leggings, a T-shirt I found online featuring Disney princesses dressed up as rock-and-roll stars, a light jacket and my old purple Converse shoes, my untidy, unwashed hair pushed back from my face with a thick hair band. Today isn't about enjoying the sunshine. Today I'm on a mission.

Euan has never seen me like this. He's either seen me glammed up for our dates, winged eyeliner on point and heels clacking on his parquet floors, or in some state of undress. The only kind of messy I've let him see is the post-coital kind, bed-head and smudged lipstick. I feel if he ever saw me like this, he'd be whisking me away for afternoons getting lost in Ikea, rather than to fancy restaurants. When I'm around him, it feels appropriate to be ever so slightly uncomfortable. Effort doesn't come without some semblance of discomfort, I find.

Helene, meanwhile, is curled up on our sofa, sunglasses on indoors, her duvet dragged from her bedroom and pulled around her. I don't even remember her coming in the night before.

'It's not that big a deal, is it?' I try my best cool, nonchalant voice. It doesn't work on Helene.

'You've never even made me so much as an omelette. You're the microwave queen. And he's a top-class chef. Something does not add up here. Why are you trying so hard?'

'I'm not trying hard. We had a great chat the other night when he came over. We really connected. And we decided that this was something I could do for him.'

'Tamsyn,' Helene's voice croaks with disdain and dehydration. The cocoon she's made with the duvet makes her looks like a half-drowned snail.

'Helene.' I grin back at her.

'Look, I love that you're all happy right now. It's lovely. It really is. It's just . . . I didn't realise you were so serious about Euan?'

'I was always serious about Euan.'

'Never mind.'

'What? What is it?'

'I haven't even met him. Don't listen to me. I'm probably still drunk.'

'Okay, I'll admit that things are moving a little faster than I'd planned, but Euan seems to really like me. How many times will a guy ever be this serious about me? And he understands that I might need a bit more time to get to where he is.'

'So, you're going to cook for him?'

'I want to show him how much I like him back.'

'By giving him food poisoning?'

'He wants to know more about me. About my culture.'

'And what culture is that? '90s nostalgia and *Love Island* culture? Are you going to perform *NSYNC's "Bye Bye Bye" dance for him too?'

'If you must know, he wants to know more about my Jewish side. So, this morning I'm going out to try and figure out what exactly I want to make him. Want me to bring you back any deli meats? Bagels?'

Helene groans and tucks herself further into her duvet burrito. 'I won't be eating anything for quite some time,' she says, her voice muffled.

'Well, text me if you do want me to bring anything back for you.'

Helene makes more mumbled affirmative sounds from within her cocoon and I decide to go to the kitchen to refill her glass of water before I leave. As I do so, I start to think about how wrong Helene is about everything. How she can't possibly understand what's going on between Euan and me. Okay, so we're not on the same page right now, but I know I can get there. Maybe he can teach me, and this dinner is the first step. Perhaps I'll wake up one morning and realise that I'm infatuated with him to the same extent that he's infatuated with me. Maybe I just need time to feel the same way he does. I can't wait to prove to Helene just how wrong she is.

So now I'm schlepping to Golders Green for inspiration and ingredients so that I can make Euan Hegarty the perfect, traditional Jewish meal.

The thing is, I actually have no idea what a traditional Jewish meal is. The biggest meals we have are on Friday nights, maybe Rosh Hashanah or Pesach, and all that involves is a roast chicken. It's basically just a Sunday lunch but without any pork trimmings. Yes, there's chicken soup, but that's hardly any different from the ramen we ate the other night. Maybe someone might make chopped liver, or gefilte fish, but I haven't got the first clue how to make those. Besides, they're garnishes, starters or snack food, rather than actual meals. I did think about making challah for him, but I've never even made a simple loaf of bread in my life and just watching a YouTube video on how to plait the strands was enough to give me a small panic attack. Abigail's been cooking for years and even her challah was flat and sad.

So basically, I have no idea what I'm doing, and only a vague idea of what I need to do to impress him. Helene may be completely wrong about the status of my relationship, but she's entirely right about my ability to cook.

The Northern Line takes me to Golders Green just as it's approaching lunchtime and the place is bustling. This isn't the typical time I like to shop, but when it comes to all things kosher, I don't have much choice. All of the shops I would want to go to would be closed on a Saturday for Shabbat, and it's not as if I have the time to get here after work during the week before everything closes for the day.

I thought briefly about telling Mum that I was doing this, but then I imagined the barrage of questions that the revelation would instantly bring and shut the thought down. If there's one thing I know, it's that my mother must never know about any of this. At least, not until I'm ready to introduce them to Euan.

There's that churning feeling in my stomach again. Just imagining my Mum and Dad meeting Euan, the kind of things they'd ask him, all the embarrassing things they would say. I have no doubt that Euan would put on a brave face. He's a charming man, and I can't imagine anyone not getting on with him. Mum would no doubt instantly presume that we were on the road to marriage, something I'm not even sure that I want anyway, and even if I did, would they insist that Euan converts? Would Euan's family want me to get married in a church? What if both sides end up upset?

It dawns on me that if I asked Euan to think about converting, I suspect that he would at least seriously consider it, and the dark churning feeling intensifies.

After a brief walk, I'm standing outside Kosher Kingdom, one of the larger of the Jewish supermarkets in Golders Green. I can't believe I'm here, that I'm doing this. The place is swarming with busy mothers, some dressed how mine would dress, others in more obviously modest clothing and sheitls. There are men with peyot and broad black hats rushing around like they're the most important customers in there, but there are others in jeans and polo shirts whom you wouldn't know were Jewish just from a glance. I have no idea what I'm looking for, or what I'm going to buy. When I googled 'traditional Jewish meals' the search came up with so many things that either looked too complicated or that I'd never heard of, I decided to just wander around and let inspiration hit me.

Except inspiration is not hitting me. It feels like when I'm wandering around foreign supermarkets when I've been on holiday, looking at all the baffling brands and alien packaging. There's a magazine rack displaying *The Jewish Chronicle*, as well as exclusively Israeli titles covered in nothing but Hebrew, and a card rack displaying greetings for all the big occasions: bar mitzvahs, brit milahs and other assorted simchas.

'Huh,' I exclaim out loud to myself when I pick up a packet of Bissli in the snack aisle. I don't think I've eaten these since I was at Hebrew School years and years ago. I'd pretty much forgotten that they existed. In a quick moment, I see myself in the car park of our synagogue, which served as a playground during the break between Sunday classes, eagerly dipping my hand into a packet and getting wheat bits all over my fingers. I grab a few packets and regret not picking up a basket on my way in.

Wandering the aisles of Kosher Kingdom, I find myself continually surprised at all the 'normal' brands I had no idea were certified kosher, although I guess there's no real reason why they wouldn't be. Like KitKats, Kettle Chips, Quaker Oats and Kinder Buenos. Turning every corner, there's a new revelation, another light bulb moment of realisation. I'm obviously walking too slowly for one harassed mother who is pushing a cart around, one toddler screaming from within the trolley seat, another actually inside the trolley itself and chewing on the strings of his tzitzit.

'Tamsyn?'

Hearing my name is a surprise after being momentarily disorientated by the rude Yiddish mum, and I drop most of the snacks I've gathered in my arms. There are packets of Bissli all over the floor between us, and then suddenly I realise that Ari Marshall is picking them all up and handing them back to me.

'Hi,' I say, again disorientated. 'What are you doing here?'

'Shopping, unsurprisingly,' Ari replies. Sure enough, he's holding a hand basket that's filled with food. 'I think the bigger question is what you're doing here?'

The angry Yiddish mother has come back down the aisle for another lap, this time both her sons screaming from the trolley, and grumbling about us being in the way, so Ari guides me by the arm to the back of the shop where we have a little more space.

'Thanks,' I say, looking at the spot on my arm his hand was lightly touching just a moment ago.

'Thought you lived out in East London? What are you up to in Golders Green?' he asks.

'I'm not even sure I know,' I admit with a laugh before composing myself, remembering suddenly that this man made me supremely angry the last time I saw him.

'Bissli craving?' he asks, handing me the last of my dropped packets.

'I haven't had these since I was about eight or nine in Hebrew School,' I say carefully, trying to work out if he's leading me into an insult trap.

'What shul did you go to by the way?' He asks this suddenly and intensely, and I find it's a question that irritates me, because it's such a typically Jewish question.

'Mill Hill United,' I reply.

'I knew it!'

'Knew what?'

'You stopped going to cheder, didn't you?'

'How did you know that?'

'Because we were in the same class!'

'No, we weren't.'

'We absolutely were, and I didn't remember either, although I always swore I'd seen your face somewhere before.'

'How could you possibly remember me from back then?'

'Okay, I'll tell you, but you must promise not to go off on me?'

'Why, is this going to involve an insult of some sort?'

'The opposite, actually.'

My fingers tense around the Bissli I'm struggling to hold, my neck and face suddenly and unexpectedly hot.

'So, I always thought you were cool. Note, I said cool, not cold. We never spoke; I was always at the back and you tended to sit near the front. Do you remember?'

'Yep,' I chirp in response, wondering where this is going.

'But I remembered you because you always asked questions. I never had the guts to. But every time the teacher told us a story or tried to teach us a song, you always had a question.'

'And you thought that was cool?'

'I can't remember if they were good questions. I can't remember the answers either for that matter. But, well, I just noticed. And I respected it.'

'We were so young. How can you respect anyone when you're eight?'

'When you're a shy kid, you respect anyone who asks anything.' Ari's voice is sheepish now, and he's looking down at his shopping basket.

'I hated going to cheder,' I tell him. 'And I'm pretty sure those teachers hated me. When I realised that I didn't have to stay, I convinced my parents to take me out. I guess you didn't have a choice?'

Ari shrugs. Nearly all Jewish boys have a bar mitzvah at thirteen, but the girls in my family have never had bat mitvahs. So, when my parents confirmed that I didn't have to have one either, I successfully pointed out that there was no reason for me to waste my Sundays and go to the associated Hebrew classes. I left before my tenth birthday and I haven't had any formal Jewish education since.

'I'd been racking my brains to try and figure out where I knew you from, so thank you Bissli for helping me to work it out!'

We smile at each other, and then I feel silly because I'm not sure if I'm meant to be saying anything more to him. He's the worst, isn't he?

'I guess I better be going,' he says with a small sigh.

Except, I'm not sure that I want him to go.

'Wait,' I say, as he's turning away. He faces me, a confused and expectant look in his face. 'I guess that was a pretty nice thing to say. I wasn't expecting it.'

'Well, maybe if I'd remembered we already knew each other sooner, the last conversation we had wouldn't have been quite so messy.'

'Yeah, maybe.'

There's that expectant look on his face again. A look that says, 'So what's next?' Except that I have no idea what the right way to answer it is.

'I've got to cook a meal,' I tell him in a weird blurt. The expectant look shifts into one of amused confusion. 'I promised my boyfriend I'd introduce him to Jewish food. And I have no idea what I'm doing.'

I use the word I was scared to use, and I watch Ari's face carefully when I say it. He gives me nothing. Just the same easy, amiable smile as always. It makes absolutely no sense for me to be disappointed. No sense at all.

'Well, what do you like cooking? Can you do a kosher version of that?' Ari shifts from one foot to the other with a relaxed lean.

'I don't like cooking anything,' I reveal. 'Besides, I don't think he wants a kosher version of something else. He's really interested in foods from other cultures, and I think he's expecting something traditional.'

'Something traditional? From you?' There's the wily cynicism I was expecting from him. I ready myself for the insults, for him to mock my progressiveness and lack of knowledge. Instead, I just get a really good suggestion: 'Have you thought about brisket?'

'Brisket? Making a whole brisket? Me?'

'It's a lot easier than you think. You just stick the meat in the oven for a few hours. And you can make it in advance. Reheat it for when you need it. Plus, you'll have leftovers for days.'

'Brisket,' I say, warming to the idea.

'Can't go wrong with brisket,' Ari affirms.

'Thanks. That's actually a great idea.'

'No problem, glad I could help.'

He looks like he's getting ready to head off again.

'So, where do I buy a brisket from?' I wince as I ask it, which seems to only amuse Ari further.

'I'll show you,' he says with a small chuckle.

* * *

Ari is dealing with the butcher, looking at the meat in the case like he really knows what he's doing, which I guess he does. I'm hanging back and holding his shopping, which is the least I can do, considering. Once he's finished explaining what he wants, I put the bags down so that I can grab a twenty-pound note to give to him. I notice the butcher pass something else to him too, as well as the brisket, something wrapped in a white paper bag, and Ari hands over another fiver in return. Afterwards, we make our own swap, his shopping bags for my giant hulk of vacuum-sealed meat.

'Thank you,' I say. We stand outside the butchers in the blazing Sunday sunshine. 'That was really cool of you. I had no idea what to ask for in there.'

'It's okay. Not my first rodeo, as they say.' Then: 'Are you hungry? I got salt beef. There's ready sliced rye bread and mustard in the shopping somewhere.'

I don't remember how I exactly agreed to sit on a high-street bench in the middle of Golders Green with Ari Marshall, eating salt beef on rye, but here we are. We don't talk as we eat, it's too hard to. The bread is soft and the filling keeps threatening to fall out all over the place. Fortunately, I'm just in my knock-off Disney schmutter, and a dribble of mustard probably wouldn't look out of place within Rapunzel's hair, but Ari's come equipped with napkins too, which I lay out over my lap and over my front and just have to hope that they won't blow away in the breeze. I'm not worried about looking cute, or seductive, because I know it's not like that with Ari. He's seen me as a precocious eight-year-old; seeing me demolishing an overloaded salt beef sandwich is hardly something to be ashamed of, considering.

'So, what are you going to make with your brisket?' he asks me when we're finished eating.

'I've barely thought about how I'm going to cook it, let alone what I'm going to cook *with* it,' I admit.

'I'm guessing latkes would be too much?'

'I've never even seen my own mother make latkes from scratch. There's no way I'm tackling them on the first attempt.' I think about it for a moment. 'Although I suppose I could head back to Kosher Kingdom and get some frozen ones. Do you think Euan would consider that cheating?'

If Euan isn't impressed with the effort I'm already making, then I have no idea what more I can do. I realise it's the first time I've mentioned him in a while, and the first time I've said his name in front of Ari.

'You can get something fresh for dessert, to make up for it?'

'Like what?'

Ari gets up and cocks his head, instructing me to follow him down the high street, back towards Golders Green station. Then we're standing outside Carmelli's, and the aroma I sense just from standing outside the bakery on the pavement, of warm, fresh bread laced with rich, dark chocolate, is just divine.

'You say he likes food? Get him some rugelach from Carmelli's,' Ari says.

'You think?'

'If he's too full on carbs by then it's something nice to take home for later. And if he doesn't like it, he's a monster and you don't want anything to do with him.'

Ari's smile is warm, but the suggestion of breaking up with Euan breaks the magic somewhat.

'Thanks for your help today,' I say, and Ari's smile changes to something more reticent. We both know this escapade is over.

'Are you going to be okay in there?' he asks me, indicating the bakery.

'I may not be able to handle myself in a butcher's shop, but where baked goods are concerned, trust me, I'm fine.'

'Well, this was nice then.'

'It was. Thank you, again.'

'Sure.'

I don't know if we're meant to hug, or kiss cheeks, or what. He must be confused too, because we both just stand there for a moment, unsure and awkward. Finally, I turn away to head into the bakery.

'Oh, Tamsyn!' Ari calls, making me turn back quickly. 'Look, I'm sorry I was a schmuck to you that night. I was kinda playing, but I don't think it came across like I intended it.'

'I wasn't exactly the nicest person to you either, I guess.'

'But I could have been more of a gentleman. I worried afterwards that I upset you.'

'I wasn't upset,' I lie. 'Well, maybe a little. You said some pretty harsh things that night.'

'I'm sorry about that.'

'I also said some pretty harsh things. But I started out more angry at Abigail and the set-up than at you. I'm sorry, too.'

His smile is big, beaming and unabashed, before he tucks it away again and becomes more serious. 'Your Bissli?' he offers. Ari passes the snacks over to me that he was keeping in his shopping bag into the one I'm carrying for the brisket.

'Thank you, again,' I say, unexpectedly sheepish.

'No worries, this was nice.'

I turn away more quickly this time, and head into the shop. A moment too late, I think of asking Ari to walk back to Kosher Kingdom with me for the latkes, but when I turn back to look for him through the open doorway, he's already walked on.

13

I can't bring myself to call Mum. Not yet. I shouldn't need to when I have the internet and endless YouTube videos showing you how to do absolutely anything you could ever dream of.

I may not be certain about whether the baking pan is the right size, or what temperature I should ideally have our (admittedly temperamental) oven set at (Helene is trying to be useful, but she's having far more fun taking short videos of me fretting), but I figure that brisket is brisket. The essence of every blog post and recipe I can find is that you can just stick it in and then take it out a few hours later. I tied it up with string to stop it from falling apart. I've crammed some onions around the bottom of the baking tray, as well as garlic and herbs, to give it flavour. I've even basted the bloody thing with all the fatty juices.

Even so, I swear I can hear Mum in my head: 'What on earth do you think you are doing? And why? For a boy? What boy? Since when have you made anything for yourself, let alone a boy? And you want to start with a brisket? Of all things, a brisket? You should have let me make it and I could have brought it round. Or you could have come round and collected it. Is your oven even big enough?'

So now it's approaching midnight (Helene went to bed ages ago), and I'm sitting in front of the oven alone whilst I wait for my precious brisket to start falling off the bone. When I'm not staring through the oven window at my expensive meat baby, I'm on my phone checking social media for Ari's profile. I'm just curious about him, that's all. He doesn't seem to be online much. There's a private Instagram account, a Twitter account that hasn't been updated in three years and still has an egg for a profile picture, and a lamentably sparse Facebook presence too.

Of course, on Facebook I can see all the very many people we have as mutuals, including Abigail and Dominic, and a couple of Dominic's relatives, who added me during the time of the engagement and after, and I figure that if I added him now it really wouldn't be a big deal, especially considering the family connection.

But I don't. This is just curiosity.

We had such an ugly start, and then he was so unexpectedly nice when he didn't need to be, and in a way that didn't aggravate me either. Maybe there's a way I can make the kindness up to him somehow. I want to tell him that I appreciate it, but I have no idea how to without giving him the wrong impression. Because I have a boyfriend. A wonderful, hot boyfriend who I'm staying up until midnight cooking for, and Ari can't think that he's anything other than a convenient helping hand. It could have been Abigail I bumped into. Or another cousin. It was Golders Green; I'm surprised that I didn't bump into more people I knew.

But I didn't.

When the timer finally goes, I wipe my eyes with relief and take the brisket out of the oven, placing it on the counter under foil to rest and cool. I'll put it in the fridge in the morning. It smells of family, and of home. I just hope it tastes as good, and that Euan likes it.

I take a picture and then send it to Euan, along with the message: *surprise preparations for tomorrow!* He replies straight away with the heart eyes emoji. I think about requesting to follow Ari's Instagram, posting the picture and tagging him, or at least sending it to him via a DM with a note of gratitude too.

But I don't.

The next day in the office we have a planning meeting just after lunch, something that Gareth would usually attend, but he's avoiding us. He stayed in his office all morning with the door closed, leaning back in his high-backed, leather executive chair and looking flustered over the phone. When he realised that people working in the bullpen could see him, he rolled over in his chair to the corner of his office and yanked the cord that pulled the blinds closed.

'He said that he had important business to attend to,' Kerry-Ann responds when I quietly ask where Gareth is at the start of the meeting. He went out for lunch and hasn't come back.

'What's in his schedule?'

'That's the thing, nothing. Not on the shared calendar anyway.'

It took months to get Gareth to use the shared calendar online so that the assistants could see where he was and more effectively set up his meetings for him. But Gareth always preferred his A4, leather-bound portfolio diary, scribbling notes across pages in handwriting nobody was ever able to read but him. Every now and again, he reverts away from the computer, and it throws us all for a loop. Especially when it comes to important meetings like this, where I might need budget approval and final confirmation of the kind of direction we want to go in.

I thought about postponing the meeting and waiting for Gareth to come back, but that's not easy to do when he's being flighty and we have deadlines. So, I ask Kerry-Ann to take notes, and resolve to go over everything with him later. I think about making the appropriate decisions in his absence, but then I worry that he'll get annoyed and ask for everything to be changed just because he'd rather have his own way than have me look after it (something that's burnt me before). So instead, I ask everyone for their pitches, and after ruling out the bad ones, I mark everything as TBD until I can get the final approval.

Later that afternoon, I think about the brisket in the fridge, and how much I'm looking forward to seeing Euan's face after I've heated it up and got it ready for the big reveal. Then my mind wanders to Ari, and the fact that he remembers me from way back. I don't remember anyone I went to cheder with. It was so long ago and I hated my teachers so much that I quickly lost interest in learning Hebrew or any of the other religious things on the curriculum, but I do remember what I used to be like, the Tamsyn Rutman Ari remembers. I remember being mystified by my teachers in their long skirts, who made us wash our hands all the time and told us fairy tales about the Shabbos bride. We would sing songs and drop our tzedakah in the box, and then I would ask questions. Or, more specifically, I would ask one question constantly: why?

And nobody could ever answer me sufficiently.

'It's what we do,' the teachers would answer. 'It's tradition and it's what it says in the Torah.'

'But why?'

'God wrote the rules and passed them down to Moses.'

'But why?'

I wasn't trying to be an annoying brat. I genuinely wanted to know. And nobody could ever answer me. Instead, the teachers would ignore when my hand was raised, or give me special tasks that involved being very quiet and focussed whilst all the other kids got to join in songs and games. Before I quit I had migrated from the front of the class towards the back, where I couldn't bother anyone with my incessant need for answers.

But Ari was there. He might have thought I was cool, but I wonder if he saw my frustration. I wonder if he saw how sad it made me that I wasn't being included, all because I kept asking.

Eventually I didn't ask anymore, and then I told my parents that I didn't want to go. I thought they would be more fussed about my little rebellion, but it turns out they were more concerned about making sure Ross was on track. He was going to have a bar mitzvah and I wasn't, so his involvement and Jewish education became more important than mine. Somewhere along the line I think this made me resentful, and I became more detached. I know there are female rabbis now, but didn't whilst growing up, and I sometimes wonder if I would have felt like I had a place as a passionate, inquisitive girl in Judaism if I had those kind of role models back then.

'Gareth's emailed me,' Kerry-Ann interrupts my thoughts, popping her head around my door with an update. 'He says he'll be out of the office for the rest of the week and to go ahead with whatever you think is best, content wise.'

'The rest of the week? Right then,' I reply, rolling my eyes. This means staying later than I planned to finalise the decisions from the meeting earlier. I'm fuming at Gareth's apparent lack of care and consideration, but quickly do the mental calculations and work out that as long as I can be home by seven, I should be able to have dinner ready and on the table by eight-thirty, eight if I really push it. Thank goodness the brisket is already cooked.

During the afternoon, whilst taking quick mental breaks between tasks, I look up Florence Biddulphe online. Every now and again I come back to what Euan said about working in hotel PR, and I haven't been able to shake it. Sure enough, Florence works for a boutique agency specialising in PR and marketing for upmarket hotels, and their client list is impressive. It doesn't seem like her job just involves getting press coverage for hot new chefs either. From what I can tell, her line of work involves getting to be pretty creative in terms of setting the direction for their clients, coming up with ideas and designing promotional strategies. Doesn't sound too far off what I'm doing now, except there are no printer deadlines.

I twist my pen in my fingers, then start drumming it on my desk. Then I look back at my task list, and out over the top of my computer to all the other staff in the bullpen and know that I can't leave this place. I have too much to do. I've already done too much to just get up and go. Dreaming of other jobs is like scraping my knee when I first tried roller-skating. I just have to see this through, because I'm sure I can prove to Gareth that I'm the right person to promote in the end.

I get home hot and sweaty, the tube a cesspit of crowded bodies and dusty grime. I shove the brisket back into the oven on a low heat to reheat and clear the small fold-out dining table, chucking the post that was accumulating on there on to the coffee table with the piles of magazines. I realise that I probably don't have time for a shower, but I change what I'm wearing and douse myself in body spray to try and take the musty city stench off from me. I don't feel sexy. I feel rushed and frantic and worried about all the things I still need to put in the oven.

'He's a chef,' I moan at Helene, who's being very helpful and arranging a paper tablecloth over the table, as well as setting out the cutlery for me. 'Why did I ever think this was a good idea?'

'Because you want him to like you,' she says.

'I feel like this is a test I'm failing.'

'If he really likes you then it won't matter what you manage to cook,' she reassures.

Helene is heading out shortly (on my orders), but I've agreed that she can be here when Euan arrives, as she's desperate to meet him.

'Wait,' I say, freshly panicked. 'If I put the frozen latkes in with the brisket, then I'll have to turn the oven up, but then what if the brisket burns? It's meant to be on a low heat to warm it up. But if I take the brisket out, how do I stop it getting cold by the time the latkes are ready?'

The internet isn't much help, as I can't work out how to search for this exact predicament, and then I realise that the only person I know who could give me good advice is exactly the person I can't ask right now, because otherwise it would ruin the surprise.

Except, there is another person. Someone who I never thought I would want to call in this scenario, but someone who I'm sure would drop everything to help nonetheless.

'Hi Mum,' I say when she answers the phone.

'Tamsyn, what's happened? Is everything okay?' I expected Mum's worry, as this isn't my usual time to call.

'I'm fine, everything is fine.'

'You haven't been mugged have you? Deborah Dreyer says she knows someone whose daughter lives in that part of London, and she was mugged. Someone on a moped took the phone right out of her hand! I knew it was a bad idea moving to that area.'

'Mum, I'm fine. Nothing has happened. And wasn't Paul mugged in Stanmore last year? It happens everywhere. I just called for some advice.'

'Advice?'

'Cooking advice.' I'm aware of Helene watching me, smiling at my consternation whilst I try and explain things to Mum without explaining too much.

'Oy a broch,' Mum says. 'Cooking, you? Why?'

'It's just a project.'

'So, tell me about this project.'

'Brisket.'

'BRISKET?' I have to hold the handset away from my face, her voice is so loud and shrill. 'What are you doing cooking a brisket?'

The conversation I imagined in my head last night starts to play out with startling accuracy.

'It's for a thing,' I say.

'Oh really? And what's the thing's name?'

'I'm making it for Helene,' I mumble, aware that Helene is now openly staring at me, her mouth agape.

'What does your flatmate want with a brisket?'

'It's for the week. For lunches. Meal prep. Look it up, it's a thing.'

'I told you buying food from Pret and coffees from Starbucks were going to catch up with your budget at some point. Didn't I tell you?'

'Yes Mum, you told me. The brisket is already cooked, I just need to heat it up. But I don't know how to time it with the potatoes because our oven is small.'

'I thought this was for lunches? Why do you need to heat it up with potatoes if it's already cooked and it's for lunches?'

I turn in circles, frustrated that my kitchen is too small to adequately pace.

'Because we're having some now. To try it.'

I know Mum knows that I'm not telling her the truth. I can hear it in the way she sighs down the line, heavy and breathy and making the speaker crackle and distort on my end.

'You should have put it all in together,' she tells me.

'Put what in together?'

'The potatoes and the veg. You part cook the brisket, leaving an hour to go. And then when you finish the last hour, you put in everything else with it.'

'If I do that now, will I overcook the brisket? Will it burn? And will it work with frozen latkes?'

'Frozen latkes? What is it you're up to exactly?'

'Mum, please!'

'It won't kill you, if that's what you mean,' Mum says. 'Taste should be fine, but it won't feel very nice. I say the best thing to do is to stick everything in one pan and go for it. Put some foil over the meat if you're scared about it burning.'

The intercom buzzes. Euan is here. No. No, no, no, no. He's early and I'm not ready yet.

'Mum, thank you! I have to go.'

'That's it?'

'That's all I need right now.'

Helene goes to buzz Euan up.

'This is all very strange Tamsyn. Are you sure you're okay? This isn't one of those phone calls where you say something unusual to let the other person know you're in danger?'

'I'm not in danger Mum. I'm just stressed out.'

'You'll call me and explain everything?'

'At some point, maybe? I have to go Mum, goodbye! And send my love to Uncle Doodle if you speak to Paul or Terry! Okay, bye!'

I end the call and think about sitting down on the floor of the kitchen to recover myself, but I don't have time. I haven't even put my face on. I'm wearing a stupid apron and now I'm all sweaty again from being too close to the oven and letting myself get stressed.

When Helene opens the front door to let Euan in, I almost want to push him out and tell him to wait outside, but then he's there, standing in my entryway, his presence large and imposing, especially next to Helene, who is tiny by comparison and positively childlike in her dungarees.

'Bonsoir monsieur,' Helene is saying in a hammy French accent. 'And welcome to fine dining à la Rutman! My name is Helene,' (she draws out the final syllable of her name to a comedic degree) 'and can I please, perhaps, take your coat?'

'Helene!' I call out.

'The chef tonight,' Helene continues with a smile, 'she has been a-working very hard to prepare for you only the finest cuisine.'

'Helene!' I call again, this time coming out of the kitchen to greet my boyfriend. 'This is my flatmate,' I say to him, exasperated.

'Very pleased to meet you Helene,' Euan says, his eyes bright and playful. 'I've heard some wonderful things about you.'

'Likewise, monsieur, I've heard only good things about you too. Tamsyn has certainly been very happy lately.' This she says with a suggestive wink, making me blush with embarrassment and Euan chuckle.

'Helene is heading out soon, aren't you Helene,' I say.

'I certainly am. Let me know if you need me to bring back a cheeky takeaway?'

'It's that bad?' Euan smiles.

'No,' I say quickly, before adding: 'Maybe.'

Helene takes Euan through to the living room to chat whilst I get back in the kitchen to finish putting everything in the oven and boiling the peas. I manage to sneak to my bedroom to whack some mascara and lipstick on and get back to the stove just in time to stop the peas from boiling over. The kitchen is a mess. It couldn't look more disorderly in here if I tried. I honestly don't know how Euan does this for a living and enjoys it. I just truly hope that my effort is worth it.

Half an hour later and Helene has gone, and I'm serving up the food. The peas are fresh and green, and the ready-made frozen potatoes cooked through, but something is wrong with the brisket. It's not the tender, honey brown colour I'd imagined and seen in the recipe photos online, but a sloppy grey. It's tender, but maybe too tender. It certainly falls off the bone, but in the mouth it just crumbles, and the juices don't seem to have any flavour at all beyond 'oniony'.

Euan is putting on a brave face, whereas I'm fuming with myself. I spent so much time on this food. What must he think of me?

'So, this is a traditional dish then?' Euan asks.

'It's meant to be. Not quite like this though. I'm sorry, it's a mess. I did tell you I couldn't cook?'

'You think that it's the food that matters?'

'I wanted to impress you.'

'Tammy, I am impressed. So, the food doesn't taste great, but you know that this wasn't what everything was about.'

'I hate cooking.'

'I know you do, but you did it for me.'

'If you ask me to do something like this again, I'll kill you. You know that, right?'

'Don't worry, I'm well aware.'

I'm leaning on the table, the plate in front of me unfinished, trying not to think about how I'm going to have to clear up the mess in the kitchen and throw out the rest of the meat. Euan's demeanour helps tremendously. The way he's looking at me, like I'm amazing despite the fact that I've thoroughly proved how much I am not.

'Can I ask you something?' I look at him dead in the eyes, my head propped on my hand as I lean across the table.

'Anything,' Euan replies.

'What is it about me? Why do you like me as much as you do?'

'It shouldn't be that much of a mystery, surely?'

Except it is. I know why I like him. He's a spectacular looking human being, he makes me feel things I've never felt before in bed and, after all that, he's kind and has solid values too. If someone could carve me the perfect man, the exact man I imagined for myself post-Simon Schaffler, then it would be Euan. He's like all my wildest fantasies come to life.

'Tell me anyway,' I coax, pushing a strand of hair away from my face.

'Well, you're beautiful for starters.'

'You think so?'

'Of course. Great hair, dark eyes, you're not like a lot of other girls I meet. All made up in cocktail dresses and layers and layers of make-up. There's something authentic about you. Plus, you're clever. You have that job, you know how to be bossy – something I like a lot – and you're easy to be around.'

'That's nice.' And it is. I know I'm blushing. 'Although I don't know how I feel about being called bossy.'

'It's a good thing, trust me,' Euan reassures, a sexy smirk on his face. 'I like it. There's also the fact that I can see you as someone my mum will like. Dad too. I can't wait for you to meet them. I know that I can take you home with me and you'll be real with her, and with the rest of the family too. You're just a real person, to me.'

I shuffle in my seat, switch arms so that my head rests on the other hand.

'I want to be with you,' Euan continues. 'Not just for right now. But for a long time. And I know it's early days, and you'd prefer to go slowly, but it's also something that you need to know. I need to tell you.'

I hold my breath for a moment, realising what's coming next.

'I can't stop thinking about you Tammy. I want to be with you all the time. I think about you all the time. You're someone I can see myself falling in love with.'

He reaches a hand out across the table, across the half-empty plates, and I hold it. I've never had anyone tell me something like that before, and I always imagined that when it happened, that I'd be able to say it back. But the words aren't there. So instead of saying anything, I stand up and lead him by the hand to my bedroom.

'Dessert?' I ask in that low, cool-girl voice I've perfected for him.

I may not be able to say the words he wants to hear, not yet anyway, but I can still make him happy. I can still give him everything I have in the moment, even if I might not be able to give him everything he wants in the future. I just want things to stay as they are right now. No talk of meeting parents, of how we're going to decorate our future home or what we would call our future kids. No future, only the right now, and our bodies moving together in that way that feels so, so good.

Afterwards, he lies back on my bed, holding me close.

'You're amazing,' he says, sounding sleepy.

I pull myself away to go to the bathroom, taking my phone with me. I'm sitting on the edge of the bath when I click through to Instagram and realise there's a new follow. Never not intrigued, I click through to see the name at the top is Ari Marshall. He's following me. He can see the pictures of the brisket I've been posting. I wonder if he's been thinking about it? About me?

There's a message from him too, the little paper aeroplane in the top right of my screen a bright red beacon: *hope it tasted good,* he's written.

His account is still private, but I decide to reciprocate and click on the follow request button. After a minute of waiting and realising that he's not going to accept my request promptly, I message him back: *Thank you for your help!*

I get more comfortable by sinking down to sit on the bathroom floor, rather than the edge of the bathtub, my boyfriend asleep in the next room, waiting for Ari to reply.

Then, I see his account isn't private anymore, his photos are now visible. Lots of arty shots of dappled light falling through green leaves on Hampstead Heath, and the London skyline from the top of Primrose Hill. But most importantly, there's a new message waiting for me.

No problem, he writes.

Short, sweet, but also pretty unemotional. No punctuation, and no emojis. A cold bare minimum. I don't know what I was expecting.

I use the toilet, and then head back to the dark of the bedroom and curl into Euan.

14

Ari and I have been messaging. It's really not a big deal.

We switched numbers, and I message him in the same way I would any other completely platonic male friend. In fact, if anything, I'm even more purposefully careful about not coming across in any way flirty or even a little bit cheeky, so that Ari can't possibly mistake the fact that we're just friends. If you can even call it that. We're people who know each other. Our cousins are married. We're practically related. But not closely. Or genetically.

When we text it's like texting someone at work. Which isn't to say I'm not searching for the signs of there being anything deeper going on. I watch every bit of correspondence for a hint of the possibility of anything. An errant 'x' at the end of a message, an emoji laden with innuendo, or even just a hint in the tone that something might be happening beyond what's polite. I'm only looking for this because I need to be aware of it. So that I can be honest with Euan. In case Euan ever finds my phone and sees the messages. So that I'm not caught by surprise.

But it's not as if Ari is anything but courteous and friendly. He either doesn't care about me all that much, or he's being very careful about not giving anything away. I'm on my guard just in case. It's perfectly plausible that he just wants to help me. He's just a good person like that. Exactly as much of a mensch as everyone has been telling me he is.

We're meeting up, but this is definitely not a date. I've been very clear that this meet-up is purely for research purposes. Just how he helped me out in Golders Green, I need his help again, this time to do something special for Uncle Doodle.

Even if there was the remote possibility that Ari might think this was a date, I've gone to a lot of trouble to dissuade that notion. If this was a date, I'd be touching up my make-up and making sure that I'm wearing something cute. I haven't even bothered straightening my hair. If this was a date, we'd both have been a little more enthused about even arranging it. He's postponed twice already because he's busy on an important case, and I've already told him that I can't stay out late because I've got to be fresh for work tomorrow. It's been hinted that Cooper is going to be making his first official appearance and I need to make sure I'm on good form. We're not even going to a bar or a restaurant. We're meeting at Spitalfields Market, and just going on a walk. No big deal.

This get together came about because I was on the phone with Terry, asking her how Uncle Doodle was.

'Very weak, very tired, but still a pain, which means he's fine,' she replied at the time. 'The moment he stops having a go at me, that's when I know something's wrong.'

'I want to get him something,' I told her.

'Like what?'

'I don't know. Something to cheer him up. What does he like?'

'His diet is very strict at the moment. If you get him any of the things he likes, it won't really be helpful.'

'Nothing food related. Something that will make him feel better.'

'He talks about wanting to see his old haunts again. We've been thinking about taking him for a drive. Showing him what the places he remembers look like now, but I'm worried it will only depress him. Besides, being in the car for that long might be too uncomfortable.'

That's when the idea hit me.

'You know I don't live far from where he grew up?'

'It's all changed now though, there's nothing much left of what was there before. Right?'

'I could still visit those places and take some photos. We can go through them and he can tell us his stories?'

Terry agreed that it sounded like a lovely, simple thing I could do to make him happy. Of course, I did a lot of research myself. I checked in with Terry again, and her brother Paul, as well as my dad, to get a list of all the places they remember him mentioning. I imagined creating a photo book or a slide show, and thought that maybe Ross would like to get involved helping to put it together. I started googling during my lunch hour the day after I had my big idea and was amazed at everything I started discovering about the Jewish East End.

It's always been the nature of London, I realised, to see waves of immigrants settling in the East, as far away from the upmarket West End as possible, and close to the old docks and centres of working-class industry. Uncle Doodle grew up in the East End, but by the time he was getting married and having children, his generation had already moved away, up north to Essex or over a bit to North West London. It's the track of the Jewish diaspora that many Jewish Londoners seem to have been through, a collective history that's just accepted and known from a young age. However, I'd never really thought about the streets my family lived on, or the places my ancestors knew. Plenty has changed in London, but also a lot hasn't. I was suddenly interested.

And I thought, out of everyone I knew, that Ari would be interested too.

Did you know my great-uncle grew up in Whitechapel? I texted Ari one evening. *Turner Street. That's not far from where I live now!*

I have ancestors who lived around there too, he wrote back.

I've been looking at the places on Google Street View, I told him.

You should go for a proper explore. Do one of those history walks.

I was actually going to head round there and take some photos. Want to join me? Could be interesting.

So, this isn't a date. It's homework. It's family business. It's getting curious about something with someone who would understand and be interested with you. That's not to say Euan wouldn't be interested too, but he's just so busy. Plus, he'd never feel the same about all this stuff as someone like Ari would feel. It's not like going to an exhibition at a museum, this is a part of our personal heritage. This is real.

Ari is leaning against a pillar within Spitalfields Market, next to a coffee stall that smells divine, lazily browsing through his phone. His hair is a messy mop, thick and dark with loose curls standing up at odd angles, and he's wearing a casual checked shirt in light, sandy colours over a plain grey T-shirt. Slightly too-long jeans over sneakers complete the look. It's been hot today; I don't blame him for the dressed-down cool. I'm wearing a summer dress. Nothing fancy or special. Just a regular summer dress, strappy and blue with tiny white flowers, along with some white tennis shoes. Comfortable, easy-breezy, barely any effort clothes. July is hitting us at full force, and even now at 6pm the sky is still pale and midsummer bright, with the heat pressing behind my knees and neck.

'Hey,' he says as I approach. I lean in for a friendly hug, but we're barely touching and I pull away quickly.

'Hi, thanks for meeting with me.' I know I sound too professional, but I'm not entirely sure how to be casual with him either.

'I thought lawyers always wore stuffy suits,' I tell him, remembering that he appeared at Abigail and Dominic's straight from work and dressed down too.

'Oh, I don't work at a big firm,' he says. 'Mine is pretty small. Not quite the same airs and graces. Unless I'm going to a big meeting, or court, I can pretty much wear what I want.'

'So, this isn't a big meeting then?' I tease, instantly regretting it afterwards. I shouldn't be doing any teasing in case it could be misconstrued as flirting. 'I thought you litigated in big cases against newspapers?'

'I do, but I represent the little guy mostly. Libel and defamation. Some class action type stuff.'

'Can you tell me what you're working on right now?'

'Not really,' he looks uncomfortable, and I wonder if it's all meant to be serious and top secret.

'I'm sorry. I shouldn't pry.'

'No, it's not that. It's more, well, I'm out of work. It's a nice evening. I just want to forget about it for a bit, if that's all right?'

'Fine by me,' I say brightly. He smiles back at me with relief. He has got a nice smile.

'So, have you got a plan of where we're going?' he asks me.

'Actually, I do. My dad and my cousins gave me a list of places that they've definitely heard Uncle Doodle talk about. Shall we just walk and see where we end up first?'

'I like that you call him Uncle Doodle.'

'It's a silly thing. Only my brother and I say it. It's to do with his Hebrew name.' I spell out 'Dudel' so that Ari understands the word play, as they're pronounced the same.

'What's your Hebrew name?' he asks me as we walk down Fashion Street towards Brick Lane.

I don't remember the last time anyone cared to ask me that, or the last time I cared to tell anyone. I'm struck suddenly by how few Jewish people I know outside my family, and therefore how few people know that I even have another, private name.

'Leah Raisel,' I say, but I'm quiet as I say it. I feel embarrassed.

'I'm Ariel Peleg, ben Shimon Raz,' he says, a lot more proudly.

'I can't remember my father's name,' I admit.

'It's okay. Besides, Leah Raisel is pretty. You don't want to ruin it with your Dad's name after.'

'Is Ari short for Ariel then?' I ask.

'Yep. But I don't go by Ariel, for obvious reasons.'

'*The Little Mermaid* is a great film, you have nothing to be ashamed of.'

'Ha ha,' he rolls his eyes. Then, more solemnly: 'I saw you with him at the wedding. Your Uncle Doodle, I mean.'

'Oh.'

'You really care about him.'

'Of course I do.'

'It was nice. Unexpected.'

'Well,' I pause, unsure what to say next. My instinct is to challenge him, to ask why it was unexpected. Because he didn't think I was capable of being nice? Too cold and stubborn to show care and affection for the people I love? But I stop myself, and just give him a simple 'thank you' instead.

We walk around the streets of the East End, heading towards Whitechapel not saying much besides pleasantries and small talk, and the whole time I feel like something's missing. It's like there's a force field between us, or at least a visceral line I can't cross, which when I try and consider it any more deeply just seems weird and frankly, a little mad. It's just Ari. Just this guy who insulted me and then helped me buy a brisket, and we're just hanging out. It shouldn't feel weird.

We're nearly at the Royal London Hospital when Ari says, 'I wish I had brought the names of the streets my family lived on.'

'It's okay,' I tell him. 'You can live vicariously through my relatives. We're nearly at the first place I want to go: Turner Street. According to my phone, just a couple of minutes' walk away.'

I'm surprised by Turner Street, just behind the huge hospital complex. There's a lot of urban build-up around this area, dreary housing blocks and stark, concrete brutalism, as well as the odd glass and steel commercial building, but this little road is remarkably intact, especially as we start heading south. I lead Ari up to an old stretch of Victorian terrace, the individual houses looking freshly renovated with glossy coats of paint across window shutters that match the doors.

'This is it,' I say with a sigh.

'Is this where your great-uncle lived?'

'Number forty-one. I don't think it was as trendy as this when he lived here. I think it was a bit of a slum to be honest. He moved out in his early teens, I think. Evacuated during the war, and then my great grandparents never came back. My dad told me some stories about his father and Uncle Doodle – they were brothers – and they really missed this place.'

'It wouldn't have been nice back then.'

'But it would have been home, I guess, before the war started?'

Ari steps back and looks around whilst I take some photos.

'It's lucky to still be standing,' he says when he comes back to my side. 'Round here, wherever you see a new, modern building or council block, that's where a bomb hit.'

I take more photos of the surrounding area, wondering how much Uncle Doodle would be likely to recognise. I feel a slight sombreness, and I think Ari feels it too. We catch each other at one point, our eyes meet but we don't say anything, and then he stuffs his hands in his pockets and looks away. That force field still feels cold.

'The next place I want to go isn't far from here. Jubilee Street.'

I lead the way, and stop us outside a huge, baroque stone building painted a garish red and adorned at the very top with a Star of David. Bold lettering across the front of the building proclaims, 'Synagogue of the Congregation of Jacob'.

'I don't think this is the same building Uncle Doodle would have known,' I say, marvelling up at the grand facade. 'I was looking it up last night and I think the original building was knocked down in the sixties. But still, this is pretty cool right?'

'Beats Mill Hill shul,' Ari jokes.

'Do you go to shul much?' I ask him, between taking photos of the area.

'High holidays, and only sometimes,' he replies.

'You strike me as more religious.'

'Whatever gave you that idea?'

'I don't know. You have this aura about you. This confident, capable thing. You know stuff. I guess I associate that feeling with frum types.'

'If I tell you something, do you promise not to laugh?'

'I absolutely cannot promise that.'

He turns his head and returns my mischievous smile. It's a moment, a crack in the force field.

'I went to a yeshivah. At least for a few months. I thought I was going to be a rabbi.'

'Really?' I'm genuinely surprised, and somewhat awed. I stop what I'm doing and turn to him, looking at him properly.

'It made sense, at the time.'

'What happened?'

'I'm not sure really. It's complicated and I don't know if I have a simple answer for you. I just remember slowly realising that my relationship with God might be something else, and that I wasn't going to become the kind of community leader I wanted to be through endless study.'

'So, you switched to law?'

'And then I switched to law. But not just that.'

'What else?' I question.

'Have you heard of tikkun olam?'

'No.'

He looks at me like he was expecting that answer, but it's not a dismissive or patronising look. If anything, talking about this seems to be brightening him up. He's eager to share, happy that I'm wanting to listen.

'It's about making the world better, in whatever way you can. I'm not saying that going to shul and following rules to the letter is a bad thing, many find their connection that way. But for me, I connect through action.'

'What does that mean exactly?'

'Well, I'm Jewish through my work. Trying to repair the world and help people with my job is important. But I do other things too. Earlier this year I did some pro bono work with a team in Lewisham, helping asylum seekers with their applications to stay in the UK. I've had a busy case load at the day job more recently, but I'm hoping to spend more time with them again soon.'

'You're Superman,' I tease, trying to hide just how impressed I am.

'Hardly,' Ari replies, bashful.

'Do you believe in God?' I ask him after we've walked a little further on.

'Maybe not the way you think of God. Not as some sort of supernatural person sitting in a cloud watching over us. I see God as existing in everything.'

'I vaguely remember a teacher in cheder telling me that. That God is all around and in everything. I'll be honest with you, it freaked me out.'

'It never freaked me out. If anything, I thought it was kind of awesome. That's why I work so hard. If I do what I can to feel connected to everything around me, to make a difference, that's me doing what I can to experience a connection to the divine.'

'Well, now you're just making me feel bad,' I say.

'That's not my intention,' Ari replies. After a pause he continues, 'You know what the word "Israel" means, right?'

I feel a drum of panic in my chest as I'm suddenly reminded of Simon Schaffler.

'It means "to fight with God",' Ari continues. 'We are the people who fight with God. It's what we do.'

'You remembered me because I asked so many questions,' I murmur, out loud but not really to him. Nonetheless, he smiles at me, a smile that's not wicked or sexy, not the kind of smile that Euan would give me, but a smile of recognition. Like he's been waiting for something to click in my head and it's finally there. It's a smile that suddenly makes me nervous, and tremendously shy.

'Yeah, you were a fighter,' he says.

We start to wander back through the small streets and back up towards Whitechapel tube station. The light is dying, the sun starting to set. I snap photos where I can, capturing the shadows when I find them pretty, the angles of the older brick architecture when I think that it might be something Uncle Doodle would appreciate and remember.

Ari and I don't talk much, not about anything important anyway. To be honest, I struggle to really look at him. I let my hair fall about my face to hide my eyes, and I'm aware that I'm using my camera as a prop to stop any deeper interactions. I don't know if he's aware of it. It's as if the force field that was once there suddenly isn't, but instead of hating the distance between us I was feeling, I'm now uncomfortable with what might be something like nakedness.

I'm aware of him walking next to me, of his height and his closeness. I'm aware that anyone looking at us might think we're a couple. I'm aware that if Euan saw us right now, that he might be angry with me. The guilt is overwhelming.

'I'm up for getting some food, if you are?' he asks me suddenly. It's about eight o'clock now, but even though I'm definitely hungry, I decide to say no.

'Euan is going to be wondering where I am,' I tell him.

This is a lie. Euan is working late tonight and doesn't even know that I'm out. It's also the first time I've mentioned Euan the entire evening. I watch Ari's face to see if there's a reaction there, any kind of possible indication that he might be upset or jealous or *something*. I don't see anything. Did he ask me because he wants to turn this walk into a date, or did he ask because he is just hungry and we happen to be together? I search his face, his body language, his demeanour, for anything resembling attraction to me. There was something before, something in the way we looked at each other when we talked about him almost becoming a rabbi, something that was powerful enough to make me uncomfortable, but maybe I was imagining it.

Thing is, I am hungry. And I do want to eat dinner with Ari. I want to ask him more questions. I want him to tell me more things. It's easy talking to him, and when he smiles, he makes me want to smile too. He's a friend after all. Friends eat together. Friends talk about their lives. It doesn't have to mean anything.

'The chef, right?' Ari checks.

'That's the one.'

'Sounds like you guys are pretty serious.'

'It's still new, but maybe, probably.'

'That brisket must have been something.'

Damn. I'm not imagining this. Or am I? Either way, this is feeling dangerous. He's looking away again, his hands in his pockets. I'm biting the inside of one cheek, thinking that if this had been a date, this would almost certainly be the point where we'd be kissing. If he tried to, would I stop him?

'I'd better get going,' I say suddenly. We're on the Whitechapel Road now, the entrance to the tube station in view. I can easily walk home from here, but I figure that Ari might want to head back to where he needs to be via public transport.

'You all right on your own? I can walk back with you?' he offers.

'No, it's out of your way,' I say, pushing the hair back from my eyes. 'It was really kind of you to accompany me this evening though. I appreciate it.'

'When are you going to show your great-uncle the photos?'

'Oh, I don't know. I want to share them with Ross – that's my brother – and see if he can help me put a PowerPoint together or something.'

'If you need any help, I'm pretty nifty with PowerPoint.'

'Oh, you've already done so much. And I have Ross. It'll be nice to get him involved.'

'Well, I guess I'll say goodbye then,' is that a sigh? Does he look sorry? Does he realise how hot and flustered I'm feeling? Or maybe that's just the balmy summer heat.

He reaches forward for a friendly hug, matching the one from when we met earlier, and I push away from it too quickly, nervous and awkward.

'This was nice,' I say. 'Thank you again.'

'You know, if you're ever interested in learning more about Judaism, not the old school stuff, but some more modern ways to observe, I can send you some links.'

'I'm really busy, with work and everything.'

'Sure.'

'But thank you. It's a nice offer. I can see you as a good teacher.'

He smiles in that bashful way again, hands back in his pockets.

'I'll see you around Tamsyn Rutman,' Ari returns.

'Sure, see you around Rabbi Marshall.'

His smile might be amiable and kind, but right then there was a flash of wickedness. It makes me laugh, to see his quick annoyance, followed by the laugh and the roll of his eyes.

'I shouldn't have told you that, should I?'

'Nope,' I tease.

He looks like he wants to say something else, to continue to banter, but he doesn't. He holds a hand up to wave goodbye, and then turns to head into Whitechapel tube station.

As I walk home, I go over the evening in my head. I didn't do anything wrong. Neither of us said anything or implied anything that was other than the truth. He knew about Euan, and I mentioned him. There's no chance that anyone could possibly get the wrong idea about what this evening was. So why, as I'm walking through the darkening streets back to my flat, do I feel so guilty?

15

'What kind of loser books holiday and spends it at home?' I tease Ross.

'This loser!' he grins.

We're halfway through July and Ross is back in London for a short holiday. It's so good to have him here. I feel like the last time I saw him we were both so stressed out and concerned with Uncle Doodle that it didn't really feel like a proper visit. Having him for two whole weeks is a complete luxury.

'So, what have you got planned for me today?' he asks me.

Ross is very much the kind of guy who, if given the opportunity, would just lounge around the house all day, every day, doing absolutely nothing. I swear, if nobody intervened he'd spend the entire two weeks of his holiday on the sofa. In his defence, he says he's so busy focusing and studying at work that he relishes the time at home to just switch off and let his brain rest, but he's also twenty-six years old and has the stamina of a fifty-something. So usually, it's up to me to get him out and about, at least on the weekends.

'Did you get the Facebook invite to Dominic's thing?' I ask in return.

'Yes,' Ross' face is now an oval of concern, his chin pulled into his neck, his brow furrowed.

'Please, don't tell me we're going?'

'So I just won't tell you.'

'Tamsyn, seriously? We're going to Dominic's birthday party?'

He was sitting upright on the sofa before, but now he's slouched all the way back in protest. I guess he hadn't noticed my afternoon party wear: a dark pink button-down satin dress from Zara (the top buttons left casually undone), cinched with a leather belt, with knee-high black boots. It's a look that I hope says 'I've dressed up, but it's for me, not for you.' I also spent nearly two hours blowing out my hair this morning, and then tonging it so that the waves fell glamorously, rather than in the lazy, tangled heap they usually do.

'It's not a *party* party. It's just afternoon drinks in the pub. Come on, it'll be fun! I've already sorted the present and signed the card from the both of us.'

'What did you get? No wait, I don't care, because I'm not going.'

'I didn't want to say this, but they know you're in town and you kinda need to make up for the fact that you didn't go to the wedding.'

'I was working! I had a deadline on a paper!'

'Well, you're not working now,' I gesture to his prone body, taking in his unshaven face, the stained sweater and the worn socks with holes in them. 'Come on. You don't have to dress up. Just put on a shirt and we'll take the tube. It's only in Hampstead. It's not even like we're going properly into town or anything.'

'Why are you so interested in going anyway? I'm surprised you haven't come up with an excuse for backing out,' Ross asks me, suddenly suspicious.

'It's just drinks, and I'm not busy. Why wouldn't I want to go?'

'Didn't you have a nightmare at their Friday night dinner a while back?'

'It wasn't that bad.'

'You texted me the next morning and told me that Abigail had her ketubah framed and hung up in the bedroom. That her chicken soup tasted of – and I quote – "abandoned feminism and drowned despair".'

'So, she's chosen to be religious. It doesn't mean she's a bad person.' I shrug, nonchalant and carefree. I'm thinking vaguely of what Ari told me, and wondering if observing old traditions is just how Abigail finds her connection. 'Probably the opposite in fact. Come on, just come with me. We'll only stay an hour or so. It'll be nice!'

Ross grumbles but realises that I'm not going to let this go. He slumps out of the living room and up the stairs to put on some nicer clothes.

'It's nice that you're spending the afternoon with family,' Mum says, coming into the living room. I wonder how long she's been eavesdropping. 'And I like that outfit.'

'Oh, this? It's nothing.'

'Is it a new dress?'

'I've had it ages, you just haven't seen it.'

'It's nice.'

'Thank you.'

Mum's looking at me weird. There's a twinkle in her eye, something that says she has secret knowledge.

'What?' I ask.

'Nothing,' she replies.

I do the only thing I know that will get my mum to spill whatever it is she's trying not to say. I take my phone out of my pocket and pretend not to care.

'Is Dad okay?' I ask, whilst flicking down my Instagram feed. 'Is it a golf afternoon?'

'You know he's a lost cause for the whole summer now,' she says. But she's still standing there near me, waiting, even when I decide to sit and sink back into the sofa.

I keep schtum, knowing she's plotzing, and I'm aware of the fiddling of her fingers, the nervous bite of her lip.

'Anyone special in your life right now?'

Ah. There it is. And if she knows something, it means Ross must have spilled the beans. I'll kill him.

'Depends what you mean by special?' As I say it, I imagine Euan next to me, and how disappointed he would be to see me miss out on an opportunity to tell her everything. But it's still too soon. Far too soon.

'Someone you're seeing maybe?'

'What has Ross said?'

'Nothing! Ross has not said a word, I swear!' A pause, whilst she thinks. 'Unless there's something he knows that's worth saying?'

Damn it.

'Can we talk about it when I get back?' I ask. 'It's really not a big deal. Nothing worth making a fuss over.'

There's Euan's face again, right there at the front of my mind, pure disappointment and longing, like a rejected puppy. But mind-Euan doesn't understand. Mind-Euan can't know how complex this is, how much grief I'm due to get if my mother ends up knowing all my business.

Ross manages to come back downstairs at just that moment, forcing my mother into retreat.

The weather is so nice we decide to walk to Edgware tube station together.

'You told Mum about Euan, didn't you?'

'Tamsyn, if Mum knew about Euan, you don't think she'd be going crazy right now, downloading every clip from that cooking show he was on from YouTube and posting it all over Facebook?'

'So, what did you say then?'

'I didn't say anything! I swear! Lord knows I don't need that grief either.'

'So why was she all weird with me?'

'Perhaps it has something to do with the fact you're all dressed up?'

'I'm not dressed up at all. These are my usual clothes.'

'I don't know. Your hair is all shiny too. Is it usually that shiny?'

'Just a new product I'm using. Nothing special.'

We're sitting on the tube train heading south to Hampstead when Ross brings up Euan again, asking why he's not joining us.

'He's working.'

'On a Sunday afternoon?'

'His restaurant is still really new, so he has to be there lots. His hours are all over the place.'

'Or you just don't want us to meet him.'

'Why wouldn't I want you to meet him? I just want to make sure the time is right. It's a lot, meeting our family. Plus, there's the Jewish stuff.'

'What Jewish stuff?'

'You know. Just, the vibe. He doesn't know anything and I don't want him to feel like an outsider.'

Ross considers this. He looks like how I imagine he looks when he's gazing through a microscope or marking his students' papers. The same look he used to get when he played chess as a teenager.

'That's bull and I think you know it,' he says finally, and carefully.

'You only say that because you're on the inside. I don't want him to find anything intimidating.'

'I may be on the inside, but I'm not the one trying to keep anyone out.'

The tube train winds through suburban North West London, sometimes below street level, and sometimes skimming high above the rooftops. The sky expands over Brent Cross, the tracks looming over the shopping centre and the North Circular, before dipping down again as the hills of Golders Green rise up and envelop the tracks. Then we're high again, slowing slightly as the train bridges Golders Green Road, and I turn my head so that I can peer down at the shops, looking for the places I visited just a few weeks ago. I've missed Kosher Kingdom, or perhaps it's just further down, but I do get a sweet glimpse of Carmelli's, and ever so briefly, maybe a flash of the bench where I ate salt beef sandwiches with Ari.

Dominic and Abigail have hired out the whole rear section of The Flask and it's crowded with their friends, most of whom neither Ross nor I know. The doors are open from the conservatory at the back, and the hot summer sunlight comes streaming in, lifting the dark tones and prints on the walls, the dark wood of the booths and the antique red of the leather upholstered seats.

I cast my gaze around for Ari, and don't see him. Perhaps he's just not here yet.

Before long I'm accosted by Yael and Ed, who have this time brought their baby in tow. He's dangling from a pouch wrapped around Ed's body, the baby's chubby thighs and feet hanging free and hitting at the air with excitement.

'It's so nice to see you again!' I say, forcing a smile before introducing them to Ross. They're curious about him, so I let them chat whilst I turn and look around the room again, trying not to make it too obvious. He should be here. Why wouldn't he be?

'Do you think it's a sheitl?' I ask Ross at the bar after we've moved away from them.

'No? Wait, is it?' he looks over his shoulder to try and get another glimpse of Yael.

'I don't know. I couldn't figure it out either.'

After acquiring drinks, we go in search of the birthday boy, and I present Dominic with his present, a card with a John Lewis voucher hidden inside.

'Ross! Great to see you!' Dominic reaches forward to give Ross a friendly hug before he turns to me to thank me for this gift: 'You really didn't have to. We've had so many gifts already this year,' he says.

'Well, those were for the both of you, and this is just for the birthday boy. Just something small from both Ross and I,' I say.

The chat quickly turns to sports, with Dominic taking Ross to one side to ask him something football related.

'Boys,' Abigail tuts. 'But how are you doing Tamsyn? We haven't really spoken since the dinner at ours.'

'I had a really good time that night. The food was lovely. You outdid yourself.'

'Is it weird to say I enjoyed it? It was stressful, but I just felt so fulfilled afterwards. I don't want to say that cooking and cleaning and being a wife is fulfilling, because that's very anti-feminist. But putting together a dinner like that, coordinating it all and getting the ingredients and the timing right, it just felt so good to get it all done, you know?'

'Sure,' I respond. That would be the perfect moment to tell her about Euan, because I'm pretty sure that what she just described is what Euan feels every day. But I don't.

'Of course, I hear you know all about that. What's this about a brisket?'

'Oh, did Mum tell you?' I ask, embarrassed.

'Auntie Liddy didn't say anything. But Ari mentioned it. Said he bumped into you in Golders Green?'

'He did? Is he here today?'

'Oh, Ari's not coming,' Abigail says, downbeat.

'Really? I thought he would be. Isn't he close with Dominic?'

'They're hanging out during the week. But Ari's girlfriend just got in, and they're spending some quality time together.'

My heart shouldn't be thudding ominously in my chest, and yet it very clearly, and painfully, is.

'Girlfriend? I thought Ari was single. Didn't you try to fix us up?'

'Oh, they're newly back together. It's one of these long-term, on again, off again, kind of things. Complicated. They haven't seen each other in a while, but apparently it's been rekindled and now she's coming over for a long stay.'

Ari didn't say anything about a girlfriend when I last saw him. Why wouldn't he say anything about a girlfriend?

I hope that Abigail thinks I'm only asking for gossip reasons, rather than from any sense of deeper interest, when I ask: 'What's she like?'

'Dalya?'

'Is that her name?'

'To be honest, I've not met her. Dom knows more about it than I do. You should ask him.'

'Oh, it's not important, I'm not going to bother him,' I start before Abigail interrupts to continue.

'But here's what I do know: she's Israeli, went into modelling after doing her national service. I've seen her Insta. Basically, you have to imagine Gal Gadot but with honey-coloured hair. A bit like Gigi Hadid?'

'Ari's going out with a model?'

'She wasn't a model when they met, I think, but essentially, yeah.'

'Wow. Good for him.'

'I know, right? I'm so pleased for him. I hope they work it out. He's such a great guy.'

'Yep. Completely. So great.'

I excuse myself, and as I walk away, I have a clear picture in my head of a blonde Wonder Woman, with Ari by her side. I want to wonder how a girl like that would end up with someone like Ari, but deep down I know. He's cute, he's intelligent, he's a lawyer, but more than that, he's a good person. He's basically perfect. Of course, he's going to want to be with someone equally perfect. Of course, someone perfect is going to recognise him for who he is straight away and snap him up.

'You okay?' Ross asks me after seeing me finish my glass of wine far too quickly.

'Did I ever tell you about Ari?' I reply.

'Nope. Who's Ari?'

'A cousin of Dominic's. I sat next to him at their wedding. Then he was at Abigail's Friday night thing.'

'Oh wait, I remember you talking about him. Wasn't he incredibly dull or something?'

'I thought he was. Anyway, turns out that he's going out with this Israeli model.'

'Well, you're going out with a celebrity chef. When it comes to the game of life, it's not like you've lost out?'

I feel stupid for dressing up. I feel stupid for doing my hair. I feel absolutely ridiculous for even holding a glimmer of hope that Ari might like me like that. Of course, he doesn't. I was rude to him, and I rejected him outright months ago. When I bumped into him in Golders Green, or when we went on our walk around Whitechapel, he was just being nice, because that's the kind of guy he is, not because he felt any sort of affection towards me. I feel so stupid.

Meanwhile, I've barely given Euan any thought, and he's been right there, eager to be with me, and eager for commitment too. I'm a fool. A complete fool.

I hang around to see the cake and to sing happy birthday with everyone else, but nudge Ross soon after.

'We should go home,' I tell him.

'You sure?'

'Absolutely.'

Ross senses my mood on the tube train back. He's sitting opposite me, giving me a look that says I don't have to talk about it, but that if I don't, he'll just do stupid things to annoy me. Like raising his eyebrows, isolating each one independently, and then both together, when I least expect it.

'Stop,' I warn.

'What? I'm not doing anything.'

'Yes you are. Stop it.'

A minute or two later, and his eyebrows are dancing again, the rest of his face impassive.

'Ross!' I whine.

'What?' he replies, mimicking my tone.

'Stop the eyebrow thing. It's annoying.'

'You're annoying.'

Here we are, a thirty-one-year-old and twenty-six year old, both behaving exactly how we behaved when we were children.

'I'm going to tell Mum and Dad about Euan tonight,' I finally reveal as the tube train emerges from the tunnel between Hendon Central and Colindale.

'Cool,' he replies.

'He's serious about me, and I'm serious about him.'

'Of course you are.'

'What's that supposed to mean?'

'I mean you seem serious, but it's more like pissed-off serious rather than in-love serious.'

'I'm fine. I'm just tired.'

'You were so excited about going to Dominic's party. And then suddenly you get there and you're miserable.'

'I just realised that I missed Euan, obviously.'

'Right.'

'I'm really getting tired of your cynicism.'

Ross tips his head back, feeling for the rush of air behind him from the circulation vents. He knows I'm lying. I know

I'm lying. But I'm not about to admit it. What kind of girl gets the man of her dreams, only to figure out that she prefers someone else who has given no indication that he's into her?

I'm a commitment-phobe, I decide right then. This isn't about Ari at all. This is all entirely about Euan. I'm just overwhelmed by the pressure he's putting me under and the intensity of our combined feelings. It's only natural to think about other possibilities when your long-term future looms in front of you. Long-term futures are frightening. Euan is an impossible dream come to life. Of course I'm nervous. Maybe I don't like Ari at all. I'm just an insecure maniac who refuses to see what's right in front of her. Euan. It's Euan. It has to be Euan.

When we get back, I can hear Mum and Dad watching an old *Law & Order* episode and playing their favourite game, guessing who is Jewish from the credits.

'Dick Wolf could be Jewish,' Mum says. 'It's a Jewish name, right?'

'Look it up,' Dad replies.

'You look it up. Richard Belzer. Definitely Jewish.'

'With that schnoz? You don't say!'

They pause the TV after Ross and I have taken off our shoes and come into the living room.

'Nice time?' Mum asks. 'Was she drinking?'

'I saw Abigail with a glass of wine,' I tell her. She makes a disappointed grimace in return.

'Did you make amends for not being at their wedding?' Mum asks Ross next.

'I supplicated on all fours and begged for mercy,' Ross replies, prompting Mum to symbolically swat him away before leaning back and preparing to continue what she and Dad were watching.

'Actually, Mum and Dad, before you get back to your show, I've got something to tell you.'

'You're not pregnant, are you?' Mum asks.

'What? No!'

'Well that's a relief.'

'Mum!'

'What?'

'Let her speak Lydia,' Dad interrupts, TV remote in hand, clearly getting impatient.

'Mum, you were right earlier, and I want to tell you both about a man I'm seeing.'

'I knew it! There's something about how you are right now. You've lost weight. Your skin is clear. I knew it!'

'Mum, seriously?' My neck is hot and I'm already half furious. 'Can you just let me tell you?'

'Is he Jewish?' Mum continues regardless. 'It doesn't matter if he isn't,' she adds diplomatically, 'we'd just like to know.'

'He's not Jewish. His name is Euan Hegarty, and he's a chef. I've been seeing him for about six weeks, and it might be something serious.'

'Right,' Mum and Dad both say in unison.

'How serious are we talking?' Mum adds.

'Well, I'm telling you guys about him. So pretty serious.'

'Six weeks is nothing,' Dad tuts. 'You can't know if you're serious in six weeks.'

'Didn't Grandma and Grandpa get engaged within about two months?' I point out.

'Well,' Dad grumbles. 'Times were different then.'

'How did you meet?' Mum asks. She's sitting up now, the lines on her forehead prominent, whilst she tries not to let her desire for knowledge get too intense.

'Actually, I interviewed him for my magazine. He's a bit of a big deal in the cookery world. He was on that show on Channel Four, the one with the blindfolds and the knives?'

'I'll have to download it. Joseph, can you download it for me?'

'Do we have to do that now?' Dad sighs.

'If Tamsyn's boyfriend is on TV, we should see it!' She turns back to me. 'We're very happy for you. And when can we meet Euan?'

'Well, I was going to see if he's free to come along to Jacob's bar mitzvah in a couple of weeks.'

The thought comes to me in the moment and is out of my mouth before I have a chance to properly consider the implications. Euan's already told me that if he's not already off, that he can move things around for urgent or important reasons, it's just that nothing urgent or important has come up yet. I know that he has a nice suit, and that he's dying to see what my family is really like, so I guess this would be the perfect occasion. Despite this, an icy chill extends to my fingertips as I watch my parents take the news in.

'You can't just bring someone to a bar mitzvah. He's not invited,' my Dad says.

'Actually, he can have my seat,' Ross interjects. 'I won't be here after all. I thought I could extend my summer holiday, but I really have to get back to the lab. Those test tubes won't stare at themselves!'

'But what about the seating plan? What if you're at different tables?'

'Mum, when have you ever known anyone to not sit Ross and me next to each other at one of these things?'

'You'll have to clear it with the Galinskis. They might not like it.'

'You really like him enough to bring him to a family function?' Dad checks with me.

'Yes,' I reply as earnestly as I can, my fists clenched by my side.

'Then bring him to a family function. If he can survive that, he can survive anything. Now, can we get back to *Law & Order*?'

I look at Mum's face. She's trying to be happy, but she looks rattled, unsure. I feel that stubborn streak, the part of me that's always desperate to prove her wrong and show her how clever I am. But this time, the pride battles with my own unease.

'I'm going to head back home,' I tell my parents.

'You sure?' Ross asks. 'I thought we could hang out more. Maybe order take-out together later?'

'I should go. I'm wiped and work is always busy on a Monday.'

'Well, you can tell your Euan that we're looking forward to meeting him,' Mum says in her posh voice.

'I'll let him know.'

Ross accompanies me to the front door.

'Are you okay Big Sister?'

'I'm fine Little Brother!'

He looks at me, his expression remarkably similar to Mum's earlier. He's always looked more like her. I take after our dad.

'Something weird happened at the pub today Tamsyn,' Ross says more seriously. 'You know you can talk to me about it.'

'Honestly Ross, there's no need to worry. I think I just had a revelation, that's all.'

'About Euan?'

'Yep. You were right. I have been keeping him out, and it's probably time I let him in.'

'Tamsyn,' Ross pauses, looks down at the floor as he searches for the words. 'Just as long as you're doing what makes you happy.'

I feel like I might cry, but I blink back any tears that threaten to make an appearance. I've made a good decision.

I've been brave, and bold, and I'm opening myself up to someone who seems to deeply care for me. Why wouldn't I be happy? I'm getting everything I always wanted.

'Don't worry about me,' I say affectionately. 'I can't wait for you to meet Euan. He's a great, genuine guy. Really down to earth. I think you're going to get along.'

'Well, maybe you two can visit me up in Edinburgh some time?'

'Sure.'

'Love you Big Sister.'

'Love you too Little Brother.'

16

'Are you sure I look okay?' Euan's asking me.

He's wearing the same outfit he wore on our first date, the dark velvet suit over a black shirt. His trousers are fashionably tight and he's also wearing these black suede slip-on shoes without socks, his ankles prominently visible when he sits down.

'What, something isn't right? Just tell me?'

'You really don't have any socks you can wear?'

'I am wearing socks. They're invisible liner socks.'

'But there are going to be a fair number of older gentlemen at this event who won't know that you're wearing invisible liner socks,' I warn him. I imagine my dad, mystified at the unnecessary ankle exposure.

'You really think people are going to be concerned about my socks?' Euan asks.

Yes, I want to tell him. Yes they will be. These are Jewish parents we're talking about. And their friends and family. Everybody is going to be scrutinising everything. Especially if you're the goyishe boyfriend who is turning up with Tamsyn Rutman.

Mandy Galinski was thrilled at the news I'd be bringing Euan along, and pointed out (much to my father's horror) that there wasn't going to be assigned seating at the event anyway, that it was designed to be a much more carefree affair and they weren't too fussed about numbers.

'You should see Jacob's guest list. Fifty of his closest friends one minute, one hundred the next. They'll all be in and out throughout the evening, so I don't want you to worry about bringing one more,' Mandy assured.

'Did you tell her that Euan was replacing Ross? What did she say when you told her that Ross couldn't come?' Mum asked me on our follow-up phone call.

'She didn't say anything about Ross. I'm not sure she minded that he wouldn't be there, though.'

'They'll forget he exists, sure enough. You can't just go missing weddings and bar mitzvahs and expect people to know who you are. He wouldn't get a minyan at his shiva at this rate.'

'Mum!' I hear Ross call in the background. 'Can you not talk about my death please?'

'People know who Ross is,' I intervene. 'And they also know that he's supremely busy doing very important medical research.'

'Tamsyn says you're supremely busy doing medical research apparently,' she calls away from the phone. 'You wouldn't know it with the amount of time he's spending on his tuchus these last couple of weeks!'

'Leave Ross alone. Everyone deserves a holiday,' I laugh. 'Besides, he's been doing a great job helping me on my special project for Uncle Doodle. And he'll be heading back up to Scotland in a couple of days anyway. You'll miss him when he's gone.'

'Well, at least I have one child who is doing me proud,' Mum replies. I know she's saying it in earshot of Ross just to push his buttons, and that I shouldn't take the comment seriously, but it does something else to me too. The thought that I was making my mother happy, even in this very tiny way, didn't feel quite as bad as I was expecting it to feel.

'So tell me more about what these parties are like. Where is it taking place again?' Euan is asking me as he oils his beard.

'It's at a place in the West End called Club Metropole.'

'I've not heard of it.'

'It's in the tabloids a lot. Apparently Rita Ora was seen falling out of there last week.'

'Who's Rita Ora?'

I've noticed recently that Euan rarely gets my references. Being on his schedule means that he doesn't often have time to watch TV or be that involved in pop culture. He listens to podcasts whilst he's running or working out, but they tend to be focused on motivational, life-affirming topics, like the one he listens to by a retired Olympian about how to reach your full potential, and another one on business ethics he insisted would be worthwhile for me to listen to, that actually sent me to sleep within five minutes (I'll be putting it on the next time I have insomnia).

We don't watch the same shows or listen to the same music, and whilst in the beginning Euan used to grin and look like he understood what I was talking about, lately I've been wondering if a lot of that was an act to appease or impress me. We've been together less than two months, and already we're struggling to stay on the same page as each other. Maybe it's my fault. Maybe, once again, it's me not giving him enough time or letting him in enough.

'I've been to a lot of these parties. Normally they're sit-down affairs in hotel ballrooms. Think weddings, except all centred around a thirteen-year-old boy,' I tell Euan as I'm straightening my hair. I'm at his place to get ready so that we can head to the party together. 'Some families are more low key of course. But from what Mum's been telling me, I think this one might be more way out.'

'But essentially, it's like a birthday party?' Euan asks.

'No, a bar mitzvah is not like a birthday party at all.'

'I know there's some religious stuff involved, but when you're looking at it from the outside, it's basically a grand birthday party, you have to admit.'

Some religious stuff? I guess it's my fault for not bringing Euan to shul with me yesterday, but my cousins' shul is one where men and women sit separately, and there was absolutely no way I was leading Euan into that lion's den. Except, I guess it means that he missed a lot of the point of the bar mitzvah.

'Come on, I thought you hated all the traditional stuff anyway?' Euan says, drawing me close to him for a kiss. I look at us both in the mirror together, how perfect we look, and how perfect everyone is going to think we are tonight.

'I do hate it,' I protest, searching for the arguments I've used so many times before and coming up shorter than usual. 'And I'm not convinced that all kids are old enough at that age to really understand the responsibility anyway.'

'Right. So, it's just a party. Doesn't mean I'm not looking forward to it any less. You have no idea how hyped I am to meet your family.'

I want to talk to him more about what I'm starting to recognise, that all the stuff I dislike is not what's actually important. That I don't know enough about the stuff that is. Jacob did something really brave yesterday. He had been working towards that moment for years, researching and studying, and then stood up in synagogue in front of everyone and sung his portion of the Torah with confidence. I may not think that all kids are ready at precisely the age of thirteen to be able to do this, but Jacob definitely proved he was. The party is just the celebration of that. A night of joy and relief after all the hard work. The Galinskis may be known for their grand parties, but really they're just proud parents doing what proud parents do.

'It may look frivolous on the outside, but it is an important moment, you know?' I tell Euan.

'I get it,' he replies with a smile. But I'm not convinced he does. 'What was your brother's bar mitzvah like?' he then asks me.

'I was doing A-levels and then in my first year of university for most of the planning, so I don't really remember much of the lead up to it. But I do remember how stressed Ross was, how much pressure he was under to get everything right. You have no idea how much studying and homework is involved, really. And I remember him standing on the bimah – that's the platform in a synagogue that you stand on to say prayers – and being so nervous that he stuttered, several times. And he's never stuttered before or since, that I know of. He had to sing too, which was frightening.'

'Sing? In front of people? At thirteen?'

'In front of the whole congregation. You have a set bit of text you have to sing out, a whole section of the Torah.'

'And Jacob did all this yesterday?'

'He did, and he was pretty great,' I say, thinking back to yesterday in shul. After he sang his portion in Hebrew he delivered a speech about the main themes from that section, which happened to be about tithes and debts. I would have thought it would be a tough topic for a thirteen-year-old to speak about and reflect on, but Jacob made it relevant by talking about charity, privilege, and doing good deeds in the community. It made me think about what Ari said regarding tikkum olam.

In synagogue, I peered over the balcony looking for him. I didn't realise I was doing it until I caught myself checking each face, each man's relative height to the next, the slight variations in stripes on the tallis and colours of kippah. Apparently one of the reasons that men and women are kept separate in old-school synagogues is to stop the men and women distracting each other – I never really understood it until that moment. Then I realised that we'd be less distracted if we were actually sitting together and getting on with whatever we were meant to be doing. If anything, the separation and the distance exacerbates sexual tension, rather than relieves it, surely?

But there was no Ari. Not unless he'd found a place to pray that was out of my eye-line, maybe under the point where the women's balcony overhung. Maybe he wasn't invited. I tried to work out the genetic calculations, but he isn't really attached to this side of the family, except via his cousin's marriage to Abigail. As far as I know.

I shouldn't have been thinking about Ari. There was nothing to think about. And I definitely shouldn't still be dwelling on my guilt for thinking about him as I'm using Euan's mirror to apply a final coat of mascara and lipstick.

'You know that Uncle Doodle didn't get his bar mitzvah until his thirties?' I tell him in an attempt to change the subject in my head.

'Doesn't it have to be when you're thirteen?'

'That's the tradition, but it doesn't have to be at that age. Uncle Doodle's was postponed because of the war. I was wandering around the part of London he grew up in a few weeks ago, and I guess it didn't really click until now just how traumatic it must have been back then.' Not thinking about Ari. Definitely not thinking about Ari. 'His parents would have been so hopeful, so looking forward to it. But they had to wait until the war was over, after they moved home to escape the bomb damage, and then they wanted to wait until they really felt like they could celebrate before going through with the ceremony and throwing a party. It's funny, now that I think about it, that what Jacob did yesterday and what my brother did years ago is the same thing people have been doing for centuries. For thousands of years. I guess I never thought of that connection.'

'That's really amazing. Is that when you took the photos for his present?'

I briefly told Euan about Uncle Doodle's gift when he discovered me pulling my hair out over a website that arranges your photos into keepsake books, like an album but with all the snaps professionally printed out. Getting the layouts right, along with the notes and captions, was proving so stressful I nearly ended up chucking my laptop across the room. You'd think a few years of doing that kind of thing professionally would give me an edge, but the website I was using was crude and flimsy. And then, after finally getting everything sorted how I wanted it, they told me the finished product would take a month to deliver.

'Huh?'

'When you were wandering around that part of London. Is that when you took the photos? I could have come with you, you know. For company.'

'Oh, it was fine. I didn't need you there.'

Then we're standing by his front door, waiting for the notification from the Uber driver to arrive. I smooth down the velvet of his jacket, pick off a tiny piece of lint from his shoulder.

'You really think your parents are going to be okay with me?' Euan asks.

'They've already been super cool,' I say. 'I think my mum is your new biggest fan.'

'It means a lot to me that we get on. I don't want to let you down.'

'Well, the first thing you can do is make sure you never refer to tonight as a birthday party.' It was meant to sound affectionate and teasing, but as soon as I say it, I realise that I came off as prickly. Euan is nervous, more nervous than I've seen him possibly ever, and I know that the way I just said that really didn't help.

'I know it's not just a birthday party,' he concedes, but with tension in his tone. 'Let's just make sure that we both enjoy the evening, okay?'

'Why wouldn't we enjoy it?'

I hate myself sometimes, I really do. I can hear myself picking a fight, but it's like the sensible part of my brain is on holiday. The problem is that I don't want to be coddling and reassuring Euan all evening. I need him to be the strong, grizzly-bear human he looks like he is, and take everything in his stride. Sensitive, nervous Euan is not someone I want to be dealing with on top of everything else.

'Sorry,' I say with a deep breath, placing both hands on his chest, wide in front of me. 'I'm scared too, okay?'

'You look beautiful,' Euan says, the tension easing as he leans down to kiss me on the forehead (he knows that we can't kiss properly with the freshly applied lipstick I'm wearing). His hands trail down the back of my dress (tight, low-cut and black but not too sexy as to scandalise my parents) and rest on my hips.

'Maybe we can just stay here instead?' I suggest, provocatively raising an eyebrow.

'Tonight is for your family. Let's get this right, okay? No messing around.'

He lets go too promptly, and I feel cold without him close to me.

I want to talk more in the taxi ride to the club, but at the same time I don't. I'm looking out of my window, and he's looking out of his, and I'm scared that anything I say will come out wrong or hurt his pride somehow. I've given him everything he needs to know about my parents: what they like to talk about and what they don't, and spent most of the last week reassuring him that he's going to be adored no matter what he does. He's a cook! At a prestigious hotel! And he has a nice place to live! Okay, he's not Jewish, but we'll deal with that whenever we have to.

Me, on the other hand, these are the people I know. A lot of them are people I can't stand, but a lot are equally people I absolutely adore, and bringing Euan into that circle is a huge thing for me. I know I've told him that he's the first boy I've brought home to meet my parents since my first-ever boyfriend, but I wonder if Euan actually gets it. If he understands what I'm doing for him.

Club Metropole sits in a street just off the Tottenham Court Road end of Oxford Street. The cab drops us outside the building, which looks like a newly built office block, all glass at street level, and we walk around the corner to get to the club entrance. I thought from the address that the place was going to be below ground, but in fact the entrance leads us into a glamorous lobby, all sumptuous red velvet drapes and soft lighting in golden sconces.

'Ah! Step this way! Step this way!' a man in a red-tailed coat and top hat says when I display the invitation to him.

'Is this normal?' Euan asks me.

'I think normal went out the door a while ago,' I reply.

I knew that Mandy Galinski wasn't going to throw a traditional bar mitzvah party for my cousin Jacob, but this really seems like something else. The exuberant man in the top hat gestures to a lift that's waiting for us, inside which is a showgirl in full feather regalia acting as the operator. I have never had such an uncomfortable experience in a lift, and I say that as someone who's been in a rickety lift with Gareth Parkinson after he's had a liquid lunch.

Up close, the showgirl's stage make-up is obnoxiously thick, her smile heightened, stretched wide and forced.

'Come here often?' I ask her with a knowing smile, hoping to make a joke of the awkwardness.

'Shh,' Euan nudges me unexpectedly, before mumbling, 'let her do her job.'

I turn my head sharply to look at Euan. He's never told me what to say or do before, and he knows damn well that I can be a little snarky sometimes. It's part of my charm, one of the things he likes about me, and even if it wasn't, what I said wasn't that bad. I wanted to show her that we were on her level, bringing some levity to a job that surely must be weird for her. It's definitely weird for me anyway.

I'm almost certain that Euan's comment did not go unheard, and when I turn back to the showgirl, she's looking away, her stage-smile still fixed, but her body language telling both of us that she really would rather not get involved.

I don't get the chance to bring it up with Euan because as soon as the lift doors open we're faced with a short corridor, the walls and floor all a glittering onyx-black, and then at the end another showgirl is waiting to open the doors to Club Metropole.

Inside is wonderful. A large open space, the entire back wall of which is just one long glass window with views over London. It's not totally dark yet, so we can see a deep navy sky fading into lilac and hitting a streak of light blue on the horizon. One side of the room is put aside for a grand buffet, and then on the other a range of beds for lounging. Actual beds, each one strewn with lush throws and metallic cushions. The light in the room is low, spotlights picking out areas of golds and warm pinks, the decor sitting somewhere between Moulin Rouge and old Hollywood, with posters on the walls for old silent films, and showgirls prancing around with headpieces and oversized feather boas presenting trays of nibbles. There are already a hundred or so people enjoying the party, some clambering over the food, some mingling around the drinks tables, and some, scandalously, already reclining on the beds whilst they eat and drink.

'This is something,' Euan says, his eyes wide and his mouth wider, before he repeats: 'Is this normal?'

'Absolutely not,' I reply. 'I did warn you that the Galinskis like to party.'

There's a receiving line of black-suited waiters holding out trays with cocktails, and I pick a pink one in a martini glass, festooned with a fluff of cotton candy. Euan goes for something that resembles a mojito, but it's hard to be sure. He winces when he takes a sip in any case.

At the end of the receiving line await my relatives, the parents of the bar mitzvah boy. Whilst John Galinski, Aunt Davina's brother-in-law, is dressed conservatively in a dark suit (he's patting his already sweating bald head with a matching black handkerchief), his wife Mandy is dressed to match the spectacle around her in a grand mermaid-tailed ballgown, lush and black and embroidered all over with fine gold flowers. The waist is as small as can be (I know my mum must be jealous) and her neckline boldly low. She looks like she's ready to attend the Oscars, not her son's bar mitzvah.

'Mandy, you look incredible!' I tell her. She really does – it would not surprise me if she's been dieting and training for a year just so that she's able to wear this dress for the one night. 'And this place? Unbelievable!'

'Isn't it something?' she says, confident and pleased.

'Mazeltov, Mr and Mrs Galinski,' Euan says, standing beside me. I can see my relative's eyes widen as she takes Euan's full form in. He does look particularly handsome right now.

'This is my boyfriend, Euan Hegarty,' I announce.

'Oh Euan! We're so pleased you could make it!' Mandy says. 'Please enjoy yourself, help yourself to food – don't blame me if it's bad, blame the caterers!'

Euan's eyes sparkle and he gives a genuinely happy smile. 'Don't worry, I'm off duty tonight,' he says kindly.

'Now we've got the main room in here, but don't forget to check out the other rooms, too. We've got all sorts going on here tonight. And there's a special musical performance happening at 11pm, so make sure you're around.'

'Thank you, truly, this all looks amazing,' I say. 'And mazeltov. You must be really proud of Jacob. He did great in shul yesterday.'

'He did, didn't he?'

'Are my parents here yet?' I ask them just before we move on so that they can greet the next lot of attendees who have arrived via showgirl-operated lift.

'I think they've commandeered a bed at the back,' John says with a smile.

We say our goodbyes for now, and I hold Euan's hand as I guide him to the side of the club with the large beds, searching through the low lighting and rotating, disco-like spotlights that swirl around us to try and find my parents.

'Ready?' I ask him.

I feel the tension from earlier dissipate. We were both nervous and feeling stressed, I tell myself. We weren't in sync because we're not used to being with each other when we're both nervous and stressed. It's something we'll have to learn to work on, and it will be part of our journey together. Euan looks down at me and smiles, and then leans down for a gentle, chaste kiss (there is family about, after all). He tastes of the mint from his mojito, and I wonder if I taste of cotton candy in return.

When I finally spot my parents, I want to laugh. They're propped up on their bed as if they were an old married couple in a retro sitcom, Mum on the side she would usually sleep on and Dad on his. They look formal and staged, except for the plate of food that's on my Dad's lap. I'm guessing they saw when we arrived, watched our greeting with Mandy and John, and got themselves ready. They've been waiting to receive us, on their best behaviour but looking weirdly awkward too, my mum especially, her hands arranged neatly in her lap, her posture too prim and certain.

'Hi Mum and Dad,' I say. I'm not sure how these introductions are meant to go, so steeled by my bright pink drink, I decide to just go for it. 'This is Euan!'

Euan, admirably, steps forward and kneels like a prince so that he can face my parents at their level. I let myself admire the tightness of his trousers in that posture for a brief moment before I decide to sit down too, positioning myself towards the end of the bed, leaving Euan more room to talk. The music is loud in here, a bass line thumping from the other side of the club, but not so loud that I can't hear them talk.

'It's really so great to meet you,' Euan says, the broadness of his Geordie accent more pronounced as he speaks up. 'I've heard lots about you.'

'We've heard a lot about you too,' Dad returns, his tone reserved and serious.

'Tamsyn said you were good looking, but I really had no idea!' Mum suddenly says, making me wonder if she's had more than the drink she's currently holding. 'I've seen you on TV, but it doesn't prepare you! Look at your eyes!'

'Mum,' I shush, smiling, but Euan seems to be taking it in his stride.

'You're very kind Mrs Rutman.'

'Oh, call me Liddy!'

'You can still call me Mr Rutman,' my dad says, I hope only half seriously.

'You know, I saw that episode with the soufflé,' Mum says.

'Mum,' I warn. I've never actually spoken to Euan about his time on the TV show, and don't know how sensitive he is about it.

'I just want to tell Euan that he was robbed! And he shouldn't have been sent home for it!'

'Well, it was a pretty gnarly soufflé,' Euan admits with a laugh.

'But that other chef, the one with the hair, he did so much worse!'

'Well, I'm not fussed about it. Wasn't easy to deal with at the time but look where I am now! I've got a great job that I love, and I've got Tamsyn by my side too.'

It sounds like he's reading from the Perfect Boyfriend script, and I appreciate it. I reach out across the bed to hold his hand and give it a squeeze. My heart flutters when he squeezes it back. We both know that this is going well.

'Shall we come and talk to you later? I want to get some food!' I say to my parents.

'Oh, you go. I'll stay here and chat,' Euan says. I'm encouraged by how relaxed his smile is, and how happy my parents seem to be too. This is right. This is perfect. I can't remember why I was so concerned.

'Want me to get you anything?'

'It's okay. I'm not hungry just yet. You go and explore and let me know what's on offer.'

'Okay,' I say, and I lean down for another of those chaste kisses before I stand up. It's like I'm proving a point to my parents, showing them how mature our relationship is. We kiss like grown-ups who are comfortable with each other! But that doesn't mean I also don't steal the opportunity to whisper to Euan: 'They like you!'

We're still holding hands as I back away, as if reluctant to be parted, and I'm all at once filled with a rush of affection and longing, because he's looking at me with such devotion, and such care. He loves me, I realise. He really, absolutely loves me. My heart thumps with the knowledge, in time to the beat of the music surrounding me.

I'm still thinking of him when I reach the buffet tables. I'm thinking of what a life with Euan will look like, whether our children will come out blonde or brunette, whether I could get used to living in the countryside one day (a dream I know he has). Suddenly I'm not hungry anymore.

My heart still thumping, my thoughts still with Euan who is currently schmoozing my possibly slightly drunk parents, I decide to head over to the bar, hoping to get another of those pink candy-floss drinks.

'Oh, hey!' sounds a scarily familiar voice.

I turn to my left, and who is standing at the bar waiting for his order, but Ari.

17

'Ari? What are you doing here?'

I know it's a rude question and not quite the normal thing to ask when you bump into someone at a party who could always very reasonably be at that party, but I'm shocked to see him. I wasn't expecting it, and I wasn't prepared.

'Getting a drink?' Ari replies with a question, and then smiles. 'What are you doing here?'

'I just didn't think you knew this part of my family all that well,' I say. 'I mean, I know you know the Galinskis via Dominic and Abigail, but I didn't think you knew Abigail's aunt and uncle?'

'Well, I haven't had much of a chance to get to know young Jacob, but my mum and Mandy go way back. I think they still do hot yoga together, along with Deborah Dreyer. You know the Dreyers, right?' I nod that I do.

'It's good to see you,' I lie. It's weird seeing him. Especially when he's all dressed up and formal. He looks good dressed up and formal. 'Were you at shul yesterday?'

'Oh no, I couldn't make it. I had some case files to finish up. I wasn't just trying to get out of shul, if that's what you're implying.'

'No! I wasn't implying anything! I just thought that I would have noticed you if you were there, and then I would have known to look out for you now.'

I sound stupid. I know I'm sounding stupid, but I'm rattled. I'm really God-damn rattled. My hot boyfriend is on the other side of the room making good with my parents, and here I am getting flustered over a guy who may not even like me very much. At least certainly not in the way I want him to like me. And I shouldn't even be wanting him to like me! I had started to think that this crush wasn't real. Now I very much want it to go away.

And then, as if my blood pressure weren't already high enough, the most gorgeous woman I have ever seen up close comes and stands next to Ari, wrapping herself around him in a manner I can only describe as feline. She's wearing a red strappy dress, tight and frankly obscene in the cleavage department. I have nothing but admiration for how her boobs appear to hold themselves up as that kind of dress leaves no room for any form of support structure or undergarments, but then my eyes travel up to her face. Maybe it's her undertones, or maybe it's the lighting, but her skin looks like it's made from gold. She has cheekbones set to attack mode, and an eyeliner wing drawn with an inhuman, mathematical precision. Finally, there's the sweep of honey-gold hair, lush and loose and sweeping in a way that even when she runs her hands through it to push it back, still falls around her face and shoulders like art.

Dalya. Glorious and other-planet beautiful Dalya. Damn. No wonder Ari doesn't fancy me. I feel like the schlub of the century next to her.

'Who's your friend?' Dalya asks, her Israeli accent pronounced.

'This is Tamsyn,' Ari tells her, taking one of her hands in his. 'She's Abigail's cousin.'

'Dalya,' she says by way of introduction, extending her free hand towards me.

'Oh, the Rutmans like to hug!' I say, reaching forward and forcing her to break away from Ari in order to hug me. Wow, she even smells divine. 'And we're all mishpocha here!'

'Ari mentioned you,' Dalya says once we break away. 'Are you the one who works at the magazine?'

'I'm the managing editor,' I say proudly, whilst inside I'm thinking, *Ari's mentioned me? What's he said?*

'I have experience of magazine work – it's an exciting industry.'

'Oh, really?'

'Yes. Well, I say experience. I don't really know what it's like to work at one. But I've appeared on the cover of several in Israel.'

'You don't say.'

Seriously? She's gloating about the magazine covers she's been on? I'm not surprised she's been on them, by any means, but a little surprised that she's rubbing them in my face after just meeting me.

'What are you up to now, in the UK?' I ask her.

'Right now, I'm taking a breather from all that commotion. It's wonderful to just get the time to spend with my Ari. He works so hard! But he's making such a beautiful life for the both of us.'

Ari is oddly quiet, and staring at the floor, but his arm is around Dalya's waist, and she is glowing with contentedness. I hate her. I hate her so, so much.

'How are you doing Tamsyn?' Ari asks me after taking a drink, but before I can reply, I feel an arm wrap around my own waist, and suddenly Euan is there. My tall, gorgeous Euan. His tattoos may be hidden under his blazer, but I'm pretty sure that both Ari and Dalya sense that he has them.

'I was wondering where you'd got to,' Euan says, leaning down to kiss me.

'Just bumped into some friends,' I say. 'Euan, this is Ari, he's a cousin of the person my cousin has just married, practically family! And this is his girlfriend Dalya. Ari, Dalya, this is my boyfriend Euan Hegarty.'

I use his full name, just in case there's a chance Dalya has heard of him.

'Really nice to meet you Euan,' Ari says, seeming suddenly bolder. He's standing up straight, and his voice is booming in a way it wasn't just before.

They shake hands. Am I imagining the tension there?

'Euan Hegarty. That's a good name. It sounds strong.' Dalya says.

'Thank you,' Euan replies, beaming. 'It's Celtic, my family are from the north of England.'

'I've not been to the north. Only seen London, but I hear that other parts of the UK are quite magical. Is this your first bar mitzvah?'

'Actually, it is! But I hear I missed the most important bit yesterday.'

'Don't worry, I missed it too,' Ari says.

'Speaking of which, we should probably find the bar mitzvah boy and say mazeltov,' I say, starting to guide Euan away. 'It was lovely to see you both, and lovely to meet you Dalya.'

'Lehitra'ot,' Dalya replies. 'We'll chat soon, I'm sure!'

'Who were they?' Euan asks as we walk away.

'Just people,' I reply. 'You want to check out the food? Also, you must tell me absolutely everything you spoke about with my parents. To the word!'

We drift around the party, grabbing small plates of food here and there, bumping into family members and introducing them to Euan (Abigail and Dominic are particularly stunned to meet him, which is only fair, considering I hadn't mentioned him to them before). We fall into a routine with it, and after a while his answers start to annoy me. He's so perpetually charming, and so keen to be involved and ask questions. It feels like we're on a parade together. A never-ending parade of flattery and small talk.

Ari keeps coming into my line of sight. I'd like to think it's by design, but who am I kidding, we're at a crowded party and as long as we're in the same room, there are bound to be moments where we're able to catch glimpses of each other. I do actually catch him looking at me at one point. A gentle, sad look. When he notices me noticing, he turns away quickly, leaving me to wonder if it happened at all. Dalya attracts a crowd wherever she goes, especially when she agrees to pose for photos with Jacob and his friends. Soon there's a whole line of thirteen-year-old boys waiting for selfies, and I notice Ari standing to the side, beer in hand, watching with fading amusement.

Euan and I discover more party rooms down a corridor away from the main club space, including a games room complete with PlayStation console rigged up to a large projector screen and a karaoke room populated by a gaggle of young girls (all the spawn of my various cousins), who seem to be competing to see who can sing 'Let It Go' the best. One girl is actually dressed up as Elsa for some reason, but she's only five years old and seems furious that the other girls aren't giving her a turn on the microphone. There's a photo room too, manned by a guy guarding a props chest, ready to take pictures against a big green screen.

'Want to have a go?' Euan asks me.

'Maybe later?' I suggest. I don't really feel like I'm in the mood to start smiling for pictures. Not so soon after watching Dalya posing with all her adoring teenage fans.

Finally, we come to the chill-out room, where the pumping music feels muted, scented candles are burning on high shelves, and upright lounge chairs are clustered around tables of nibbles and drinks. This is where the older generation seem to have made their home.

'Uncle Doodle!' I cry, leaving Euan's side to rush up to the elderly man. 'I didn't know you were here. I would have thought this might be too much for you?'

'He shouldn't be here.' Terry makes a face at me as she steps over from the other side of the room. 'He should be resting and taking things slow. Doctor's orders.'

'Pah,' Uncle Doodle scoffs.

'But he insisted. Wouldn't stop giving me grief.'

'What do the doctors know? Celebrations are important,' he says to his daughter, before turning to me again. 'I never miss a party. And shall I tell you why?'

'Why Uncle Doodle?'

'Because after the rain, there is always a rainbow. After all the suffering, all the grief, as Jews it's our duty to celebrate. We find joy where we can, and we live.'

'L'chaim!' someone across the room toasts in agreement.

He may be dressed up and on fine form, but Uncle Doodle has lost so much weight, even since the last time I saw him. We've been speaking lots on the phone, but I had no idea just how different he would look. His jacket almost seems comical, the shoulders dramatically oversized, the sleeves hiding half his hands. The way he's hunched in the chair, it's like he's nothing but a skeleton shrouded in clothes. It breaks my heart to see him this way.

'Uncle Doodle, would you like to meet my boyfriend?' I ask.

'Is this the special one? The one that makes you happy?' he asks me back sincerely.

'Euan is very special, yes.' I beckon Euan over, and he crouches down between us so that Uncle Doodle can see him clearly.

'You have the heart of a very special lady,' Uncle Doodle says solemnly after all the introductions are made. 'This one is something else, I'm telling you. And you must be very special to have her heart too.'

'Tamsyn means a lot to me,' Euan says. Then he pauses, as if he's catching his breath. I'm about to ask if he's okay, before he continues on: 'In fact, if I may be so bold sir, I must say I've fallen in love with her.'

I'm floored. He's telling my great-uncle that he loves me before discussing it with me first. Has he told my parents? We've been dating two months. It's far too soon for this. Far, far too soon. I force a smile, and grip tight on Uncle Doodle's hand.

'Well, love is it?' the elderly man replies, his tone affectionately cynical. 'Love is a fine thing, indeed. I wish you well. I wish the both of you very well.'

'I'll come back and see you later, okay Uncle Doodle?' I tell him. 'Are you going to stay in this room for the evening?'

'The music is so loud out there,' Uncle Doodle complains. 'But come back and see me. We'll still have our dance, yes?'

'Of course we'll dance,' I say. 'Pasodoble this time? Are you up for it?'

'Am I up for it she says? We'll paso until the sun comes up!'

'I'll come back for you soon.'

'I know you will meydeleh.'

I kiss Uncle Doodle on the forehead, and then say a quick hello to a few other relatives in the room before heading back out to the noise and the lights with Euan.

'You said you loved me?' I check.

'I did.' Euan looks so proud of himself.

'Did you say that to my parents?'

'Should it be a big deal? You must know how I feel about you.'

'We talked about going slow Euan. This isn't going slow.'

'It's how I feel.'

We move out the way as one of Jacob's friends suddenly charges past us with the microphone from the karaoke room, followed by all the young girls who were singing the *Frozen* soundtrack moments before. Now they're just screaming and paying no attention to any grown-ups they might be annoying.

'I need some air,' I tell Euan.

'There's a door that leads to a rooftop terrace,' he replies, his tone cold and unsure. 'I'll come with you. We'll talk.'

'No, I need some space for a moment. I'm sorry. This evening has been overwhelming. Just give me a moment. Go and enjoy the food.'

I leave Euan behind as I head back into the main club room on my search for the door to the terrace. There's a corridor that runs behind where all the lounging beds are, and I figure there must be a way out there. Of course, I pass my parents as I go. Both are now reclining on their beds as if they were Roman emperors, laughing with some friends. I hurry by, hoping that they don't see me. I don't want to hear what they say about Euan. I don't want to know just how perfectly he's been charming them.

The door to the terrace is propped open to allow for the cool August night air to flow through to the main room. I step outside and behold the twinkling lights of London at night. It's like a magical fairy scene. This high up, the noise of the traffic below is barely noticeable, and whilst there's still the steady thud of music playing from the club, it's softened by the night and feels like a hazy dream left behind. Inside is madness, and out here feels solid and real. Like breaking the surface after almost drowning.

Standing by the balcony, looking down across Oxford Street and beyond, is Ari. I can't turn back now. He's seen me. He toasts me with his champagne flute, almost as if he's been expecting me.

'Crazy in there, right?' I say, feeling nervous as I head over to stand next to him. 'No Dalya?'

'Dalya is very popular this evening,' Ari sighs with a glib smile.

'You never mentioned her,' I say. I keep my tone quiet, cautious. I don't want him to think I'm annoyed with him. I don't want him to think I care as much as I do.

'I didn't think there was anything to mention,' he says. I think that's the end of it, and don't push any further. But as we look out across the sparkling city, he sighs again and continues: 'I don't always know where I am with Dalya, but right now it's good. We've spent a lot of time apart, and that helps I think.'

'Absence makes the heart grow fonder?'

'Sometimes, yes. But other times, I think that we're a bit like celestial bodies orbiting each other. Sometimes we're closer, sometimes we're further apart.'

'If it works for you, then it's good you have that rhythm.'

'It doesn't.'

I can hear my own heartbeat, pulsing with the steady drum from the club inside. What am I meant to say to that? How do I say how I feel without ruining absolutely everything?

'Euan is telling everyone he loves me,' I manage to reveal.

'That's nice,' Ari replies. There's a coldness there, a bitterness. I'm not imagining it; I know I'm not.

'I don't love him. I've been trying to. I've been trying to convince myself that he's perfect because I know how much he cares for me, and because I thought he was everything I always wanted.'

Ari turns away from the view to look at me seriously, but he doesn't say anything. He's here though, listening to me, taking all of me in, and that's enough.

'You were right about me. Ages ago when you called me out. You said I was cold. And stubborn.'

'Don't make me remember when I said that. It was mean.'

'No, you were right. I was a cow. I was self-absorbed, and I thought I knew better than everyone else. Well, look at me now. Euan is incredible, I really can't fault him, and he adores me too. So, what's wrong with me?'

'There's nothing wrong with you Tamsyn.'

I flush with the warmth of his words. He looks away from me again, and I follow his lead and gaze out across the wide expanse of the city.

'I'm sorry,' I say after a moment of silence.

'What for?' he asks quietly.

'I'm sorry that I was harsh to you when we met. I'm sorry that I didn't see you when I should have done. If I could change that now, I would. I'm sorry for everything.'

We're standing so close to each other, and he's about to say something, he's about to *do* something (I know he is), but we're interrupted by a commotion behind us. Back inside the club, it's loud and bright. We look at each other, both knowing there's more we want to say and reveal, but also knowing that the timing is impossible. He looks sad, and tired. I want to reach out to him, to tell him that I recognise it and I feel the same, but I can't. Euan is just on the other side of the window, along with Ari's girlfriend and the entirety of my family. Now is not the time.

'We'd better see what's going on,' I say, trying to regain some of my party spirit before turning and heading back inside. Ari doesn't follow me.

What's going on is the speeches. A huge projector screen has emerged on the stage in front of the DJ deck, and an insanely well-produced video is playing, showing all of Jacob's closest friends and family delivering well wishes and hopes for the future. Then Jacob's siblings appear on screen to perform a version of the Backstreet Boys' 'I Want It That Way', the lyrics changed to refer directly to Jacob and his quirks. The performance looks as good as a real music video, produced with snazzy camera angles and special effects. This is followed by specially recorded messages from men I soon gather are players for Chelsea Football Club. Half the room cheers with joy and wonder, the other half (the Tottenham and Arsenal supporters) playfully boo and hiss. It's ludicrously over the top but also hugely entertaining (and certainly more interesting than watching family members stand up and deliver more formal speeches).

I spot Euan standing near my parents and go to stand next to them. We look at each other – if he's annoyed with me, I don't sense it in his expression towards me – and then he reaches down to take my hand to hold. I let him, and notice my parents watching us. They look pleased for me.

Mandy Galinski appears on stage in her magnificent dress, the grand mermaid tail swishing about her legs as she moves.

'I just want to thank everyone for coming tonight. John and I couldn't be prouder of our Jakey, and as one final treat to see the evening through, I'd like to welcome to the stage a very special guest. We certainly like the shape of him! Ladies and gentlemen, please welcome Ted Sheeran!'

Excuse me? *Ted* Sheeran?

The man who graces the stage looks almost exactly like Ed Sheeran, but just not quite. Same loose flannel shirt, unkempt ginger hair, and with the familiar stickers arranged just so on his guitar. He's accompanied by a couple of backup dancers, and the vibe is suddenly so hilarious and energetic that it doesn't matter that I barely listen to this kind of music, I'm suddenly knock-off Ed Sheeran's biggest fan.

'He's not real!' I yell out to Mum over the noise. 'He's a lookalike!'

Mum is baffled, but she's smiling and having a bit of a bop, her hips moving from side to side as she enjoys herself. Then Euan takes my hand and spins me around, holding me close to him as we move into the centre of the dance floor. I'll never get over the feel of his arms around me, his heaviness and warmth, the solid hardness of his muscled chest. He swirls me around, and then brings me back towards him with an easy grace. I never even knew that he could dance, and then a thought plummets through me and hits my stomach with the weight of a stone: this is the only time we're going to dance. It's not going to ever happen again.

Ted churns through the big hits, 'Shape of You' followed by 'Sing' followed by 'Thinking Out Loud', Jacob and his siblings even going up on stage to mimic the backup dancers and play air guitar, and the older crowd generally having a good time, moving and swaying to the pop tunes, even if they don't know much about Ed Sheeran or haven't heard the songs.

'I need to dance with Uncle Doodle!' I yell at Euan as she goes into her third song. 'We always have a dance! I promised him!'

He lets me go, and I make my way to the chill-out room, although less of a chill-out room at present. Even with the door closed behind us, Ted's performance is so loud you can hear it clear as anything in here anyway.

'Where's Uncle Doodle?' I ask Terry. She's still in here with a few other of my relatives and older family friends and has in front of her a bowl containing what looks like a waffle drizzled with chocolate syrup and sprinkles.

'Oh Tamsyn, sweetheart, he wasn't feeling very well so Paul took him back home.'

'Really? I promised him a dance.'

'I don't think he would have been up to a dance. You know how fragile he's been lately. But it's nice of you to think of it.'

'I should have said goodbye though,' I say.

'Give him a call in the morning. I know he'll like that.'

'Sure, will do.'

There's a flicker of something like panic stirring with the thought of Uncle Doodle going home and not being well, but I wonder if that's just me reacting to the emotional stress of this evening. I'm sure he's fine, and the overwhelming nature of this party couldn't have been easy for him, despite there being a designated quiet room.

Back in the club space, I've discovered that the contents of the food tables have been replaced by dessert items. This must be where Terry found her waffle. But I don't have the heart or stomach for any of it. That weighty stone of dread and panic is still sitting there, and however good everything looks, I just don't feel like I deserve the luxury right now.

'Everything okay?' Euan asks when I get back to him.

'I think I want to go home,' I say.

'I'll get an Uber for the both of us?'

'Actually, I was thinking about heading back to my own place tonight.'

'Are you sure?'

'I am.'

'Let me call you an Uber anyway, so that I know you'll get home safely.'

I appreciate the concern and the care he has for me and don't try to stop him. I do the rounds, saying goodbye to friends and family, and give my mum a long hug when I reach her.

'Euan is amazing,' she tells me, clearly tipsy and kvelling with pride.

'I know,' I reply.

'And I don't want you to worry about the Jewish thing. We know he's wonderful.'

'I'll ring you during the week,' I say before leaving her.

Euan and I both head downstairs. He's going to see me off in my taxi before he takes his own one home.

'Are you sure everything is okay?' he asks again once we're outside on the pavement.

'No,' I admit.

'I'm sorry if I overstepped before. We should talk about it.'

'Not now. Tomorrow though. If that's all right?'

'You know it is.'

'I don't want you to think that I'm upset at the thought of you falling in love with me.'

'But you're not falling in love with me back, are you?'

I feel the tears come when he says it out loud.

'We'll talk properly about this tomorrow. When we haven't been drinking. I'm sorry.'

'I'm sorry too.'

I cry in the Uber home. Tiny, quiet sobs that I contain as best I can so that the driver doesn't get too worried or nosy. But I'm not thinking about Euan. I'm thinking about Ari. About sad Ari standing out on the terrace, about the connectedness there, about the longing that I know now isn't just a stupid crush to distract me from Euan. He wanted to kiss me, but he was hurting too, for his own private reasons. I wonder how things might be different if only I had allowed myself to notice him back at Dominic and Abigail's wedding, and then a few weeks later at their dinner party. He was right there all along.

18

As if I wasn't already feeling rotten and full of angst, Gareth calls me into an important meeting first thing on Monday morning.

'It's about Cooper Radcliffe,' he says. I can tell from the tone that this isn't going to be good news. He's been distant the last few weeks, barely coming in and disinterested in all our important meetings. On calls he's been pacing his office, face puce and neck muscles stretched, plus I overheard Kerry-Ann talking about spotting an empty bottle of whisky in his bin. We all know that something has gone very wrong with Cooper Radcliffe, or that he's just taking his time and playing hard ball in whatever contract negotiations are going on behind the scenes. Whatever it is, Gareth has been more stressed about it than any of us have ever seen him. If we manage to see him at all.

'I thought it had gone a bit too quiet on that front,' I admit.

'He's decided that the world of hotels isn't quite for him,' Gareth says with heavy-hearted finality. He's got white bits accumulating in the corners of his mouth.

I'm not surprised. I don't think someone like Cooper, if he was ambitious at all, would be eyeing up a trade magazine as his next endeavour. Unless he was planning for the magazine to take a big shift, like a pivot to online and social. Doing something like that could be the making of a career. Except, considering his resistance to all my pushing, if this was on the cards, I don't think Gareth would be seriously considering giving him the job in the first place. Gareth wants his legacy to continue after he's gone. A traditional, conservative publication doing what a traditional, conservative publication has always done. But look where that's getting us. Less and less budget for staff. More and more pages dedicated to cheaper and cheaper advertisements. So, either Cooper Radcliffe had exciting plans that scared Gareth off, or he just wasn't being offered enough money. The fact that I know there's not that much money to offer, makes me suspect the latter rather than the former.

'So, of course, this leaves me in quite the pickle,' Gareth continues. 'Because I was really starting to get excited about my retirement, of course.'

'Of course,' I say.

'I think we might have to expand the candidate pool beyond those that I'm generally typically aware of.'

'I think that's a pretty good idea.'

'Fresh blood, new ideas. Something a bit different to really invigorate things. Don't think I'm not unaware of the landscape for our industry. But that's not to say there isn't still a market for what we do.'

'Absolutely.'

'So your task over the coming weeks, if it's all right, is to put those feelers out. Get in touch with head hunters, attend parties, network, whatever it is that people do nowadays, and find us an editor-in-chief.'

'That's a big responsibility.'

'Well, whoever he is, you'd be working with him the closest. This is a good idea, no?'

'It is. Definitely.'

'Thank you, Tamsyn. That's all for now.'

I'm about to leave his musty, yellow-ceilinged office when it occurs to me that now is the time to stand up for myself, and to ask serious questions. This is the job I'm desperate for after all, and he's leaving it in my hands to cover. Screw hoping and waiting for him to see me.

'I was wondering Gareth,' I say, strategising as I go. 'What are your feelings regarding a possible internal hire?'

'Internal? As in someone at *Hotelier Monthly*, or someone at another publication in this building?'

'I was thinking about someone who is in the room with you right now.'

He laughs. Gareth Parkinson actually laughs. A bold, animal-like guffaw that feels like it sends tremor waves through the room and beyond. I'm startled by the intensity of it.

'You? You mean you?' he bellows.

'Is that so crazy?' I ask. 'I'm already the managing editor. I know how this place runs. I'm one of the longest-serving staff members. And I have ideas too, about taking this magazine digital, about expanding out from our usual remit and embracing modern ideas.'

'Oh Tamsyn,' Gareth says with a sigh, 'I do apologise for my outburst, but you really took me by surprise. I thought there was every chance that you were joking.'

'I'm not joking.'

'Dear girl,' I prickle when he says that. Like hearing nails scrape a blackboard. 'Dear girl, you're a valued colleague and this place wouldn't survive without you, for sure. But you're not really of the background I'd envisioned for the role.'

'Background?'

'You know what I mean, don't make me say it.'

'I just want to make sure that I understand your thinking.'

'You're a young woman. You've barely travelled. You haven't seen the world. We need someone dynamic, forward thinking, who understands what he's talking about.'

I don't miss the use of pronoun at the end, but I don't bring it up either. I already know I've lost this battle, and that

Gareth is a sexist buffoon. If I start rallying against him now, I'm sure he'll just call me hysterical. I also hear the insinuation regarding being *barely travelled.* Not only am I a woman, but I'm not rich either. He has an image of the kind of person he wants in charge of the magazine, and I'm the complete opposite of it.

'Is this about money? Are you after a pay rise?'

'What? No. This is about the job. Why would you even think that?'

'Well,' he starts, but looks like he's not sure if he should continue. I don't interrupt him. I give him the space to finish. 'I know what you're like.'

'What *I'm* like?' I feel the horror of what he's insinuating before he finishes.

'Well, maybe not you, especially. But, you know.'

'No Gareth, I don't know. Why don't you tell me?'

'Well, now you're trying to make it a thing, when you know that it's not my intention. If anything, I'm being *sensitive* to your background.'

'And what background is that Gareth?'

'Now you're getting hysterical. Haven't you got work to do? I know I certainly have.'

I stare at him, open-mouthed with shock and anger.

'This was a lovely chat Tamsyn, please do let me know how you get on with your search, and when we're ready to start interviewing.'

He says this as though the last part of our conversation never happened. I leave his office feeling winded. Like he's physically punched me in the gut and I'm left struggling to stand from it.

When I go back to my office, Kerry-Ann comes to see if I'm all right (she must have heard the raised voices from Gareth's office), and I tell her I'm just a little hungover from the night before. I've already shown her the photos and videos on my phone from the bar mitzvah, so my current demeanour isn't entirely inappropriate. She eventually leaves me alone, but she knows something isn't right.

What am I still doing here? Why didn't I hand in my notice ages ago when it became clear that Gareth was never going to promote me? I knew the old codger was sexist, but that was the first sign I'd ever had of any hint of antisemitism. Or was it always there, bubbling under the surface, and I'd just been oblivious to it? I didn't realise that Gareth even knew I was Jewish. Worse than that, a woman and Jewish. He's never going to promote me. He's never going to give up his job if he suspects that I'll end up in charge.

I bring up Carmella's resignation letter on my computer, the one I wrote for her ages ago. I change the date and replace her name with my own. I hover the mouse over the print button, and bite the inside of my cheek as I seriously consider pressing it, but ultimately I decide not to take any action right at that moment. I'm upset and angry, and if I am going to resign, I want to do it with a clear head.

I do, however, send a friendly email to Florence Biddulphe, asking if she'd like to meet for a chat about future projects.

Mum calls me at lunchtime, but I ignore it. I text her to say that I'm fine, just a little tired. She texts back, repeating what she said the previous night about being proud of me and really liking Euan.

Would he like to come to a Friday night some time? Mum asks.

I should be grateful at how embracing my parents are being. I thought they would be more sceptical, maybe uninterested, or at worse dismissive of him. But instead they're rolling the red carpet out, which only makes what I'm about to do so much worse. I think about confiding in her, about telling her that I got it wrong, but I start imagining the inevitable 'I told you so' moment and reply: *I'll ask him* instead, before switching my phone on silent and stuffing it into my handbag.

I head to the Clarence the moment I can reasonably escape the office, my heart hammering the whole walk over. He must know that this is coming. He hasn't messaged me all day (although to be honest, I haven't even taken my phone out to look since after lunch), and I haven't sent anything to him either. But after last night, he must know. Will he make me spell it out for him? I never wanted to break anyone's heart. I never even completely realised that I had a heart in my grasp to break.

Somehow the Clarence seems more imposing now than it did when I was first here back in the middle of June. All that crisp, rose-scented luxury feels oppressive rather than comforting.

I make my way to the bar, and then on through to the entrance to the restaurant. It's busier now, people here for evening meetings or early dinners. I can hear the clatter of cutlery hitting plates, the shining ring of crystal and behind it all, a piano being played softly in a corner.

'Yes?' the maitre'd asks when I approach.

'I'm here to see Euan Hegarty,' I say. The man looks at me sceptically, and I wonder suddenly if Euan has had any fans try and reach him this way. 'I'm his girlfriend, Tamsyn Rutman. He's not expecting me, but it's urgent. Can you get him?'

When the maitre'd leaves to go to the kitchen, I think about running away. Euan might be busy or annoyed to see me. I've never actually seen him in the kitchen; what if he's in a fearsome mood?

So, when he emerges from a side door looking soft and scared, his emotions evident behind the burly facade, I nearly crumble. If he were angry with me, or even just annoyed, I would understand, but here is a man who loves me, and I have no idea why.

'Are you okay?' he asks, rushing forward and embracing me in his arms.

'I'm fine.'

'They said it's urgent. I hadn't heard from you all day and I was worried.'

I feel like I'm going to be sick. Him hating me would be so much easier than this.

'It's not urgent. Well, it is, but not like that. Have you got time to talk?'

'Give me a moment. I just need to finish something in the kitchen and I'll be right out.' He turns to the maitre'd standing close by: 'Can you find us a table? Somewhere discreet?'

I'm led away to a quiet corner of the bar area, to a booth that's well shielded from anyone walking by. Without asking, I'm also brought some water with a slice of lemon. It's a considerate touch that makes me feel even more guilty.

When Euan comes back, he shuffles into the banquette opposite me and takes both my hands in his. I slowly remove them.

'I'm sorry,' I say, my voice a husky whisper. I reach for the glass of water. He waits for me to continue, giving me room to breathe. But I can't. I don't know what I'm meant to say.

'I think I know what's coming,' Euan murmurs.

'Do I have to say it?' I ask.

'You have to explain it,' he replies.

'You're the best person. You really are. You're literally my dream guy.'

'Don't say that. Don't make it worse.' His accent comes out hot and broad.

'I'm just not sure that the guy I had in my dreams was really the right one for me. I think I made that dream for the wrong reasons. So, when I finally found you, when I got you, I realised that I'd made a really big mistake.'

'Tammy,' I recoil when he says my name like that, 'this doesn't make any sense. You know how I feel about you. I know you're attracted to me, that you care about me. Why would you introduce me to your parents if you didn't feel the same way as I did?'

'I thought I would learn to feel that way. And I am attracted to you. I'm insanely attracted to you – please never doubt that. I just don't think you're my person, ultimately.'

'Not your person?'

'I'm sorry. I don't know how else to explain it. Do you really think that I'm the perfect one for you? Really, truly? We don't want the same things. Our ambitions are different.'

'We don't even know each other well enough yet to know that.'

'You don't see that as a problem?'

'Tamsyn,' he pauses after using my full name, and I recognise the seriousness of what he's about to say. 'I thought I had found everything I had ever wanted in you. You may be confused, or uncertain, but I know that you're my dream girl.'

'Why, though?' I didn't mean to interrupt him, but I have to know.

'We've been here before.'

'We have, but I still don't understand it.'

'Well, initially it was your looks. You're sultry. You reminded me of a femme fatale from one of those old black-and-white films. I thought you might be the death of me. But then, when I got to know you, I realised that you were smart too. The fact that you are Jewish, I thought that was wonderful, and it fascinated me.'

'My Jewishness fascinated you?'

'Not like that, it came out wrong. You know what I mean.'

I want to give him the benefit of the doubt, but my conversation with Gareth earlier has left me rattled, and on edge.

'Having different cultures come together, like what I try to do with my food. Don't you think that's a beautiful thing?'

'I don't think that's the reason you should want to be with someone.'

'Come on Tamsyn, you're putting words into my mouth now.'

Except I'm not sure that I am. I don't like feeling different from him. I don't like that he's pointed out that we're different, as if it's somehow a feature and not a bug.

'We barely have anything in common either,' I continue, referring to our hobbies and interests, rather than our backgrounds.

'My parents have nothing in common. You should see them. We can like different things and still love each other.'

I look down at the table, feeling his words fill me up and wondering whether it might still be worth it after all. Whether I'm just being silly and reading far too much into his comments. It's not like it was with Gareth. Euan's not coming from a place of hate, but of love. So why does it feel so similar?

'I was never a femme fatale,' I say.

'I obviously know that,' Euan interrupts. 'It was just a way of describing something.'

'What I mean is that I was never really myself with you. Not in the beginning. Not even now, to be honest. It's not like I was setting out to trick you, but at the same time, I never really imagined that we'd be serious. I thought we were just going to be fun.'

'It was fun. We are still fun.'

'What I'm trying to say is that I thought this was just going to be about living in the moment. About eating good food and having great sex. All the family stuff, all the serious talk.

That's not fun for me.' He doesn't argue. 'We want different things. The things you want, a settled future, routine, houses with gardens to kick a ball about in, they scare me. And I thought that maybe I could want them too, but I don't. I tried to want them, and I worked really hard to show you how much I was trying. But it shouldn't be this hard, don't you think?'

'I thought we had something.'

'We did have something, don't you see?'

'Was it really only ever about sex for you?'

I struggle to find an answer for him, one that's honest but won't hurt his feelings. The soft sounds of piano, silver and crystal muffle through the upholstery of the banquette, and for a moment I almost feel like I'm underwater, with everything around me filtered through a haze of panic and feeling.

'I don't understand this at all,' Euan says with a sigh, leaning back and running a hand over his forehead and through his hair. 'I don't understand you at all.'

'I'll admit that I never made myself particularly easy to understand.'

'I want to hate you, but I can't.'

'You're being too kind to me.'

He's studying me. I'm looking down at my hands around my glass of water, but I know he's watching, and trying to work me out.

'I'm sorry,' I say again.

'I know,' he replies. 'I should have warned you that I have a habit of falling hard and fast.'

I'm going to cry, but I work hard at composing myself. I don't want to be someone who cries in public, especially when the public place is her ex-boyfriend's place of work.

'You're going to find someone who is perfect for you,' I say. 'You're going to ride tandem bicycles through the countryside and she'll bake bread for you on your days off from work.'

'And what will you be doing?'

'Scowling, probably.' That makes him laugh. He sighs again, this one sounding like a real release.

'Ah, the sex was pretty great though, right?'

I feel the corners of my mouth curl up in amusement, and I dare to look at Euan straight in the eyes. He's looking back at me, sad, clearly, but also definitely not angry. He looks lighter. I feel lighter.

'The sex was flipping fantastic,' I admit.

'Couldn't have done it on my own.' The look he gives me then, his eyes filled with a familiar hunger, almost makes me want to reach across the table and kiss him. It's not fair.

I pull myself away from temptation by reaching into my bag to check my phone.

'What's wrong?' Euan asks when he sees my face.

'Three missed calls from Mum. Two from Ross. And the family WhatsApp group is on fire.'

My heart has stopped. The world has stopped. I can't even hear the piano playing any more.

'Tamsyn, darling,' the voicemail from Mum tells me. 'It's Uncle Doodle.'

I can't listen to the rest of the message. I don't want to. I knew this day was coming, we all did, but I'm still not prepared. I only saw him last night. I can't say that he seemed fine, but I didn't think he was that bad. I thought there would still be time.

'Tamsyn?' Euan checks, coming to sit on my side of the table with me, and wrapping an arm around me.

'He's gone,' I say.

'Your great-uncle?'

I call Ross, and he picks up before the first ring has completed.

'I'm getting on a plane. Where have you been? Mum's been trying to get hold of you all afternoon!'

'I'm sorry, I'm sorry.'

'I've got to go. I'm about to go through security. I'll speak to you later. Call Mum!'

Mum tells me that Uncle Doodle passed away around lunchtime, peacefully in his favourite chair. He had been talking with Terry just moments before, remembering the time he first danced with Gloria, Terry's mother, and then he closed his eyes, and was gone. The funeral will be tomorrow, late morning in Bushey, with the shiva at Paul's house for the rest of the week.

The underwater feeling that envelops me is only mitigated by the gentle pressure of Euan's arms, and him offering soothing words in my ear.

'You don't need to do this,' I tell him. I won't let myself sob, not here, but there's now no stopping the tears trailing down my face.

'Of course I do.'

'Please, stop being so nice to me. Stop being so good.'

'It's okay. It really is. I'm sorry this is happening.'

'But we're broken up now.'

'We're both still human beings, last time I checked.'

I turn my head and lean into his chest. He smells faintly of chopped onions and garlic.

'Don't you have to work?' I ask him.

'Nope.'

I don't believe him, but I'm grateful.

'I'm so sorry Euan,' I say against his heart. 'I'm so sorry. I wish it was you. It would be so much easier if it was you. You have no idea.'

'We don't have to talk about that right now. You've had a shock.'

At some point in the last few moments, he's arranged for a glass of sherry to be brought over. I drink it with shaking hands, marvelling at how much it tastes like kosher wine.

'Baruch atah Adonai, eloheinu melech ha-olam, borei peri ha-gafen,' I murmur under my breath. I don't know why I say the bracha. It doesn't make any sense and it's not the appropriate time and place. I know it's ridiculous, but I feel the need to say important words, and there aren't very many I know off by heart. I find I'm embarrassed, wishing I knew more.

'Where are you going to go now?' Euan asks me. 'How are you getting home?'

'I don't know.'

'Do you need to go back to your parents' place?'

'I should probably go there. I'll need to go to my flat first to pick up some things.'

'Let me arrange for a cab back to your flat.'

'You've done too much already. I can't accept.'

'It's either me ordering you a cab, or me accompanying you home on the tube myself. What's it going to be?'

'Cab,' I mope. I still don't like that he's paying for me, but at least I know it's not going to happen again.

He walks me outside to the front of the hotel once he gets an alert that the Uber is nearly here.

'I'm sorry,' he says it this time, 'if I ever put any pressure on you.'

'I wanted to fall in love with you, believe me,' I admit.

'That would have been nice.'

'You don't seem to be hating me much right now, but it's okay if you do. I hate myself a fair bit.'

'Don't hate yourself Tamsyn.'

We hug for the last time as the car pulls up to the pavement. The Clarence doorman steps forward and opens the car door for me.

I gaze at Euan as the car pulls away with me in it, my stunning Viking bear, his tattooed arms wrapped around himself defensively, but I don't have any regrets, not now. I imagine Uncle Doodle sitting next to me, holding my hand, telling me that I've done the right thing. I imagine him so firmly that it hurts when I look to my side and don't see him there. When it hits me that I'll never see him again, I let the sobs overtake me, and don't care what the driver thinks.

19

The prayer hall is baking hot. It's mid-August, and even with all the doors and windows open, we're schvitzing like crazy.

I've been careful to refer to my great-uncle as David Rutman around everyone, but when the Rabbi calls him by his Hebrew name, Dudel Aharon, I look across the aisle, where Ross is standing directly opposite me, and we smile at each other.

The back wall of the prayer hall is constructed of amber-panelled glass framed by concrete, which looks almost like a honeycomb, and the light streams through and on to the plain, pale wood coffin in streaks of gold and copper. The women stand on one side, and the men on the other, and I'm holding my mum's hand, or she's holding mine. It's hard to tell which. I look at Ross on the other side of the room, standing with Dad, and marvel at how we found ourselves here. How we all found ourselves here. The tangles of ancestry that led us from the villages of the old Russian territories and other parts of Eastern Europe, through East London and right to this spot. The room is overflowing with people who dropped everything at a moment's notice to make sure that they were present to say goodbye. It astounds me, the depth of feeling and the connection.

This is how it's done. This is how it was always done, and this will be how it's done long after I'm gone. I wonder if realising this should be filling me with dread, because it doesn't. It's reassuring and beautiful.

Terry says a few words, as she was the one caring for Uncle Doodle the most in the last few months, then the mourners say Kaddish.

I'm holding the prayer book in my hands, looking down at the words of the mourning prayer printed in Hebrew on one side, and in English on the other. I think of all the times I've been to synagogue and never bothered to look at the prayer book nor taken the time to really understand what all the words mean. I said that bracha yesterday on instinct, repeated it because my family have said it over wine every Friday night for as long as I can remember, but even so, I don't know what it means. I don't know what any of the words actually mean. I'm an editor, and these are words that belong to me, and yet I've never taken the time to truly understand them.

When the prayers finish, we parade out of the hall and to the funeral ground just beyond, the principle mourners following closely behind the coffin and then the rest of us trailing after. I'm still holding Mum's hand, and Ross is now on my other side. He looks stern but collected. When I reach out to hold his hand, he grabs on to it, his palm hot and sweating.

More prayers, and then dirt shovelled on to the grave. We all do it. We all bury Uncle Doodle together and say goodbye. My brain won't let me process that he's in there. I know he is, rationally, I know this, but I refuse to imagine it. It's ugly and frightening.

There's no shade in this part of the cemetery, and the heat is intense, pushing down on my shoulders, making my feet feel like they're melting into my shoes and into the ground beyond. We're on a vast field of gently rolling land, the graves evenly spaced but packed tight. No flowers anywhere, but many of the graves have clusters of stones and pebbles placed on them to show that they've been visited, and that the person buried beneath is remembered.

My mum wants to visit her parents on the way back. The four of us, Mum, Dad, Ross and me, all place a stone on both my grandparents' graves. The tombstones match, although they were actually buried a couple of years apart. I was too young to go to the lavoyah back then, but I did attend the stone-setting, a ceremony just under a year later to mark the end of the official mourning period, and the unveiling of the tombstones. But Mum didn't finish mourning then, I know she didn't. She still feels lonely. Dad too. His parents rest in the Willesden Cemetery. I've never been there; Dad tends to go alone when he visits.

I cling to Ross as Mum stands in silence over the ghosts of her parents, and then we walk back past the Holocaust memorial to where Dad has parked the car.

There are a couple of voicemails waiting for me when I check my phone. One from Kerry-Ann saying how sorry she is to hear the news, along with a not-so-subtle indication that Gareth isn't particularly happy that I'm taking time off last minute again.

'He was asking questions about how close you are,' Kerry-Ann says on the message, her tone apologetic. She doesn't want to tell me this, but she also wants to make sure I'm prepared. We all know how Gareth is, and I'm not annoyed at her. 'And he wants to know if you'll be in for the Thursday meeting.'

I'll reply to her later. That magazine is the least of my worries right now.

The other message is from Euan.

'Hey, I know I probably shouldn't be calling, and I know I should be pissed off with you, but that doesn't stop the fact that you're going through a lot right now, and I'm sorry. I just wanted to know how you are and wanted to let you know that if you need me, even if it's just as a friend, then I can be here for you.'

It would be so easy. Too easy.

There are many things I could settle for right now. I could settle for my job, always being second in command and never seeing out my full potential, with a boss who will never regard me as an equal. And I could settle with someone like Euan too. I know I'd never be happy, not really, and it would be a second-best life, but what if I never have a chance to do better? Shouldn't I be feeling grateful for what I have right now, instead of aspiring for anything else?

'I broke up with Euan,' I tell Ross at the lunch being thrown at Paul's.

Paul lives in Hampstead Garden Surburb, not far from Henly Corner, in a house that might have been impressive a few decades ago, but now feels like a shabby relic, the last one on the street that hasn't been extended in all directions with the driveway paved over. Even the interiors I can imagine through a sepia filter. Busy carpets, the furniture all made from a dark and highly polished wood, and overly ornate frames around tiny oil paintings. It used to be his father's home, but Uncle Doodle moved into the flat in Hendon when he started to find it hard to manage stairs, and Paul stayed on. The kitchen was redecorated more recently and is starkly silver and shiny compared to everywhere else. This is where the food has been laid out, all brought by people paying their respects. There are platters of bridge rolls filled with smoked salmon, egg salad or cream cheese, boxes of biscuits from Sharon's Bakery, and a thick brick of babka ready sliced.

'When? Didn't he come with you to the bar mitzvah on Sunday?' Ross asks, astonished. We're standing close to the kitchen (it feels better to be standing where it's busy rather than around the moping relatives) and I'm wondering how I can possibly explain the truth. It sounds stupid, even in my head:

He fell in love with me, but I wasn't in love with him.

We didn't match, he was too wholesome and I feel like too much of a mess.

There's somebody else. It's hopeless, but he exists and it's breaking my heart.

Every explanation I try sounds ridiculous. All good reasons to break up with someone, but none seem to fit with why I broke up with him right then, the next day after introducing him to my parents and the whole Rutman clan. So, I don't say anything.

'Do Mum and Dad know?' Ross asks next.

'No. I don't know how to tell them. Mum loved him.'

'Blimey Tamsyn, you don't half love a bit of drama sometimes, do you.'

'Uncle Doodle said I should be with the person who makes me happy,' I say, reflecting on the last proper conversation we had. 'What if I don't know what happy is?'

'You've lost me,' Ross says.

'What if my idea of happiness is completely skewed. What if I was happy with Euan, but I just didn't realise it?'

'I'm not going to say we don't both have issues, but we're not that broken. You know what happiness feels like.'

'What does it feel like to you?' I ask him.

'Well, now you're asking.'

'I am. I don't know anything about your life in Scotland. I don't know if you're happy. I don't even know why you're up there. Aren't there universities down in London you can research in?'

'I moved to Scotland for love,' Ross says with a heavy sigh.

'I didn't know that.'

He moves me around the corner, out of the way of any busybody relatives who might be able to hear.

'Who was she?' I ask.

'He,' Ross murmurs.

'He,' I correct myself, trying not to display my surprise.

'He was called Will, and I was an idiot. He was the reason I moved to Scotland, because he was moving there. When that ended, I stayed.'

'You never told me.'

'I didn't want the attention.'

'Who else knows?'

'The only people who know are up in Scotland. And Uncle Doodle. Remember when we went round there? I told him everything, and I'm pleased I did. He was kind.'

'I'm sorry you never felt you could tell me.'

'I knew I could. But the time was never right. There was always something going on. I didn't want the fuss.'

'Ross, I'm so sorry.'

'There's nothing to be sorry about. Anyway, I've made a life for myself up there now. Sometimes London doesn't even feel real anymore, you know?'

'I should have realised. I should have made time for you.'

'Please don't worry.'

We stand together in silence for a while, watching our relatives pick at the food, their sloped shoulders, the tentative starts to any and all topics of conversation.

'You may not know what happiness is, Big Sister,' Ross tells me. 'But you should trust your instincts on what made you unhappy.'

'I wanted to be happy with Euan. And he's a good man. I wish I could feel the same way he feels about me.'

'There'll be others.'

'There already is,' I admit.

'Let me guess, the one with the supermodel?'

'How did you know?'

'You think you're this deep and mysterious person, Big Sister, but you're really not.'

'And I suppose you are, Little Brother?'

'I've known I was definitely gay since I was fourteen and none of you lot even had an inkling, as far as I can tell. What does that say?'

'It says that I'm embarrassingly self-obsessed. That none of us took the time to notice.'

'Well, that and a few other things,' Ross chuckles.

'Stubborn, self-obsessed and cold. Maybe haughty too.'

'Who said all that?'

'Nobody important. But it's true. I'm an awful human being. I don't know why I get so stuck on some things. I don't know why I let the opinions of others bother me so much. I should have made more time for you, when you needed it. I feel awful Ross.'

'I blame the parents,' Ross says, drawing me close for a brotherly hug. 'But you're okay.'

'I feel like Uncle Doodle would know the perfect thing to say. He'd have the perfect Yiddish proverb, and he'd treat me like a princess no matter what mess I'd got myself into.'

'You're not going to say anything to Mum and Dad, are you?'

'No. And you're not going to tell them I broke up with Euan, right?'

We link pinky fingers in a promise.

'You know, Mum and Dad really surprised me?'

'They did? How?'

'Just in how they were with Euan. Maybe shocked at first, but really cool afterwards. I mean it when I said they loved him. Just before we broke up, Mum asked me to invite him to Friday night dinner.'

'Wow.'

'I know, right? I don't think you have to worry about what they'd say as much as you think.'

He brings me in for a tight hug.

'I want to be a better person,' I tell my brother. 'I'm going to come up to Edinburgh and we're going to spend some proper time getting to know each other, okay?'

'That'd be great.'

We go home after lunch and I nap in my childhood bedroom before it's time for a light dinner and then back to Paul's house for the evening prayers. Ross decides to stay home. He's exhausted from the early morning flight and the funeral and will attend the shiva the following night.

I wish I could fix everything for him. I wish he wasn't scared of telling my parents, and the rest of the family. I wish he didn't feel the need to keep us all as far away as possible, for fear of us seeing the real him. I wish I had known sooner. I could have done my job as his older sister and made the path easier for him. There's so much I wish I could change.

Paul's place is packed. Only close family came to the lunch, but now it's an open house, with anybody who wants to pay their respects attending to give well wishes to the mourners, and to help them pray.

I hover in the corner of the living room, watching the multitude of strangers who are here, marvelling at the number of people who Uncle Doodle knew. Paul and Terry are sitting on their low chairs, their expressions wan, Paul's face left all rough and unshaven. It's been little more than twenty-four hours and already the shadows on the lower part of his face are deep.

I feel like I'm not here. The real me is somewhere else, watching everything through my eyes. These aren't my feet, but I can move them; these aren't my fingers, but I use them to nervously twirl my hair regardless. I don't feel solid.

And then Ari arrives.

He doesn't see me at first. I'm hidden in my corner by the bookcase, and he's busy greeting people he knows, and trying to figure out where he needs to be.

I like being able to just watch him. He stands out from everyone else, a little taller, and then taller still with all that hair. He's tried to tame it, but it's outrageously thick, his kippah precariously clipped in and holding on for dear life. He's wearing a flannel shirt over a T-shirt, and dark jeans over his sneakers. You'd never think he was a lawyer to look at him. A comedian maybe, or a writer. It's a sad evening, but he can't help but smile when he meets people, and shakes hands with warmth and intention. I'm looking out for Dalya, but I don't think she's here. He's not checking around for anyone, nor does his body language suggest that he intends to make any introductions, so I'm guessing she isn't accompanying him. It doesn't surprise me. She's a newcomer, and busy shivas are hard when you don't know anyone, as well as being intensely depressing.

When he spots me, it's like the world stops for a moment. Instead of feeling detached from the world, it's suddenly like there is no world, only me and him.

Ari walks over, making a beeline but being casual about it, and when we're close enough, he reaches across for a hug. I cling to him and sink into the pressure of his arms wrapped around me, the smell of his neck and the texture of the flannel shirt. I let out one of those ugly sobs, the kind of sob that only forms when you've been holding it in for too long, and then instantly apologise, embarrassed. But he doesn't let me go. He doesn't say anything back to me in that moment, but he doesn't let go either.

I'm the one who pulls away, scared suddenly because we're in a crowded room surrounded by my family and other acquaintances, most of whom know I was parading around another man just a couple of nights before. Not to mention the supermodel Ari was parading around with himself.

'I'm sorry,' I say again, gathering myself and wiping my nose on a tissue.

'It's all right,' he murmurs, suddenly reserved. 'You're going through a lot right now.'

'Thank you.'

'I wish you a long life,' he says after an uncertain pause.

'I'm not one of the mourners,' I point out, nodding my head to where Paul and Terry are sitting on their low chairs.

'But you're mourning,' Ari returns.

We smile at each other, a smile of understanding. I want to hold him again, but I don't know if it's due to desire or grief. I notice him clench his hands and stuff them in his pockets. A now familiar move.

'No Euan?' he asks.

'No. He's not here.' I say it with the full stop, firm and with meaning. I just hope Ari hears it.

'Right,' he murmurs in response.

'It's nice of you to come,' I say. 'You must be really busy, but it's nice. Thank you.'

'I met your great-uncle at Dom's wedding, remember? He was a good man.'

'I remember.'

'I watched you dance together.'

'You did?'

'He was a great dancer. You could really see it. He had proper training, didn't he?'

'Among many things he did when he was young, yes. I always loved dancing with him.'

I think about the bar mitzvah party, about being so caught up with my own drama that I didn't have a chance to say a proper goodbye. I was starting to enjoy smiling with Ari, but now the tears are threatening to start again.

'Well, you did need the practise,' Ari fools, one corner of his mouth curling in amusement.

Just like that, he's caught me and pulled me back to a smile.

'I'm sorry,' Ari says, composing himself again. 'I shouldn't tease. I know you loved him. And that he loved you too. You must miss him a lot.'

'I think it's too soon to miss him. I only just saw him. This process, what's happening right now, it's mystifying. In my head, he's still sitting in his chair in his flat, still available to tell me stories when I need them. It feels insane.'

'It's not insane,' Ari reassures. 'You were close. My mum told me after hearing about what happened from Deborah. I knew you'd be here tonight, and I wanted to make sure you were okay.'

I look into his eyes and my own well with tears again. I can feel my heart liquifying and sending faintly pleasing chills all the way through my body. I shudder from the intensity of the feeling, knowing that it's heightened by my grief.

'I'm good,' I tell him, even as a tear rolls down my cheek. 'Thank you.'

He wants to hug me again. I can feel it. He's not stepped any closer, not made any moves at all, and yet I feel it. Like the feeling before a kiss, the pressure of the imminence, the thrum of static just under my skin. I know he feels it too. It's the same as when we were out on the balcony together a couple of nights ago. This isn't the kind of feeling that happens alone, it only happens because someone else is feeling the same way.

'Prayers are going to start soon,' he says. I look up and notice people moving, preparing to allow the men to stand near the front by the mourners. Ari feels for his kippah, adjusting it on his head so that it's more secure. He turns back to me before he walks away and says: 'We'll dance.'

'What?' I ask, not quite hearing him.

'We'll dance. I mean it. I'm not as good as your great-uncle, but you should know that someday soon, we'll dance.'

'Okay.'

The thrum under my skin is electric. I can't move. I can't look anywhere but at him. Can't think of anything else but that promise.

And then he's gone into the crowd of people, and I feel cold. I head into the kitchen where Mum has made her base and allow her to hold me as I hear the people in the other room say Kaddish. Whilst they pray, I imagine Uncle Doodle watching me, watching Ari too, and think of what he'd say.

'Man plans, and God laughs,' I mumble.

'What was that?' Mum asks.

'Just thinking of things Uncle Doodle used to say.'

'That's an old saying, that one. My father used to say it too.'

'I think God might be in hysterics watching me,' I say.

Mum tightens her grip around my shoulders, and I slouch and let my head fall on her, not easy considering that I'm taller. I don't care if I'm uncomfortable, because right now uncomfortable feels appropriate. I can just about see the back of Ari's head from where I stand, and as the mourning song swells, I close my eyes and let God laugh.

20

The last month has been a mess. A crazy, lonely mess.

I had planned to take the whole week off to spend with my family, but Gareth had other plans. Uncle Doodle died on the Monday, the funeral was on Tuesday, and Gareth called me first thing Wednesday to ask when I'd be back. He didn't tell me to return exactly, but he didn't have to.

'So how long do these things take, usually?' he had asked. No mention of our last conversation, his tone was sharp and brutal.

'You mean grieving?'

'But it wasn't a close relative, was it now, so how much time do you really need?'

'I need a week Gareth.'

'A whole week? That's quite a lot. Is that a normal thing in your culture? I haven't heard of it.'

I wanted to ask how many Jewish people he really knew and, of those, how many had dealt with death in the time that he had known them. There was also something in the way he said 'your culture', something distasteful and ugly, almost as if he didn't quite trust that I wasn't up to something. The desire to quit right there over the phone frothed in my mind like venom. But this wasn't even about my culture. This was about needing to spend some time with my family, for the sake of my mental health.

'Surely he should understand?' Mum asked me afterwards.

'No, he really wouldn't. Gareth doesn't even believe that depression is real. He thinks it's something made up to get you out of taking responsibility for your actions. He's a disaster. But I'm really not in the mood to argue with him. We had a bit of an ugly conversation the other day, and it's just not worth making any extra fuss.'

'What did you say?' Dad demanded to know.

So I told them. I felt worn down and exhausted, any barriers I would usually put up between my parents and my private life paper thin. I told my parents that I'd suggested myself for a promotion, and been laughed out of the room. I didn't tell them what he'd said afterwards, his presumption that all I wanted was money. They didn't need to hear that too, not right now.

'Why do you still even work there?' Mum asked. 'It doesn't make you happy. Not like it used to.'

This is where I would usually stand my ground, stick up for my job and my ambitions there, as well as remind my parents that jobs didn't have to make you happy, they just had to pay the bills. All I had to do was wait until Gareth retired. I had dreams, and plans, and great ideas, and surely it wouldn't be much longer until I had the chance to take action on them? Except, it had become horrifyingly clear to me that Gareth had no intention of ever letting me rise up. The fight I would usually put up in a conversation like this with my parents, the determination that usually thrilled through me, urging me to prove everyone wrong and end up victorious, all gone.

I looked at my parents after I told them everything about work and wondered why I worked so hard to resist their help and advice. Even when it might have sounded like disdain, or there was a quiet threaten of 'I told you so'. My parents love me. They want the best for me, and they want me to be happy. I've seen it in their faces throughout my life. There's no desire for schadenfreude, just genuine concern and hope. How did my brain manage to scramble it all up so much? It's like I've been stopping myself from being happy out of spite. What kind of person does that?

'It doesn't make me happy.' I said the words out loud, in front of my parents. Neither laughed at me. Neither 'told me so'. They both just looked at me, feeling sorry and helpless.

'Do you want to tell us about Euan?' Mum asked next, carefully, like the words might crack something in me, and break me apart.

'There's not much to say,' I admitted with a shrug.

'I liked him. Both your father and I did.'

'He was tall,' Dad said stoically. Coming from him, this was a gleaming compliment.

'It just wasn't right. It wasn't what I thought it was,' I told them.

'Yes, well,' Mum sighed. 'It was exciting to meet him regardless. Whoever you bring to meet us, whoever you end up with, you know we just want what's best for you, right?'

'I do know.'

'We're not going to judge. We're never going to be those kind of parents.'

'Well, hang on a minute here Liddy,' Dad interjected. 'I have every right to judge if I want to.'

'Oh, stop it Joseph!' Mum hissed with good humour before turning back to me. 'Tamsyn, Jewish or not, tall or not, good in the kitchen or not – although, let's face it, you're never going to be the cook of the couple – nobody knows what's right for you apart from you.'

'Do you mean that?'

Mum looked pensive, chewing over her thoughts. 'Well,' she continued with a half-smile, 'I am your mother. At the end of the day, I have a pretty good idea of what's right for you.'

'And what's right for me right now?'

'I think you know that.'

I wonder how many times in life you face moments that unpick fundamental parts of your personality. I'm not saying that everything changed in that moment, after I spoke honestly with my parents, but something definitely clicked. Everything I had built up, all the snarly, prickly traits I'd developed to protect myself, always because I believed I was doing the right thing and had to be prickly in order to get by, suddenly seemed so useless. I had always thought I was so tough. What had I been punishing myself for? What was I building up those defences against? Was it even that much of a big deal if someone laughed at me once in a while? Especially if it was only my parents, who I knew loved me no matter what?

I didn't quit my job, not right then anyway.

One of the pitfalls of being a managing editor is that it's incredibly difficult to take impromptu time off. There are so many tasks I need to delegate, so much to handover, that the only thing that would ever make sense is just to do the job myself. So, I went in on Thursday and did everything I needed to do, including appearing to be okay in front of Gareth because the last thing I wanted was for him to build any sort of case against me, or nurture the thought that I might not be tough enough. I was not going to allow myself to be fired before I'd really given time to let my escape plan fall into place.

After work on Thursday and Friday, I went straight over to my parents' place, had dinner with Mum, Dad and Ross, and then we all headed over to the shiva together. Afterwards, they dropped me at East Finchley tube station and I took myself home, where Helene checked that I was all right before I went to my room for a quiet night, the echoes of the kaddish still ringing in my head.

Time crawled by. Each night of the shiva I hoped to see Ari but didn't. I waited for him, and I hoped, but he didn't show. Maybe it was too much for him, maybe too little. Maybe he was just busy and I'd been reading too much into his kindness. He paid his respects, he did the right thing, and then he went back to living his own life. I thought about messaging him, but I could never figure out what to say.

The following Monday, I saw Gareth lead another eager, red-chinoed toff into his office and realised that my time at *Hotelier Monthly* was finally over. I asked Kerry-Ann to find out the guy's name, and after some light digging on LinkedIn, discovered that he came from the world of investment banking, no experience in journalism or editorial whatsoever. I saw myself working for another rich, entitled arsehole, doing all the work for none of the credit, and with no hope of promotion.

I don't need to be here, I told myself. Was there really any job that someone else couldn't pick up in my absence? Was I really so crucial that the magazine would fall apart without me? There was no internal panic, no anger or resentment, just a quiet internal acknowledgment that the time had come. I was finally done.

'Gareth?' I knocked on his door after I saw the man leave. Gareth's cheeks puffed with annoyance when I stepped into his office before he had agreed to let me enter. 'I'd like to talk.'

'Well, I'm very busy. Could you not put something in the diary?'

'Was that another candidate for the editor position?' I asked, ignoring him.

'Edwin Winstead-Duke,' Gareth says. 'I used to go golfing with his father. He's a bit bored at his current job and looking for a challenge.'

'Has he worked in publishing before? Any journalism experience?'

'He's got an excellent pedigree and a solid decade in high-stakes project management. Ruthless too, I hear. Could be just what this place needs.'

Whilst Edwin Winstead-Duke had been in Gareth's office, I had printed out my edited version of Carmella's resignation letter. The one I originally wrote for her in May.

'What's this?' Gareth asked me, refusing to take it.

'My notice.'

'Your what?'

'I'll stay here until you secure a replacement. Or for another month. Whichever comes first.'

'Is this some kind of strange joke? Is this what the millennials are doing these days? Are you filming this for the TikTok?'

I thrust the letter forward and waited for Gareth to take it.

'It's my notice Gareth.'

'Have you got a new job? You never said you were looking! I expect to be informed of these things so that we can make arrangements!'

'No new job. Nothing on the horizon.'

I didn't tell him about the lunch I had booked with Florence Biddulphe the following week, or how excited she was to hear from me and learn that I was exploring new avenues. It's not as if anything had been offered at this point, it was just an informal lunch, so technically I wasn't even lying.

'Well then, you're a fool on top of everything else. In this economy? I don't know what kind of game you're playing, but I'm not impressed.'

'I'll work until you secure a replacement, or for a month, whichever comes first,' I repeated, before I placed the letter down on his desk, turned on my heels and left before he could say anything else.

I came home that evening and buried my face in a cushion on the sofa. I didn't even realise Helene was home. She stood over me with her arms folded, a blue brush pen behind one ear and multiple more stuffed in the front pocket of her bright orange dungarees, and asked if I needed wine.

'You're my best friend, you know that?' I told her three quarters of a bottle later.

'I know, you soppy cow,' she replied with a hug. 'But have you thought about how you're going to keep up on the mortgage? I don't want to get weird about it, but I kind of like living with you, you know?'

I finished my glass of wine quickly and then instantly regretted it. Turns out that grief and anxiety doesn't quite make for a sunshine happy drunken state.

'I'm going to have to write a CV,' I moaned to Helene. 'I haven't written one since uni.'

'I could help you with that,' she replied. 'You could go bog-standard Word document, but if you want to stand out, you should do something more graphic. Something with wow factor!'

'You'd really help me with that?'

'I can't write it for you, but if you could get that going, I could work my magic on it?'

Helene found a website and showed me all these incredible examples of unusual and exciting CV designs.

'I'm going to get the best job Helene, I promise. I'm going to get a job that makes me happy and has actual career potential, and it's going to pay the bills too.'

We listened to Taylor Swift songs as loud as we dared without risking bothering our neighbours in the adjoining flats, and ordered take-out, getting steadily more and more drunk as the evening went on. The sense of freedom, mixed with the alcohol, made me feel deliriously untethered, like a balloon let loose from a child's hand and allowed to float up high into the sky.

'Are you drunk enough for me to ask about what happened with Euan?' Helene asked me.

'Yep! Ask away!'

'He was so hot.'

'He was. He really was so hot.'

'And he could cook.'

'That too.'

'And he was so nice!'

'Nice. Definitely nice.'

'So, what happened?'

'I developed the biggest crush I've ever developed in the history of crushes on another guy.'

'The one you had the row with that evening? The Jewish one?'

'Yes! How did you know?'

'Because you hated him so much. I figured you were either going to murder him or sleep with him at some point.'

'But why didn't I know back then? Why didn't I know Helene? How did *you* know when I didn't?'

We ended the evening with the light turned down low, huddled over Helene's phone, stalking the what-might-have-beens of our lives. Helene showed me pictures of her ex-boyfriend's wedding, the bride an eerie replica of Helene.

'I know,' she said, tilting her head and squinting to examine it even more closely. 'It's like he went from me to the upgraded version of me.'

'Downgraded, more like,' I told her.

But it was eerie. Same feathery blonde hair, similar geeky glasses and bright, colourful clothes.

'It sucks, because I wonder if he was looking for something particular, and thought he found it with me. But then I ended up not being good enough, you know? What if I was the lesser version, and he found the more perfect one?'

'Helene,' I said, drawing her close. 'You are completely perfect. Just not for him, that's all.'

'That's sweet. I wanted to be perfect for him though.'

'I know exactly what you mean.'

Euan has an Instagram account for publicity purposes, and I guided Helene to it. He never posted much on there before, it was all professional shots done to celebrate him starting work at the Clarence, and then before that promotional shots for the TV show he was on. But in the couple of weeks since our break-up, it appeared he had been on Instagram a fair bit.

'Wow. Did you know his arms looked like that when you dated?' Helene asked, now squinting and tilting her head at a bulge of tattooed bicep almost as big as Euan's whole head.

I just sighed in reply, remembering those arms around me.

'I think this is what the young folk refer to as a thirst trap,' she flicked through to a mirror selfie of Euan working out at the gym, sweaty and intense and all his muscles primed and glistening. 'Do you think he's sending a message to you?'

'A message?'

'Trying to show you what you're missing?'

'I don't miss him.' I didn't realise it until I had said it.

'You don't? Wow, that was a quick recovery.'

'I've been broken up with him for a quarter of the time we were together.'

'Well, when you put it like that.'

'Look up Dalya Malka.'

'Who?'

'She's a model. Just look her up.'

Helene did as I asked and her pictures came up, each one as stunningly perfect as the last.

'Who is she?'

'She's Ari's girlfriend.'

'Wow. Okay.'

'I know.'

There was a series of pictures from Jacob's bar mitzvah. No pictures of the kids she was perpetually surrounded by that evening, and no indications that it was anything other than a glamorous club event. Just Dalya and her legs, or Dalya and her miraculous cleavage in that red dress. Anyone looking at these pictures would just think it was a regular (albeit dazzling) private party. There was even a picture of her and the tribute act together, although she's gone ahead and tagged the real thing, maybe hoping her followers will believe it's really Ed.

'Scroll down,' I told Helene.

'What is it?'

'There's no pictures of her with Ari.'

'You're right.'

'I know he's pretty private. He doesn't really do social media. But you'd think if they were dating, and if they were serious, that there'd be some couple pictures, right?'

'I don't know. This looks like a model account, as in, it's more for work than it is for real life. I think she's an influencer. Look, this picture has a tag for a foreign toothpaste company.'

'Now scroll up,' I directed. 'What's the date on that picture? Is it recent?'

It was a bikini shot, Dalya looking stunningly perfect, her body posed and pristine to a supernatural degree.

'Yesterday,' Helene affirmed.

'And where's it tagged?'

'Tel Aviv.'

'So, she's gone back to Israel. Maybe that's why he didn't come to the other nights of the shiva. He's probably gone back with her.'

'Could be an old picture?'

'The caption is "It's great to be home", sunshine emoji, heart emoji, champagne emoji. Heart emoji and champagne emoji? Is she celebrating? Why would she be celebrating?'

'Maybe she's just happy to be home?'

'Maybe she's happy to be home with Ari.'

'Now you're overthinking.'

'How can I be over my boyfriend, but not over another guy I was never even with? Nothing makes sense!'

'More wine?'

'Absolutely.'

'You broke up with your boyfriend, suffered a bereavement, and quit your job all within ten days? Are you sure you're not having a nervous breakdown Big Sister?' Ross called me straight after I texted him my news the next day on my lunch hour.

'Not a breakdown, but maybe a breakthrough?' I admitted.

'I'm still worried about you.'

'I'm fine, I promise.'

'Well, I won't know for certain until you come and visit me up here.'

'After all the holidays, absolutely.'

'After the holidays? Since when did you go frum?'

'I'm not frum. I don't even know if I believe in God.'

'Then what?'

'I just want to be around everyone right now. It's comforting to feel connected. I'm starting to wonder if this is what it's all about.'

'Does this mean you're going to start going to shul?'

'I'm not even a member anywhere. But I've been thinking, over this summer and with Uncle Doodle now gone, I don't want to lose this feeling, whatever it is. Didn't you feel it? At the lavoyah?'

'I think I know what you mean.'

'It just felt real, and solid. To have everyone there, it felt like a safety net for the soul, somehow. It's weird how I never felt it before.'

'I always thought you hated being Jewish,' Ross said.

'I think I did,' I admitted. 'I never wanted to be different from other people. I guess I thought it was something to be ashamed of somehow.'

'This is some breakthrough. Can you send some of it my way?'

'I'm still trying to make sense of it myself. Listen, I've got to go. Are you sure you're not going to come down for Rosh Hashanah?'

'You know what I'm like around the whole family. It's hard for me.'

'I know. I love you Ross.'

'I love you too Tamsyn. Happy New Year, I guess. And no more big life-changing decisions for now, I beg you.'

Summer is over when Rosh Hashanah arrives, with apple dipped in honey always tasting like autumn. This year Auntie Davina and Uncle Marc Galinski are putting on lunch in their house in Radlett, although Mum is making the honey cake. My cousins Abigail and Sarah will be there of course, plus Dominic and his parents.

It's been one month since Uncle Doodle died, and the celebrations feel a little empty with it all being so recent. We're going through the motions, and doing all the things we'd usually do, but there's none of the pep and smiles. This'll be the first yom tov without him that any of us will have known. I miss him tremendously, and I hate that missing him is accompanied by so much guilt. I could have spent more time with him. He had so much wisdom, and I had (still have) so many questions, but I always thought that there would be time. He may have been elderly, and I know that he felt satisfied with his long life, but that doesn't stop me from feeling the unfairness of losing him. It was too quick, and I wasn't ready.

The printed album containing all the photos I took around Whitechapel arrived a few days ago, and I bring it around to my Aunt and Uncle's house as a surprise. I filled out the pages with other photos, sepia-stained images of relatives I never had the chance to meet, pictures of Ross and me as children sitting on Uncle Doodle's knees, and pictures from Abigail and Dominic's wedding too. Dad cries when he first sees it. He lost his own father such a long time ago, and Uncle Doodle was like a second father to him. Auntie Davina runs her fingers over the images, reading them as if she was reading braille, trying to feel the lines and shapes across the flat page. She complains about one of the pictures Ross and I chose to include though, moaning that she wishes we hadn't selected a picture where she's wearing glasses, as we can't see her eyes properly. I know it's not a real complaint though, that both her and my father find complaints much easier to deliver than compliments. Her hands shake as she hands the album around to the next person, trembling with emotion, and afterwards she comes over to me and holds me close in a firm, serious hug.

'It doesn't feel right, does it,' Abigail says to me in the kitchen. She's busy preparing the kneidlach and checking on the chicken soup. Our dads are at shul with Dominic and his parents, and we're waiting for them to get back before we have lunch. My mum and Auntie Davina are upstairs going through her wardrobe, seeing if there's anything Mum wants before Davina gives it to charity. I can hear them both clunking around above our heads, their voices sometimes passionately loud.

'I guess this is how it's meant to be,' I respond. I glance over into the conservatory where my other first cousin is struggling to brush the family dog, a frisky Pomeranian called Starsky (Hutch the rabbit died a few years ago now).

'No Starsky! No!' Sarah is calling whilst the dog hops around on her lap fighting to get away.

'Tell me something good,' I ask Abigail, fixing my mouth in a dramatic downward droop. 'What's been going on with you?'

'Honestly?'

'Honestly.'

'I'm exhausted most of the time,' she admits.

'Really?'

'I just feel like I'm putting a lot of effort in, marriage wise, and sometimes it's like I'm on my own a bit with that.'

'You're not on your own,' I tell Abigail. There might have been a time where I would have judged her choices, but I think I understand her a bit better now, or at least, understand where she's coming from. She's just trying to feel connected too, in her own way.

'You know, I caught Dominic watching the Spurs game before Shabbos had gone out a couple of weeks ago. I lost it with him. Really lost it. Here I am sticking to the rules, making cholent every weekend and taking off my make-up in the dark because we don't have a time switch on the light in the bathroom, and he's there watching football like nothing's wrong. What's the point? Why do I bother?'

Abigail recognises that I don't quite know how to respond to that and continues. 'I always knew that Dominic wasn't as religiously minded as I wanted us to be. We talked about it a lot, and I know that on some level he wanted to be more relaxed about the rules, but I thought we could have a fresh start once we were married. We discussed it. We agreed that we wanted to bring children into a family that respected the traditions.'

'But you never observed that religiously growing up. I used to come over on Saturdays and play The Sims with you.'

'Something happened when I went to university. I learned a lot there, and afterwards. I found a community, and I found a way that I wanted to live my life. I thought Dominic knew this and agreed with me.'

'I think you need to talk to him about finding your own ways to honour Shabbos, without it causing problems for the both of you. You don't want to feel overworked, and he may not have realised that he was giving up something that was important to him.'

'Is the football more important than me?'

'He probably doesn't even see it as a choice between one thing or the other. He may feel that there's room for both of you. Does his family observe like you do?'

'No. They're more like our family. His parents only go to shul on high holy days. But I really thought we could start our marriage right and follow all the rules. I thought it would be a spiritual journey for the both of us.'

'But you can drive yourself crazy with all that if it's something you're not used to. You'll both adjust and find a compromise.'

'Shabbos isn't really Shabbos if you're compromising the things that make it Shabbos though,' Abigail said pointedly.

'Look, I know you probably look down on me sometimes – don't make that face, I know you do – but surely there's a way to observe that's right for the both of you together?'

'I don't like the idea of picking and choosing what you want and leaving out the bits of Judaism you don't like.'

'I know, but someone once told me that the word Israel means 'to fight with God'. Maybe it's not about choosing the bits you like, but it could be about picking your battles? Or maybe, even better than that, think about it as though you're creating your own traditions to honour your heritage. Then it's not about picking and choosing, it's about making it work together?'

'Tamsyn Rutman, what's gotten into you? That almost sounds profound.'

'It's been a weird summer.'

Abigail puts down the ladle she's been using to stir the pot of soup and looks at me.

'Tell me the truth, am I being a cow about Dom watching football? Is it even a big deal? I feel like I've made it a big deal, but then shouldn't it be? Am I going crazy?'

'I think if you don't stick to all the rules it doesn't make you any less Jewish. I also think that you can feel fulfilled and connected to something powerful and spiritual in other ways too, not just by following the rules to the very letter.'

I'm saying it to myself as I'm saying it to her, thinking about all the times I didn't feel Jewish enough, or the times where I saw others openly and happily being Jewish and felt like a different species altogether. I was Jewish enough for Gareth to make his stupid remarks though, wasn't I?

'You know, a boy once told me I wasn't Jewish enough for him?' I continue.

'What?'

'Simon Schaffler. He was my first boyfriend.'

'I never knew about that.'

'You were younger than me. I don't think your Mum would have liked me telling you about boys and sex and everything.'

'You're right on that front.'

'We were eighteen, and although we weren't serious, we were serious enough. We did it for the first time in his car, if you can believe it.'

'Oof, sounds uncomfortable.'

'It wasn't that bad,' I smirk, before continuing. 'It's not as if I expected things with Simon to last because university was coming up, but I didn't think it would end like it did. He went to Israel for the summer, and when he came back, he was like a different person. He didn't want to touch me anymore, and all he could talk about was how incredible Israel was.'

'Well,' Abigail looks like she's about to launch into a defensive speech, but I stop her quickly.

'I know, I know. It's just not for me. I don't feel it like you do. I was already starting to feel like an outsider, but Simon Schaffler was the person who cemented that feeling and made it real. He said it right to my face, after I told him that I didn't think I was the type who could ever make aliyah. He literally said, "I'm just not sure you're Jewish enough for me."'

As I say it out loud, for the first time in about a decade, I find that it still hurts. Simon Schaffler might as well have physically punched me, and I'm still feeling the bruise.

I'd never really questioned my Jewishness before then. Even when I withdrew from Hebrew School, it was more from frustration than a concrete feeling of otherness. But from that moment, I decided that I was not going to let my Jewishness define me. If anything, I was going to be keeping it at arm's length as much as I possibly could. I'd find other things to be defined by instead. This resolution also extended to Jewish men. It wasn't worth it, not if they wanted me to end up as a wife and mother, make Seder every year and then eventually insist I go live in Israel.

I was a girl raised by Carrie Bradshaw and Geri Halliwell, and I refused to be held to a standard I felt detached from. Simon Schaffler had shown me a side to my culture that was old-fashioned and, frankly, scary. What I wanted was the future. I could have anything if I aimed high and worked hard enough. I didn't want what people told me I was supposed to be wanting. I'd make my own rules.

'This explains a lot,' Abigail says now.

'You know what's really messed up? I believed him. Maybe not fully, but definitely in part. I always had this sense that I could never be Jewish enough. Not just for him, but for anyone.'

I think about telling Abigail how I always felt like my mum compared me to her. Like I was some rogue nuisance, and there was Abigail, perfect and wonderful. I don't, because I don't want to upset her, but also because from looking at her now, I wonder if she knows. She looks sorry. Even if she doesn't understand, it looks like she has a sense of it.

'You should never feel like you're excluded. You belong. You're one of us. No matter what you do or say or eat or whether you never set foot in shul again. We're family, right? And I'm sorry if I've ever made you feel uncomfortable about that.'

'I did a lot of this to myself,' I say sadly. 'I shouldn't have let Simon Schaffler decide for me what Jewishness was. I should have worked it out on my own.'

'Sounds like you've got there now?'

Abigail brings me in for a hug, and then quickly goes to turn the hob off to stop the soup from boiling over.

'Abigail,' I look closely at her, waiting to see if she's going to catch on. When she doesn't, I continue: 'you turned the hob off.'

'So?' she's confused for a moment.

'So today is a yom tov. You've broken the rules!'

'I forgot! We use a hot plate at our flat but Mum doesn't have one and then we were talking! I wasn't even thinking!' she says, flustered.

Knowing that she won't be able to turn it back on, I reach over and do it for her.

'Thank you,' she says, still flustered. 'Don't tell my mum. She thinks I've gone too far with the strictness. I feel like she's just waiting for me to mess something up so that she can have a good laugh.'

'You're doing great Abigail,' I tell her. 'And we all mess up from time to time. Maybe Auntie Davina will surprise you?'

Abigail takes a long, deep breath, and lets it out slowly.

'I don't know what's happened to you over the summer Tamsyn, but this is nice. Seriously, thank you.'

'New year, new me,' I reply, before reaching over to give her a hug.

21

Lunch is nice. A little more subdued than normal maybe, but still nice. Uncle Marc sits at the head of the table and is busy telling us about how appalling the shofar blowing was this year, as Auntie Davina and Abigail serve up.

'Every year they get some poor schmendrick up and they think they know what they're doing. And every year is farkakte. Do they even practise? It's a horn. There are only three notes to learn! How hard can it be?'

'The Dreyers were in shul,' Dad tells Mum. 'They asked how everyone was.'

'What did you tell them?'

'That we were fine.'

'Did you ask them how they were?'

'Of course I did. Why wouldn't I ask that?'

'You never said. How am I meant to know that you asked about them if you don't say you asked about them. You only mentioned that they asked about us.'

'Well of course I asked.'

'And?'

'And what?'

'How are they?'

'They're fine!'

'Honestly Joseph,' Mum gets up from the table in a huff to help take away the empty chicken soup bowls. 'If you've embarrassed me in front of the Dreyers.'

'How have I embarrassed you? We're fine, they're fine. Stop making a broyges out of it.'

'And then,' Uncle Marc continues with his story, 'when the poor schmo tried to blow it again, it sounded like a wet fart!'

He laughs, and Dominic laughs along with him, but I see the look he gives Abigail, a look that says 'I love you, therefore I'll laugh at all your father's jokes'. It's nice. I'm happy for them, but I feel sad too.

After lunch we all go out for a walk. Abigail loops her arm through mine as we drift through the leafy Radlett streets, watching as our parents stride ahead, talking loudly. I can make out my dad saying something about a curb not being dropped satisfactorily, a driveway not being paved properly, a tree not being cut back the way it should.

'If there's something to complain about, my dad will find it,' I sigh.

'You're lucky all your dad does is complain,' Abigail replies.

Marc Galinski is ferocious about setting the world to rights. My dad likes a good grumble, but Uncle Marc likes to bring tyranny on those who he believes did him wrong. I wouldn't be surprised if he isn't drafting a letter in his head to the shul about the dismal shofar playing as we walk.

'Abigail?' I ask. She looks at me curiously. 'If I told you that I wanted to learn more about Jewish stuff, what should I do?'

'Really? This is something you want to do?'

'I don't think I belong in a Masorti or United congregation, maybe not even Reform, but I don't know yet. There's so much I don't know. So much I've ignored over the years.'

'Have you heard of Limmud?'

'No.'

'They might be a good place to start. They're non-denominational, and all about learning and enrichment. Do you remember Becca from Friday night dinner? She does some volunteer work with them. I can ask if she thinks there are any events it might be worth going along to.'

'That might be good.'

'You can look into liberal Judaism too. If you're more interested in learning about things from a more cultural, heritage standpoint. Although that movement isn't quite so big in the UK.'

'You definitely wouldn't look down on me if I don't end up following all the rules and become religious?'

'I think what's more important is that you feel like you belong. We're all on our own different paths, with our own beliefs and attitudes. But just because we're all different, that doesn't make us any less Jewish.'

Ahead I can see some people gathered at the side of the road. They're looking down where the road passes over a small babbling stream, davening with their heads down.

'What's going on?' I ask Abigail, confused.

'Tashlich,' Abigail replies. 'I'm going to do it with Dominic tomorrow afternoon at the Dollis Brook near our house.'

I've heard of this ceremony, but nobody on my side of the family observes it, and I certainly wouldn't have the name of it ready if anyone asked. But I know it involves throwing the sins of the past year into flowing water, atoning and getting ready for the judgement that will come on Yom Kippur. As we get closer to the group of people, I can hear the murmur of their quiet prayers. They are all dressed formally, except for the men wearing bright sneakers, a custom for Rosh Hashanah, when leather is forbidden but wearing white is encouraged. I see a woman toss a breadcrumb beneath her as she prays, then another, and another.

But we walk past, we don't stop and we don't take part.

'I wish it was as easy as that, shrugging off your sins in one go,' I say to Abigail, meaning for the comment to be light-hearted.

'I don't think it is easy,' she replies more soberly. 'I think it takes a lot of courage to face wrongdoing, and to atone for it.'

The image of Ari's face suddenly flashes in my mind, how I told him I was sorry at the bar mitzvah, and again at the shiva, of how hard it was to say it, and how desperately I felt it needed to be said. It still doesn't feel enough. Then I imagine him far away on a hot beach, Dalya lovingly coating his back with sun cream. Fat lot of good atoning did for me then.

'Do you have anything you need to atone for?' I ask Abigail curiously. 'And you're not allowed to say switching off the hob earlier.'

'Honestly?' she looks at me, and I look back. 'Among many, many things, I'm sorry for turning into a bridezilla over the past year. I'm sorry for crying and getting angry at the bakers for the cake being slightly different from how I imagined it. And I'm sorry for trying to set you up, twice. It was pretty awful of me to do something like that without checking in with you first. I thought I was doing the right thing, but I guess it backfired.'

'Oh,' I say, stunned. 'I didn't think you were going to say that.'

'Well, I am sorry. If I'm really atoning properly, I should probably apologise to Ari too, to be honest.'

'I don't think what you did was awful.'

'Are you kidding me? You hated the dinner I threw. I made it so awkward for you!'

'Abigail,' we stop in the road, those atoning for their sins are a little way behind us. I feel the words I want to say, and the stubbornness working to stop them getting out, knowing that once they're said then there's no going back. 'I like Ari. Not at your wedding or dinner maybe, but afterwards. You actually did a pretty good matchmaking job, I just wasn't paying attention at the time.'

'Excuse me, Tamsyn Rutman?' she's astonished, taking me in with wide eyes.

'We became friends. But I was with Euan and I was trying to make that work. But now of course he's with Dalya, so I messed up there. Maybe one day when we're both single at the same time again? I don't know. It's probably too late now.'

'Tamsyn,' Abigail interrupts me. 'He's not with Dalya.'

'What do you mean he's not with Dalya? I saw them together at Jacob's bar mitzvah.'

'And you were with Euan then. Doesn't mean you're together now, does it?'

'He hasn't gone with her back to Israel?'

'What? Why would you think that?'

I know exactly why I would think that. Because somewhere in my heart there's a boy I really liked who went to Israel and forgot all about me. Because that boy broke a part of me, and I was so sure that history was repeating itself.

When we get back to my uncle and aunt's house, Abigail finds Dominic and sits him down for a chat.

'What have I done wrong now?' Dominic asks, his face pale.

'Nothing. Why, is there something you're feeling guilty about?' Abigail checks with a raised eyebrow. 'This is about your cousin Ari. You need to tell everything you know about him to Tamsyn right now.'

'Why, is everything all right?'

'Just tell Tamsyn what happened between him and Dalya!'

By this point, both our mothers have come into the living room and are watching the conversation intently. I'm conscious of Mum prying, but figure if I send her away or try and find any more privacy, it will only make things worse. Besides which, I'm discovering that I don't care what she knows. What I care about is learning everything I can about Ari, and whether he's actually single.

'Well, I don't know everything,' Dominic admits. 'But it's probably the same story as before. They get together for a bit, fight, and then they split up. Then he'll go through this big depressive phase over it and then, when he's finally better again, she'll appear and ruin it all. It's been going on for years.'

'When did they split up this time? When exactly?' I ask.

'Is everything all right?' Dominic asks back.

'Dominic,' Abigail interrupts, 'my darling angel, it is imperative that we have all the facts and find out absolutely everything that's going on here.'

'Why?'

'Yes, why?' Auntie Davina chimes in.

Suddenly I'm surrounded by them all. Dominic sitting in his chair looking up at me, Abigail brimming with something like excitement and fury mixed together, and both our mothers, worried and interested and all of them crowding my space and my thoughts.

'What's going on Tamsyn?' Mum asks.

I tell them everything, and it's not nearly as bad as I think it's going to be, except for when my mum says with a certain degree of pomp and jubilation: 'See, why didn't you listen to me? I told you so. We all told you so.'

But even hearing the words I've dreaded for so long just didn't really seem to matter. Yes, I should have listened. Yes, I got it wrong. Except, how can I even be sure that I'd feel the way I'm feeling now if I had listened? Maybe going through those trials was a part of the journey.

I say this as if everything is settled, as if Ari is right there on a plate ready for the taking. But he's not. He doesn't know that I'm single. I don't know for certain how he feels. What if he's in this so-called depressive phase after splitting up from Dalya again? I don't want to be a rebound blip before they get to their happy ending.

'Wait,' I announce loudly, stopping all the conversations around me. 'Please, promise me that none of you will do anything.'

'Do anything? Like what?' Mum asks.

'I don't know. Whatever it is you're all thinking and planning. Whatever is going to happen, let it happen in its own time.'

'If we let things happen in their own time, they may not happen at all,' says Auntie Davina.

'I mean it though. I don't like meddling. It just makes me angry.'

'This, we know,' Mum sighs.

'So, please listen to me this time. No setting up, no phone calls with him behind my back, nothing like that. I really, really don't want to be embarrassed.'

'But Tamsyn!' Mum complains.

'Mum, I mean it!' I snap back at her. 'It's been a hectic few weeks and I've got to sort all the job stuff out. I have too much going on and I don't need romantic drama to go with it. Do I have your word?'

'You have my word,' Mum assures.

A week later, and it's my final day at *Hotelier Monthly*.

Gareth has been furious for the entirety of the last month and has barely come into the office. Fortunately, this means that I've had plenty of time to go through all my tasks with the staff writers Nadine and Mark, as well as with Kerry-Ann, who will be taking the brunt of the workload after I've gone.

'Get out as soon as you can,' I warn her. 'Unless he makes some positive changes, hires an editor who knows what they're doing and doesn't get here via nepotism, then promise me you'll get out.'

'This place is going to fall apart without you,' she replies sadly. 'Gareth is going to fall apart without you.'

'I couldn't care less about what happens to Gareth after I'm gone. I should have left ages ago.'

'What are you going to do next?'

'Do you remember Florence Biddulphe?'

'No?'

'She was the PR person looking after the Clarence when I went to interview Euan.'

'Wait, you're not going to be working at the Clarence, are you?!'

'Oh God no. Absolutely not. But Florence works for an agency that specialises in hotel publicity and PR. We met for lunch recently, and then I had a meeting with her team. It went well.'

'Hotel PR? I feel like you're crossing to the dark side.'

'And I feel like I've been on the dark side for too long. Now I get a chance to cross to the light. Anyway, it's not a done deal yet, I still have another meeting with the CEO to go, but it's looking good. They seem excited about me. And before you say anything, Florence does know that Euan and I dated and no, she does not care.'

I breathe a sigh of relief as I clear my desk. I did think about asking for a meeting so that I could air my grievances, telling Gareth right to his face what I thought about him, how he could disappear for a week and nobody would notice, but if I was unexpectedly gone for a day then everyone would panic. And how even though everyone knew this, I never got the credit or the appreciation for the work I put in. Every time the budgets were cut and the staff head count got lower, I took on more and more work without the associated pay rise. Running this magazine was never about sailing a calm ocean, but every month feeling like you were about to sink under the waves and fighting for survival. And meanwhile, through all of this, was Gareth, with his expensive holidays, long lunches, his country home and his pervy wandering eye.

I thought it would make me feel powerful and in control, that Gareth deserved to hear all those truths. But then I realised that it was unlikely to achieve anything. Gareth was never going to change, not this late in the day, and not if he didn't want to. I don't have the energy for that much anger. It's over now. I need to get out and start looking towards the future.

I fast on Yom Kippur.

I've not fasted since I was young, and even then rarely all the way through. It's easier that I don't have work to endure at the same time, but this doesn't feel like it's about endurance. I don't have anything to prove to myself by doing this. It's more about honouring something I've maybe been ignoring for much of my life, and about reconciling it.

Never usually that hungry first thing in the morning, I decide to take the opportunity to go for a walk. I'm not going to go to synagogue with my parents, or even pray. They don't even know that I'm doing this. Whatever it is I'm doing. I may not be following the rules, but I feel like I'm doing what's right.

I wander aimlessly, heading south through the City, and eventually find myself at Tower Hill, and then the Thames. I start to walk over Tower Bridge and then stop, watching the river flow down beneath me, surging faster than I thought it would do in eddies of silver and green.

I think about the people I saw in Radlett huddled over the tiny brook and tossing breadcrumbs representing their sins into the flowing water. Digging into my pocket, I feel an old receipt and pull it out to tear into pieces instead. I don't know the rules, and I don't know the words either, but I know how to feel sorry, and how to atone.

Silently, in my own way, I pray.

One by one, the small torn-up receipt gets scattered into the water below, falling like confetti. There goes everything I was. Everything I was pretending to be. So much pent-up anger and stubbornness that made me blind to the truth.

I'm sorry about Ross, about how I never worked hard enough to build a relationship beyond us being silly, squabbling kids. I never took the time to get to know him. As outcast and alone as I felt, he felt it even more keenly, and I never noticed it.

I'm sorry about Euan, for not being honest with him at the outset, for letting him believe what he wanted to believe about me, and for not seeing him for who he really was. He only wanted from me what I couldn't give him.

I'm sorry about Helene, and Abigail, and even Kerry-Ann at work, for always being a little distant, a little cold, for thinking that I was better than them because I was cynical. I could have been a better friend. I could have put myself in their shoes more often.

There are my parents too. Uncle Doodle, who I took for granted, and who indulged me, maybe a little too much.

And then finally I think of Ari, who I have already said sorry to, and who dwells in my mind like a daunting shadow. I honestly have no idea what to do about him. I don't know how to make first moves (not when there are serious feelings involved, at least), and he doesn't know that he can. And even if a move was made, there's no guarantee of anything happening. As promised, my family have not gone to him. They've left me alone with my guilt and my embarrassment and my flaws. Maybe I'll do nothing. Maybe this summer was a bizarre chapter of my life that needed to happen, and then needed to close so that I could move on and be a better person.

'Having a good laugh?' I mutter under my breath as I watch the final sparkling flecks of white disappear into the cold river. Then I look around me, at the murky foam that gathers where the water slaps against the supports of the bridge, at the seagulls hovering and squawking looking for food, and finally up to the sky, dull white and heavy. I don't know if God is here, and if he is, if he cares about my silly mistakes and my awkward love life.

My stomach growls. It's only eleven and I have hours to go before I can eat again.

And then, whilst I'm still looking up to the sky, as if someone has seen me searching and trying and thinks it's the funniest thing they've ever seen, it starts to rain.

22

Brent Cross shopping centre was built in the 1970s in North West London and was one of the first American-style malls to be built in the UK. From the moment it opened, it became central to the Jewish community. There's even a joke: 'When I'm dead, bury me in Brent Cross so that my daughters will visit me.' You don't just go there to shop, you go there to be seen. Never in my life have I ever been to Brent Cross and not bumped into someone I know, whether a relative, a friend of the family, or someone I went to school with.

Which explains why Mum is giving me hell this morning.

'You're not wearing that. You look like a schloch!'

I do not in fact look like a schloch. I'm wearing an oversized shirt dress from COS over a pair of leggings with ankle boots. My hair is pulled back into a scrawny bun, fine strands of wavy dark hair falling about my face. But that's the best you're going to get on a Saturday morning, especially if I've stayed the night because I couldn't be bothered to schlep back to my flat after coming over to my parents for Friday night dinner.

Spending Friday nights with them is a new, and not altogether unpleasant, thing. We don't make a big thing of it, but it's nice to have a good, home-cooked meal once a week, to talk to them about how things are going in my life and theirs, and then to sit on the sofa afterwards watching silly TV until I decide it's time to head home or, like last night, decide I'm too tired and head up to my old bedroom to crawl under my teddy-bear bedsheets. I used to hate staying here because it made me feel too much of a kid. I'd return home and return to juvenile behaviour. Nowadays, even though nothing has really changed in terms of how my parents treat me, there's been a change in how I react to it.

So now, when my Mum nags me about what I'm wearing, I don't feel the same tired fury that I did before. She's just being my mum and trying the best she can.

'You must have some other clothes here? Something more flattering than that sad sack?'

I've agreed to go with Mum to Brent Cross as she needs to return some things at John Lewis and thought it would be a nice opportunity for us to have lunch together.

'I look fine Mum.'

'You look like a teenage boy. What's the point of having your figure if you're not going to show it off? Go on, for me, put on something nice? Something with a waist?'

'I'll find a belt if it means you'll stop nagging me,' I tell her.

It just so happens that there's a bunch of my old clothes in the wardrobe in my room, schmutter that I haven't worn in ages, and I manage to find a skinny leather belt that I can pull out from an old pair of jeans.

'You're keeping your hair like that?' Mum asks after she nods at my newly cinched waistline.

'Mum, my hair is fine.'

'But it looks so pretty when it's down.'

'All my products are at home, and it's greasy.'

She's being unusually insistent about my appearance, but I put it down to the fact that we haven't had a mother/daughter day out together in years. Yes, it's just Brent Cross, and we're just going to grab some lunch after running some errands, but I also know this might be a big deal for her. If we bump into anyone (which we undoubtedly will), she's going to want to show me off. My final concession to her demands is to brush my hair one more time and arrange the bun so that it's a little less scrappy, the strands that fall down outside it just a little less frizzy.

I haven't been to Brent Cross in ages. There was a time when I was a teenager that I seemed to spend every weekend here. If I wasn't shopping for clothes, I was visiting friends who found their first jobs in the big WHSmiths or Gap. For the longest time, Brent Cross had the closest Starbucks to me, and it was where I had my first Frappuccino. It's not changed much over the years, but as long as the original dumb-bell layout remains the same, with a huge John Lewis at one end and the huge Fenwicks department store at the other, it will always feel familiar.

After she parks the car in the multi-storey, Mum checks her watch.

'Everything all right?' I ask.

'Just checking that we have enough time,' she says.

'Enough time for what? It's John Lewis, then lunch, then home, right?'

'Oh, I have a few other errands I need to make. We might have to pop to Boots as well at some point.'

'That's fine. I could do with picking up a few things.'

But Mum's behaviour does concern me a little. She has a nervous, frantic energy about her. She's checking her phone more than usual, as well as the time. She's trying to hide it, saying that she's got a lot on her mind and that she doesn't want to forget anything, but it's weird.

After she makes the returns in John Lewis, it's even worse.

'Mum, are you sure you're all right?' I ask. I'm thinking the worst to be honest, early-onset dementia perhaps.

'I just didn't think that would be so quick to do. John Lewis was empty. You'd think there'd be more trade about on a Saturday. It's too early for lunch, don't you think?'

'It's half past twelve. I'm pretty hungry. There's a Wagamamas we could go to?'

'No, let's head down towards Fenwicks. There's something down that way I want to look at.'

'What exactly?'

'Just a thing.'

We're walking one way through the central plaza, past Marks & Spencer and the escalators, when she checks her watch and then turns to walk the other way. Just when I'm about to make another comment, maybe even suggest that Mum finds a place to sit down and rest, she exclaims loudly: 'Deborah!'

Suddenly Deborah Dreyer is there, and Mum looks suspiciously relieved.

'Liddy! Fancy seeing you here!'

'I know! What a coincidence!' Mum agrees.

Yes. What a coincidence indeed.

'And Tamsyn, so nice to see you too! Your mother has been telling me about your job situation. Any news yet?'

'Actually, I got an offer on Thursday.'

'You did? Mazeltov!'

'Thank you.'

'Still magazines?'

'I'll be working with magazines sometimes, but my new title is Marketing Manager. I start a week on Monday.'

'Well, that is good news. Isn't that good news Liddy?'

'It is,' Mum agrees.

'I must tell you what my Nina is up to at some point. She works with all these young people. They're called influencers. It's really quite something. Tell you what, are you busy? We could do lunch and I'll tell you everything! How about right now?'

'Oh, Mum and I already had plans,' I say quickly, but not before I'm interrupted by Mum.

'We would love to!'

I look at her, but she's not making eye contact with me. My suspicion intensifies.

'Well, that's fabulous. I'm just about to go and meet a friend of mine, and you're more than welcome to join us.'

'Lead the way!'

'Mum,' I say quietly. 'I thought we were having a mother-daughter day together?'

'We can have that anytime, don't worry.' Then she turns to Deborah again. 'Who's your friend? Have I met her?'

'Oh, I'm not sure. It's someone I know from way back. Jenny Marshall?'

It would be easy for me to stop dead in my tracks and demand an explanation, to turn on my mum and one of her best friends and try and work out what exactly is going on. Because hearing that last name sends fireworks of panic racing through me, and suddenly everything makes sense. Mum's insistence on me looking nice today, the constant checking of her watch and phone. She was timing everything to conveniently bump into Deborah, and then Deborah was going to lead us straight to someone with the last name Marshall.

'Mum,' I say urgently, holding on to her arm and stopping her from walking. Deborah stops a little way ahead, waiting for us.

'What?'

'What's going on?'

'What do you mean?'

'Jenny Marshall? MARSHALL?'

'What?'

'You know damn well what.'

'I don't know her. She may not even be related. I'm sure there are lots of Marshalls out there.'

And then she goes to catch up with Deborah, leaving me lagging behind.

We're led to a restaurant called The Kanteen, a place that serves a pretty decent range of food, all kosher. It's tucked away down a side corridor by John Lewis, relatively quiet compared to the rest of the shopping centre. It also means that my apprehension has plenty of chance to build and build. We turn the corner, and I almost stop right there to tell Mum that she should go ahead and enjoy her ladies' lunch, whilst I go and do some shopping and meet her later. It seems ridiculous me being here, and preposterous that I should even find myself in this kind of situation. But then again, there's another more rational voice telling me that this could be nothing. I don't know the names of any of Ari's relatives, and this could be a nobody. This person may not even be aware that Ari and I know each other. It's this rationality that keeps me moving and stops me from saying anything further to Mum.

And then I see him.

Even though it's only the back of his head, I know it's him. He's sitting with a woman who looks a lot like him. Thin faced, with all this thick black hair, although whilst Ari's stands up in crazy tufts, the woman's (I presume Jenny Marshall) is perfectly blown out and coiffed around her shoulders.

'Oh, isn't that Ari?' Mum says innocently to me. Too innocently.

Deborah marches forward and makes a huge display of greeting Jenny, and then she introduces us.

'And I'm surprised you don't know my good friend Lydia Rutman. We just bumped into her! She's here with her daughter Tamsyn.'

That's when he turns his head and our eyes lock. He's clearly just as surprised to see me as I am to see him, but whereas I'm filled with the queasy terror of embarrassment, his face settles almost immediately from shock into an easy, amiable smile. He's pleased I'm here. He's pleased to see me.

I'm pleased to see him too. Really pleased. But not pleased enough to forgive my Mum quite yet.

'What's going on?' I ask her.

'Nothing's going on.

We just bumped into Deborah. It's all a marvellous coincidence, don't you think?'

There's space enough for us all at the table without having to move any chairs around. As if it had all been arranged.

'Did you know about this?' I ask Ari as I take the seat opposite him.

'I was wondering why my Mum was so keen for me to join her for lunch, and why we needed such a big table, but no. I can assure you I was not involved in this one bit.'

It's so good to be with him, to be sitting right here in front of him, that I almost forget that I'm meant to be furious.

'Tamsyn, can I introduce you to my mother, Jenny?' Ari offers.

'Nice to meet you,' I reply cordially, and then return the favour to him. 'And this is my mum, Lydia.'

'Liddy! Call me Liddy!' Mum says, her voice too loud, her smile embarrassingly wide. 'I've heard so much about you Ari! It's so good to meet you properly.'

'Likewise.'

'Have you ordered yet?' Deborah asks. She looks so smug.

'We're just about to,' Jenny says. She's a quiet woman, I realise, and she's keeping herself polite and guarded. Her voice is soft, but I've noticed her sharing warm smiles with her son.

'What are you going to get?' Ari asks me.

We keep looking up at each other, catching each other's gaze, and every time I find that it triggers a smile so wide it makes me want to laugh. Even if I wanted to, I can't hide how

I'm feeling right now. I don't think he can either. Even when he's looking down at the menu, one side of his mouth remains in a permanent upward quirk.

'I don't know. What are you having?'

'I was thinking of a smoked salmon bagel. But it's a shame this is a milky restaurant. I wouldn't mind salt beef on rye right now.' The look he gives me then is something more focused, more purposeful. I think of that sunny day in Golders Green, of sitting with him on a bench under the blue sky, and how tasty that sandwich was.

'I think I'll have the same,' I reply.

'So, Ari, how are you? What have you been up to?' Deborah asks.

'I'm well. Busy at work, but nothing out of the ordinary.'

'Your mother was telling me you've had a break-up recently?'

The air around the table tenses when Deborah says that. Ari's mother looks down, jaw clenched, embarrassed and uncertain. Ari too, looks uncomfortable, and won't meet my eye.

'Yes,' he confirms. 'But it wasn't important. I'm fine, it wasn't a big deal.'

I may be completely mad in searching for hidden meaning in his answers, but what I'm hearing is that he's not stuck on Dalya, and that it isn't a relationship that's going to get rekindled again either. It's over, and he wants me to know.

'I had a break-up too,' I tell the table. Mum looks up at me instantly, surprised that I'm disclosing this kind of information, but I need to make sure Ari is fully aware.

'Oh, I'm sorry to hear that,' he says. 'Euan seemed nice.'

'He was. But he wasn't the right dance partner for me.'

Is Ari blushing? It's as forward as I'm willing to be with our mothers and Deborah Dreyer present, but I'm yearning for more.

Our food arrives, and conversation drifts to what Deborah's children are up to, and other inconsequential gossip.

'Sorry,' Ari says nervously when his foot accidentally bumps against mine under the table.

'It's fine,' I say, nudging him under the table right back. Eventually our feet come to rest together, close even whilst we're focussed on our bagels.

Whilst our mothers talk and laugh, getting to know each other, Ari and I don't say anything, but that doesn't mean we're not talking. We're sharing glances as we laugh along with the others, we're smiling and nudging each other with our feet like naughty children not wanting to get caught.

'Well, this was lovely,' Jenny Marshall says after we're done and we've all grabbed a mint from a bowl in the middle of the table. 'Tamsyn, it was so nice to meet you and your mother. And good luck with the new job!'

'Thank you,' I reply. 'It was really nice to meet you too.'

'Hey Tamsyn,' Ari asks. 'Want to go on a walk for a bit?'

He's asking me in front of our mothers, just like that? That's top marks for bravery right there. I guess it's my turn to be brave as well.

'Sure. You don't mind Mum?'

'I don't mind at all!' Mum's face is a picture of delight. 'We'll all stay here and have a coffee. You kids go and have fun.'

As Ari and I walk away from the table, I know that we're being watched and cooed over. I know that the three of them are probably feeling very pleased with themselves. I almost think I can hear my mother yelling 'I told you so!' but we're far enough away from the restaurant that it's possible I'm just imagining things.

'So,' Ari says as we turn the corner into the main shopping precinct.

'So,' I return. My mouth is so dry with apprehension it's hard to finish the mint I'm still sucking on. 'That was weird, right?'

'Very weird.'

'Is this what they call a shidduch?' I ask.

'Well, that would be implying quite a lot about what's going on here. I think some formal conversation would need to take place. I don't think we can really call it a shidduch until your father has agreed a suitable dowry.'

'Do me a favour. As if that's even a thing in this day and age?' I punch Ari in the arm playfully. He pretends it's more painful than it is.

'Ow,' he says. 'Is this how it's going to be?'

'If you keep playing a fool,' I tease.

We fall into silence as we walk, and I'm suddenly painfully aware that we haven't kissed yet. And also, how much I want to kiss him.

Then he stops on a balcony that looks from one level of the shopping centre down to another, and I stop with him. We're facing each other, and he's looking at me seriously.

'Listen,' he starts, biting his lip as he tries to work out what he wants to say.

'No, let me say something,' I interrupt. 'I just feel like it was me who got us started on the wrong foot, so it should be my responsibility to get us on the right one.'

I'm holding his hands in mine. Standing across from each other like this, hand in hand, all we'd need is some music and we'd be dancing.

'I feel like I'm going insane with how much I like you. And I'm so angry at myself for getting everything wrong earlier in the year. It's been a strange summer for me, and I've learnt a lot. I felt disconnected before, and I didn't know what I wanted. Or at least, I thought I did, but that was only because I was angry, or wanted to prove a point to my parents.'

'And now?' Ari asks.

'I want you,' I reply.

'I want you too.' He shuffles his feet, our hands still firmly intertwined, but he's still not looking me in the eyes. 'I've liked you forever. Even when you were younger and a brat, I never forgot you. And then I saw you at the wedding, still bratty mind, but somehow I just knew.'

'How?'

'So, you know how I was looking after your great-uncle, and you came to talk to him before the wedding ceremony?'

'Vaguely.'

'And then you went back, and asked me to watch him again? We had a chat. He told me how much you reminded him of his late wife, and how special you were. But I think I already had a sense of that anyway, just from the way you were talking with him, and later, dancing. I didn't realise that you were the same girl from cheder then, but I could tell we were connected somehow, or at least I hoped we would be.'

'I wasn't very nice to you that night.'

'No, you weren't.'

'Or the next time we met.'

'No,' Ari sighs when he smiles, and his eyes meet mine again. 'But I knew.'

'You did?'

'I hoped I did.'

'But you were with Dalya?'

'Dalya and I,' Ari starts to blush. He looks to the ceiling, scrambling for words. 'We had history. She's beautiful, and talented—'

'I'm well aware,' I tease.

'But she's not you.' Now it's my turn to blush. 'And besides, I thought you and Euan were a done deal. When I saw you both together at the bar mitzvah. He's very tall. Very handsome. Did you ever notice that? A neck like a car tyre. I mean, talk about intimidating. No wonder you didn't fancy me when you had a whole human hunk of ribeye steak waiting for you at home.'

'Oya broch,' I groan, squeezing my eyes shut with shame. When I open them again Ari is still in front of me, still smiling. So I lean forward and kiss him. Nothing compares to the rush I feel when he starts kissing me back, the feel of him right there, so close.

'It starts here,' he tells me when we finally break apart. 'Let's forget everything that happened before. We start right now.'

'Agreed,' I say.

I reach up and pull at a tuft of his hair, twirling it within my fingers. He leans down and lets his forehead rest on mine.

'Do you think our mothers are planning our wedding?' I whisper, too aware of the closeness and curve of his lips.

'Probably,' he admits. 'We should get back to them and put a stop to it.'

'We really should.'

But we don't move. I bring my arms together around his neck and then we're kissing again, and I never want it to stop. We're standing in the middle of Brent Cross, and I don't care how many relatives or potential friends of my mother see us. This is real. This is something true. Even as we're kissing, I know that this is bigger than the kiss, that this is everything.

THE END

GLOSSARY

The following is not designed to be a comprehensive nor exhaustive explanation of Jewish customs or Yiddish terms. Traditions can vary hugely between communities, therefore I've chosen to present definitions that reflect my personal experience within the Ashkenazi community of London. I'd encourage using this list as a launchpad for further investigation and learning!

Yiddish is a Russian/Polish/German/Hebrew hybrid language, spoken amongst diaspora communities as they moved through Europe (whether through choice or persecution). It was always written using the Hebrew alphabet, so there is no definite or 'correct' way to spell these words in English. Where I can, I have used the generally accepted English spellings of Yiddish and Hebrew words, although there may be times that I've used variations that reflect the pronunciations I am more personally familiar with.

It's also worth noting that Yiddish is a language rarely spoken in full today, although many words and phrases live on and have been absorbed into English, particularly in America (see the words glitch, nosh or klutz). Each generation speaks less and less, and as the words become muddled or misused, it's common for there to be slight variations of use even between families in the same community. Even though Yiddish can be seen as dying out, this doesn't mean it can't still evolve!

Aliyah	Means 'ascent' or 'going up' in Hebrew. Can be used to refer to 'going up' to do a reading in synagogue, but also refers to the spiritual and physical move to live permanently in Israel.
Alte kacker	Yiddish, literally meaning 'old man'..
Ashkenazi	Jewish ethno-group, comprised of diaspora communities settling in areas now comprised of Central and Eastern Europe, and Russia. Yiddish developed as a language linking this population, as they moved and resettled over the centuries, often uprooted due persecution. The families in my story are Ashkenazi.
Baruch Hashem	A Hebrew phrase, similar in meaning to 'thank G-d', used to offer praise after a small miracle.
Beshert	Yiddish for fate or destiny, used to refer specifically to finding your soulmate.
Bat/Bar Mitzvah	The Jewish coming of age ceremony, usually held at thirteen for boys (twelve or thirteen for girls) marking the age that they are considered responsible in the community and able to partake in adult religious ceremonies. Often accompanied by a big party!
Bimah	The raised platform in synagogue where ceremonies are conducted, and the Torah is read from.

Bracha	Hebrew, meaning 'blessing' (plural, brachot). The set prayers you say before eating some foods or undertaking certain activities.
Brit milah	Also known as a 'bris', the circumcision ceremony conducted on a baby boy at eight days old.
Broyges	Yiddish, an argument, feud or falling out.
Bubbe	Yiddish, meaning 'grandmother'.
Bubbeleh	Yiddish, a term of endearment for a small child or grandchild.
Challah	The traditional bread eaten at the sabbath, typically plaited, and enriched with eggs or oil (never dairy).
Cheder	Hebrew school, usually attended on Sundays at shul, and not just for learning Hebrew, but for Jewish learning in general.
Cholent	A traditional Ashkenazi dish, developed to provide hot food on the sabbath, where many tasks are forbidden to perform. Basically a slow-cooked stew.
Chupah	Crucial element of Jewish weddings, this is the open-sided but covered structure representing the home that the couple stand under for the ceremony. Other traditions that take place

	under the chupah: the bride circling the groom, symbolising the creation of the private world between her and her husband, and the crushing of the wine glass, acknowledging that marriage is never easy and that the couple embraces the hard times as well as the good.
Chutzpah	Yiddish, meaning showing extreme confidence, cheek or audacity.
Davening	Verb, 'to daven'. The act of Jewish prayer.
Evelyn Rose	A Jewish cook, her book 'The Complete International Jewish Cookbook', first published in 1976, is still considered an authority in the modern Jewish (Ashkenazi) kitchen.
Farkakte	Yiddish, referring to something that's messed up, broken or of poor quality.
Frum	Yiddish, used to denote someone who is religious.
FZY	Standing for the Federation of Zionist Youth, the UK's oldest Jewish youth movement. They arrange social gatherings for Jewish teens, as well as the summer birth right 'tours' of Israel, most commonly experienced at the age of sixteen or seventeen.
Gefilte fish	A traditional Ashkenazi dish consisting of boiled or poached white-fleshed

	fish. Usually served with carrots and chrain.
Goy	Yiddish, a derogatory word referring to non-Jews. Plural: goyim. Adjective: goyishe.
Haimish/haimisher	Yiddish, meaning homely. If a family is described as haimisher, it would denote that they are a nice family.
Halacha	Jewish religious law.
Harmotzi	The name for the bracha said over bread, typically on Shabbat before eating challah.
Hava Nagila	Probably the most famous Israeli folk songs, traditionally sung and danced to at celebrations.
Hebrew name	A tradition throughout diaspora communities. The Jewish naming system does not include surnames, you are named as the son or daughter of your father. At the latter end of the nineteenth century and throughout the pogroms of Eastern Europe, Jewish families were forced to 'register' with the local government and adopt more typical locally recognised names. Sometimes these were forcefully assigned. Names that are nowadays associated with the Ashkenazi Jewish community are the result of this. Many families choose to give their children Hebrew names as well as

	western, legal names. These are used throughout their lives in religious contexts and in prayer.
Hillel House	An international campus organisation, engaging and supporting Jewish students at universities all around the world.
Horah	Traditional folk dance performed in a circle, familiar throughout many communities in Eastern Europe (not just Jewish!). Usually accompanied by Klezmer music or songs like the Hava Nagila.
Jdate	The most famous Jewish dating app.
JFS	The Jewish Free School, based in Kingsbury, North London. One of the largest Jewish secondary schools in Europe.
Kaddish	An important prayer meaning 'sanctification', said at all prayer services. Mourners will participate in this prayer and recite it throughout the rest of their lives, not just during the official mourning period.
Ketubah	The Jewish marriage contract.
Kibbutz	An Israeli commune.
Kiddush cup	Kiddush is the ceremony held by the family to welcome in the sabbath or a holy day. The Kiddush cup is where the family would typically drink the

	wine from, once the bracha has been said. These come in a range of styles, from simple small cups that people can drink from individually, or ornate goblets shared by the whole family.
Kinderlech	Yiddish, meaning little children.
Kippah	The skullcap worn by Jewish men. Some men might wear it all the time, others only on religious occasions. Also known as a yarmulke (mostly in America) and in Yiddish as a koppel. When a kippah is not at hand and a prayer needs to be said, a Jewish man might cover his head with his hand.
Klezmer	Ashkenazi Jewish folk music.
Kneidlach	Singular: kneidl. Otherwise known as matzah balls. A traditional dumpling served in chicken soup, made from matzah meal, eggs, water, and fat (also known as schmaltz).
Kosher	Referring to the Jewish food laws. The main components of these laws involve not eating anything from the pig, nor shellfish, and not mixing dairy and meat in the same meal.
Kvelling	Yiddish, verb: 'to kvell'. Describing the feeling of bursting with pride.
Lavoyah	Jewish funeral ceremony.
Lehitra'ot	Modern Hebrew way of saying goodbye, meaning literally 'see you again'.

Ma Nishtana	The traditional song sung at Seder Night, the first night of Passover, traditionally by the youngest capable person present (most often a child). During the song, they will ask four questions, the first of which is captured in the song's title: 'why is this night different from all other nights?'
Maccabi	Jewish youth movement, running social clubs and athletic games.
Machatunim	Yiddish, referring to the relationship between the parents of the bride and groom.
Mazeltov	Hebrew for congratulations.
Mensch	Yiddish, meaning a particularly good person, someone of a noble character, who acts with honour and integrity.
Meshugana	Yiddish, meaning a silly or crazy person.
Meyne kinder	Yiddish term of endearment, meaning 'my child'.
Mezuzah	Fixed at a specific angle on the entrance to every liveable room in the Jewish home or workplace (bathrooms, laundry rooms etc. don't count), including the front door, this decorative case contains a tiny scroll upon which is written the Shema, one of the principle prayers in Judaism. Seen by some as a device to protect

	the home and its occupants, it also serves to constantly remind the person passing through the door of the Jewish way of life and the connection to G-d.
Minyan	Formed of at least ten men, a minyan is needed to perform public prayer and other religious obligations. Once a boy has had his bar mitzvah he's considered responsible enough to be counted in a minyan.
Mishigas	Yiddish, meaning silliness or craziness.
Mishpocha	Yiddish, meaning family. A term used to be inclusive of close friends and extended family formed by marriage, as well as by blood.
Oy	Yiddish, an exclamation that captures pretty much everything.
Oy a broch	Yiddish, the word 'broch' translates as 'curse'. When coupled with 'oy' this conveys a sense of disaster.
Oy vey	Yiddish expression, conveying exasperation or dismay. Similar to 'good grief!'
Pesach	The Hebrew word for the festival of Passover.
Peyot	The Hebrew word for the side curls worn by religious men (sometimes called payos), as per the commandment in Leviticus to 'not round the corner of your head'. This is also why

	very religious men will sport full beards. Peyot styles will differ between communities and traditions.
Plotzing	Yiddish verb, 'to plotz', referring to someone who is about to burst with emotion.
Punkt	Yiddish, meaning literally 'point' as in 'full stop'. Usage would be identical to someone who exclaims 'period' to put a firm end to a sentence.
Rosh Hashanah	Jewish New Year festival.
Rugelach	Ashkenazi Jewish pastry, similar in look to a croissant, but filled throughout, usually with chocolate.
Schloch	Yiddish, meaning something of low quality or value. To look 'schlochy' is to dress shabbily.
Schlub	Yiddish insult, used for a lazy, worthless or unattractive person.
Schmendrick	Yiddish insult, used to describe a stupid person or fool.
Schmo	Yiddish insult, used to describe a fool or a jerk.
Schmuck	Yiddish insult, meaning literally 'penis'. Used to describe someone particularly obnoxious or contemptable.
Schmutter	Yiddish, meaning rags. Can be used to refer to clothes more generally, to an

	individual rag perhaps used for cleaning, or to any material deemed worthless. If you wear your schmutter, you risk looking like a schloch!
Schnoz	Yiddish, meaning literally 'nose'.
Schtick	Yiddish, referring to someone's gimmick or signature style. Nowadays associated with comedians who have a known routine.
Schtum	Yiddish, meaning silence. To 'keep schtum' is to shut up about something.
Schvitzing	Yiddish, verb, 'to schvitz', meaning literally 'to sweat'. As a noun, a schvitz would be a bath house or steam room.
Seder	The service and dinner held on the first (sometimes first and second) nights of Pesach.
Shabbat	The Hebrew word for sabbath. In Yiddish, 'shabbos'. This is the day of rest, a time for prayer and family, where no 'work' can be done. This includes making a spark of any kind, so you can't turn on or off anything electrical.
Shabbat shalom	The Hebrew greeting on the sabbath. In Yiddish, 'gut shabbos', meaning literally 'good sabbath'.
Shayna meydeleh	Yiddish, meaning 'beautiful maiden'.
Sheitl	Yiddish, referring to the wig some religious women wear to oblige the

	commandment to have their hair covered after marriage.
Shickered	Yiddish, meaning to be drunk.
Shidduch	The process of Jewish matchmaking, sometimes used just to refer to the actual arranged marriage itself.
Shiva	This is the week long mourning period immediately after a person has died. First degree family of the deceased are said to be 'sitting shiva' during this week, referring to the custom of sitting in low chairs whilst visitors are received to pay their respects and say prayers.
Schlep	Yiddish, meaning literally to drag or to haul. Can refer to carrying something heavy, or going on an arduous journey.
Shoah	Hebrew, meaning literally 'catastrophe', and now used to refer specifically to the Holocaust.
Shofar	A rams horn blown at religious ceremonies, most significantly at Rosh Hashanah.
Shtetl	Yiddish, referring to a small town, village or Jewish community in Eastern Europe.
Shul	The Yiddish word for synagogue.
Simcha	Hebrew, meaning joy. Typically used to refer to a celebration, like a wedding or bar mitvah.

Sukkah	A sukkah is a temporary hut built for use during the autumn festival of Sukkot to specific requirements. One requirement is a roof through which you should be able to see the stars, so many are covered with loosely laid tree branches and then decorated with hanging fruits or other plants. Those observing Sukkot will eat all their meals in the sukkah.
Tallis	Yiddish for tallit, the Jewish prayer shawl.
Tashlich	A ritual for atonement performed during the 'days of awe' in the run up to Yom Kippur.
Tchotchkes	Yiddish word referring to a small item, like a trinket or knick-knack.
Tentsl	Yiddish, referring to a dance.
Tikkun Olam	Hebrew, meaning literally 'world repair'. This has come to mean the pursuit of social justice, or taking meaningful action to make the world a better place.
Tisch	Yiddish, meaning literally 'table'. Can refer to any festive meal, but more usually refers to the celebratory 'knees-up' held by the men shortly before a wedding ceremony.
Torah	The five books of Moses, that also make up the first five books of the Old

	Testament. Only one part of the complete Jewish holy writings, which are collectively known as the Tanakh.
Tsedrayte	Yiddish, meaning confused.
Tsuris	Yiddish, meaning worries or problems.
Tuchus	The Yiddish word for bum!
Tzedakah	Hebrew, literally meaning 'righteousness', used to refer to charity. Tzedakah isn't seen as an act of generosity, but a spiritual and physical obligation, and a fundamental component of leading a good Jewish life.
Tzitzit	Hebrew, literally meaning 'fringes'. Refers to the 'day wear' version of the tallis, worn like a poncho under normal clothes, with the strings or fringes hanging out over the trousers.
Yeshiva	Can refer to any school that provides a Jewish education, but more typically refers to a college or seminary that focusses specifically on the study of Jewish texts.
Yom Kippur	The holiest day in the Jewish calendar, a solemn festival where we atone and ask for G-d's forgiveness, accompanied by a fast of twenty-five hours.
Yom tov	Hebrew, literally meaning 'good day'. Refers specifically to high holy days, festivals where Shabbat rules apply.

ACKNOWLEDGEMENTS

I am who I am today because of my family. To the Bursteins and the Matteys, the whole mishpocha, thank you. I went through a tough time in my teens, struggling to embrace my Jewishness and my heritage. For me it was moving away from North West London to University (and becoming President of the Durham Jewish Society!) that made me realise who I really am, and what I'm a part of. I hope this book goes some way to honouring our connection, the amazing celebrations we've experienced together, as well as the sad moments. We come out stronger every time.

To my agent Bryony Woods, and the team at Coronet, especially Melissa Cox and Morgan Springett – you guys are amazing! Thank you for believing in this book, and for understanding my commitment to getting it right.

Thank you to the maven Keren David, my guide and my cheerleader, for covering my blind spots and helping to make this book the most wonderful version of itself. I would have pissed so many people off without your wisdom and input!

A very special mention to my friend Chloe, for whom the last year has not been easy, but who has never failed to be a bright light of good cheer. You are an amazing human, and in a way, without you Ari Marshall would not exist. The actor Ben Schwartz may be out of reach (for now . . .), but your undying, unquenchable thirst for him provided endless inspiration when crafting my hero. You are awesome, and I can't wait for us both to be horribly embarrassed about this paragraph in years to come.

I wrote this book whilst the world seemed to be descending into turmoil and uncertainty, and if it weren't for my friends, I don't know what I would have done. You all know who you are, but special mentions need to go to my graphic novel book group chums, we've met most Saturdays on Skype to talk about anything and everything. I like to think we've kept each other sane? Thank you for never failing in your support and enthusiasm. And a very special thank you to Felicity, on whose doorstep (at least six feet away) I vented all my concerns and who, when I was worried about how to bring the main characters together at the end, suggested Brent Cross Shopping Centre. Of course! How can a Jewish novel set in North West London not culminate at Brent Cross?! You are a star.

Finally, a thank you to my team at the day job. I wrote this novel whilst learning to be a manager for the first time, in the middle of a pandemic. It's not been the easiest ride, but without the support, compassion and friendship of my colleagues I never would have managed all of it. Particular thanks to Dimple and to Hannah, but also to everyone I work with. I recognise how lucky I am, and I'm truly grateful.

Whether you are Jewish, curious about Jewish life and culture, or just in the mood for a romantic yarn, thank you for picking up this book. Don't be scared to embrace who you are, nor ignore the myriad of possibilities right in front of you.